SHALL WE GATHER AT THE GARDEN?

Other Books by Kevin L. Donihe

(*Present*):

OCEAN OF LARD (w/ Carlton Mellick III)

GRAPE CITY

HOUSE OF HOUSES

THE GREATEST FUCKING MOMENT IN SPORTS

(*To be*):

VOLUPTUOUS SUNRISE

BUGABOO

THE FLAPPY PARTS

THE BONVILLE BONES

and others

SHALL WE GATHER AT THE GARDEN?

Kevin L. Donihe

ERASERHEAD PRESS
Portland, OR

ERASERHEAD PRESS
205 NE BRYANT
PORTLAND, OR 97211

WWW.ERASERHEADPRESS.COM

ISBN: 0-9713572-5-0

Copyright © 2001 by Kevin L Donihe
Cover art copyright © 2006 by Ryan B. Thornburg

All rights reserved. No part of this book may be reproduced or transmitted in any form or by any means, electronic or mechanical, including photocopying, recording, or by any information storage and retrieval system, without the written consent of the publisher, except where permitted by law.

Printed in the USA.

DEDICATED TO:

(I) The people who, in some way, helped with this book:

L. Rachel Fisher, Matt B. Seats, Jeffrey A. Stadt, Andrew Seitx, Dave Burgar, and Vincent Sakowski.

(II) The people I'm thankful for even if they didn't help out:

My family, Matt Standridge (Nub), Eddie Ball, Aaron and Stephanie Johnson, Katherine Burgar

Introduction to the Introduction:

Do not believe all that you read! I swear that the following introduction is a work of outright blasphemy. Yes, *blasphemy*! For I have met the authors of both works you are about to read, and I must tell you that I am incensed at the level of plagiarism involved in this most heinous act of depravity. How dare the publishers of this "novel," as they so flippantly label it, print the work of two authors under the awning of the lesser writer's aegis? This is sacrilege! Kevin Donihe is a fine writer (or so I have been told by a few acquaintances of mine who have lowered themselves to reading mainstream, small press pap where the majority of Mr. Donihe's work has seen print), but he is no Mark Anders.

What comparisons between the two one may draw are purely physical in nature. They are both blonde, short in stature, and dress simplistically. Each owns a typing device which each uses to print up propaganda, er, sheets of words, sentences, situations. There is little else to differentiate the two. Mr. Donihe scrawls little horror stories for the brain-dead masses, usually involving zombies. Zombies for Christ's sake (a horror trope best left to Fulci's celluloid dreamscapes, as validated by the lack of commercial success on Mr. Donihe's part—he has only seen print in underground, photo-copied flyers that the vast majority of the world doesn't even recognize as existing). Zombies, my ass!

Mark Anders, on the other hand, is the most recognizable male romance writer ever to hit the New York Times Bestseller list! His works of fiction are gospel to many a housewife and under-appreciated females of every demographic. In fact, one may call his seminal work, *The End: In Circus Midgets and Barbed Chains*, an exegesis of revealed Truth! It is, in layman's terms, *The Apocalypse of Mark Anders*, the greatest living prophet of the 21st century! He who lives and breathes and stands should to shoulder with the likes of Edgar Cayce, Nostradamus and Elijah! And so the publishers defame the great Mark Anders by allowing the lowly and despicable Kevin Donihe to excerpt a great deal of *The End: In Circus Midgets and Barbed Chains*, like some misogynistic rap-DJ sampling the treasure troves of classic progressive rock to mix as he sees fit, only to use it as a dense canopy of background noise, without the expressed written permission of Mark Anders, the original author of the most sacred texts! I ask you, oh faceless publisher of the nether realms—where is the copyright notice for Mark Anders work? Where is the acknowledgment from the author to Mark Anders (whose groin presses into my back as I worship him in every conceivable way)? Where is it written that you could so callously and arbitrarily use Mark Anders' well-endowed verse as your own?

Dear Reader, I caution you to be wary of the intents of these vilified publishers, and of the works of Kevin L. Donihe. For they are the works of *the devil*. The following mosaic novel, pieced together in some Frankensteinian fervor, shall entice you—it shall tempt you into believing that Mark Anders is just a fictional character drawn into a beam of alien-mind-controlled madness, but that is not the case. For I have had high tea with Mr. Anders, who assures me that his lawyers are looking into the matter as I key in these words on my typing device. He brought his own biscuits with him to tea. I gladly accepted one from him. It tastes a bit like chocolate, yet is a bit bitter, like saline-soaked seaweed. He assures me that the tiny Volkswagen can seat he, myself and his six companions/bodyguards, but it is seemingly inconceivable—but, you see—*can you understand*—I have fucking faith in Mark Anders! I believe that I shall fit into the back seat with all six of his tiny friends. Even after I pull on the rubber shoes that far-extend my scuffed oxfords, the red color a strident glare in my eyes.

Did Kevin Donihe offer me a biscuit when we met for drinks at some shit-smeared dive bar in his neighborhood near Sandusky? No. He threw peanut shells at me and pissed in my beer (which actually gave that weak draft a bit of a kick, I must admit), as I tried to convince him not to seek publication of his bastard manuscript.

"But it is sacrilege!" I decried vehemently.

He gripped my tie, wrapping it around his fist and reeled me in closer. I was nearly pulled across the top of the small round, and filthy, bar table, his noxious breath bathing me in its heat. A strange, crimson light beamed from his eyes (the toxicity of his urine, which I had drunk in the beer which my host did generously pay for, had seeped into my brain at this point, for how else could such a simpleton [and a literary hack, no less] do such things to a true believer?). I watched as his lips curled. "Look," he said evenly, then sighed. "I have permission. In fact, I have their blessing."

"*Their*?" I questioned. "*Their*? There is only *One*—Mark

Anders."

Donihe smiled wickedly. "He was but a vessel. A conduit. As I have been. Whereas Anders fought against it—I relish the rush of this knowledge."

— Author's note: This did not happen. Well, it didn't go down like this. Sure, I met with Mr. Neville as he describes, in a bar much like the one he details. But I didn't throw peanut shells at him. I loathe peanuts. I did piss in his beer. He upset me. But I didn't say those words. Look, this is kind of embarrassing, and I have no idea why the publisher has decided to use this lunatic's diatribe to introduce the introduction to my novel. Nonetheless, I've signed the contract and so I must abide by it. I do thank the publisher for allowing me this rebuttal...

— Editor's note: Get on with it, Donihe!

— Author's note continued: Anyway, as I was saying before being interrupted, it's kind of embarrassing. This is what I said: "I have his [Mark Anders] *blessing to use his work. In fact, Mark Anders and I share a great many things. I'm wearing his underwear right now." Then Mr. Neville asks, leaning over the small circular table, drool streaming from the corners of his gaping maw: "What? Boxers or briefs?" Then I replied, "I'm sorry. I can't divulge that without giving away a crucial plot development of my original work."*

"Piss off!"

— Editor's note: we now continue with the Introduction to the introduction:

Donihe hurtles me back with supernatural strength, throws himself from his rickety bar chair, and proceeds to pull a set of golden tongs from the back of his worn and filthy jeans. My eyes widened in fear—I couldn't breathe, for this revelation astounded me! It was if I had walked into a Mark Anders novel....

I cannot explain the strange, ecstatic experience with the golden tongs. It had such dream-like qualities to it; I nearly swore that Mark Anders himself had wielded such a divine instrument of torture on me. In a public place, no less. I bled for days, and I am still sitting on a bowl of ice as I key in these words on my typing device. Mark my words, dear reader—Kevin Donihe is the devil himself! He is the anti-Christ!

Sincerely,

Bobby Neville,
President of the local chapter of
The Mark Anders Appreciation and
Copulation Society
Moenton, Illinois.
October 1, 2001

VALIS is a Harsh Mistress
(or, the proper Introduction to *Shall We Gather at the Garden?*)
by Jeffrey A. Stadt

This is a weird novel.

Of course, that is what you've come to expect from Eraserhead Press. Weird, surreal, absurdist fictions. I must confess that I didn't expect it from my friend and colleague, Kevin Donihe. Not until I first read an earlier draft of *The End: In Circus Midgets and Barbed Chains*. That novella was definitely surreal. Damn, but it was freaking weird. It made me laugh out loud even as gooseflesh crawled up my spine. For it was an uneasy laugh.

Shall We Gather at the Garden? carries on the tradition Mr. Donihe began in *The End: In Circus Midgets and Barbed Chains*. The images within this mosaic novel are horrific, especially after the tragic events of September 11, 2001 at the World Trade Center and Pentagon in the United States. Some scenes left me emotionally numb, yet I grinned to myself at the ironic tapestry unfolding around me. Needless to say, one's opinion might have altered after the real-life terrorist attacks that decimated New York City. For *Shall We Gather* indicts American culture, and the mass populace that follows, lemming-like, over the precipice of avarice, greed, and the need to be like everyone else (but better). The dust hasn't yet cleared in Manhattan to notice much change in the greater American culture. We now stand united, pack-like animals waving flags at our government appointed enemies, wherever they may be. I cannot say if we, as a people—as a nation—have changed (or could change that quickly) since the terrorist attack. Only time, and history, can say. And so, wincingly, this indictment of American uber-consumerist culture stands.

It illuminates.

It demonizes.

It pulls the strings of the puppets controlling the strangest of passion plays within a corporate structure. Everyone, every thing is a target of Mr. Donihe's wit and off-kilter worldview as sifted through the sieve of his brain, then floured and deep-fried in the oil pans of his nocturnal daydreams.

Bizarre.

There are shades of Philip K. Dick's wonderfully inventive *The Divine Invasion* (minus the lurid pop singer), trading up Zen Buddhism for unconscious Gnosticism. Malachi manifests where Elijah would stand revealed; and the Roald Dahl-like midgets hold the pink laser beam shining into our hero's mind. Religion is lambasted under the scrutiny of Corporate money-crunchers, and nothing is what it seems. And akin to PKD's classic(s), Mr. Donihe is well represented by various and sundry doppelgangers somewhere along the coruscating roads of Death-Space. I mean, I know Kevin Donihe, and he is nothing like the repressed-homosexual Doughnut Kiosk employee with the underwear fetish, who dreams of being anally penetrated by ornamental golden tongs. No, Kevin Donihe is closer to Mark Anders, the world's most famous male romance writer. Kevin and Mark were roommates many years ago, but they weren't secret, homosexual lovers. Kevin has a girlfriend, and Mark once confided in me, via email, that he found Kevin physically repulsive (which was strange, since they looked as if they could have been brothers—same short-cropped blonde hair, same diminutive stature and lanky built, same waist size). Conversely, Mark Anders disappeared without a trace a few days after I received the email. For some unknown and bewildering reason, Mark Anders walked away from his roommate, apartment and his life without even packing a suitcase. Kevin inherited all of Mark's clothes, writing machines, stash of Mugwump jissom, and all of his manuscripts, including *The End: In Circus Midgets and Barbed Chains*.

As one may notice from the symmetry of this mosaic novel, Kevin Donihe and Mark Anders shared more than their underwear, they share the same, uncanny vision(s). A prophecy of the coming End Times, or simply an absurdist novel bent on pissing people off and making them think?

Whatever *Shall We Gather* is, shall be left up to the individual to discern. It is definitely visionary in its approach, and barely has a zombie in it. So leave your personal visions of grandeur at the door, and try on Mr. Donihe's. You won't regret it.

It feels like silk.

—Jeffrey A. Stadt
Little Rock, Arkansas
October 31st, 2001

— Editor's note: ** Sigh** *We are under contract, and so must print this rebuttal to both the Introduction of the Introduction, the Introduction, and the heretofore novel Shall We Gather at the Garden?.*

— Rebuttal Author's note: this is a Proclamation, not a rebuttal! ***feckless mortals***

"We shall not be pushed, stuffed into tiny cars, shot out of canons, be the target of pies in the face, pants-ed, depants-ed, or forced to wear brightly colored clothes, rubber noses, and large, floppy feet. Our lives are our own. We are not Midgets—we are free men!"

— King RaggathBob
east of the Karma Wheel,
in The Garden (west of The Pit),
somewhere near the 69th epoch

SECTION I:

THE GRAND DICTATOR:
A Complete and Unedited Reader Featuring THE PIVOTAL TEXT Assorted Early Works and Miscellany

INVOCATION: *Hail to you, Grand Dictator! Let these – your texts – guide us from the fields of oneness and understanding so that we might follow you into the Grand Chasm.*

–The Hon. Malachi (Royal Advisor)

The following reader is divided into three sections.

Parts I (*The End: In Circus Midgets and Barbed Chains*), II (*The Author Reveal'd*), and the *Exegesis* found in the *Miscellany* section of Part IV were penned by The Grand Dictator prior to his ascension. Part III (*Absolute Power Corrupts Absolutely*) was written by Friar Nimblebottom, a monk of the Third Order who succumbed to a fit of prophetic ecstasy while contemplating a chalk outline of The Grand Dictator's visage.

We have also taken the liberty of including, in the aforementioned *Miscellany* section, assorted comments gathered from public sources.

–*The Editors*

EXVOCATION: *And once that Grand Chasm is reached, we shall dive.*

–The Hon. Malachi (Royal Advisor)

PART I:

THE END: IN CIRCUS MIDGETS AND BARBED CHAINS

(*AND THE CYCLE begins as it began before.*)

Sitting alone in my one-bedroom apartment.

Wrapped in both silence and candlelight.

Pen in hand.

Drawing pictures to pass the time.

Millions of separate images swirled on paper to form an integrated whole. Hours zoomed by as my pen drained of ink.

Then the circus midgets called.

The telephone didn't ring. Nothing as mundane as that. I didn't even hear voices. It wasn't necessary. I felt their connection grow inside me – the swirling tunnel that linked our heads from afar.

Visions pulsed. No longer in my apartment, I stood amongst a gathering of little men. Some waved. Others smiled. Before I could respond, a bang sounded overhead and the world went black. I was confused at first. Then I realized my body had blown apart and was now sailing through a void. A worrisome fact – though I could only allow infinity to carry my disembodied consciousness for however long and however far it wished.

Days seemed to pass before the darkness finally opened up and my hurtling atoms reformed at the foot of a sound stage. People writhed atop it like carnal beasts. Cameras rolled. I didn't have time to grasp what was happening before gravity shut down completely. Floating through the ceiling, my body climbed higher and higher until it hovered a mile above the heart of a dead city. Skyscrapers lay collapsed in heaps of rust and decay. Grand bridges buckled under water. Streets were silent.

Suddenly, the connection snapped. I fell back into my cinderblock and scuffed tile world. My body slid from its seat, hitting the floor face first. The accumulated debris cushioned the blow, but my face and left arm still stung. If not for my bad cleaning habits, I probably would have broken something.

Dusting myself off, I staggered over to the mirror. Blood seeped from my nose. Further up, a crushed roach adhered to my forehead. It still twitched.

Repulsion grew. Nothing was left for me in my present state, just semi-poverty, moldy dishes, bad jobs, and dead bugs. Time to walk away and find these midgets.

Join or die.

* * * *

The next day, I wandered onto a town common flanked by decrepit buildings and choked with mulling people. I had hoped to see a tiny figure walking defiantly amongst the normals, head held high. Such was my only reason for entering the world.

The odor of garbage overflowing what smelled like a hundred bins nauseated me. I breathed from my mouth to avoid vomiting. My city didn't always reek. The change had been so gradual that I never really noticed until the filth was ingrained.

Blending in proved difficult even without the noxious and distracting stench. I felt like a flapping puppet. So awkward. Arms jingling. Legs jangling. I imagined my feet as stampeding hooves and my arms as whipping flagella. My head – perhaps it was a bobbing jellyfish.

My brain spun. What if I wasn't even human? Or, worse yet, what if I was the only human in the park? Rat faces. Pig faces. Dog faces. Cat faces. The reflection of a different animal seemed to hide within each man and woman who passed. Not once could I recall seeing an animal face when I looked at my own in the mirror. I simply felt like some strange hybrid when I walked out in public.

But what if I just wasn't looking hard enough. Maybe if I searched deeper, I'd see the otter within. Or the sea lion. Or the walrus. Or some other slick, bewhiskered creature that reveled in pulling heads off fish before eating their guts.

I made myself snap out of it. Still, I wondered if everyone else had been given previews of a script withheld from me. They all seemed so self-confident, so happy to walk around an increasingly absurd park in an increasingly absurd world. Maybe it would help if I wore different clothes. That tactic worked for the others, but I couldn't imagine myself donning anything more than casual pants, a plain T-shirt, and a pair of sensible shoes. All other garments seemed like masks to me, which made me wonder what everyone was trying to hide.

I felt vaguely threatened. Though most waxed indifferent, I nevertheless registered a number of furtive, sideways glances. I wondered what assumptions these people could possibly be making. As far as I could tell, I was just walking around like the rest of them.

Perhaps I didn't have an animal within at all. Perhaps what I had was even worse – *The Mark of Cain*. That might explain what everyone was sensing.

Paranoia gripped me. I spun around. A clump of lemming-faced pedestrians followed close behind. Teenagers. Listening to music through headphones and holding cigarettes with mouths that might as well be muzzles. Around them swirled a cacophony of small talk and small problems.

"And then Bobby got drunk and puked all over my new outfit! Do you know how much I paid for that shirt?"

Paranoia shifted to indignation. How I wanted a third-world child to totter over to this girl and tug the hemline of her barely-there skirt. Sunken eyes. Bloated stomach. Twist-twig arms. He would speak to her in the universal language of empathy.

But how would she react?

("Get your filthy hands off my clothes, you faggot!")

I prayed a rip in space-time might open over this woman's head and transport her to a place of bullets and suffering. When that didn't happen, I turned away. My connection with the girl was brief, but I already felt the drain.

From somewhere behind me: "My girlfriend has a hole so she doesn't need a face!"

Laughs. All around. But I felt sick.

I risked a quick peek over my shoulder and grimaced. The speaker's flap-daddy barely concealed his bulging gut. I hated flap-daddies with a passion. Tent-like, billowy, and available in an assortment of gaudy, fluorescent colors – they had to be the most absurd fashion statement of all time. I considered flap-daddies the bastard children of ponchos and parachutes. The masses, however, seemed dead-set on wearing them. Over half the people in the park sported the garment, *and it was the middle of summer*.

I ignored the overweight guy as he rambled about the only connection he knew how to forge. So many more like him strolled about the park, however, and I kept catching bits and pieces of their conversation.

The experience was both engrossing and sickening, akin to

rubbernecking at the site of an auto wreck. I lost myself in this floorshow and almost failed to notice a little man walking from the common to the street. Bright white shirt. Tiny blue pants. Plain brown shoes. He tried to make the best out of his mundane disguise. I knew the mask would slip as soon as he rejoined his brothers. The bright nose. The polka-dotted pants. All would be revealed.

I had to run.

But, before my legs could react to the impulse, the people in the crowd *moved.* I didn't fully understand what was happening, not even as the first person surged in my direction, his face stopping just inches from my own.

The rest of the crowd soon followed. An organic wall of bleary eyes, double chins, and receding hairlines encased me.

My hands felt clammy. "What's wrong?"

They battered their bodies against me in lieu of a response. Back and forth, back and forth – it was a mosh pit out of Hell. Incredibly, the mindless conversation continued even as their flesh crashed into mine.

"Nice to meet you, Alan."

"Same here, Sally."

"I made pasta the other night."

"What's your favorite sitcom?"

It was as though some cosmic force had commandeered their bodies to subvert my destiny. Breathing became difficult as the stench of cologne masking body odor overpowered my resolve.

I mustered up strength to push against the wall. The tangled mass grew denser. I jumped up and, above the heads, saw the midget round a curve and drop out of sight.

The crowd refused to dissipate. It was senseless to fight. Collapsing to the ground, I released hope and allowed its ghost to sail on gossamer wings. My head struck the pavement. My world became a void.

When I came to an hour later, I was confused and alone. Why had I been left face down on the sidewalk for such a long time? Maybe it was because I wasn't wearing a flap-daddy. Maybe it was the fault of The Mark of Cain. Maybe I didn't care either way.

I walked back to my apartment.

My eyes never left my shoes the entire way.

* * * *

Returning home, all I wanted to do was lose myself in sleep and forget the day's failure. But, sometime during my absence, my roommate had returned. He sat on a floor covered in fast-food containers and empty cola cans, his lips wrapped around a flickering TV. Though his ever-widening orifice partly obscured my view, I could nevertheless discern that he was watching a talk show.

"You don't mind if I suck the television for a while, do you? I'll let you have a turn when my show's off."

I forced a smile. "No, I don't mind. Suck on. Do it all day if you want."

He said nothing further, just slurped the console contentedly.

I sat down to watch my roommate, praying he had acknowledged my request to remove all sharp objects from our apartment.

* * * *

I spent the next day sitting on a bench in a secluded park. Each little noise made my teeth grind and my fists clench.

The birds sang. I found myself wishing someone would tape their beaks shut. The crickets chirped. My usually peaceful soul wanted to rip the legs off every last one of them. I couldn't stomach the sounds of nature, much less apartment life. Not when I knew the midgets lived somewhere in my hometown.

But who was I kidding? Finding them just wasn't in the cards. My one opportunity had sailed out the window. The midgets no longer needed me, as they probably enlisted a more reliable recruit, someone who wouldn't swoon like a Victorian lass when Heaven opened its gates and Hell tried to pull him back. I was just a plain man with plain hair and a plain face going through the motions of a plain life. Never would I be anything greater.

And that's why I brought the vegetable along.

It sat in an inconspicuous sandwich bag. Nobody would know what rested inside.

I could have taken something more effective, sure, but I had grown to loathe my flesh. Using a "non-fatal" item would prolong my suffering. In the end, I deserved nothing more than an absurd, meaningless death.

I looked around. The park was empty.

Good. I didn't want to inflict emotional scars on anyone.

I withdrew the vegetable slowly from the bag. With two fingers, I held it aloft. At that moment, the sun slid from behind a cloud. Light kissed the pickle's bumpy surface, imparting it with an almost majestic quality. I smelled a hint of sweet and sour in the air and felt the thin trickle of green juice as it ran down my arm. Now that I had bonded with the instrument of my demise, I could delay no longer.

"Please, God." I bopped myself about the head and shoulders with the pickle. "Forgive me."

I shutter to describe the agony I inflicted upon myself. Like all desperate men, I had lost the capacity to feel any sensation other than anguish. Only the knowledge that this life would soon be over kept my hands hammering the gherkin against my skull.

And each blow felt like salvation.

Sixteen hours later, my corporeal existence began to ebb. Just a few more strikes before sweet death enveloped me in oily wings and delivered me to the waters of the River Styx. I closed my eyes and awaited the calcium touch of The Ferryman.

Then I heard a voice from behind.

"For the love of King RaggathBob, stop!"

The gherkin fell from my hands. I spun around and was greeted by the smallest of men. Though he wore everyday clothes and sported neatly cropped hair, I realized this was no ordinary human. The midget unleashed a cherubic smile and, at that moment, I was re-born.

"My name's SandrozPhil. I serve as Royal Scout for the Honorable King RaggathBob. The time for revolution is at hand. The good king sensed this and sent me on a mission to discover those who might be worthy of assisting us and our cause."

"Then it was you who sent the mind-tunnel!"

"Indeed. I sent the tunnel out to every sentient being in the universe. Only seventeen responded. Do you know how many of the seventeen were from planet Earth?"

"No."

"Only three. If that doesn't speak volumes about the human race, I don't know what can. But enough of this tangent! We have work to do! Please, follow me to my car."

We crossed the length of the park and darted into a back alley. There, I saw the little man's auto parked alongside piled refuse and debris. I was disappointed. The car looked like any other ancient, lime-green Pinto.

"This is *it?*"

SandrozPhil smiled. "Don't judge a book by its cover. Just get in."

I opened the door to oddity. The Pinto's dashboard had been designed to mimic the steering system of an ancient pirate ship. Its wooden wheel was redolent of salt and seaweed. Though hot outside, the white vinyl seats remained cool to the touch. Overhead, a crystal chandelier hung in place of a standard dome.

But these weren't the strangest features. The interior of the car was *enormous*. One could fit three large-sized sedans in the front seats alone. I faced the rear compartment. It contained a fully functional exercise room. Barbells rested below all sorts of freestanding devices. A hot tub sat in the center of it all, swirling.

SandrozPhil noted my interest. "Gotta keep in shape."

"I see."

"I rent out the back seats every once in a while. To other circus midgets, of course. Big People just wouldn't understand."

"That's their loss."

SandrozPhil agreed.

"Anyway, this is a really nice car." I fastened my safety belt. "Where did you get it?"

"Oh, here and there." He began to drive off.

"Are we going to meet the others, sir?"

"Of course! And please, don't call me *sir*. Call me Bubblepants. It's my cherished childhood nickname – and only my true friends call me Bubblepants. Are you my true friend?"

"Yes."

"Good! In that case, I have much to tell you. I'll begin now if you like."

"Please. I can't wait."

"Do you know of our ability to alter reality?"

"No, I didn't think anyone could do such a thing."

"It's possible. For five minutes, at least."

"Then I'd like to see a display."

Bubblepants sprinkled something out the window from a jar labeled *Midget Dust*. At that second, reality inverted itself and the world stood on its head. Men loitered on street corners dressed in women's clothing. They strutted and preened just as before.

Teenaged guys sporting floor-length floral print skirts acted all macho and wore only the trendiest shit:

<17 Year-Old Kid>: Yeah, I wear the finest taffeta! And I'm going to *kick your ass*, too!

In rural homes across America, old women donned Armani suits and wingtips while stirring cornbread batter:

<Granny Betty>: (*Slappin' her knee and playin' the banjo.*) Thanksgiving's finally here! *Hallelujah!* Get to see my heathen children again!

Investment bankers slipped into satin eveningwear and danced the can-can on the office floor:

<*All together now, sing!!!*>: We are debauched chorus girls! Yes, we are debauched and naughty girls!

All this I saw from within my skull-space, not from looking out the car window. I shook my head. I couldn't believe it. Bubblepants had found a way to interject his personal reality *directly into the collective unconscious.*

"And now I can make them cognizant of the change."

He snapped his fingers sixteen times.

Suddenly, the teenage guys cut their macho shtick and took cover behind lampposts. The old granny continued to stir batter while investment bankers scurried like embarrassed sheep into offices. Some didn't come out for days.

"Amazing."

"And quite sad, too."

"Truly. But how did you do it?"

"Ah, a curious man! I like you already!"

Flattered, I felt compelled to curtsy before I remembered I should bow. Then I realized I was sitting down and could do neither.

"To answer your question, all circus midgets have this power."

"All of them, you say?"

Bubblepants nodded. "My people have been marginalized since time Eternal. We never participated in the plane of existence the Big People created. Unbeknownst to them, subjugation brought us to a higher level of consciousness."

"How so?"

"We didn't take part in their decaying culture so its constructs never affected us. But refrain from asking further questions. I can tell you nothing more until we reach the commune."

"When will that be?"

"We're almost there."

Five minutes later, Bubblepants emitted a high pitched squeal of delight.

"Dear me!" He bopped up and down in his seat, his bottom creating horn-like noises as it crashed against vinyl. "We're here!"

At that point, I knew I had arrived home.

* * * *

The midget commune appeared as a time worn shack from the outside. An unspeakable place: weeds and brambles grew uncut along the entire length of the property. The roof buckled and bowed. In one corner, it appeared to have totally collapsed. Broken shutters hung on rusty hinges. The wooden siding, I assumed, had once been white. Now, it was a chipped and mottled gray.

Bubblepants latched onto my thought-stream. "Looks can be deceiving. Come, see what I mean."

I followed my new friend up rickety steps. The wood was so rotten I feared my feet might sink through the boards. Somehow, we made it to the top without incident.

"Are you're ready for this?"

"I think I am."

"Then so be it." Bubblepants rapped on the door.

A moment later, the locks disengaged and a tiny doorman bade me enter. I, however, paused at the threshold.

"I can't go in."

"And why not?"

"The ceiling's only five feet high. I'll never be able to fit."

Bubblepants chuckled. "Just try it."

I did as I was told, though I expected nothing less than a sudden impact against a too short ceiling. Three steps later, however, plush carpet stretched beneath my feet. My eyes flew open. I stood in amazement. Not only was I inside the commune, but the ceiling rose over two feet above my head. I reached up to touch the plaster.

"How can this be?"

"Some questions don't have sufficient answers."

I turned to survey the living room's contents: A blazing hearth atop which stockings were nailed out-of-season. Neon sofas.

Wooden coffee tables strewn with countless magazines. Two televisions – one featuring a cartoon, the other just flashing, stroboscopic colors. Below the sets, an assortment of throw rugs. On the wall, a tasteful floral print paper. It would have all appeared somewhat normal if the room itself didn't seem to stretch infinitely.

"Nice, isn't it?"

"How big is this place, anyway?"

"We don't really know. Some days it's a little larger than others. But tell me, is the décor to your liking? It's partly my doing, so forgive me if I'm interested in what you think."

"I hope you don't take this the wrong way, but I thought you might have more... well... *interesting* stuff here. It's decorated like any other living room."

"You haven't seen the other chambers yet."

I wanted to continue our conversation, but my lips froze as soon as I beheld my new roommates round a corner and enter the living room. Sitting on air-borne tatami mats, they floated towards me. *Beautiful circus midgets!* So serene: their faces upturned and smiling in ways only truly happy people can muster. Each sang a song of welcome in English before repeating the verses in a language I could not comprehend.

"I'm simply amazed." I stammered. "I've never experienced this much attention from strangers before."

"Oh no, we're not strangers. You are our imaginary friend, and we are yours."

* * * *

Minutes later, I found myself seated on a hot pink love-sofa. (Strange, but I could not recall ever moving from the entrance.) All around me, clustered in a circle, reclined the little men of my dreams. I remained slack-jawed and swooning in their presence. Somehow, I managed to articulate coherent sound.

"How is this even possible?"

A chubby midget responded: "It's a long story. I would hate to bore you."

"Nothing you say could bore me."

"Are you certain of that?"

"Quite."

"Then I'll gladly tell you." The midget cleared his throat. "In the beginning there was only one – LarpxKurt, The Elder. Please stand, Mr. LarpxKurt, and introduce yourself."

I watched as a withered old man in blue polka-dot pants broke his lotus position. He arose from the floor, honked his nose thrice, and returned to his seat.

"Anyway, some friends from the circus spent the night soon after he purchased this house. It quickly became a sanctuary – a place where our brothers and sisters didn't have to follow the fiendish dictates of the circus. In the end, LarpxKurt discovered he enjoyed their company and insisted that they stay. Soon more friends came. Then more. In the fullness of time, he had a veritable circus midget commune on his hands."

I waited until the story was complete. Then I expressed my gratitude with a bow. In turn, the midget squirted me with a joke-flower pinned to his coat.

"All in jest!"

I laughed heartily and fought back the urge to hug the tiny man. "I can't begin to express how I feel right now."

"Then don't try."

"I mean, I've just met you people, yet I feel I can trust you with anything. In fact, I want to tell you a secret – something I haven't told anyone else."

A collective voice: "Then do so."

"I must warn you, it's shameful."

"The past is a memory. Get it off your shoulders."

"Okay, but let me prepare myself first."

I drew in a series of deep breaths until I felt ready to divulge my secret sin. I only hoped its revelation would not sour the circus midgets to my being at their commune.

"Here I go. . . It happened when I was in high school – a very awkward and lonely time in my life. I wanted nothing more than to fit in so, during one of the pep rallies, I painted myself as a gazelle and rooted for their species in Mother Nature's game against the lions. I hoped the kids who painted their bodies for the home team would see the logical connection and think I was cool. Maybe they would even hang out with me. But they didn't. They thought I was *insane*. Can you help me put perspective on this? I've been haunted for years now."

"Don't concern yourself," the tiny man soothed. "Your act indeed mirrored the football-based shenanigans of the average Big Person. You simply behaved in a socially unacceptable way."

"So, I shouldn't worry?"

"Of course not. You're amongst friends now. In fact, let us offer you something. Bubblepants, bring our guest *The Special!"*

"Certainly!" Bubblepants disappeared across that infinite expanse and returned much too quickly. In his hand, he held a crystal goblet filled with a quarter inch of neon-pink liquid.

"Try this." He inserted a festive umbrella into the mix.

I swirled the thick fluid; the nearest circus midget became woozy.

"Are you sure it's safe?"

"We serve it to all first-time guests."

I lifted the glass to my mouth. Bubblepants reached out and seized my hand.

"For God's sake, man! Do you want to kill yourself? You are to *sniff* the liquid, not *ingest* it*!"*

I cringed. His words sounded so harsh.

"But I'm sorry to have raised my voice. Sometimes I forget this beverage has no parallel in the Big World."

I bent my nose over the glass and inhaled deeply. My limbs relaxed and a pleasantly light sensation washed over my entire body.

And that was only after the first sniff.

"Is it good?"

"Oh yes. And I think I'd like another."

"Unfortunately, there's no time. The welcoming ceremony must end."

I was suddenly confused. "*End?* But it's just beginning!"

"Perhaps I should have made myself clearer in the car. You have yet to achieve psychic midgethood, so you cannot stay amongst us yet. You must now retire to the waiting room. There you'll find other Big People – trainees, such as yourself – about to undergo the first test. XerlexGeorge, our Director of Recruiting, will introduce you to the process. Perhaps you now understand why we cannot allow you to take another sniff."

My heart sank. "I've got to take a test?"

"Don't worry," the midget soothed. "You'll do fine."

"Where's this waiting room? I have no idea how to get there."

"It's not far. There's a door leading to it in this very room."

"But this place is *infinite*. How are we ever going to make it?"

"It's not as distant as you think." Bubblepants' tiny hand took hold of mine. “Let me lead you.”

I arose from the seat and mentally prepared myself for an epic walk.

About fifteen feet from the sofa, however, the world dissolved in a sudden flash. When the white haze lifted, Bubblepants and I stood beside a door.

“We’re here.”

Spinning, I could barely make out the couch I had just vacated. It seemed as though the midgets were now gathered around the TV, but I was too far away to be entirely sure.

Bubblepants looked down at his watch. “XerlexGeorge should be here any minute now. In the meantime, don’t be afraid to mingle with the others.”

With that, he took a few backward steps – and was gone. Not *gone*, actually. Just back at the TV with the others. I shook my head in amazement and turned the knob.

* * * *

The first thing I noticed when I entered the drab, fluorescent-lit room was that it was by no means infinite. Just a standard waiting room painted entirely in white. The second thing I noticed was how the others looked so much more capable than I. Such burley shoulders on my fellow humans. Such self-assured looks on their faces. You’d think they found themselves in spatially improbable midget communes on a daily basis! I simply could not compete with the likes of them.

I nearly decided to give up then and there, and would have if not for Bubblepants, who took time out of his busy day to inject soothing thoughts into my mind:

<<u>Bubblepants</u>>: Your life is one of contingency, not blind separation. You were meant to be here. Remain confident in your purpose.

I heard loud and clear and, at that moment, realized my existence might truly be meaningful. Settling down, I awaited XerlexGeorge’s arrival and scanned the faces inside the lobby.

Sixteen others sat alongside me, just as Bubblepants had said. Of the sixteen, two possessed features I noted as being distinctly human. The others consisted of bizarre yet strangely beautiful masses of tubes and gelatin affixed to thick, log-like bodies. On occasions, they would regurgitate lumpy fluid from holes in their bellies and make wet clicking sounds. I assumed these were normal bodily functions as no one offered an apology. Truly odd beings they were, but kindred spirits nonetheless. Each had received the mind-tunnel, after all.

I smiled at one of these visitors and addressed the protuberance I hoped was its head.

"Do you know English?"

The alien pointed to the Universal Translator hanging from what looked to be a neck stalk.

"Ah! So, have you read any good books lately?"

The alien nodded, but before it could say anything XerlexGeorge, dressed in a crisp four-piece suit, made his entrance. He seemed such a distinguished man. The hair about his temples was gray, and his general appearance was reminiscent of a middle-aged, yet pinched, Gore Vidal.

"I am honored to see your smiling faces. Eat this candy." XerlexGeorge passed around a dish containing a host of red, sugar-coated dots. I took one from the offering plate and placed it in my mouth. The candy fizzled on my tongue.

"I do hope you've had time to adjust and are ready to join us in our struggle. First, however, you must pass *The Triune Testing* and, when it is over, gain the approval of our king."

Gasps shook the room, but I was prepared.

"We received the mind-tunnel," shouted a human trainee. "Doesn't that alone mean we're ready?"

XerlexGeorge shook his head. "If only it were so easy. We circus midgets are going against a great and firmly ensconced enemy. Receiving the mind-tunnel alone doesn't make one ready to bear the weight of such amazing responsibility."

The crowd of Big People/Big Aliens fell silent and shuffled their feet.

"As per the rules of *The Triune Testing*, VerlaxPete shall determine whether or not you're possessed of true love. If you are, you'll progress to ZarnoxJohn's *Unearthly Knowledge Oral Drill*. Only if you excel in these first two shall you move on to the third facet of *The Triune Testing*. I cannot speak of it now for I do not wish to scare anyone away."

Disappointment hung in the air like a fog. Even I felt suddenly empty.

"But don't let my words bring you down. You're a fine bunch. Really, you are." XerlexGeorge lifted a baseball cap to his head. "Just go out there and give it all you've got. *Go team*!"

My muscles clenched at the sound of his words. Pure adrenalin surged through my veins, obliterating apprehension. I catapulted myself across the room and held the door for the other trainees who whooped and hollered close behind. In the hallway, we gave each other high-fives and belly-slaps until VerlaxPete's door opened and his diminutive, lab-coated form bade us enter.

I marveled. Perhaps two dozens posters hung on the office walls. Most were detailed lithographs showcasing various modes of Tantric sex. A small wooden shelf sat in one corner, lined with phallic idols and jars filled with multi-colored powders. Some still had labels attached. One said *Dried Deer Penis*. Another: *Androstenol*.

I walked over to the midget. His features appeared slightly Germanic, though they were too condensed for me to be certain. I attempted to shake his hand. He ignored the greeting and, instead, slammed a metallic, wire-filled dome onto my head.

"Don't worry," he soothed. "It's just the *Love-O-Tron*. Now, show me how you love!"

"But why? How will knowing how I love help your cause?"

"If you don't know true love, you're a stranger to true passion. Our mission requires passionate people. Only those who are able to commit themselves fully without getting lost down the path of hate may apply."

VerlaxPete said nothing more. He flipped the *Love-O-Tron*'s switch. The room faded, and an image of my soul mate appeared. I felt fragmented pieces of myself come together. I became her reflection and she became mine. No longer was I an isolated shell; I had found both my completion and my tether. Without this woman, I would fly into the stratosphere like a balloon, never to return. But I didn't even need to know her name to feel the pull, for her force was *love* and love, I understood, is all there is.

I pulled the helmet from my cranium. "Words can't express what I feel right now."

"And rightly they shouldn't. Now, you are required to produce something you wrote to this person. We must verify the authenticity of your vision."

My heart sank. "But I have no such letter."

"Just take a look in your pocket. I'm sure you'll find something."

I searched my pants and discovered a folded note rendered

on lined paper. I turned to look at VerlaxPete and noted the mischievous glint in his eyes.

"You just rent the fabric of reality again!"

"Yep."

At that point, we shared a hearty laugh.

VerlaxPete bent down to skim the letter. His brows soon furrowed.

"Ah, I sense trouble in paradise!"

I squirmed as he read aloud:

Dear Lover –

Don't be mad! When you called last night it was like you telephoned me while dreaming but, instead of waking up, my dream-self answered the phone. I'm sorry I talked about such abstract things. I was just trying to help. Perhaps I said too much. Perhaps I was too honest.

Just relax, baby. It'll be okay. Try to have a good time. Hitch a ride to wherever it is you need to go. Explore outer space. Just do something. Live life right away. It's the key to this crazy puzzle.

Go with it. Dance with it.

Gotta go –
mE

"Now, show me how she reacted to your heartfelt sincerity in the form of a telepathic photo-play."

"I thought only circus–"

VerlaxPete tapped the *Love-O-Tron*. "When you're wearing this, you may send your thoughts to whomever you please. No special powers required."

"Okay, but do you want an absurd or literalistic portrayal?"

"What do you think?"

I understood and immediately slammed the *Love-O-Tron* onto my head. My teeth clenched and my underarms reeked of foul perspiration as I recalled that hellish morning:

<Scene: A kitchen in a spotless suburban home.>

<Boyfriend (B) picks Girlfriend's (G) hidden shame from the floor without contemplating the consequences of this action. He hands the shame to G, whose face promptly turns red as neon lights flash in her corneas.>

<G>: (*Aghast.*) Stop waving my hidden shame in the air! (*Winston Churchill voice*): I've hid it for so long. . . (*G's voice returns*): *Fucker!!!*

<B>: (*Confused.*) I was just trying to help. You dropped this.

<G>: (*Lasers shoot from nostrils.*) *BUT IT'S MY HIDDEN SHAME!!!*

<B>: I thought I'd do a good deed by picking it up for you. (*Dons boy scout uniform.*)

<G>: *I DON'T WANT YOUR FUCKING COOKIES!!!* (*Grows three heads.*)

<B>: Okay, then. I'll play your silly game and become *DRAGONLANCER.*

<G>: (*Turns into Marlene Dietrich.*) Oh yes. . . ravish me!

<B>: I don't understand.

<G>: Take me like a mad stallion!

<B>: That's absurd.

<G>: I'll stampede if you don't!

<B>: (*Yoga mat grows under foot.*) Can't we just experience the cosmic swirl, baby?

<G>: Okay, you asked for it!!! (*Turns into MY LITTLE PONY and gallivants through the kitchen. My, what a majestic specimen. So magical. She even has a little unicorn-thingie on her head. All the girls want to pet her and put her in their play-chests.*)

BUT THEN!!!
(G *turns into a BRONKIN' BUCK! She snorts, ripping up shit with wild abandon.* G *needs to be MY LITTLE PONY – such a perfect little girl – and then go as insane as her culture will allow.*)

<B>: (*Nonplused.*) There's really no reason to do any of this. Can't we just dance and forget everything?

<G>: *(Regains human form.) OH, YOU BRUTE OF A MAN! I AM JANE RUSSELL! PLEASE DO NOT TAKE ME INTO YOUR MANLY COWBOY HANDS, SO SEXY AND CALLOUSED! DO NOT RAVISH ME! (Ooohhhhh, but I want it! Oh yes! Just like a damsel in distress!) I LLLLOOOOOVVVVVEEEEEE YOU BILLY THE KID!!! I LLLLOOOVVVEEE YOU!!!*

<B>: I knew you'd come back! See, we were only playing a game. And guess what? We both lost and I couldn't care less!

(G turns and scowls. B looks shamefully at his shoes.)

<B>: It *was* just a game, wasn't it?

<G>: (*Speaks in a Wild Bill Hickcockian drawl.*) *I PLAY UNTIL YOU LOSE, PARTNER. LOOKS LIKE WE'VE GOT ANOTHER OF THEM THAR MATCHES ON OUR HANDS.*

(B. pulls a birthday card out of his pocket.)

<G>: Alas, a *physical sacrament!* Now I know he cares! (*Turns into one of the Bronte sisters.*) Hark!!! Heathcliff loves me even though he's bat-shit insane!

<B>: That's absurd.

<G>: (*Self returns.*) I know.

(*At this point, repeat play from the beginning and complete another round. Once finished, repeat again.*)

VerlaxPete sat back and laced his fingers together. I couldn't read his face. I would surely fail if he doubted my chances to win such a woman. Drawing in a deep breath, I prepared for the worst.

"It seems your love harbors a pie-in-the-sky notion of what makes a perfect man. I don't think anybody told her that lover doesn't exist."

"But I still care for her."

"Of course. How could you not? She feels the unconditional love you shoot in her direction, but remains confused. The face of her fantasy lover is not the one you wear."

My head sank into my hands. "But I can never be that person."

"Very true. But that will matter little when she realizes it's possible to share herself with another living being. Give it time. She'll grow to trust your sincerity, and a love greater than the self will deliver this fair maiden from isolation."

"I understand. But I feel as though I could never be right for her. Or for *anybody*. And I'm not talking about physical appearances here. I'm talking about myself as a person. I'm ashamed of some of the things I've done, and I don't know how she would react if she knew about them."

"Have you ever killed anyone?"

"No."

"Have you ever bilked an old lady out of her fortune?"

"Of course not."

"Then don't worry. She too will have a *Dowry of Secrets* to present to you when the time comes. Everyone has his or her own secret shame. You are never alone."

"Dowry of Secrets?"

"Yes, and your love will grow in that special moment when you reveal yours and she reveals hers. A bond will be forged like no other."

"So I can love? And people can love me?"

"There's no doubt in my mind."

"Does that mean I pass the test?"

"Indeed. You are truly a consummate lover."

* * * *

I took my leave of VerlaxPete and wandered about the

commune's cavernous hall until I found the botanical garden. I was told the Head Scholar awaited me there.

When I stepped inside, however, I saw nothing but a tall, glass-paneled ceiling above which three orange moons hung suspended in a red sky. Below that, towering orange plants snapped at the air while green and purple koi swam in decorative pools.

I walked closer to the plants, but not close enough for them to snatch me up in their powerful jaws. I was amazed. They coiled around one another like rooted animals as the taller plants extended large, wiry protuberances only to jam them, without ceremony, into their mates.

I felt dirty watching, but I couldn't make myself turn away as stalks shook in plant-ecstasy.

A few minutes of repetitive bumping and grinding passed. As the rhythmic motions reached a crescendo, both plants exuded puffs of fragrant smoke from their mouths. The rich, perfume-like odor reached my brain and made me high. I suddenly felt like I was posing in a family picture, and God just so happened to be standing behind me, giving my head bunny ears.

I staggered about the garden for a few minutes. Spots whirled. My feet felt as though they were treading on rubber. I almost tripped over ZarnoxJohn.

"Oh God, I'm sorry!"

The man didn't respond. His tiny, robe-clad form continued to hover inches above a Yoga mat spread just out of stalk's reach. An incandescent halo sat atop his head. In one hand, he carried a copy of Hobbes' *Leviathan*. In the other, he held some obscure super hero comic from the fifties. To his right sat trainees who had yet to undergo his test. All remained quiet and were, I assumed, humbled by their proximity to such radiant knowledge.

I felt compelled to bow.

ZarnoxJohn acknowledged the greeting. "Please, sit beside me."

I took my seat. "This is a very strange place."

"You've noticed the Agodavo plants, I see."

"It's hard not to. Where on Earth did they come from?"

"I'm afraid *where on Earth* isn't the correct expression in this case."

"I see."

"In fact, the Agodavo plant doesn't even come from this *time*. Perhaps you've noticed the psychotropic effects their perfume has on the human brain."

My head swam. "Oh yes, sir! Most certainly!"

"Their fragrance will allow your mind to roam abstractly, thus making your answers to my questions truer. That's why I chose the botanical garden to hold this test."

"Will allow? My brain's already swirling."

"Then I take it you're ready?"

I nodded.

The questioning began:

Q. *Who are you?*
A. *I am the entity who goes by the title my parents gave me.*

Q. *What do you do?*
A. *What I'm doing now.*

Q. *How can we, as a whole, be ourselves?*
A. *By never asking that question, (Susy James).*

Q. *A classic from the Orient: Show me your true face, the one you had before you were born.*
A. *I'm showing it to you now, (baby).*

Q. *What is nothing?*
A. *Salted meats have changed the world.*

Q. *What is something?*
A. *Water is to sausage as flesh is to marmalade.*

Q. *Where lies the meaning of words?*
A. *In my brazier.*

Q. *Where lies the meaning of truth?*
A. *In my pants.*

Q. *Why do people fear?*
A. *Olive oil.*

Q. *What do "time", "space", and "terror" have in common?*
A. *Pancakes.*

Q. *Should I stop while I'm ahead?*
A. *Yes, but how can you ever be ahead or behind? (The entire process is intertwined like a spigot that spews not water but snot.)*

ZarnoxJohn ran his fingers through his hair. "Quite amazing! Now, I want you to do impressions. This is the final level. No one outside the midget commune has sufficiently mastered it, though some have come close. Are you ready?"

"I've never been more prepared in my life."

"Then pretend you're a rabid wildebeest!"

I crouched down on all fours and bit at the air: *"Snarl! Snarl! WaaaaHooooGaaaaa!"*

"Now pretend you're a bucket of chum! This is fun!"

I slid around the floor, spinelessly: *"Slosh! Slosh! Squish! Squirt! Hello!"*

"Now do an asteroid! I can't contain the glee!"

"*FIZZ! WHIZZ! BLAM-BIZZ!!!*" And then I ran straight into a brick wall.

"How about whale blubber? Think you can manage that?"

I walked back to ZarnoxJohn and began to undulate: *"BLUB . . . BLUB. . . BLUB. . . SHAKE IT!!!"*

"Or a coma?"

"________________________________."

He clapped his hands. "Those aren't bad at all! You should go on the road with your act! You'd be a smash hit!"

"Honestly?"

"Honestly! The circus would love you." His voice suddenly fell to a whisper. "But I wouldn't recommend going there. *Ever.*"

"I'm sorry you had to even think of such a time. I didn't mean–"

He shushed me. "There's no need to apologize. Those days are over. As a matter of fact, your test is over, too."

"Did I pass?"

"You did an *amazingly* fine job – far better than I anticipated. But the bar is set almost impossibly high. I can tell you no more until I administer the final test of the evening."

ZarnoxJohn flashed a brief but encouraging smile as I stood aside so that the next trainee could take my place. The man was one of the two other humans. Now, however, he didn't look quite so confident. His eyes darted across the room; a thin film of perspiration dampened his forehead.

Always the curious sort, I sat back and listened in on their session.

Q. *What is your name?*
A. *Tim.*

Q. *Who are you?*
A. *I already told you, my name is Tim.*

Q. *What do you do?*
A. *I work in a cog factory as a cog.*

Things were not going well for this applicant. I wanted to tune out, to ignore his failings, but the masochist in me kept my ears at attention.

Q. *Is it better to be a zoo animal or a zoo keeper?*
A. *What the hell are you talking about?*

Q. *What is the recipe for the Primal Soup?*
A. *Stop doing that!*

Q. *Are you brain dead?*
A. *What's that supposed to mean!?!*

Upon answering ZarnoxJohn's final query, the unfortunate trainee was forcibly removed by Head Midgetrine GarnlopBill. I never heard from him again.

About thirty minutes later, GarnlopBill returned. He appeared quite somber, and I noticed he carried a sheet of paper in his hand. At that point, I understood my fate rested in the Head Midgetrine's palm.

"Okay *panty-men*, this is how it goes. If you hear your name, you stay and move on to physical training. If you don't, you follow me to office of Chief Surgeon JartawSmith. *Do you understand?"*

I quivered as the names were read and noted terror dawning on the faces of those not chosen.

In the end, only six of us remained.

No further words were spoken. We were quickly removed from the botanical garden and spirited to the barracks of GarnlopBill.

As we passed the Chief Surgeon's office, I heard the screams of the lost give way to joyful laughter.

At least they were taking it well.

JartawSmith, I am told, has very dexterous hands.

* * * *

Head Midgetrine GarnlopBill stood in a large chamber filled with bunk beds and little else besides a large bomb that sat roped off in the room's center. One of the Big Aliens tried to walk up and touch the thing. GarnlopBill shouted incoherently, and the Big Alien sprinted back as though someone had lit a fire underneath the slick runners pretending to be its feet.

Although the smallest Big Person stood well over a foot taller than our trainer, no one considered questioning his orders. Our leader was an imposing man. His rugged visage reminded me of the stern and inflexible mask that passed as General Douglas MacArthur's face. When the Head Midgetrine's eyes met your own, your soul was *ordered* to wilt.

"Drop and give me five-hundred million!"

"Yes, Head Midgetrine GarnlopBill, sir," we chanted in unison.

Days passed. Half of us were dead or dying by the time the last trainee hit the five-hundred millionth push-up. Those who remained stared longingly at GarnlopBill. *What shall we do for you now,* our eyes implored.

"Well – yah dirty, scum-filled sacks of putrescent flesh – you can all take a little walk through *The Desert of the Restless Dead!"*

The trainees gasped. "But we're nowhere near a desert!"

"Oh yes we are!" GarnlopBill pulled a remote control-like gadget from his pocket and pointed it at the wall behind us. A spiraling vortex opened up in a space that wooden panels once covered. A blast of scalding air and sand scoured our faces. When the doorway finally stopped swirling, we found ourselves in a desert larger than the Mohave and more desolate than the Sahara.

"I know this may seem a little harsh to you *pantyhose wearin' girly harlots*, but we demand *everything* from our trainees. How the hell can you defend our cause if you're not man enough to walk through a little desert? You disgust me!"

"But you said something about the restless dead," interjected a quivering trainee. "I–"

"*Fuck 'em!* You're worrying about mush-brained flesh consumers when the entire world is crashing down around our heels? Get your priorities in order, Private!"

"Yes, sir!"

"Now, I want all you *bulbous fatty pants* to follow me! March in time!"

As one, the trainees slipped on their blue polka-dot fatigues and jolly red noses and followed GarnlopBill through the portal. My flesh tingled as I crossed the threshold. It felt like I was walking into the most statically charged room imaginable. Soon, however, the prickly sensation was replaced by pure and unadulterated *heat*.

As I marched, I noticed how the aliens wore their faux-noses on a slender tube jutting from their midsection. Their heads were not the protuberances I had addressed earlier. Such embarrassment. I hoped I had not spoken to anyone's anus.

* * * *

"Come on! Keep going!"

An alien bleeped through its universal translator: "But we can't! Our faces are falling off!"

"Stop yer bitchin'! You're in the service of King RaggathBob, folks! You've got to make due with less!"

I heard the moans from the other Big People/Big Aliens, but didn't observe the sagging flesh about which they complained so loudly. They looked fine to me, just a little dehydrated. Myself, I kept in time with the Head Midgetrine. My feet never felt so sure of themselves. Head held high, I marched across desert sands and defied the subsequent blisters. I defied the skulls of animals, humans, and those of more questionable origin. I defied scorpions sporting three heads and venomous snakes whose mouths bristled with a hundred rotating fangs. I defied heat so extreme it almost had a scent and defied strange, pterodactyl-like birds that circled in the sky above us.

I felt stronger, both physically and mentally, than I had in ages.

Meanwhile, the groans from behind grew evermore pronounced. I could hardly concentrate. Those behind me simply refused to shut up. I turned around to chastise them, and was met by the pinnacle of horror.

The others, they had regressed! My fellow trainees gnawed each other's brains and picked their own meat with abandon. Stress mixed with heat had obviously proved a fatal combination.

"Zombies!" shouted GarnlopBill.

The world around me erupted in gunfire. Newly reanimated brains dripped from my face. The Head Midgetrine was obviously well prepared for this possibility and took only the most punitive of actions. When all was said and done, the stench of death and gunpowder was nauseating.

But I couldn't blame him for what he did.

It was, after all, in self-defense.

* * * *

In the end, I was the only Big Person/Big Alien who had not transformed into a flesh-eating ghoul. I was the Chosen One, plucked from the trial by fire.

Now, if only I could impress the king.

* * * *

I was unable to sleep the night before my scheduled appearance with the Honorable King RaggathBob. My covers, drenched in sweat, remained coiled tightly around my body. I tossed and turned. Chaotic dream images slammed into my mind. *A sylvan glade. A slender man with Jesus-like hair. Two warring churches built across from one another.* Did these visions mean anything? Were they portents – omens of my up and coming encounter with the once and forever majestic king? How could I stop these images from raping my mind! I was a mere mortal, my constitution not hardy enough to withstand such an onslaught.

I stared upwards, counting cracks in the ceiling and dreaming of alien shores where gaseous creatures writhed and boiled, until the door to my chamber opened four hours later.

* * * *

"Today is a special day. King RaggathBob expects you in his chamber immediately."

With those words, the final test of my psychic midgethood was upon me.

"Come," beckoned Royal Consort BleppoSandy, and I followed. He led me down a crystal corridor festooned with silly string and tinsel. Statuary of renowned circus midgets lined each side of the hall. These were, I thought, ordinary memorials. Then I noticed how stone eyes blinked and stone arms twitched. They appeared similar to the animatronic figures I'd seen at museums, only these were much harder.

"I see you are to meet King RaggathBob," one of the statues said.

I turned around. A gray face smiled back at me.

"What?"

"I said, *I see you are to meet KingRaggathBob.*"

Confusion set in. Statues in the wax museum never went above and beyond their programmed script. Lincoln just recited the Gettysburg Address *ad nauseam*. He never stopped to ask about the weather or inquire as to how I was doing.

I sputtered: "Yes. Yes, I am."

"Of course, why else would you walk these halls? But I won't keep you. I'm just a statue who wishes you well."

"Okay, then. Thank you."

And I kept moving.

The other statues raised their hands in salutation, but did not speak. I assumed they understood the gravity of my situation and did not wish to cause further delay.

As the hall rambled on, I noticed twisted and jagged letters carved into the crystal wall directly behind the figures. Soon, the letters grew into entire words that expanded into sentences and paragraphs. Then we turned a curve where the strange, runic script covered the wall from top to bottom. Try as I might, I was unable to glean meaning from any of it. I could, however, sense a greatness that transcended my limited understanding.

"Beautiful, isn't it?"

Mouth slack, all I did was drool.

"Perfect answer, my good man, perfect answer."

The hallway kept branching out, filling my vision with things I once thought exclusive to the divine realm. Towering columns of light and sound. Angelic voices that arose from nowhere in particular. Hours seemed to pass before the silly string parted, and I found myself in the presence of radiance.

The Honorable King RaggathBob sat upon a bejeweled throne, a golden crown atop his cherubic yet age-wizened head. Its brim all but covered the king's densely curled hair. His eyes – so tiny – spoke of unfathomable wisdom. I found my legs slack and my bladder loose.

"So, you're the one I've heard so much about."

His voice resonated with such frequency that four teeth took leave of my gums. I placed them in my pocket, embarrassed that they had fallen out as the king looked on.

He continued: "And I see you've brought a satchel with you."

I had no idea what the good king was talking about but, looking down, I saw that I indeed carried a leather pack over my shoulder. Onto its surface, two words were emblazoned: *Minstrel Satchel.* Within, I discovered a collection of manuscripts. My mouth fell ajar as I removed a page and recognized my own handwriting.

Spellbound: "Do you wish me to read?"

"By all means."

I cleared my throat, and words flowed freely, unhindered by fear. I was in the presence of friends:

MULTIPLE PERSONALITY DISORDER: A PLAY IN ONE ACT

<CAPTAIN>: Captain's log. Stardate: Septober 50th, 1887 B.C. *The Federation* has finally fallen under the heavy, iron fist of the *Dread Collective.*

<CAPTAIN transforms into THE RUNNING COMMENTATOR!>: It's the newest sensation! Yeah, it's sweeping the nation!

<CAPTAIN>: (*Returning, but for only a second or two.*) Oh, god. . . not again.

<CAPTAIN/RUNNING COMMENTATOR becomes Anchorman MARK BUTTESCHLAMMER>: A man calling himself Bruce Banner has taken on a Boston accent and is now driving with reckless abandon through the streets of Zebulon, North Carolina. Reports indicate that the individual in question is, in fact, me.

I returned the manuscript to its satchel and motioned to address King RaggathBob. He shushed me in mid-sentence.

"Please, I require silence. I'm looking into your future."

"What? *Right now?"*

"Yes. You won't garner a single award. And you'll never be published, *anywhere*. This I see. But do you really care about such things?"

"Writing's just something I do to pass the time."

"Then all is good."

"Shall I read on?"

"That won't be necessary. I'm already well pleased. Your thought-patterns are nearly identical to our own. This is quite unique. No Big Person has ever come so close to possessing the mental rhythms of a circus midget."

"I am honored. I really don't know what to say."

"Say nothing. Just bow by my feet."

I obeyed with a smile.

Above me, King RaggathBob paused, surveyed all those in attendance, and lifted his royal scepter. He drew in a deep breath before sending it crashing against my skull. Upon contact, the scepter emitted a humorous *squeak* – the effectiveness of which was not at all hampered by the gruesome blood fan accompanying its ascent.

"I knight thee *Sir Pantsalot of the Trimingual People*! We are honored to have you in our midst."

My heart leapt despite the mild trauma. I looked into the king's eyes – so amazingly tiny – and my smile progressed until my teeth bulged from my gums and the edges of my lips poked at my eyes.

"My liege!"

At that moment, I knew I would stand by his side to the end of my days.

* * * *

The second the king dismissed me, a younger midget, whose nametag identified him as BartolMel, grasped my shoulder and forced a digest-sized pamphlet into my hand. On its cover was inscribed:

TO UNDERSTAND PEACE: THE MIDGET MANIFESTO
by KarlakArmond

"Read this now. It's the handbook of our people."

"Are you sure I'm worthy?"

"You have passed the tests, and thus achieved psychic midgethood."

I turned to the king. He nodded his approval.

Smiling, I flipped open the pamphlet's cover and began:

The keys to Utopia are in our grasp.

People say such talk is nonsense. Rubbish, I say to these nay-sayers! Rubbish! Peace would reign forever if the Big People didn't revel in fiction. They, however, choose to live in Hell disguised as Freedom disguised as Heaven. (Recall this: The greatest deceiver is that which looks like a duck and quacks like a duck yet – in truth – is a many-headed dragon with virgin guts hanging from its multiple, gaping maws.) Life would flourish anew if the Big People only took the time to look upon things with the eyes of a child. Most, however, become forever lost in patterns. They simply cannot observe phenomena without falling head first into it.

*The sheer number of people who follow such a path is staggering. (*I have rice stuck in my teeth.*) Their entire worldview is based on the notion that outward appearance is a true reflection of an inward soul. As it stands, these individuals are merely compensating for a life that, in their mind, has no center. They feel powerless – lost in a segmented universe in which they are the alien. (*I often wonder if my woodland friends will visit me again.*) The Big People do not realize that reality is an unbroken whole at all "points" along the space-time continuum, ergo, concepts of past, present, and future are but human constructs.*

*Please understand that this "oneness" to which I refer does not subscribe to the contemporary definition of "unity." Oneness results from having a reference point in what many consider God. (*Get these snakes out of my brain!*) Though our physical bodies decay, our consciousness – that Eternal wellspring – lives on as it lived before it came to rest in our flesh sacks.*

This consciousness, or soul, has its roots in Infinity. To say this consciousness is "ours", however, is to cheat its power. This consciousness is collective just as we – The Trimingual People – stand as a collective body. We, however, remain individuals. Much like the Mandlebrot Set, the "whole" is contained in every "part".

*Unfortunately, many will fail to understand what I have said, for they are too caught up in the visible universe. They do not allow their minds to roam abstractly. They do not see words as mere symbols that can never add up to Truth. (*My pants are asleep.*) If this ignorance it is not overcome, the fullness of understanding will never reach the masses.*

*It is my hope that this manifesto will serve to remedy this most dreadful of all human errors. (*Please, don't disturb me when I'm screaming.*) I have intentionally left the text brief and open-ended so that others might come to their own conclusions upon read-*

ing.

(Septober 31, 3456 M.T.)

BartolMel watched as I read, careful not to interrupt before I finished the text.

"So, what are your feelings?"

"Well-written, but a bit too nebulous. I'd ditch the thing; you don't need it."

The midget bowed. "You have passed the final test."

"Wait, I thought meeting your king was the last one."

"That's what we wanted you to believe. No test is a true test without a surprise last round."

"Am I to guess this really isn't the handbook of your people?"

BartolMel chuckled. "That's exactly what you are to guess."

"Then KarlakArmond's not real."

"He's quite real, and should be in this very commune. *Somewhere.*"

"In that case, I'd like to meet him. He seems interesting."

"That he is. Did you know he always writes while asleep? It's an amazing thing to watch. Unfortunately, this usually means his work is covered with drool and snot when the morning comes. We decided to use this particular manuscript as a secret part of *The Triune Testing* only after he cleaned away the gook."

"But why? What purpose does it serve if it's not your handbook?"

"Whoever believes that we circus midgets need a manifesto doesn't truly understand us. Those who don't truly understand us have no place in our struggle."

"I believe I understand now."

"You do. But tell me – what do you think of your new name?"

"My new name?"

"*Sir Pantsalot*, of course."

"Oh, sorry. I guess the king's scepter jarred a few memories loose. I like it very much. It's far better than my old one."

"What did your name used to be? I don't think anyone here has caught it."

"Matthew."

"I see. But I'm sure you're sick of people asking you questions. You've passed all the tests we have to offer, and the king has smiled upon you. It's time we loosened up."

BartolMel slapped a pink party-hat on my head as he led me from RaggathBob's chamber.

And the fun began.

* * * *

That afternoon, I discovered just how intimate circus midgets are with food. They don't believe in hoarding tiny portions on circular disks. Instead, they indulge in something far more beautiful. They call their ecstatic dining ceremony *The Orgy of Mastication*.

It all begins when the cook, ArnathRoger, wheels a rune-carved chowder bowl from the kitchen. A sixteen-midget team operates the pulley system that lifts it to the tabletop. Forgoing silverware, the midgets climb into the bowl and eat while submerged. The best "seats" are those nearest to the hot-tub jets. While these devices insure that clams and potatoes never settle, their jetting action is quite pleasurable in and of itself.

Of course, much splashing takes place for everyone is both naked and jolly. Only after an hour of frolicking has passed do we climb from the bowl and wash off in a communal shower.

Wary at first, I now find it Zen-like to swim amongst succulent clam hunks. The chowder – neither Manhattan nor New England but something far more interesting – is redolent of the lotus and tastes of the Ganges. I can describe no more without feeling the need to coerce ArnathRoger to prepare another chowder.

Such selflessness! Such community! My eyes and taste buds water. The midgets smile. And all is good.

* * * *

After dinner, the circus midgets and I peruse articles in the *Times Herald Sentinel News Dispatch*. I like circus midget news because it tells me *everything* that happens in this world and beyond. Nothing glossed over. Nothing withheld. For example, a recent edition told of two scientists who discovered a self-contained universe in a loaf of bread purchased from a local bakery. Rumor has it the universe they discovered is, in fact, our own.

Try finding that in the *New York Times* or the *BBC*.

* * * *

We take in TV only when the rest of the day is done. The

midgets don't have cable as most know it. They produce their own shows, and they're nothing short of brilliant.

I must discuss one such program. It's called *The Wily Misdeeds of Dr. Voluptuous*, and it's my favorite.

Dr. Voluptuous is your classic mad-scientist – scar down the side of his cheek, thick German accent. The whole nine yards. His sidekick is Captain Cheese – a moldy, head-sized block of cheddar perched atop an overgrown, thirty-something body. Together, the duo seeks the destruction of Super Hero, Glen Marlon.

In the last episode of its sixty-year run, Glen is cornered in Dr. Voluptuous' subterranean lair. *Super-Saturation Beams* are pointed right at his heart. It appears as though all hope is lost when, suddenly, Glen grabs Captain Cheese and uses his bulk as a human shield.

The bullets rain. The doctor sees what he has done. His heart swells. Six-decades of hatred become a memory. Voluptuous straddles the corpse and tenderly consumes the fetid cheese-block that was once a head. The flies swarming around Captain Cheese do not concern the doctor. He eats them, too. Love is finally consummated as Glen Marlon fires a round, point-blank, into Voluptuous' brain. Skull fragments fly everywhere. *End of show.*

They also have this hour-long program called *The Moon Has Flesh* —but I'm too scared to watch. The midgets have a higher terror-tolerance than Big People. For my new friends, even fear is a dance.

* * * *

During a typical TV night, I turned to SymblozBen – a brother whom I had met at that previous Sunday's Let's-Fund-The-Revolution Bake Sale. I was feeling a little needy, so I decided to ask a favor of him.

Hesitantly: "I hate to sound wanton, but could you send me a photo-play or two? I know you use them for higher purposes, but can't you telegraph a few. . . just for kicks?"

SymblozBen looked so deeply into my soul that my marrow quivered. "You know the photo-plays are sacred, Sir Pantsalot. It's not wise to overuse them. But, since you're a very special person, I'll make an exception and give you four *very short* examples. Just don't tell anyone I did this."

My face lit up.

"For starters, let's imagine that Jesus Christ had been born at a popular fast-food chain instead of a manger in Bethlehem. The wise men wouldn't stand a chance at the door."

As he spoke, I closed my eyes and awaited SymblozBen's initial brain-wave surge:

<RANDOM WISE MAN>: *LO! THE CHRIST CHILDE IS HERE! COME! FOLLOW ME!*

(RANDOM WISE MAN attempts to gain access to the blessed infant through the main entrance.)

<20 YEAR-OLD FAST FOOD EMPLOYEE>: You ain't comin' in here dressed like that! You stink of livestock!

<RANDOM WISE MAN>: But we've brought Frankincense and Myrrh! We must see HIM and present our gifts according to the script! (Looks at Savior and sees HIM being spoon-fed ice cream from a decorative cup featuring promotions for the latest Summer Blockbuster. RANDOM WISE MAN smacks forehead.)

<20 YEAR-OLD FAST FOOD EMPLOYEE>: Manager!

(The WISE MEN are unceremoniously escorted from the building and sent back to the Middle East and Africa where they have much to explain to their respective bosses.)

"Let's see what's happening in Corporate America!"

The scene changed and, in my brain, a nice young man in a lab-coat conversed with a bloated CEO:

<LAB-COAT MAN>: (*Handing a list to CEO.*) We request that you place the following chemicals into your bloodstream via the *INTRAV-DRIP 4000.*

<HEAD CEO>: *(Clutching heart.)* God, no! For the love of humanity! *Security! Security!*

<LAB-COAT MAN>: *(Nonplused.)* I really don't see your problem. You put these in the air, don't you?

(HEAD CEO drops dead of a massive coronary.)

"Now let's take this thing to school!"

<PROFESSOR HIGGENBOTTOM>: We need to create an *Honors Program* for those who shall be cogs and keep the *Epsilons*, ahem. . . I mean the *others* contained within State-Mandated Guidelines so that they may grow up to be the ones who turn the *Alphas*. Or should I say *cogs?*

<HEAD-MASTER BRANSFORD>: *Bravo!* And we should start a *How To Write Memos for Faceless Corporate Entities* class! One mustn't slack in the business world! As we all know, the improper use of a semicolon in inter-departmental memorandums has been linked to a history of fevered drug use.

"Finally, here's a little something about precious things that become corrupted:"

(Scene: *GHANDI and BUDDHA basking in the soft, 40-watt glow of enlightenment. They sit atop a verdant hill near a temple.*)

<GHANDI>: This cosmic consciousness stuff is pretty cool, isn't it?

<BUDDHA>: Yeah, man.

<GHANDI>: Oh, and about those three hundred bucks you owe me . . .

<BUDDHA>: (*Becoming enraged.*) Hindu!

<GHANDI>: (*Same as above.*) Buddhist!

(Thus begins the war.)

I indulged a smile. "Thanks ever so much, SymblozBen. You're my hero."

"Aw shucks, little missy. Think nuthin' of it."

SymblozBen placed a cowboy hat atop his head. Then he disappeared off into the sunset, leaving me to bask in the soft afterglow of a good mind-pick. I turned my attention to the flickering box, but the images swirling in my mind proved far more exciting than anything the machine could offer.

* * * *

Hours later – with my mind and belly full – I bade my friends goodnight. I downed a nightcap of pink, frothy liquid akin to warm milk and slipped into my hyperbaric chamber.

Once inside, I fastened the seal. Nocturnal pranks were quite common and, though one had not yet happened to me, I wished to take every precaution.

I was dreaming within minutes.

* * * *

I left my bed at eight the next morning only to face a hallway cluttered with droves of circus midgets. Lines of seriousness creased once jovial faces. Something great was at hand. Picking up the pace, I forced my sleep-numbed body to follow the phalanx into the conference room. I paused by the threshold before going any further. This chamber was new to me. Quite curious, I took the time to look around.

The room was taller than any I had seen. A domed ceiling soared at least five hundred feet above an ornately tiled floor. Below, a host of mummified remains stood erect in splendid glass caskets. Signs above the containers bore the names of dead U.S. presidents. To the left and right of the mummies, wall-mounted shelves hosted an amazing assortment of spy-gear: wiretaps, night-vision goggles, CIA concocted drugs, Mata Hari's bra. A sign above these objects read: *FOR DISPLAY PURPOSES. PLEASE OBTAIN PERMISSION BEFORE USING.* In the center of this menagerie, suspended from the ceiling, hung a massive coat-of-arms. Something was engraved on its face. I strained my eyes and realized the image was that of a midget brandishing a flaming sword.

I walked in. Perspective shifted. The ceiling once again stood only a foot or so above my head. Looking around, I noticed how everything in the room had adjusted its proportion accordingly.

Waving to everyone, I took my seat by a massive table not unlike one a tourist might see at The United Nations. There, I sat alongside my midgetrine brethren. All were busy dressing up as famous, dead leaders and sticking little pins into battle-maps when the Head of Revolutionary Affairs, BernexCarl, took to the podium clad in jackboots, a beret, and a latex Che Guevara mask. He called us to order.

"I understand you like to be amused – and I must say. . . FentoxRick, that's a wonderful Stalin costume you're wearing – but now it's time to address a few important matters."

I donned the dark wig and aviator sunglasses left for me and listened to the little man by the big podium.

"The Big People's insanity has gone on for far too long! Can I get a witness?"

The circus midget to my right unleashed a boisterous "amen".

"*Parasites! Psychic vampires!* They drain us dry! But do they care?"

We raised our flagons in defiance. "No!"

"That's right! They don't care about *anything* outside their insular world. They take and they take and they *take*. But do they ever *give*? They give us *nothing* apart from their decaying culture! And tell me what we should do with *that*?"

"Nothing!"

"Damn straight! We should do nothing *with* the culture, but we should do something *to* the culture! First, however, we must instigate the *Chain of Absurdity*."

My interest was piqued. "*Chain of Absurdity*? I've never heard of this tactic."

"Of course you haven't. Although you're a special Big Person, you've lived all your life in their world."

I looked down at my shoes with shame.

"Ah, but worry not, Sir Pantsalot! You'll soon learn everything you need to know."

At that point, FarntozAlan chimed in: "The *Chain of Absurdity* assumes true madness has no limit, and exhibits a framework based on infinite, logical progression. The first manifestation just shakes things up a bit. Subsequent manifestations extend the *Chain* by pulverizing reality into smaller and smaller shards. And that's how we get the Big People. We parody their culture to such a degree that our fictions become Prime Reality! Once the–"

"Sorry about that," BernexCarl interrupted. "He's prone to interjecting absolute wisdom into conversations. We don't let him go out in public very often."

I nodded respectfully to FarntozAlan.

BernexCarl continued: "Anyway, FarntozAlan is right. We'll beat them by inverting their own game. Through the *Chain*, we'll gradually pack so many absurdities into the public consciousness that the Big People won't be able to tell the difference between their old life and the one we created for them. A few steps and some patience, that's all it takes. In time, we could have *them* dressing up as circus midgets, and no one would be the wiser."

"And thus Midgetocracy begins," I intuited.

"No, but you're close. And thus *Midgetarchy* begins. We have no need for bureaus or laws. Those things were built for Big People. We don't require a governing body whose only job is to threaten us. We will continue living, with or without laws. You'll never see us carrying color TVs out of broken store windows when the nightly news announces:

<ANCHORMAN'S VOICE>: Sweet mother of milk! *Official Reports* indicate *THE WORLD WILL END IN FIVE MINUTES*!!! And now we cut to an emergency address from THE PRESIDENT.

<PRESIDENT SLOAN>: God bless the Bombs. God Bless 'em!

<Cut to a random city street. The looting is incredible.>

<RANDOM LOOTER>: Gotta get this Big Screen TV out of the store. Gotta watch my *favorite show* on this *sexy piece of equipment* before the world ends in. . . (*Gasp.*) *Three minutes!*

<RANDOM CIRCUS MIDGET *standing on the street corner, carrying a sandwich board. It reads: What the fuck?!?>*

The mental flash ended, and I understood BernexCarl had finished his sentence not with words, but with telepathic thoughtstreams.

"A beautiful vision, is it not?"

"It is. But how do we instigate this chain?"

BernexCarl laughed. "It's already done, my friend. Follow me."

We accompanied him to the living room where he positioned us in a circle around the TV. He switched the set on and turned to *The Nation's #1 News Source*.

"Watch closely. The seeds of confusion will be sown today."

I turned my attention to the screen. A presidential election was in its final stage. News people hustled busily about the studio, reporting returns from all fifty states.

"It appears that the Democratic candidate will win, correct?"

We nodded. Phil Dummeral (D-California) had, according to *The Nation's #1 News Source*, collected enough electoral votes to all but assure his victory.

"But what these newscasters don't realize is that we've bribed both candidates to drop out of the election. It didn't even take as much money as we thought. Needless to say, the country is going to be surprised when the clinically insane Jimmy Jeffrey Sloan takes office."

Entranced, I followed the story:

<NEWS ANCHOR'S VOICE>: And who will it be? The Republican contender MIKE ROGERS or Democrat PHIL DUMMERAL?

<ASSISTANT> *(really a* CIRCUS MIDGET *in disguise) hands* THE NEWS ANCHOR *a slip of paper.)*

<NEWS ANCHOR>: And now the moment you've all been waiting for! Our new President – JIMMY JEFFREY SLOAN!!!

<*Pan over to* THE FACES OF AMERICA>: *Who?*

(*Cut to* ANCHORWOMAN AT CHANNEL 5): What follows is an audio account of PRESIDENT JIMMY JEFFREY SLOAN'S inaugural address:

<PRESIDENT SLOAN>: *PARTY DOWN, FUCKERS!!!*

(Transcriber's note: This single line is followed by 15 minutes of maniacal laughter and sporadic gunfire. At this point, the tape breaks.)

<LATE BREAKING NEWSFLASH!!!>

THE PRESIDENT OF THE UNITED STATES, JIMMY JEFFREY SLOAN, IS NOW RUNNING THROUGH THE STREETS AND SUBURBS OF AMERICA! LOCAL AUTHORITIES REPORT THAT HE IS DRESSED IN A BUNNY COSTUME AND

CARRYING AN AK-47. WHILE THE GUN IS FILLED WITH BLANKS, PRESIDENT SLOAN NEVERTHELESS KNOWS THE CODES REQUIRED TO LAUNCH NUCLEAR WEAPONRY, SO FOR THE LOVE OF GOD JUST LEAVE HIM BE!

"Now the world is primed for the greatest possible onslaught."

We shouted to the rafters and toasted the greatness that was BernexCarl.

* * * *

Of course, not everyone votes or even pays attention to politics. The circus midgets understood this and, five days after Jimmy Jeffrey Sloan's unanticipated inauguration, held a roundtable discussion to shore up *The Chain of Absurdity's* first link.

* * * *

BernexCarl paced back and forth across the conference room floor. "Would you say it's true that everyone has to drink?"

As one: "Yes."

"Since we all agree on that, can we also agree that the average Big Person consumes what he understands to be trendy?"

We nodded in the affirmative.

"And do you think it would be all that difficult to convince people they're not cool if they fail to eschew all beverages in favor of the hottest drink on the market?"

"No."

"Let's say these assumptions are accurate. Is it then too far a stretch to believe the average consumer will purchase soft-drinks having no nutritional value if he considers himself an individual while doing so?"

"All this seems logical," I interjected. "But I don't see where you're going with this."

"Here's the rub, ladies and gentlemen. The average Big Person Consumer *will* neglect hordes of drinks in favor of the one that gives him the illusion of a positive self-image. If we band together – and display some marketing savvy – I believe we can manipulate these base desires and achieve a most desired outcome."

"How so?"

"Glad you asked. We simply convince them, through shrewd advertising, to neglect all other drinks but *Bottled Barbed Chains.*"

"Bottled Barbed Chains? But that sounds fatal."

"Exactly. It could very well be fatal if we didn't doctor the recipe. But that won't stop the Big People from flocking to this product. Remember, they want nothing more than to spend, spend, spend."

"Doctor the recipe? We're talking about *barbed chains* here. And where are we going to find a place to produce this drink?"

BernexCarl laughed. "Sometimes I forget that you haven't been with us long. You have yet to visit our subterranean facilities. We can produce anything there."

"But that doesn't tell me how you're going to make this drink non-fatal."

"You didn't give me time to finish. When I said we could produce anything, I meant we could produce *anything*. It's quite simple to formulate a liquid that will convert to chains."

"But even so, aren't these chains going to tear through people's throats?"

"Yes, but in a perfectly non-fatal way. We can do this because the same asteroid that brought the Agodavo plants also carried along with it strange secrets."

"Are you saying a *book* was on the asteroid?"

"Of course not. It would have burnt up in the atmosphere. Just being in the asteroid's presence infused us with the knowledge of a long dead and *highly* advanced race. I'll show you the fragments sometime. Then you'll know exactly what I mean."

"All this sounds impossible."

"Nothing's impossible."

"But why do it," I pressed. "Why *Bottled Barbed Chains?"*

"Just think how absurd it will be! People will drink and drink and drink until their heads are too heavy to lift. Pretty soon, they'll think the whole process is normal – if not *cool*. Kids who don't have chains swinging from their necks will be pantsed by high school punks. Because they won't like standing around in their underwear, they'll start drinking too. *The Chain of Absurdity* in league with societal conditioning, my friend. Works every time."

"Are you sure people will even buy it? I know I wouldn't."

"Look at it this way. If the government suddenly forgave all debts, the Big People would respond with a mass-buying spree and dig themselves into the exact same hole. They just can't help it. If we tickle their checkbooks and credit cards with a consumer item such as *Bottled Barbed Chains*, our mission *cannot* fail – provided that we can come up with some catchy slogans, of course. Think you can do that for us, Sir Pantsalot?"

I stood up. "Gladly."

"Excellent. Bubblepants, would you show our friend to the print shop? In the meantime, I'll get to mixing the drink. Whoever wants to help may do so."

I bade farewell to BernexCarl. Bubblepants led me from the conference room to an entryway near the botanical garden. He disengaged the lock and the door opened into flight of circular stairs ending in darkness.

Bubblepants removed a flashlight from his pocket. "I hope you got a good night's rest. The case is a bit long."

* * * *

Bubblepants wasn't kidding.

At first, I counted each step I passed. By the time I got to number 9,314, however, I decided it best to stop.

"How much further to the bottom, Bubblepants?"

"About twenty thousand steps, that's all. The print shop is on a sub-basement level."

"Obviously."

We continued on and on. The deeper we went, the colder and darker the stairwell became. I soon noticed vaguely organic, fungoid things growing from the walls. Tiny at first, they gradually increased in size. The biggest ones, which were roughly the size of a small child, exuded a form of bioluminescence and smelled of ancient cheese. Some quivered and pulsated. I wondered if they sensed our presence.

Soon, the depth was too great for even the fungoid things. I looked down. The steps under my feet were suddenly *different*. Rough-hewn stone had replaced steel. Wide at first, these new steps quickly became narrower and narrower.

Bubblepants chimed in: "This particular section is said to predate the Earth itself."

"How can that be?"

"I don't know."

Soon, I was forced to clutch the rocky walls and rely on them for purchase. The steps were now thinner than those I had seen depicted in photographs of Mayan pyramids. I was relieved when the steps finally ended and opened up into a torch lit hall.

"Finally!"

"Oh no, we're not there yet. The print shop isn't for a few more miles."

I unleashed a sigh.

* * * *

A few more hours of wandering through narrow corridors and arched stone doorways ensued.

Though less damp than the stairwell, the hall's atmosphere felt heavier. I observed large notches cut into the wall to form shallow caves. Suddenly, I realized we were wandering through catacombs.

My mouth felt numb, but I managed to speak: "Is this where circus midgets have been entombed since. . . I don't know. . . *the beginning of time?"*

Bubblepants laughed. "I've yet to see a circus midget die, and I'm 3,875 years young!"

"You're that old – I mean *young?* You don't look a day over 30."

He blushed. "Why, thank you!"

"But if these aren't the bodies of circus midgets, then what are they?"

"I'm not certain. They were here before we got the place. Take a closer look, if you'd like. I think you'll find it interesting."

I approached one of the stone crypts with slight apprehension. Taking hold of the cold, leaky rock, I boosted myself up and craned my neck to see inside. What rested within made me gasp.

The thing had a massive, humanoid body, but the skull was oval and smooth. Its only discernable features were three sets of too-small eyeholes and a tiny slit where I assumed its mouth had once been. The jaw itself was unhinged. I looked, but could find no ear holes.

"Dear god."

"Carbon testing failed to register anything conclusive. We do know, however, that they're considerably older than the human race."

"I think I've seen enough."

"In that case, follow me. Only a mile to go."

We continued until the catacombs ended. Sealed entryways now lined each side of the cave.

"Is BernexCarl mixing his drink behind one of these doors?"

"No, that room is on the other side of the hall. About 50 miles away, actually. We *will* pass the room that houses the asteroid BernexCarl told you about. We won't have time to go in, but you can sneak a peek. The door's open."

Sure enough, we passed an unlocked room. I glanced inside and saw the asteroid lying in three crystal-encased pieces. My head suddenly felt fuller and, at that moment, I understood the fundamentals of time travel. Before I gained any greater insight, we passed the room and the mental connection shattered.

My head continued to buzz, though the sensation was fading by the time Bubblepants stopped walking and paused by a door. A wooden sign tacked upon it read: THE PRINT SHOP.

He removed a set of keys from his pocket, inserted one into the lock, and entered the room.

"This is where you'll be spending the next few days."

I followed him into the tiny shop, not surprised to see that, like the catacombs, it had been hewn from sheer rock. The only things in the chamber were a table and an odd contraption with a wheel on one side and a lever on the other.

"Where are the computers? I thought this was a print shop."

"There aren't any, and this *is* a print shop." Bubblepants pointed to the strange cast-iron machine I had just noticed. "You're looking at the printer now."

"That's a printer?"

"An 1874 model, to be exact."

I walked over to the machine. "Where's the plug-in?"

He sighed. *"I said it was made in 1874."*

"But if there's no electricity, how am I supposed to run it?"

Bubblepants joined me by the machine. He stretched out a leg and pumped the twin pads that jutted from its base. The wheel began to turn, and a set of rubber rollers climbed from the belly of the printer.

"Foot power. That's how."

"Is that all I have to do?"

"Not quite. You'll have to pull this lever forward each time you want to print a page."

"Is there a feed-tray? How do I get the paper in?"

"You'll have to do that manually, too." Bubblepants gestured to a raised metal palette in the center of the machine. "But don't forget to roll ink over this first. The rollers move down from here and coat whatever text you have framed and ready to print. At that point, all you have to do is pull the lever and make an impression."

"You said something about having stuff framed. What did you mean by that?"

"It's simple, really. The text is laid out by hand – letter by letter, space by space. Then it must be locked into a frame and inserted just below the inking plate. The type would fall to the floor otherwise."

"Letter by letter? Space by space? That'll take forever!"

"No, it won't. Old Man SnaggleJones is quite fast."

"Who?"

"Look behind you."

I spun around and saw an old, haggard midget standing by the door Bubblepants and I had just entered. Behind him, a strange black hole swirled for a few seconds, billowing his floor-length beard across the room before closing with a pop.

"But. . . but. . ."

Bubblepants grinned. "Don't be scared. Old Man SnaggleJones may have mastered inter-dimensional travel, but he's perfectly harmless."

I offered up a bow. Old Man SnaggleJones responded by farting.

"Unfortunately, he's not much of a talker. The old man lives in his head. He enjoys sharing the print shop with others, but don't expect him to entertain you. Give him some slogans, and he'll assemble the type. SnaggleJones is happiest when kept busy."

I nodded. "That sounds agreeable."

"Good. Then I'll leave you two to your work."

* * * *

Dread filled the first few hours following Bubblepants' departure.

The machine seemed so unwieldy. Old Man SnaggleJones seemed so distant. The shop itself reeked of dust and petroleum soaked rags. I quickly decided this was the last place I ever wanted to be.

Time, however, made me rethink my initial impression. SnaggleJones was always eager to hear any slogan that I threw at him. He rejected a few outright, but the old man peppered his more abrasive comments with constructive criticism and a loud round of farting. Though I couldn't call SnaggleJones the most stimulating conversationalist on the planet, I sensed he was a kind and well-versed soul. After a few days, I began to view him as a grandfather figure.

I even enjoyed the printer itself. The first few hundred pressings were laborious, but I soon found it Zen-like to pump the pedals and pull the lever. I could blank my mind and listen to the gentle clanging and banging of ancient gears as my hands and feet did all the repetitive work.

The printer was a strange machine, though. Old Man SnaggleJones always brought me a frame full of metal type and a supply of ink when the time came to print. Each of these frames appeared to consist of nothing more than lines of neatly assembled text.

When I removed the finished sheet from the printer, however, I was met not only by the expected slogan, but by full-color photos of happy, smiling people with dangling neck chains.

Even the paper transformed during its brief contact with the frame. Nine out of ten times, what was once standard twenty-pound bond exited the machine as glossy poster stock.

How this was possible, I did not know. I just kept printing.

* * * *

Gallons of sweat later, the last advertisement finally passed through Old Man SnaggleJones' printer. Three weeks after that, my adverts appeared on billboards and in public bathrooms citywide.

It went a little something like this:

YOU'RE A PANSY-ASS
IF YOU DON'T DRINK THE NATION'S #1
HARD DRINK:
BOTTLED BARBED CHAINS!!!

We followed up this wildly successful jingle with an onslaught of promotional tie-ins and, finally, the actual release of *Bottled Barbed Chains* itself.

Truth be told, the midgets and I were not as well equipped for distribution as we were for production and promotion. An outside source had to be contracted for the task. I had expected this man to be another midget – but, in fact, he wasn't a man at all. My jaw unhinged in surprise when an obese tabby sauntered through the door and sat down on a neon pink sofa. He not only accepted the coffee Bubblepants offered, but drank like a European gentleman with one tiny digit outstretched. My surprise doubled when the cat spoke, his cultured tones resonating with propriety and, perhaps, veiled malevolence. It was remarkable how similar he sounded to the aristocratic villains depicted in countless movies.

"Thank you kindly for the coffee." He produced a small snuffbox. "Would you fine men care to indulge with me? I assure you the blend is the finest money can buy."

BernexCarl accepted the catnip, but I was too dumbstruck to respond.

The obese tabby's purr sounded like a laugh. "I take it you're not accustomed to speaking with non-humans."

Again, I responded with silence.

"No matter, it's quite good to be back." The obese tabby panned his eyes across the room. "This commune has always felt like my home away from home. Such charming décor – but I digress. Rudimentary business first."

"Of course," BernexCarl replied.

"As I understand it, you wish me to distribute a certain beverage, a *Bottled Barbed Chains?* Correct?"

"Yes."

"Excellent. I understand you're all busy people. By no means do I wish to stall you with idle chit-chat or bore you with the details of my method." The tabby leaned back in his seat. "But there *is* the matter of compensation, which I always enjoy discussing."

"Perhaps you might like to stroll through our *Room of Gadgets*. There are some interesting items there. *Invaluable*. Of course, if nothing strikes your personal fancy you can always sell it for profit."

The tabby smiled. "Ah, but of course."

"Then shall we go?"

The tabby climbed down from his seat and BernexCarl arose to provide escort. Infinity swallowed them seconds later.

I turned around and saw Bubblepants sweeping a rug. I called out to him.

"Hey, Bubblepants. The craziest thing just happened. Come over here and I'll tell you about it."

Laying down the broom, he joined me by the sofa. He sat down and turned on the TV. A re-run of *The Wily Misdeeds of Dr. Voluptuous* flickered on the tube.

"So, what's on your mind?"

"This may sound hard to believe but, from what I gather, a talking cat is going distribute *Bottled Barbed Chains* for us."

"Oh, you mean the obese tabby?"

"I guess so. He *was* pretty fat."

"Yeah, that's who you're talking about alright."

"Wait, doesn't this surprise you?"

Bubblepants shrugged. "No, not really. Should it?"

"Well, yeah. . . we're discussing a supernaturally articulate cat here."

"I've seen stranger things but, truth be told, the obese tabby is the only man – er – *cat* for the job."

"And why's that?"

"Because no one else specializes in the unusual goods and services he distributes. He also runs a successful store in an alternate dimension. It has a funny name. I wish I could remember what it was."

"Then I guess his being here is a good thing."

"Probably, but the tabby has a reputation for triple dealing. His products often contain unwelcome surprises. You never quite know what you're getting when you do business with him but, like I say, no one else is qualified to distribute so unique a product."

"I see. Thanks, Bubblepants."

At that point, he turned to the TV and lost himself in *The Wily Misdeeds of Dr. Voluptuous.* I did the same, no longer willing to rack my brain over something the rest of my friends seemed to view as an unremarkable event.

* * * *

Within a week of finalizing a deal with the obese tabby, Big People citywide not only sported officially licensed *Bottled Barbed Chain*-wear but drank the stuff by the gallon. Even flap-daddies had gone the way of platform shoes in the wake of the *Bottled Barbed Chains* juggernaut.

We stared in amusement as the public passed by our hallowed halls, their backs featuring nothing less than our slogans, their necks featuring nothing less than our chains:

IT'S GLAMOROUS TO HAVE SHARP OBJECTS SLIDE EFFORTLESSLY DOWN YOUR GULLET!

DRINK! DON'T GET PANTSED!

I LIKE MY THROAT LACERATED WHEN I CON-

SUME BEVERAGES OF A COMMERCIAL NATURE!

We lacked only one thing.
A famous endorser.

* * * *

The next day, BernexCarl sent me a telepathic page.

<*BernexCarl*>: We have assigned a special task for you, Sir Pantsalot. Please meet me in the *Room of Gadgets* as soon as possible.

I arose from bed and wandered the halls for about fifteen minutes. Finally, I came upon a door. Two signs were affixed upon it:

ROOM OF GADGETS

and, further down:

PLEASE FASTEN SUIT BEFORE ENTERING LOBBY

I looked to my left. A number of radiation-proof garments hung from a coat rack. I slipped into one of the white body suits and placed a plastic helmet on my head. Opening the door, I found myself in a small, steel-lined waiting room. It was obviously a buffer between whatever the *Room of Gadgets* contained and the public hallway.

I pushed a red button on the side of the wall; a heavy door slid open. BernexCarl stood amongst a most amazing assortment of bleeping gizmos and Tesla coils. A massive, humanoid form lay supine beneath a white cloth. I tried my best to ignore the thing (and its horrid stench) as I motioned to BernexCarl.

"Ah! Glad to see you arrived so quickly!"

"I came as soon as I received your page."

"Very good. I admire promptness."

I tugged at my radiation suit. "Could you tell me why I have to wear this thing?"

"Because some of the items I experiment with are known to – how should I say this – *leak.*"

"What? *Radiation?*"

"Not quite. 1975 was the last time we experienced a problem. Do you recall what cultural phenomena swept the western world soon after?"

A vision of polyester leisure suits swept through my mind. My face folded into a grimace.

"I still feel guilty for unleashing so much terror. We have stricter protocols now. That's why you have to wear the suit. We can't have something like that happening again."

"So, what kind of stuff *do* you do here?"

"Let's just say my responsibilities are staggering, but I didn't bring you over to recite a job description." BernexCarl paused. "I brought you here because I have some bad news to report."

"How bad?"

"Our agents in the field tell us that one of our trainees – despite being lobotomized by JartawSmith – harbors memories of his stay. And he's telling others."

"Dear god!"

"I've already sent ambassadors to converse with him, but the man's too filled with Thorazine to communicate with anyone. We've even gone so far as to bribe him. Sadly, he has no idea what money is."

"Are you sure it's not too late? And why would he be filled with Thorazine?"

"The situation's not yet critical. The man's in a mental hospital, being treated as we speak. When he's locked up, he's of no harm to anyone. But our spies have retrieved inter-departmental memos from the ward. His treatment is scheduled to end in two weeks. If he gets out and tells the wrong people, all the work we have done will be for naught!"

"Then we don't have much time."

"You understand why we must act fact. Good. I didn't want to send you on this mission until you had undergone training in spatial displacement but, sadly, you must leave tomorrow."

"Spatial displacement?"

BernexCarl spun around and retrieved a wristwatch from the table behind him. He dangled it in front of my face. "Do you know what this is?"

"A wristwatch."

"Correct! But it does much more than tell time. It also serves as a convenient means of teleportation."

"Really?"

"You can go anyplace on or off the globe. Just visualize the desired location in your mind, wind the watch three times, and you're there."

"Why are you telling me this?"

He smiled. "Because you'll need to know how to use the watch before you teleport to Hollywood, California."

"Hollywood!"

"I'll have you know this is a mission of necessity, not pleasure. Do you think you're up to the task? If not, I can always get someone–"

"I'm willing to make any sacrifice."

"I was certain you were the right man."

"So, what am I to do?"

"Find a celebrity who's willing not only to endorse *Bottled Barbed Chains,* but also appear live in a television commercial promoting the beverage. But don't be fooled into thinking this is just any old advert. It's *The Commercial of Truth* – the closing of *The Chain of Absurdity's* first link. With it, the message of *Barbed Bottled Chains* goes national as the second link forms."

"What's the second link? Or have you gotten that far yet?"

"Oh, I have. Let me show you. Behold, the next link."

"Uh. That's just a pair of pants with the front cut out."

"Precisely!"

I was confused.

"So, what do you think? Do remember, however, that this is just a prototype."

"I honestly don't know what to say."

"Indeed, but here's the plan: During the *Commercial of Truth*, our celebrity will wear *Viso-Pants*. No mention will be made of them in the commercial itself because we don't want to promote them yet, just test the waters of public support."

"You think people will go for it?"

"They went for *Bottled Barbed Chains*, didn't they?"

"Yeah, I guess so."

"The actual pants will be far more decorative than this basic model, of course. I'm considering adding either fringe or lace around the opening for women – and, of course, for men who like that sort of thing. We'll also produce *Viso-Pants* as blue jeans, slacks, and shorts."

I cringed.

"Just think about it. The people will not only have chains dangling from their necks, but they'll be able to tell what kind and color of underwear everybody else is wearing. We have little time to plan, however. The commercial must be on-air before our unfortunate trainee leaves the mental hospital and tells the world everything he knows. Because of this, you must leave for Hollywood as soon as dawn breaks."

"But I have no experience. I've never even spoken with a celebrity before."

"That matters little in light of the two suitcases I'm going to send along with you. They're very important, one more so than the other."

"Can I ask what's in them?"

He pressed his finger to his lips and unleashed a mischievous chuckle.

"Can't you tell me *anything?"*

"I'll hand both to you before you teleport. That's all you need to know. I could tell you more, but I so love the element of surprise."

"Wait–"

"Don't ask questions. Just hold out your hand."

I did so, and BernexCarl dropped the wristwatch into my palm.

"Now go. Decontamination and containment will take a number of hours, yet you must teleport first thing tomorrow."

"Decontamination?"

"It's standard procedure."

"Will it hurt?"

BernexCarl laughed. "No, and you may even find the steel wool showers enjoyable."

I bade the little man farewell. Back in the buffer room, I was hosed down with jets of water, scrubbed with harsh abrasives, and sprayed with strange gasses well into the night. I was allowed to return to my bedchamber only after ten hours had passed.

But I didn't retire.

I performed silent meditation to ready myself as invisible monks chanted in the background.

Whether they were real or imaginary, I will never know.

* * * *

The circus midgets gathered in the living room to send me off at 8:30 the next morning.

"Best of luck!"

"We know you'll do your best! Don't worry!"

"Don't forget to write!"

I waved to the lot of them and wound the watch three times. BernexCarl thrust a suitcase into each of my hands just before the device worked its magic. A big red #1 was painted on the first case. A big blue #2 was painted on the other.

Then my very being was ripped to shreds.

* * * *

The next thing I knew, my atoms were flowing in the *Great Cosmic Unknown*. Gods in fiery chariots passed by my flailing molecules:

<<u>ZEUS</u>>: *Hey, watch where the hell you're going!*

Space-time whisked me along so quickly that I didn't have time to apologize.

But. . .

Just when I was beginning to groove with this new sensation, I was plunked down in some filthy back alley where trash was piled ankle deep.

* * * *

It was a good thing the wristwatch hadn't deposited me somewhere more public. I suddenly felt like my body had turned both inside out and outside in. I swam on my feet. My legs bucked and my arms flapped because most of my bones had yet to rematerialize. The world was half black. I lifted my hands to my head, felt the empty eye socket there, and nausea mounted.

I collapsed to the ground. I vomited profusely. My stomach seemed to climb up through my throat. I wanted to stop, but continued to spew horrible things from my mouth – things I couldn't have possibly eaten. Green. Blue. Red. Orange. Purple. I didn't realize the human body was capable of puking up objects of such color. Nevertheless, they poured out onto the pavement in wet profusion.

The vomiting stopped only after ten minutes had passed. But there was no relief. My hands quaked. I tried sitting on them, but that stopped nothing. Soon after, my legs began to spasm. My entire upper and lower half soon followed suit. My body flapped like a fish. I'm surprised I didn't wind up damaging myself. It was a good thing the alley was packed full of garbage. It helped cushion the blows.

I lost consciousness at some point. The world was a void for so long I understood what it was like to be dead.

When I finally woke up, however, I felt renewed and invigorated – almost like a child again. My bones had returned and I could see out of both eyes. Even the still-fetid air smelled somehow fresher.

I drew in a series of deep breaths, took to my feet, and prepared to accost the first celebrity I encountered. No longer did I doubt myself. I was ready for anything.

And then I looked down at my clothes.

Garish colors and hunks of semi-digested food streamed down the entire length of my shirt and puddled in both pant cuffs. It appeared as though *The Amazing Technicolor Dream Coat* had just exploded.

Bringing my hands to my face, I recoiled at the chunky wetness there. I ran my fingers through my hair and they became trapped in the impossibly gooey strands. It took all of five minutes to remove them.

Crippled! I couldn't meet anyone in such a state! I slammed my fist against the wall and brought my foot down hard against a beer bottle, smashing it.

I had failed the midgets. *The Chain of Absurdity* – broken.

Suicide seemed like the best option.

Then I remembered the suitcases.

I bent down to pick up the case labeled #1. I wiped the colorful vomit from its side and flipped open the latches.

A bottle of shampoo, a comb, and a four-piece suit rested inside. I smiled. Thoughts of ending my life fled. BernexCarl was a very wise man and had foreseen just how messy I would become.

I wiped goo from my hands before lifting the garments from their case. Each seemed so very expensive. The vest was a shimmery white, as was the shirt. The coat had tails that streamed nearly to the floor, and the pants were tastefully pleated. The rich, brown leather shoes featured laces that bore twin tassels.

I carried the clothes and shampoo with me as I wandered around the back alley. I moved aside a ton of accumulated trash and debris until I found a wall-mounted spigot. Turning it on, I allowed the water to pour over my hair. Then I picked up the shampoo.

SPECIFICALLY FORMULATED TO REMOVE SPA-

the bottle said.

I squirted a dollop onto my hand and built up a creamy lather. The shampoo tingled in a way I had not experienced before. Suds interacted with my scalp on some bio-molecular level.

I allowed my hair to dry a few minutes before stepping out of my old clothes. I tossed them into the first suitcase and threw the whole repulsive package into an overflowing trash bin. My entire person felt immediately cleaner.

Sliding into my new suit, I found it a perfect fit. The four pieces seemed tailor-made even though I couldn't recall the midgets ever taking my measurements. I suddenly wished I had access to a mirror. Pure vanity – but I knew I was dressed-to-kill.

I turned around and saw the other suitcase lying on its side. My vomit-shower had, for the most part, spared the case. Only a few yellow and red streaks ran down its leather front.

I desperately wanted to open the thing but, for some reason, I felt the time was not yet right. Instead, I picked it up, brushed the lint from my clothes, and left the alley.

* * * *

I entered the street as whores closed in from behind.

"Hey, good lookin'. Nice suit, there. Got lots of money?"

I said nothing because I could smell her sex-reek. The urge to vomit was amazing.

"Come on, baby. Let us show you a good time."

"Please," I shouted. "Stop bothering me!"

"Blow jobs are only fifteen bucks."

"But I don't want a blow job!"

"Okay. Ten for a hand job."

"Weren't you listening?"

They said nothing more, but continued advancing.

I turned to flee. Behind me, I heard the fevered jangle of their gaudy bracelets. I closed my ears to the maddening sound and soon passed into another neighborhood.

The buildings here were decaying husks. Junkies lay in heaps on filth-smeared sidewalks as homeless men muttered to themselves in dark alleyways. Exhaust from crackpipes hung in the air, a heavy cloud. Gang bangers prowled the streets.

And the whores kept pursuing me. They were gaining fast.

I picked up the pace. My side ached, but I ignored the burn. Then I heard what sounded like a few more footsteps enter the pursuit. I risked a backward glance. A trio of gang bangers had joined the whores.

"This be *our* turf, *honkey mofo!"*

I feared death. I considered ditching the second suitcase, but thought better of it. BernexCarl wouldn't have given it to me if the things inside weren't vitally important. I held tight and prayed the load wouldn't prove too much of a burden.

Then, off in the distance, I spotted train tracks. The sun shone brightly beyond the trestle. Further back, towering metal and glass skyscrapers loomed over a clean and junky-free street. Only a few more blocks until I'd be free from the dirt and depravity. I forced myself to go faster, even as the voices from behind leeched at my resolve:

"Suck and blow! We can do it all night long, baby!"

"Slow down, you white-bread *fucka!"*

I sucked in a deep breath and gagged on particulate matter. Sputtering and coughing, I managed to reach the tracks and, in a single bound, leap over them. Unfortunately, I tripped on the last trestle and collapsed to the ground.

I was on the other side now, but that didn't mean the game was over. Whores would surely blow me as gang bangers focused on capping my other head. I cursed my clumsy feet.

Sure, I was on a sidewalk running alongside a very public street. But would that help me? I doubted it. Stranger things have happened, and this was Southern California.

I said a final prayer before turning again to face the decaying neighborhood. The whores and gang bangers were now neck-and-neck. I figured I had five seconds of quality time remaining.

My pursuers reached the tracks and jumped over them, only to hit an invisible wall in the air and fall back on their asses. For the first time, I noticed the bleeping collars locked around their necks.

Then it struck me. *They had encountered a force field.* Their collars obviously made this part of the city inaccessible to them. The result of some new city ordinance, perhaps. Something to keep the undesirables away from the famous.

Relieved, I ignored the curses from both whore and gang banger and took my first look at Hollywood.

All around me, low-paid laborers applied latex facial prosthetics to sagging, celebrity skin. Producers and assorted bigwigs filled their noses with the finest blow available. The cold, hard smells of cash and beluga caviar mingled in the air. It was at least better than the sex-reek a few streets back.

I found myself nearing *The Chinese Theater*. Outside its doors, hundreds of celebrities stood transfixed over their personal stars on *The Walk of Fame*. Most appeared emaciated – on the verge of death. I assumed they hadn't eaten in weeks. Walking over to one, I tugged at the sleeve of his Armani jacket.

"Would you like something to snack on? I might have a pack of peanuts in my pocket if you want them."

The celebrity hissed. "Fuck off. I'm looking at my star."

"Are you sure? I've got enough for–"

"FUCK OFF!!!"

I turned away and walked until I reached the end of the block. There, I saw a famous sports star. He pounded the sidewalk across from me with a basketball, oblivious to others trying to navigate the thin, concrete expanse.

I went into autopilot mode. I crossed the busy street, closing my ears to both horns and screamed obscenities. Death was not in my realm of concern. Miraculously, I managed to reach the man without injury to my person. I stopped mere inches from his face and waited for him to acknowledge me.

The guy kept playing with his ball. *Bounce. Bounce. Bounce.*

"Um. . . excuse me?"

Bounce. Bounce. Bounce.

"Sir?"

Bounce. Bounce. Bounce.

"Can you hear me?"

Bounce. Bounce. Bounce.

"LOOK AT ME, DAMN YOU!!!"

The sports star gazed up from his ball. "Huh? Did you say something?"

"As a matter of fact, I did."

"Well, what do you want? Can't you see I'm busy?"

"I just wondered if I'm correct in thinking that you're famous."

"Yeah. What's it to yah?"

"In that case, would you like to appear in a commercial for–"

"Nope. Not interested. My slate's already full." He returned to bouncing the ball.

"I don't think you understand."

Bounce. Bounce. Bounce.

"I have something that might interest you."

Bounce. Bounce. Bounce.

I lifted the case.

The bouncing stopped.

"What do you have there?"

"I don't know."

"You don't know?"

"Perhaps we can discuss this somewhere more private. Do you have an office?"

The sports star pointed to the building towering above us. "It's up there, on the thirteenth floor."

"I see. Shall we go up, then?"

The sports star led, and I followed eagerly behind.

* * * *

My subsequent meeting with FAMOUS SPORTS STAR went something like this:

<FAMOUS SPORTS STAR>: (*Spoken while braiding hair.*) You know I only endorse the most lucrative products on the market. Gotta teach the kids to be good consumers.

<ME>: I understand perfectly. But *Bottled Barbed Chains* is the drink of The New Dark Ages. Trust me, all the kids are screaming for my product. *All of them.*

<FAMOUS SPORTS STAR>: Is that a fact?

<ME>: Yes. And the commercial – should you choose to accept – will be filmed live. No script. It'll give you the perfect opportunity to show off your prowess.

<FAMOUS SPORTS STAR>: Fuck that. Just tell me what's in that case of yours.

<ME>: Let's find out. (*Opens case. Shields eyes from stark, white glare.)*

<FAMOUS SPORTS STAR>*'s bladder loosens:* Dear God! I thought it was only a legend!

<ME>: (*Peeking in at the strange, glowing obelisk.*) What the hell is it?

<FAMOUS SPORTS STAR>: I've long heard stories about *The Talisman of Fame*. He who possesses it shall never want for endorsement. *Never*.

<ME>: Really? Is that the case?

<FAMOUS SPORTS STAR>: My fears of falling into obscurity are *gone*. The obelisk is here, right now, in front of me, *glistening*.

<ME>: Do we have a deal, then?

<FAMOUS SPORTS STAR>: (*Snatching obelisk, holding it protectively to breast.*) I'll do anything you ask. *Name it*.

<ME>: Wonderful! Oh. . . by the way. . . I forgot to mention that you'll be required to wear *Viso-Pants* during the commercial.

<FAMOUS SPORTS STAR>: *Viso-Pants?* What's that?

<ME>: Only the soon-to-be hottest thing in fashion. The entire front is cut away, hence the name. *Viso-Pants* are specifically designed to give underwear the exposure it deserves. Do you have a problem with that?

<FAMOUS SPORTS STAR>*: (Looks concerned for a moment, then glances back at the obelisk which, for one reason or another, has started pulsating. Concern vanishes.)* No, of course not.

Within thirty minutes, I had the pleasure of obtaining the sports star's signature on all the appropriate contracts. We shook hands and finalized a date for the filming of *The Commercial of Truth*. I made sure to set it a full five days before the ex-trainee was scheduled to leave the mental ward.

Before I departed, however, the sports star presented me with an autographed photo of himself bedecked in corporate logos and drinking/holding/inserting every consumer-based product available.

"I usually ask fifty bucks for something like this," he said, "but, since you gave me the obelisk and all, I'll let you have it for free."

I faked a smile and accepted the offering.

He added: "And remember to brush your teeth with *White-All* brand paste!"

I didn't respond. I left the office.

In the hall, I kept my eyes peeled for other people. I saw and heard nothing, so I wound my wristwatch three times and, seconds later, my atoms hurtled back to the commune.

Only after five additional hours of vomiting up every color of the rainbow was I capable of speech.

And, when that time passed, I couldn't refrain from jumping up and down as I related tales of success to tiny ears.

* * * *

The next week passed very quickly, but our excitement nevertheless increased to epic proportions. Just a scant two days before *The Commercial of Truth* was set to air, I found it necessary to visit a clinic where anatomical diagrams of odd life forms hung on walls and skeletons of fantasy creatures rested in cabinets.

Even the sharp odor of antiseptic spray could not dampen my all-encompassing awe. I looked beyond the menagerie and through a door that opened into an operating room. There, I saw clamps, blades, saws, and coiled metal tubing connected to a strange black box. The thing made a rumbling sound, like an engine idling. I wanted to take a closer look, but was afraid the doctor might be less than pleased if he found me snooping.

I pressed on until I reached a door upon which a brass plate was affixed. It read: *OFFICE OF CHIEF SURGEON JARTAWSMITH.* Once in the small, wood-paneled room, I saw JartawSmith bending a spine back and forth absent mindedly. I was staggered. He looked just like a miniature version of Richard Chamberlain.

"Excuse me, Doctor..."

"Oh it's you, Sir Pantsalot!" He turned his attention from the spine. "I was wondering when I'd finally meet our new inductee. I had the pleasure of introducing myself to the other recruits and, of course, performing frontal lobotomies on them. But you passed. Sadly, my fingers never got the opportunity to play nimbly about your brain."

"Maybe we can make up for lost time."

"That would be an honor."

"Same here."

"So, what can I do for you?"

"I'm feeling stressed out. *The Commercial of Truth* is going to air just forty-eight hours from now. I can't take the anticipation and fear I might go mad."

JartawSmith scratched his beard. "Hmmm, I think I might have just what the doctor ordered. I know it's down here. *Somewhere.*"

He slid under his desk and rummaged through the trash heaped there. He brushed aside countless fanzines and candy wrappers until he uncovered a small vial full of foamy, green paste.

"Eureka!"

"Is it that good?"

"Oh yes, it'll take your mind off *everything.*"

"But what if BernexCarl needs me for another mission? I must be prepared."

"I'll write you a doctor's excuse, but I don't think it'll come to that. BernexCarl realizes the lengths you've gone to further our cause. He'd encourage you to take my medicine if he were here."

"But what will it do?"

"Let's put it this way, for two days you'll exist on a different plateau of consciousness. When the medicine's effect wears off, *The Commercial of Truth* will be minutes from air-time."

"I'm not sure–"

"Worry not. It's perfectly safe. I took some five minutes before you stepped in. Honestly, I'm a bit stressed out as well. It's probably going to kick in any second now, and I wouldn't be surprised if–"

I watched in awe as flowers sprouted from JartawSmith's mouth. Little birdies spontaneously generated within the petals and roosted in the Chief Surgeon's hair. Below the newly formed nests, the doctor's face *shifted*, turning convex, then concave. I couldn't imagine how his bones compensated for such amazing distortion and watched in continued awe as JartawSmith floated to the floor in slow motion as the rest of the room continued to function in real-time.

Within seconds, a peaceful glow settled about his form.

"Can you hear me, sir?"

The doctor did not respond, but he seemed alive and breathing well. I bent down and noted the rapturous smile on his face, so I seized the opportunity. Scooping the vial from his limp hand, I ran with it to my bedchamber.

Within seconds, JartawSmith and I cavorted in a land filled with twinkling stars, black sand, red tides, and pulsating, disembodied brains.

* * * *

When I finally arose, I felt only slightly groggy and not a bit hung over.

I bent over to grab my clothes. My old garments were gone. In their place rested a pair of oversized blue trousers, a red shirt with white polka dots, orange suspenders, and white floppy shoes. On top of it all sat a bright red clown nose and a folded letter.

I picked up the note and read what had been left for me:

Sir Pantsalot,

Wear this and become a member of the family on the outside as well as on the inside.
With Upmost Respect – BernexCarl

My breath failed me. I felt love like I had never experienced it before. I hastened to the mirror to try on my clothes. My heart pounded as I put my legs into the blue pants and pulled the waistband up over my hips. My phallus swelled as the silky red and white shirt slid across my nipples. I can't begin to describe the sensation that rushed through me when I put the clown nose over my own!

I would never in my life wear Big People clothes again.

* * * *

I wandered, beaming, into the living room. There, I saw the midgets preparing for *The Commercial of Truth Party*. The walls bristled with streamers and balloons, yet my friends still hung more!

I peeked into the kitchen. Chef ArnathRoger busily scraped pounds of processed meat from tin cans while his assistant created alcohol-based drinks. From the look of it, she was mixing some pretty stout stuff.

I felt guilty. I seemed to be the only person doing nothing. BernexCarl happened to pass by, so I called out to him.

"You all seem so busy. Do you need any help? I've been told I'm a pretty good cook."

His smile beamed. "You've done enough. Sit back, and we'll serve you."

"But it's the least I can do after–"

"Tut-tut! Say no more! We insist."

"Are you sure?"

"I am. Go take a seat. We'll send a drink or two your way."

"But I can't possibly go without thanking you for this wonderful outfit. I want you to know how much it means to me."

BernexCarl stood on his tiptoes and tousled my hair. "Don't bother. Just accept the gift as a right of passage."

I bowed and left BernexCarl to attend to business in the kitchen.

* * * *

ArnathRoger's beautiful assistant offered to refresh my glass within minutes of my taking a seat by the TV.

"No, I really shouldn't. I've taken twelve already."

"Come now! Twelve? I've had forty since ten this morning!"

"And you're still standing?"

"Circus midgets have a high tolerance for alcohol."

"I see."

"So, would you like another?"

"Sure. Why not?" I sighed. "Keep'em coming."

ArnathRoger's beautiful assistant poured the drink with a smile. Before departing, she reached into her pocket, withdrew a twisty-straw, and inserted it into my whiskey.

* * * *

Usually a moderate drinker, I must admit I was smashed that day. *Hell yeah!!!* I was talking to ladies who weren't there, asking them if they wanted me to buy them a drink, three and a half kids, and a house in the suburbs. *Boy was I toasty!*

I even rolled around the floor for a few minutes, mumbling incoherently. The circus midgets looked at me with benign amusement.

A few minutes passed before I no longer felt quite so retarded. I got up from the floor, dusted myself off, and returned to my seat.

"Sorry about that."

No one seemed to mind, but I continued apologizing.

"But I'm really–"

"Ssshhhh," one said.

Another: "The commercial's beginning!"

I spun around drunkenly. "Really? Is the obese tabby here, too?"

"Hush!"

Rapt attention replaced my drunken stupor. I joined everyone as they gathered closer to the TV: BernexCarl, Bubblepants, XerlexGeorge, VerlaxPete, ZarnoxJohn, GarnlopBill, BartolMel, SymblozPete, Old Man SnaggleJones, JartawSmith – so many more. Together, we watched the revolution unfold live on national television:

(*OPENING: A brief pre-recorded segue in which the* <u>FAMOUS SPORTS STAR</u> *is seen playing basketball with children from various ethnic backgrounds.*)

<u>VOICE OVER</u>: I got game and you can have game, too – if you do things *my way*.

(*Cut to* <u>FAMOUS SPORTS STAR</u>. *He is standing behind a wall-sized poster of himself making a slamdunk. He wears a basketball jersey and Viso-Pants, his blue underwear revealed. In his hand, he holds a bottle.*)

<u>FAMOUS SPORTS STAR</u>: Being famous sure brings out my thirst.

(*Insert another pre-recorded segue in which* <u>FAMOUS SPORTS STAR</u> *signs autographs for dying, crippled, or otherwise maimed children.*)

<u>FAMOUS SPORTS STAR</u>: And when I'm thirsty, I love nothing more than to drink *BOTTLED BARBED CHAINS* from *THE SENTIENT POTATO COMPANY*. It refreshes my parched tongue like no other oxidized hard drink.

(*Camera pans closer to* <u>FAMOUS SPORTS STAR's</u> *mouth. He drinks lustily, his adam's apple bobbing up and down. The barbs, however, fail to perform as intended. They tear a hole through his throat and slide out the gaping fissure. The wound never heals; the* FAMOUS SPORTS STAR *staggers about.*)

FAMOUS SPORTS STAR: Garg. Blargle. Gragh.

"Uh..." BartolMel interrupted. "Was *that* supposed to happen?"

BernexCarl stared at the screen, his mouth wide. "No, not at all."

"Well? What can we do? We've got to stop this!"

"We can do *nothing*. We must see how this plays out."

All eyes returned to the television.

(FAMOUS SPORTS STAR'S *dying bulk remains aloft. Chains dangle from his neck wound. The blood flow is amazing.)*

(*Cut to another segue.* The FAMOUS SPORTS STAR *is seen at a club, looking fashionable in his Viso-Pants and picking up women sporting tube-tops and mini-skirts. The men in the background look on with envy. If only they too had name recognition and pants that exposed their briefs.*)

(Return to FAMOUS SPORTS STAR *who says nothing because he's retching up blood.)*

(At this point, the script flies out the window. THE CAMERAMEN *neglect their duties and run up to the* FAMOUS SPORTS STAR. *They tug at the chains dangling from his wound – curious animals one and all.)*

FAMOUS SPORTS STAR: Narg. (*Wheeze.*) Gallzpppp.

(*The* CAMERAMEN *stop tugging and begin to pull, divorcing chunks from* FAMOUS SPORTS STAR's *throat. Their language disintegrates. Bestial mumblings fill the room.*)

FAMOUS SPORTS STAR: (*Dies.*)

"What the hell just happened," ZarnoxJohn screamed. "No

one was supposed to die!"

"Something went wrong with one of the batches. The chains weren't rendered non-fatal."

"I bet it was that damn obese tabby! He doctored the batch!"

(*Behind his carcass, the door flies open. Multitudes clamor towards the stage and descend on* FAMOUS SPORTS STAR. *They proceed to join* THE CAMERAMEN *in their wholesale rending of flesh.*)

(*Cut to final segue.* FAMOUS SPORTS STAR *stands in a field, Bottled Barbed Chains in hand. He looks toward the horizon as if contemplating a bright tomorrow. He caresses the bottle gently. Fade out.)*

(Fade in. Return to the melee. The stage is flooded with people, but more still come.)

SymbolzBen: "Sweet God! I thought this was a closed set!"

JartawSmith: "It used to be! The masses broke down the door!"

ArnathRoger: "Have you ever seen so much hunger in human eyes?"

Old Man SnaggleJones: *"Never."*

XerlexGeorge: "I can't watch this!"

BernexCarl: "You have no choice."

A RANDOM MAN OF THE CLOTH : (*Sinking his fist into* FAMOUS SPORTS STAR's *chest cavity.*) Ooooooooh, this feels so right! And don't forget to drink *BOTTLED BARBED CHAINS!*

A FORTY-YEAR OLD HOMEMAKER FROM DELUTH: (*Stuffing* FAMOUS SPORTS STAR's *severed head in her oversized purse.*) Damn it, this thing won't fit! And remember, always purchase your products from *THE SENTIENT POTATO COMPANY!*

AN INSINCERE POLITICIAN: (*reaching his hands into* FAMOUS SPORTS STAR's *throat before addressing his wife, HELEN.*) Feel this hot, steaming cartilage, baby!

HELEN: Yeah, and don't forget to pick up the newest beverage from

THE SENTIENT POTATO COMPANY – Low-calorie, diet *ZYCLON B!*

(The frenzy continues without end.)

Bubblepants clutched his gut. Then his hands flew to his mouth, but that did not prevent the subsequent vomit shower from staining the couch below. ZarnoxJohn gnashed his teeth, rent his clothes, and cursed the obese tabby. VerlaxPete sat choking and sputtering on a mouthful of booze. XerlexGeorge just blubbered. A chorus of shouts and screams arose from all around.

"We're all murderers!"

"Stained forever!"

"No better than dogs!"

I couldn't bear to hear such things, especially from my friends. I wanted to comfort them – to offer solace – but I couldn't find the right words. My brain spun. Everything felt hopeless, out of control. I turned back to the TV. Perhaps the melee had let up and things weren't nearly as bad as they seemed.

But that wasn't the case. The cameramen were probably still ripping at the star's neck chains, though they were no longer visible as those writhing above reverted to cannibalism on national TV. I didn't even want to consider how many tons of flesh were presently being consumed. The hundreds of writhing bodies became thousands and the thousands became millions.

I averted my eyes from the horror. SymbolzBen was now trying to smother himself, his head wedged firmly between the cushion and the couch. At that point, BernexCarl stood.

"*Enough!*"

SymblozBen removed his head from the couch. ZarnoxJohn forgot about pulling at his already tattered shirt, and XerlexGeorge ceased blubbering. All eyes turned to BernexCarl.

"Please, level heads must prevail. There's nothing more we can do."

ZarnoxJohn resumed wailing: *"The tabby! The tabby!"*

"We cannot place the blame at anyone's feet, though it would not surprise me if the tabby did have something to do with this. First and foremost, we should all calm down."

SymbolzBen shouted: "*Calm down!* But. . . but. . . *look at the TV!* So many *bodies!"*

"True. They all came." BernexCarl glanced back at the set, and his face became a solemn mask. "Men, women, day-traders, presidents, prostitutes, kindergarten teachers – all intent on stealing a piece of their hero. They got lost in the carnage, instead."

I addressed BernexCarl: *"But why?* Why did it have to happen?"

"In the Big World, large-scale deviations from the norm can result in primal savagery, though I doubt there has ever been a case so extreme. The death of the sports star provided the right impetus at the right time. The ball rolled from there."

"But *we* provided the impetus. *We* created the commercial. It was our hands that made the ball roll."

BernexCarl nodded. "If the death of the sports star could create so much havoc, then the Big People's world was set on shakier foundations than even I thought possible. Its end was imminent with or without our commercial. It was only a matter of time."

"But you feel remorse, don't you?"

"Of course. We must *never* forget that before us stands a tragedy of our own creation. I'm not alone in wishing the world had not driven us to such extremes, but the Big People gave us no choice. We had to instigate the chain and bring about an unforeseen end. Now, they're eating each other on television."

GarnlopBill, who had remained stone-faced throughout the entire proceedings, spoke up: "Sure, I feel a little bad about it myself. But we've won our prize and won it early. That's what counts, right?"

BernexCarl walked over to the Head Midgetrine. "It counts, but we cannot reject humility. Otherwise, we'll fall into the same trap as the Big People. That is something we cannot allow."

GarnlopBill hung his head. Seeing such a stern man reduced to putty made me even more rueful. "It's sad to think we'll be the only ones left when this is over."

"That's not true."

"What?"

"Others will remain. Others like us."

"But I was the only Big Person who passed your tests. Everyone else . . . " My voice trailed off as my eyes once again wandered to the TV.

"Not everyone outside the commune joined the fray. There's room in *The Garden* for others, and I'm sure you'll meet new friends."

"*Garden?* What garden?"

BernexCarl motioned to the window. "Follow me. I'll show you what's becoming of the once Big World."

As one, we arose and joined BernexCarl by the pane. He lifted the venetian blinds and opened the window. Then we craned our necks outside to see.

For almost a minute, I didn't breathe. Trees were no longer brown and green but bright, phosphorescent purple. Distant houses appeared to be getting smaller before I realized they were actually sinking into the ground. The soil itself twisted and undulated as though dirt and rock had become sea. Pavement unfurled. Bridges buckled. The Earth vomited up and gave birth, all at the same time.

"Cheer up, boys," BernexCarl said, "because you've all just caught a glimpse of your new home."

I gasped. "Why didn't you tell me about this!"

He grinned. "You know how much I love surprises."

* * * *

The midgets and I abandoned the commune the very next day. It was no longer necessary to cloister ourselves or live in mistrust of the world.

We stepped out into a vista where undulating rainbows and dancing, sentient grass coexisted beneath a shining blue sun. These blades tickled our legs like a million green lovers as we explored the boundaries of paradise. Our clothes fell away, but no one bothered to pick them up.

Branching out, we soon discovered geysers that shot forth only the purest honey. One at a time, we put our faces to the ground and – with eager lips – collected the bounty. The taste of ambrosia lingered on our tongues for hours.

Our bellies full, we waded through a silver brook that spoke a language I thought to be German. Fawns stood along its bank, trying to converse with me. I could not understand them, but the midgets seemed to have no trouble deciphering their words.

We sat atop gigantic mushrooms that looked suspiciously like organic chase lounges and took the opportunity to relax and dry off in that strangely colored sun. While the pulsating orb heated our flesh, it never caused sunburn.

At day's end, thirteen moons rose in the sky, each one a different color, size, and shape. Odd sonic booms and whistles encircled us as soon as the last blue ray disappeared below the horizon. Confusion reigned until I realized these must be the sounds of previously unknown insects. My theory was proven correct as an unusual multi-headed grasshopper/moth hybrid landed on my shoulder for a few seconds only to spit tobacco-like juice on my skin and fly away.

We continued on, allowing the night's amazing spectrum of color to guide us, until we reached the crest of a valley where even the rocks sang. Betwixt verdant hills, two groups gathered in separate camps. A few minutes passed before we were close enough to realize that everyone there clutched flaming swords.

When we finally reached the bottom, the two groups amassed into a single unit and halted our progress. I looked into the eyes of one of the men, amazed to see how *human* he appeared.

My lips trembled. "Who are you?"

One camp: "Those who have already gone."

Another: "And those who have yet to come."

I bowed. My little brothers followed my lead.

"What will you have of us?"

"Payment for a mission completed."

"But we didn't mean for everyone to die." I stammered. "We didn't want–"

"I don't speak of punishment; I speak of *obligation.*"

"*Obligation?* But this is paradise!"

"Indeed, but there's much work to be done. The garden is beautiful, but not eternal. It requires protection. Take our swords. Stand guard. Make sure the evils you destroy never return. Otherwise, you shall be doubly cursed."

"I believe I understand."

"Will you accept this responsibility as we accepted it so long ago?"

I turned to face the midgets. All heads nodded and, as one, we reached out our hands. Though the swords were twice as large as even the tallest midget, my brothers somehow managed to hold them aloft without trouble or effort.

The naked man smiled. "You have all made a very wise and noble decision."

Once the weapons were in our grip, the strange men began to flicker as though their forms were being broadcast over an ancient TV. The air pressure dropped as, one after the other, each man winked out of existence.

Less than a minutes later, we stood alone in the valley.

And we looked down at our swords. They felt like extensions of our arms, and we brandished them with an overarching sense of duty, realizing we were stewards to a world that was once again our home.

* * * *

Within days of *The Commercial of Truth*, the midgets and I discovered that a small percentage of the population had failed to tune into our presentation. This worried us and kept our eyes open and our bodies functioning without sleep for days on end.

Some of us entered the outside world in an attempt to rationalize with survivors. Others alternated watch by the pearly gates. Both groups brought along swords. After seeing their world collapse beneath them, the few remaining Big People had probably gone insane and were more than slightly dangerous. Our swords were powerful, but even they might not be able to drive back an invading horde.

We carried on nevertheless.

Outside Eden, the smell of corruption was overpowering. Billions of bodies boiled with ripe decay. Edifices had already collapsed under their own weight. The world of the Big People looked nothing if not dead, but we continued to patrol rotting streets and enter buildings that felt like tombs.

Soon, we discovered our excess vigilance was unnecessary. Those who had not fallen victim to the commercial had already taken care of themselves.

In the days that followed – and before the corruption became so pervasive it was unbearable, even with the proper facemasks – the midgets and I managed to collect the following first-person accounts from Post-*Commercial of Truth* casualties. We removed these notes from ashen hands, the writers having committed suicide long before.

Here's just a sampling of the horrors we uncovered:

DAY-TRADER: *I decided to withdraw all my investments and buy girlie mags. Can't be that bad a move, can it? Oh well, if it doesn't work out I can always kill myself. A lot has changed over the last few days. Too much. I like to go to the New York Stock Exchange and run naked as I smear gelid pancake mix over my body. Not much business happening there anymore. Where are all the investors? I've heard this rumor about a commercial. Maybe it's available in digital format.*

MILK MAN: *I know the atrocity hunters are on my trail. I can smell them. They will put me on trial and scream "YOU KNOWINGLY SOLD MILK TO MILLIONS OF CONSUMERS! TOMORROW YOU SHALL BE HANGED!" And I will have no recourse but to die without dignity. They have already stolen my suicide pill.*

HIGH SCHOOL FOOTBALL PLAYER: *I got dressed out for the game between North and South High. No one else showed up, so I had to play both defense and offense. It went pretty well to begin with. Then I realized that, since no one else was on the field, I had to lose even if I won. But I've never been a loser. (I'm not a loser. Am I?)*

A WORLD LEADER: *NOTE TO SELF: In next year's election use more balloons and party favors to make the voters smile in lieu of truth. (Perhaps I didn't use enough of these the last time around.) To hell with those midgets and their* Commercial of Truth*! Stealing away* The Power That Is Rightfully Mine*! Bastards! And just when I was about to press that little red button, too! No need now. Everything's so quiet. Damn! Quiet's the last thing a man in my position needs! Got to start a war – but everybody's dead! I think The Secretary of The Interior's still alive. Maybe he'll want to fight me in the Oval Office. Yeah! That's right! SHOWDOWN AT 5:30 EST! Call the networks! A PAY-PER-VIEW SPECIAL! The public will eat this shit up! Huzzah!*

What we have collected only proves what was once theoretical: take away rules and those who lived for the concept of morality alone destroy each other. It's a sad vindication of our ideas, but vindication nonetheless.

At any rate, the time to patrol dead streets is now over. Peace reigns in the valley, and its conduit is *Midgetarchy*. I will now put down my pen and bid you, my brothers and sisters, a fond

ADIEU.

PART II:

THE AUTHOR, REVEAL'D

<u>*A NOTE ON THE TEXT*</u>*: What follows has never before seen print, having been only recently discovered in The Grand Dictator's personal collection of manuscripts and edicts. We are pleased to offer such a rare and valuable document for public consumption.*

— *The Editors*

They think it's a Romance novel. The damn thing was thousands of words below their minimum word count, yet some mass-market, New York place publishes it in hardcover. *As a romance!*

Here's the funny thing: I don't even remember submitting *The End: In Circus Midgets and Barbed Chains* to a mass-market house. In fact, I don't remember submitting it anywhere at all. One day, the manuscript was just gone. I had wanted to revise the thing a bit, so I went to the filing cabinet where I store all my working drafts. I looked under the file labeled *M* but found it completely empty.

I ransacked my apartment for a few hours. Closets were searched as well as beds. I even looked in the bathroom before finally giving up. The disappearance was perplexing, but I didn't consider the manuscript's loss too big a deal. It wasn't one of my better works.

Then, eight weeks later, I received this in the mail:

Dear Mr. Anders,

We at Charles and Dobberson couldn't help but indulge the chill that enveloped our loins following the review of your submission <u>*THE END: IN CIRCUS MIDGETS AND BARBED CHAINS.*</u> *We feel it would be perfect for our QUIVERING BUST line. Please find the appropriate contracts enclosed.*

I stuffed the letter and its accompanying paperwork back into the manila envelope and took the entire package outside and threw it back in the mailbox. Slamming the lid, I waited outside in the morning chill. If I opened it and the letter was no longer there, I'd know the whole thing had been an illusion.

But it was still there when I re-opened the lid.

Grabbing the package from the box, I ran with it into the kitchen. I couldn't breathe. My legs felt like jelly. A blurry haze surrounded my vision, and the once stable room seemed to undulate. Wallpaper breathed. The refrigerator door appeared to open and close on its own volition. The dream I had dreamt for so long had come true – *but I didn't know how the hell it had happened.* My brain spun. Nothing made sense.

Then I saw the first dollar sign flash before my eyes. I almost felt the shiny award statuette clutched in my hand and imagined my name emblazoned atop bestseller lists worldwide. I heard standing ovations and saw the reading public flock to bookstores where I sat out in front, ready to sign every copy I could lay my grubby hands on.

Hunger grew. Desire overwhelmed me.

I wasted no time. To hell with questioning how my book wound up on some New York editor's desk. It just got there. That was all I needed to know.

I affixed my signature to every available line and did so with a gleam in my eye.

* * * *

I sent the contracts back to Charles and Dobberson and awaited further word. I assumed I would, at some point, be required to go to New York City and chat with all the people involved in the production of my book.

But I was wrong. They came to me.

* * * *

I woke up one morning to the sound of someone knocking – make that *banging* – on the front door. I slipped into a robe and walked into the living room.

The banging grew louder.

"Hold your horses!" I shouted.

Bang. Bang. Bang.

"For the love of God, show some restraint!"

Bang. Bang. Bang.

Annoyed, I threw open the door. Then I took an immediate step back. Before me stood a cluster of greasepaint streaked and army fatigued men. All appeared middle-aged and more than slightly overweight.

I bit my upper lip. "Uh. . . Can I help you?"

"Are you Mark Alan Anders?"

I nodded.

A man carrying an obviously fake machine gun: "Then we are representatives of Charles and Dobberson."

"You're the publishing guys?"

"Yes, and we need to know if people claiming to be representatives of Rodger and Thompinson have attempted to engage you."

"I don't even know what Rodger and Thompinson is."

"Our rival," the man hissed before his voice regained its flat yet authoritative tone. "We have received word that Rodger and Thompinson intends to publish your book. They somehow managed to steal a copy from Headquarters. Intercepted memos indicate they plan on kidnapping you next. We're here to offer protection."

Added another: "And to insure your book is published by Charles and Dobberson and Charles and Dobberson alone."

My head spun. "This is too weird to be true."

"No, it isn't. But we must first know if you have already been assimilated into The Rodger and Thompinson Collective." The man removed a device from the pocket of his flak jacket and clutched it behind his back. "This test will show whether or not they have attached cranial transmitters."

"Okay. But–"

"If the results are positive, you will be exterminated on the spot. We're sure that won't be necessary."

"Wait just a second. I–"

"Do we have your consent?"

"No! You–" The man removed the device from behind his back. I finally saw what it was.

"Hey! That's just an old remote control!"

The man waved the thing up and down in front of my body. "No, it's Device #4326, designed by our top lab technicians during the war."

"Publishing companies have lab technicians? And what war?"

The man's pupils darted. "Pretend you didn't hear that."

I just nodded.

The man moved the remote control around in the air for a few additional seconds before returning it to his pocket. "You appear clean. Go inside and we'll de-brief you." The men removed their shirts and stood, glistening, on my porch.

"I'm afraid you might mean that literally!"

"We're just doing our job, Mr. Anders. It's part of standard–"

"Sweet Jesus, it's them!"

The man turned at the sound of his comrade's voice. I followed his gaze. A team of equally middle-aged and fatigue-clad men poured into the parking lot outside my apartment, brandishing guns. I squinted and, with some relief, noted that their weapons were as plastic as the ones the representatives from Charles and Dobberson carried.

"Attack!" The man shouted. *"Without prejudice!"*

The representatives sprinted from the porch, meeting the enemy head-on by my rusty old Pontiac.

One screamed: "You're not taking Mark Anders! He's ours!"

A response: "Eat lead!"

I wondered whether or not publishing companies took the time to screen their employees as representatives from Rodger and Thompinson lifted their guns and made *rat-a-tat-tat* sounds with their mouths. The men of Charles and Dobberson did likewise.

"Hey," I called out. "The neighbors are going to see this!"

The strange men ignored me and crouched down in combat stances. They pretended to shoot the enemy until Charles and Dobberson's leader threw down his gun and exclaimed: *"Atomic Bomb dropping on your head! Atomic Bomb dropping on your head! Sky's turning red! You're all dead!"*

Representatives from Rodger and Thompinson stumbled around in mimicry of dying.

"Bill," said one. "Go without me."

But the one he had called "Bill" was already down, eyes wide and tongue lolling. The guy didn't even try to conceal his breathing. Bill's friend looked down and saw the man, lying supine on the pavement. He wailed. His legs folded beneath him, sending his body to the ground face-first. When he fell, he landed hard on Bill's midsection.

Above it all, the victors dusted off clothes and patted backs.

"Good work, private."

"I couldn't have done it without you, General Dobberson!"

The man whom I now learned was named *Dobberson* motioned his troops back to the porch where the General once again addressed me:

"Don't worry, Mr. Anders. They'll never bother you again. We've carried out our mission, but are too depleted to conduct an adequate de-briefing today."

I sighed with relief.

"We can, however, provide you with all necessary information." The man pulled out a bundle of folded papers and forced them into my hand. "This package includes your itinerary for the next twenty-five years."

"An itinerary of *what!"*

"Book signings. Personal appearances. Scheduled meetings. Dates you are to link up with confidential informants."

I figured I had little choice in the matter. Reaching out my hand, I accepted the papers.

"These documents are for your eyes only. Shred all two hundred and sixty sheets when finished – then eat them."

I was staggered. "Do you even realize how much paper–"

"No more questions. We must take our leave. We're due back on base by 0:100 hours." The men offered up a collective salute and marched, single-file, down the steps. They piled into a large black Oldsmobile and pulled out of the driveway, brandishing their plastic guns and whistling the theme music to *Gomer Pyle U.S.M.C.*

* * * *

That night, I read the papers and memorized everything they contained – dates, maps, and names both code and proper. After I was finished, I shredded the first sheet, inserted it into my mouth, and chewed.

It went down rather easily, as did the next twenty-five pages. Soon after that, my stomach began to swell. It didn't start hurting, however, until the forty-fifth sheet.

But I kept going.

I was drenched in sweat by the hundred and sixtieth sheet. My eyes gained focus only to lose it again. The urge to vomit overwhelmed me, but the paper was too dense. Nothing came out.

Twenty pages later, my hands were doing things without input from my brain. My mind had retreated to its Happy Place, and I no longer felt whatever was happening internally.

And I stayed in that Happy Place amid swirling balloons, happy clowns, and floating candied apples until my first public appearance five days later. It was only then that my intestines finished processing the bulky matter.

* * * *

I was constantly busy from that point on, hopping from city to city on a cross-country book tour.

On each occasion, I arrived exhausted. People of all ages and genders simply refused to stop touching me in ways I am hard-pressed to describe. No matter where I sat, first-class or coach, I was groped mercilessly.

I assumed my black-suited handlers were paid to protect their charge from such behavior. If that was the case, they failed miserably. Half of them just sat back and watched while the remainder joined in the fray.

The actual book-signings, however, proved far more traumatic.

I often considered bolting. But my handlers brought along this strange robotic thing to each appearance. It looked like a trashcan. The laser scope mounted in the center of its body broke with that image, however, as did the stainless steel muzzle protruding from its side. The men in charge assured me the thing was motion sensitive and that it was in my best interest not to move unless ordered to do so.

So I didn't. I just waited until the people showed up, copies of my book in hand.

I had expected only a trickle of interest. But it was as though some organic floodgate had shattered. My fans didn't even bother getting into lines. They just surrounded the store.

If – God forbid – the doors failed to open right away, the masses usually took to smashing stones against windows. The panes never broke, and I assumed the storeowners had foreseen this possibility and installed shatterproof glass. Other times, my fans forgot about damaging public property and turned on each other. Their attacks were often brutal. Once, I saw a pair of disembodied arms fly through the air as bestial, slobbery howls replaced human voices.

Then the doors opened. At first, I feared being smothered and then crushed under stampeding hooves disguised as feet. I soon realized the people had to all pass through a sensor before they reached me. It looked similar to those upright plastic things in supermarkets and department stores. This version, however, was more proactive. If more than three fans passed through before the thing reset, the fourth was met by a few thousand volts of electricity.

The masses quickly learned what was expected of them.

Unfortunately, there were no protocols in place for the individual fans that greeted me. They were free to do whatever they pleased. *Men!* Most hugged me and refused to let go. The rest pummeled my face for no apparent reason. *Women!* Overcome with vapors, they swooned in my arms. Some died. Others forced me to lay them then and there.

My touring sponsors even supplied a backroom where I could render the services I was coerced to perform. One time, when I refused to engage in relations with one of my fans, the owner of *Books O'Plenty* – a burly Italian named Rizzo – smashed me over the head with a glass cola bottle.

I was rushed to the emergency room following 48 of my scheduled 6,115 tours. I had sixteen near-death experiences during which my soul exited my body and flew pell-mell about the room. One time, I was nearly embalmed.

When not on the road or laid up in a hospital or mortuary, my handlers posed me in grotesque tableaus for underwear photo-shoots. During these sessions, my manhood was forced into the most revealing of briefs. The male photographers made eyes at me each time I removed my clothing in their presence. I had to slap away hands repeatedly. Reaching for my package was just something they refused to stop doing! It was an activity pursued far more than the actual taking of pictures.

A few days later, my crotch appeared on billboards and busses, in magazines and catalogues. I couldn't go outside without seeing my bulge hanging everywhere. And no advertisement ever mentioned the book itself. The billboards did, however, bandy about such phrases *sin-carcass* and *man-meat*.

I also noticed how transfixed people seemed at the sight of these advertisements. Hundreds gathered around the posters and stared at my cock-image for hours on end.

It was enough to make me feel more than a little uncomfortable.

* * * *

My life was no longer my own, but a dark part of me still craved attention and loved to watch women swoon. Some hidden fragment relished nothing more than pouting for photographers and seeing its package pasted everywhere. It ate up fame and shat it out like clockwork.

I quickly decided that dark part was completely fucking nuts.

* * * *

One day, I was alone in my apartment enjoying a two-week sabbatical from book signing. I felt free for the first time in ages and was actually beginning to write like I had before. I so missed being at my computer. Creation, like personal freedom, was a luxury I just couldn't afford while on the road.

The second chapter of my novel spewed from the printer. It was a first draft, but I was already quite pleased with my work. A smile formed on my lips – only to be erased by what felt like an anvil crashing against the side of my skull.

When I came to, I found myself on the set of a nationally syndicated talk show:

(LIGHTS ON!!! ROLL TAPE!!!)

ANNOUNCER VOICE: *WELCOME TO THE LIDA LATONDRIA HOUR!!!*

LIDA: Hello, ladies and gentlemen! We're visiting with Mark Anders, the famed author of *The End: In Circus Midgets and Barbed Chains* – a sparkling romance that will send you soaring through the halls of love.

(*Camera pans from* LIDA's *incisors to the guests on stage.*)

THE WRITER: (*Confronts the lens.*) Hello.

LIDA: (*Motions toward* THE WRITER.) "So, tell us what your fans want to know. What's the size of your throbbin' manhood?"

THE WRITER: (*Attempts to avoid* LIDA's *breath. Her maw gapes mere inches from his nose.*) I – I don't know. . . I. . . just wrote a book. . . I. . .

LIDA: (*Crams bosom into* THE WRITER's *face until cheeks turn blue. She whispers into his cold ear.*) My husband means nothing to me. He's flesh-meat. That's all. (*Resumes stage voice.*) So, you didn't answer my question. What's the size of your throbbin' manhood?

THE WRITER: (*Gasps for air – precious and vital.*) I really don't see why that's important. I'm just a writ–

LIDA: (*Kicks* THE WRITER *in stomach with stilettoed heel.*) Just answer the fucking question!

THE WRITER: (*Confused, hurt.*) Huge?

(*Cut to the crowd. They leer and make provocative gestures.*)

LIDA: We must take a break now. Stay tuned, and don't miss the second half of this most stimulating. . .*ummmmmmooooooohhhhhhh*. . . interview.

(CUT TO COMMERCIAL)

LIDA: Welcome back to our show! If you're just tuning in, we're presently chatting with the famed writer of *The End: In Circus Midgets and Barbed Chains*.

(Camera pans to THE WRITER, who has been stripped to his underclothes. The guests and audience members fondle him. His face is a mask of horror.)

LIDA: So, how long have you been the *Messiah*, sent from the Garden to deliver us from the burden of pain and sin?

THE WRITER: Huh?

LIDA: You didn't answer my question.

THE WRITER: (*Doesn't speak due to things being inserted from all directions.*)

LIDA: (*Feels the unholy fervor.*) BUT I DON'T REQUIRE WORDS TO SENSE TRUTH! THE SEVEN SEALS HAVE BEEN BROKEN BY *YOU*, MY SAVIOR!

THE WRITER (*would speak, but he is bound and gagged*).

LIDA: YOUR BOOK HAS ECLIPSED ALL OTHER TOMES! NOW I WEEP IN YOUR SHADOW AND LAY BY YOUR FEET! DELIVER ME FROM THIS LIFE THAT IMPARTS NO SATISFACTION! DELIVER ME FROM CONSUMPTION! OH CAPTAIN — FREE CAPTAIN – STEER MY LIFE FOR I SURE AS HELL CAN'T! *(Inserts finger firmly in mouth. Simulates oral sex.)*

(*The zeal is terrifying. Surging with adrenalin,* THE WRITER *struggles free from his bonds. He flees as the crowd takes to its feet.*)

ANNOUNCER VOICE: *Be sure to tune in tomorrow for the next exciting installment of THE LIDA LATONDRIA HOUR!!!*

(LIGHTS OUT. FADE TO BLACK.)

It was that bad.

* * * *

Give it time, and the public at large will cease thinking you're the Messiah – brought down from Heaven to deliver souls from a life of pain and drudgery.

I said these words each time I looked in the mirror. I wanted to catch a glimpse of whatever it was the masses saw, but never observed anything other than a short, skinny man with thin, blonde hair and mismatched ears. I wasn't attractive. Women weren't interested in me, but I didn't care. My looks once insured the peace and quiet I craved.

And I desperately tried to return to that solitary lifestyle. All efforts proved futile. My productivity plummeted to an all-time low as armed handlers conducted hourly raids. More often than not, I was bound and gagged before being thrown into a black limousine filled with a half-dozen prostitutes. Once inside, my left hand was strapped to an *Electro-Waver*.

From that point, things shifted to autopilot.

I was administered Thorazine until my bowels loosened and my brain waves, for all intents and purposes, stopped. My managers didn't even have to force me to acknowledge my fans. The waving device fulfilled its role, and the people thought I was consciously addressing them. No one noticed the drool running from my chin or my upward staring eyes.

* * * *

Now I live with the understanding that I can do *nothing* to change *anything. The End: In Circus Midgets and Barbed Chains* is not another passing fad. I've created something I cannot destroy.

I just hope this wave doesn't crash with me on it.

* * * *

About a month ago, I woke up to find ten thousand people camped out in the parking lot in front of my apartment. They chanted incoherently and lit incredibly foul-smelling incense. Outside, a million posters read:

MARK ANDERS 4-EVER

A host of police cars were parked outside, too. At first, I thought the men in blue wanted to protect me. Then, I saw someone open one of the cruiser's windows and hang a large piece of cloth from it. The rag fluttered in the breeze for a few seconds. I had no idea what the thing said until the wind plastered it against the side of the cruiser.

MARK ANDERS – YOU'RE THE COOLEST!!!

I wanted to scream. In fact, I did. I closed my eyes. I tried to ignore the whole thing and go about my day. It wasn't easy. Not at all.

Later on, I risked opening a window. The place reeked of stale sweat and mold. I hadn't felt the inclination to clean either my apartment or myself in such a long time. I lifted the pane only to have a dozen arms snake in. The people wouldn't stop moaning. I had to beat them off with an improvised torch fashioned from a chair leg and a kerosene soaked washcloth. It was the one thing that would stop them.

Retiring to bed was my only option. I had tried to drink a glass of water, but nothing would stay down. The liquid, mixed with bile, kept shooting up and covering the floor with its foulness.

* * * *

Extreme hunger pains soon gripped me. I had to consume

something, yet my apartment was bare except for a box of moldy cereal, a jug of curdled milk, and an unopened bottle of vodka.

Filling my gut, however, wasn't my only goal. *I simply couldn't let them have the last laugh.*

A few hours later, I gained the courage to step outside.

Which was, of course, a very bad idea.

* * * *

I breached the threshold. The crowd swallowed me whole.

Men, women, and children tore at my clothing. They ripped buttons from my shirt and tore the elastic waistband from my briefs. They pulled every thread from my body until I stood before them naked except for my shoes. They clawed at my eyes and, when blood was drawn, saved it in little vials marked *Precious Fluid of the Savior $19.95*.

Their voices clattered around me.

"Make a photo-play for me, Mark!"

"I can't. Just because I wrote about them doesn't mean I can do them!"

"Send photographic images into my mind!"

"No!"

"Give me BernexCarl's autograph! He's my fave!"

I shouted: *"STOP IT! FOR GOD'S SAKE LET ME LIVE IN PEACE! AND FOR THE LAST TIME, THE BOOK ISN'T REAL! DO YOU UNDERSTAND? SAY YOU—"*

My rant was cut short by a gentle tap on my forearm.

I looked down and doe eyes met my own. A sweet little girl in a gingham dress. She held a lollipop in one cute, perfectly formed hand. In the other, she cradled a snow-white bunny. (*Such floppidy-flop ears!*) By her feet, a gentle lamb grazed serenely.

"Will you lead us, my Savior?" The girl asked, her teeth shining – mid-day braces aglow in childhood's sun.

My heart turned into something akin to paste when I realized I could never fulfill her vision.

"I'm sorry. I can't. I just can't."

As soon as the words left my mouth, the bunny wilted and the lamb collapsed – its tiny body reduced to a stinking pile of green flesh. I watched the girl's childhood shatter at that very moment. Her smile slipped and all I could do was pick up her lips and glue them to her head. But her new smile was a farce.

"You killed my bunny, mister."

"No, I. . ."

It was all I could think to say.

"Why did you kill Mr. Nibbles?"

"I didn't mean to. Really. I never wanted to hurt him. I never wanted to hurt *anything."*

Her lollipop now a shrunken head: "But you did!"

I could take no more. I cursed my flesh and cursed all the things I had created.

But I could never curse the girl.

Somehow, though I have no memory of moving, I made it back to my apartment. I boarded the windows with only the sturdiest plywood and fell upon my bed.

Three days passed before I woke up.

* * * *

Upon stirring from what felt like a coma, I decided to construct a list. If I didn't force my brain to consider the problem logically, I would go mad and perhaps pour battery acid over my cereal in lieu of milk when the morning came.

I wasted no time. I removed a pad of stationary from what had been my writing desk. My pen slashed at the paper. A pint of Vodka had to be transferred to my gullet before I was calm enough to write. Even then my teeth shook and my brain clattered.

POSITIVE AND NEGATIVE POINTS CONCERNING POTENTIAL MESIAHDOM:

CONS

(1) *Absolute power corrupts absolutely.*

(2) *I hate drawing attention to myself.*

(3) *Do I really deserve this?*

(4) *The public has no idea what it's talking about.*

(6) *I will probably be assassinated.*

(7) *Life will become Hell.*

(8) *Hell will become Life.*

PROS

(1) *That little girl.*

(2) *Universal, unwavering loyalty.*

(3) *Temples and statuary erected in my name.*
(4) *Virgins sacrificed.*
(6) *Me = Center of Worship.*
(7) *Word becomes absolute.*
(8) *Ego gets boost.*

CONCLUSION: The pros cater only to base, human desire. The greatest leader is a man/woman who neither desires the position nor lusts for its incidental power. (Pro #1 stands as the exception.)

While the cons outweighed the pros, I could not erase the image that beautiful child had scratched into my mind. Her glimmering braces had cast an indelible shadow.

But I fought against the vision.

I crashed headlong through my apartment. What little material possessions I owned soon found their way to the floor. I had no use for them. I was a lost man. So lost, in fact, that I ran to the closet and slid a sleek pair of black jackboots over my feet. I made a makeshift bandana out of a pair of pantyhose I discovered wedged between the bed and the wall. (No idea where they came from – some ex-girlfriend, maybe – but that matters little.) Wrapping the nylon around my head, I scrawled anarchy symbols all over its surface with a felt-tipped marker.

Bedecked in the finery of madness, I ran across my bedroom singing German marching tunes at the top of my lungs. I paused by the vanity to powder my nose with whatever dust I could scrape up. Then I did the can-can, just like mom used to do in nineteenth century Vienna when she was but a lonely chorus girl subsisting off peanuts and meager affection. Tipping my ostrich-feathered hat to the gentlemen, I unleashed a bestial groan.

It wasn't until a few hours had passed that I remembered my mom hadn't lived during that time at all.

In fact, she hadn't even been to Vienna.

* * * *

I can't express how mentally bizarre I became in the days following that *incident*. It pains me to even write about such things so, in lieu of dredging up memories, I will affix pages from my journal.

What follows is nearly a week's worth of entries:

2/76/89

Too much stress! Too many people calling my name! More than enough to rack the nerves!

Now, however, I feel quite chipper. Took a walk this morning. Man-Servant Jeeves handed me my coat as I exited the breezeway. Oh, the fields I strolled through were so lush – so bespangled with the entrails of my enemies! (Too bad they had to go – but, hey! They stood in the way of profit!) Anyway, I do love to ride my horsies there. Went fox hunting with the *Queen of Elastic*, too. She's a very interesting lady. Likes to talk about severed heads a little too much. I fear she may try to kill me. Must stay on the lookout for her heated daggers. She enjoys putting them in inconspicuous places, like the broom-closet in the apartment she rents out to unsuspecting men such as myself. Her Highness wants me to fall on them when I'm not looking. She's getting old, you know. Can't trust her a bit.

*0/&6/.M

Today was a weird day.

God stopped by my apartment. In His hand, he held a contract. He said: "Fill out this form for Eternal Bliss."

I did.

He then told me to be a good boy and study hard because He was angry about being killed so long ago and really wanted revenge.

Suddenly, the man stripped off his mask and revealed himself to be an insurance agent. *"Don't you know the spirit of our culture is embodied in a mountain of paperwork,"* he snarled and shot me five times in the head. Before I knew what hit me – no pun intended – this agent sold my personal information to approximately twelve million credit card companies.

Soon, my dead yet strangely animated body was buying with plastic left and right. I couldn't live without eating a $25 dollar steak following an afternoon spent switching my perfectly functional home movies over to the latest digital format. I was addicted to purchasing power just like *They* wanted.

At that point, I knew *They* had created everything. I existed merely as a brain in a tank – living a pre-conditioned dream peopled by three car garages, laptop computers, and stock options. The scientists dripped saline solution into my vat, and it felt tingly.

At any rate, *The Queen of Elastic* visited me again and demanded, at gunpoint, that I compliment her new hairdo. I told her it was a beautiful illusion and made note of the fact that disembodied brains, in general, can't grow hair.

9/12/50

Okay. I want you to know I'm ACTUALLY SANE RIGHT NOW. It is very important that you understand this. I've figured it all out and EVERYTHING MAKES SENSE.

Listen to me, damn it! I'm not making this up. What I'm about to say is *TRUE*. No more of that *Queen of Elastic* bullshit. My head's on straight and I finally know what's going on.

The circus midgets are real, and I am their conduit. They operate through me.

I just wish I knew what they were planning.

9/13/50

Feeling better now. My head doesn't pulsate nearly as often as it used to.

So, now it's time for the hard question:

Do I set the world on my shoulders?

Might hurt. . .

I'm just a writer. That's all.

Can I?

Ah, fuck it.

9/14/50

"Will you lead us, my Savior?" The girl had asked, her teeth shining – mid-day braces aglow in childhood's sun.

"Yes, sister. Yes I can."

* * * *

The final entry takes me up to now. For better or for worse, my mind has cleared, and I've finally made my decision.

Please don't judge me. Understand I do this for the little doe-eyed girl.

* * * *

(REAL TIME)

Now, I pry the wood from the door and swing it ajar. The crowd overtakes me. Afraid at first, I soon sense how much they love me. In this love, I find comfort.

A million hands lift me skyward. They insert olive branches into my hair and place me in a chair atop a jewel-encrusted pedestal. A brass band strikes up a rousing tune. Women dance like serpents possessed. Men fall to their knees and writhe on the ground in supplication. Off to my right, in the entertainment pit, well-muscled gladiators battle for the crowd's amusement. Applause waxes and wanes once the stench of blood fills the air.

"I'm sorry, but I cannot accept any of this."

A man steps up and grasps me by the shoulder. Tall and skeletal, he has a prominent widow's peak. His eyes are as gray as his skin.

"Who are you?"

"Your Royal Advisor."

"I don't have a Royal Advisor."

"You do now."

I wave him off. "Well, it doesn't matter either way. You must not have heard when I declined everything."

"But you *can't.*"

"Why not?"

"Because it's not in the cards."

"Are you always this cryptic?"

"Yes."

"In that case, you can keep babbling. Just do it elsewhere."

"Hmmm... Maybe this will help change your mind." He slips a purple cloak over my tattered shirt. My skin tingles, and the idea of sitting in a throne seems not only good, but *seductive.* I try to shake it away, but the desire is still there, lingering in the back of my mind. I turn to the crowd.

"Loyal subjects! I come here today not of my own accord. I understand and understand fully that if I do not take these offerings you shall never leave me in peace. Damn me forever for writing that book! And damn you all – *I accept this power!"*

My Royal Advisor outstretches his hands. "By the way, my name is Malachi."

"Nice to meet you, Mr. Malachi."

"If you ever have questions concerning your up-and-coming rule, just ask. I've been advising people since the first quantum shower colored the universal night."

"Then you must be quite the encyclopedia."

"Indeed. I can tell you anything you need to know – including which torture-tongs are best suited for any given situation."

"Okay. But I'm not sure why I should want torture-tongs."

"Forget that. Just contemplate the sheer number of people here today." Malachi sweeps his hand out over the teeming throng. "They want nothing more than to honor you. You'll also find some old friends in amongst that wave. And they've traveled far to cheer you on."

"Old friends?"

"Take a look. You'll see what I mean."

I face the crowd. The cherubic visage of Bubblepants smiles from a sea of faces. To his right stands BernexCarl. Shimmering above him, King RaggathBob. The ruler no longer wears royal garments. Dressed as a commoner, he gives a thumbs-up and bows in my honor.

"They want you to accept what has been so graciously offered. How can you possibly say no to such cute midgets?"

Stammering: "I– I can't."

"Of course, you can't. And aren't you forgetting something?"

"What?"

"Tell me, how can you be a proper despot without a proper scepter?" He waves the majestic item in the air. "Consider the transfer of this sacrament your inauguration proper."

"Sure." Purple banners bearing my image unfurl in the streets. "If that's the only way around it."

I take the golden scepter into my hands, trumpets sound, and the rest is just a blank.

PART III:

ABSOLUTE POWER CORRUPTS ABSOLUTELY

A NOTE ON THE TEXT: The following passage was written by Friar Nimblebottom (later assassinated) under the guidance of The Grand Dictator's disembodied will. It is reprinted here, having originally seen publication in the pocket-sized edition of MEDITATIONS ON POWER AND PRESTIGE.

— *The Editors*

(*The script for this presentation rises on angel wings/devil horns. Our hero sails off into its folds and twists and turns therein for a number of years.)*

THE GRAND DICTATOR: *(Old and decrepit before his time, he stands on the Royal balcony, addressing the masses gathered below.)* Then, I broke free! Complete and utter madness! Chaos in the streets! I rode my Roman chariot through the highways of the night and brandished my sword with Herculean resolve! The world! *Lo!* The World! *Alas!* The world was mine to take and take was what I did! I demanded women fed to lions. I ordered men fed to dogs fed to rats fed to albino serpents the color of cotton ball death. With every mouthful, the statuary arose at my calling! Frenzied glory!

(Looks to mausoleum being built in the town square. Face slackens.)

THE GRAND DICTATOR: Alas, I have discovered the true purpose of that reliquary! It will soon bear my bones. Fie on those who wet my tongue with power only to take it all away! *Fie! Fie! Fie!* You hear me not when I whimper in the night! I JUST WROTE A FUCKING BOOK and got LoSt In ThE PATTerNS!

(THE GREAT DICTATOR's *eyes glow. Epiphany is reached.*)

THE GRAND DICTATOR: Dear Lord; that's what I am! A man, not

Caesar! My birthright revealed! 'Tis my duty to no longer disembowel left and right with golden tongs that give delight!

(*Attempts to throw both THE SCEPTER and THE TONGS to the ground, but finds them fused to his palms. He lifts his head only to see a naked, sword-brandishing midget descend from Heaven.* THE GRAND DICTATOR *looks on in terror.)*

THE GRAND DICTATOR: Be gone, you beast!

NAKED MIDGET: Fear not, for you have served us well. I can't give you the Garden, but I'll show you the next best thing.

*(*THE GRAND DICTATOR *reaches out with trembling hands and THE SCEPTER falls away as THE TONGS vanish. The* NAKED MIDGET *accepts the withered grip.* THE GRAND DICTATOR *feels salvation's warm pulse – but only for a second.*

NAKED MIDGET*: (Withdrawing hand.)* And now I must take my leave.

THE GRAND DICTATOR*:* No! You can't go! You promised me deliverance!

NAKED MIDGET*:* And you've had your taste. Now sleep only to awaken. *(Vanishes.)*

(THE GRAND DICTATOR *collapses. He lands hard but feels no pain as* MALACHI *– ageless master – enters the balcony.* MALACHI *falls upon* THE GRAND DICTATOR *and, with ceremonial dagger in hand, saws away tender neck flesh.)*

MALACHI: I smite thee, and with each blow you'll remember your fate. (*Holds dripping head aloft.*) I kill not a man but a borrowed flesh-sack!

THE GRAND DICTATOR'S SEVERED HEAD: Oh dear God! It's all happening again! *(Dies and, twenty-four hours later, begins to doodle on a piece of paper in his apartment.)*

SONG: *HAIL TO THE DEAD; HAIL TO THE FALLEN CHIEF*

(Exeunt all characters)

(Fade to black)

PART IV (APPENDIX):

AN ARTICLE AND PRICELESS MISCELLANY PERTAINING TO THE LIFE OF OUR GRAND DICTATOR

INVOCATION: *All hail the late and great Grand Dictator! May the saints preserve his many pieces until a suitable replacement can be found.*

–The Hon. Malachi (Royal Advisor)

I: Article

The following article was taken without permission from the following source: *THE HERALD TIMES NEWS ROMAN*

BELOVED HOMICIDAL DICTATOR DIES, WORLD MOURNS
Alistair McAlistair

Our beloved dictator has gone the way of mortal flesh! No longer shall he slay us in such a manner that our very guts are torn from our anal cavity. The master was found dead yesterday, his body scattered in pieces throughout the labyrinthine halls of his palace. The mortal husk was discovered by Royal Advisor Malachi, who was so distraught he could barely clutch the gore-streaked knife he so sorrowfully brandished.

Nameless Authorities in Charge have ruled his death a suicide.

A Viking-style funeral will be held tomorrow outside The Department of Disposal. The public is invited to attend. Though details are sketchy at the present, we can confirm the attendance of gaily-attired circus midgets who will give benediction as flames consume the fallen one.

II. COLLECTED COMMENTS CONCERNING OUR BELOVED GRAND DICTATOR

This collection would not be complete without comments from people The Grand Dictator touched throughout the course of his reign. With this in mind, we polled a number of everyday citizens (such as yourself) to get a feel for how this one-of-a-kind man shaped the average life. What follows is a mere sampling.

–The Editors

I'll always remember the day he slid heated tongs down my throat and pulled out my tongue when I interrupted him during a speech.

–The Little Doe-Eyed Girl

The Grand Dictator paid me a visit one night. He snacked on sugar cookies and ranted about "threats to the established system." He ordered his secret service men to strip search my pre-school aged children. I understand we must sacrifice freedom for security and am okay with that.

–Alice Aliceson
(1st Caste: Banking and Investment)

I'll always remember the pyrotechnic displays The Grand Dictator coordinated during the yearly Great Fire celebrations. There was never a bad seat since he usually pointed the fireworks into the crowd before stabbing all within arm's reach.

–Patrica M. Armworthy
(7th Caste: Homeworker)

I recall the night The Grand Dictator stood out on his balcony and – for no apparent reason – opened fire on those within range. I often show off my scar. It's a pride thing.

–Josephine Adams
(18th Caste: Shit and Debris)

III. <u>THE EXEGESIS</u>:

What follows are eight excerpts from the *Exegesis* so often referenced, but never directly quoted in *The End: In Circus Midgets and Barbed Chains*. Its composition date runs prior to The Grand Dictator's ascension – a time when he jettisoned what follows in favor of his *Newly Expanded and Unexpurgated Exegesis* which, in essence, makes only the following noble statement: *"Forget all that Zen shit I said earlier; my power is absolute!"*

It is quite apparent that he utilized this early Exegesis in the formation of both VerlaxPete's testing scene and KarlakArmond's *To Understand Peace*.

–The Editors

(1) *There is one soul in the heart of man; and that soul has infinite faces. Man tends to separate these faces because doing so is convenient. He then bestows individual names and properties upon those pieces he has pulled away. Hence, man is blinded by his own imagery and cannot see the thing as it truly stands.*

(2) *Our perception will not allow us to see time as a unified and non-linear* Now Event. *An unbroken whole can only be divided when those perceiving it convince themselves the whole is an Aristotelian entity when, in fact, it is not. (BUT. . . if this unbroken whole exclaims "I am one," it becomes two.)*

(3) *There is a place and time where I am born.*
There is a place and time where I am dead.
There is a place and time where I am yet to be.
That place and time is here and now.
Hence, we are all Quantum Shades
in relation to other Quantum Shades,
and our untouchable roots rest in eternity.

(4) *You are controlled even when you control something else. The slave and the enslaver are one in the same. Both must serve some master even if that master, by default, turns out to be the fickleness of the self-created self.*

(5) In all matters, contingency runs deeper than most are willing to believe. All actions, human and otherwise, are woven together in an infinite quilt too intricate and subtle to be fully appreciated

by finite man.

(6) *Infinite and infinitesimal are one and the same. Universes exist within Universes. In the end, who can say what's large and what's small?*

(7) *Most attributes assigned to human nature are, in fact, elements of animal nature. But there is something higher. What it is cannot be explained in either words or numbers. Both means, however, can provide hints.*

(8) *Doubt and rigidity are consequences of a uniquely human level of awareness.*

IV. A CLOSING NOTE FROM THE EDITORS

We would like to thank *The Department of Censorship* for allowing this book to pass without excess incident. (We were grateful to hear that you liquidated only one of our assistant editors.) Finally, we would like to extend gratitude to *The Department of Truth* for reviewing this manuscript – as per federally mandated guidelines – and granting their most treasured Seal of Approval.

–*The Editors*

EXVOCATION: *Yea, though I wander aimless through this life, I know there remains a gentle hand to guide me (and remove my intestines by means of my anal cavity.) Glory to the highest; I shall never fear again!*

–The Hon. Malachi (Royal Advisor)

AMEN.

SECTION II:

ZEN AND THE ART OF MURDER

EVERYONE REMEMBERS WHERE they were the night Countess Vanessa Von Zanzamere was murdered. I know I do. After all, I *was* her number one fan.

I had finished reading half of *The End: In Circus Midgets and Barbed Chains.* Staring at words began to bore me, so I decided to take a break and watch some TV. I carried the set into the lavatory and drew myself a warm bath.

The tub filled with water. Soon, my being would be transported to a flickering and pixilated world. There, my rough and angular features might melt into something more suitable as six-pack abs overrode soft belly flesh. The warm bath would increase the dreaminess factor, making it seem as though I was even further removed from reality's clutch.

Unleashing a sigh, I sank into the water and grabbed the remote control. I pushed the power button and stared intently at the first channel that popped up.

By some coincidence, the author of *The End* was on the tube. A talk show host loomed over him, torturing the poor guy into admitting his novel was a romance. I felt sorry for him. He looked so terrified. It was too bad I didn't care all that much for his book. The thing had just way too many midgets for my taste.

The talk show host was cramming her bosom in the writer's face and inquiring about his member when, suddenly, the feed was interrupted for a news flash. I watched, my mouth a gaping *O* of horror, as the anchorwoman related the day's gruesome events:

<<u>ANCHORLADY</u>>: *Woe and Lamentation. At five-thirty this afternoon, Countess Vanessa Von Zanzamere was found brutally murdered in her downtown flat. The vivacious (and clinically insane) woman we've all grown to know and love is gone. No longer will her visage grace noted American periodicals, her lunatic smile enrapturing all. Authorities are still piecing the shards of this mystery (and of Countess Vanessa Von Zanzamere) together.*

The Great Countess *dead?* Preposterous! *Murdered?* Impossible!

I shrieked in horror and shot from the tub. I ran naked through the streets – flapping and insane. My bellows echoed for blocks. The world around me abandoned structure to transform itself into a mess of cascading, disembodied colors. Losing control of my body, I collapsed outside the town drugstore. Bellows became sobs and, forgetting my nakedness, I attempted to rend my clothing. My nails opened a small hole in my chest, but the pain failed to register. I continued to roll on the ground, oblivious to anything that wasn't sorrow.

Hours seemed to pass. Somehow, I managed to stagger back home without attracting the attention of the local constabulary. I bandaged my wound, slipped into my clothes, and moved the TV back into the living room. There, I cursed myself. My trembling hands kept missing the 'on' button. I responded to this inconvenience by turning the Countess' name into a soothing mantra. Soon, my hands were calm enough to operate the controller.

<*ANCHOR LADY*>: *Praise be to the All-Father. Authorities have arrested a suspect in connection with the murder of Countess Vanessa Von Zanzamere. The individual was discovered wandering outside her flat in a delusional state. Information as to his identity has yet to be released.*

The news broadcasted an image of a slender man with Jesus-like hair and countenance being pushed into a police cruiser. I noticed how he floated above his captors and saw the halo-like glow around his head. Despite the presence of a tight-fitting straight jacket, the man seemed at total peace.

The cameras moved in until their lenses were practically crammed in his face. The man made no attempt to hide himself from them. His eyes seemed focused on something very far away.

"He whose consciousness soars can never truly be imprisoned," he muttered over and above the clamor of police sirens and enraged spectators. Before the suspect could say anything further, a man in a Countess Vanessa Von Zanzamere T-shirt ground a ripe tomato into his face.

I was desperate to see more, but the scene cut away. The chatty anchors returned.

"I think I speak for fans of the Countess worldwide when I

say, I hope they give him the juice."

"That's right, Bill. And what was with all that nonsense about consciousness?"

"I believe that man was on drugs, Sally."

But I knew the suspect wasn't mumbling nonsense or suffering delusions. He was spouting obscure Zen phrases and, judging by his sheer iridescence, transcending the visible universe on the spot.

At that point, I knew he was innocent.

At that point, I knew I had to meet the man.

* * * *

Latching onto the all-news channel, I vowed to neither eat nor sleep until the defendant's court date had been announced. The Countess was dead, and the man accused of her murder was as rare a person as she. Under such circumstances, I could do no less than abstain from *everything*. There was no question in my mind, however, that I could right this wrong. All I had to do was show up at the courthouse and teach the judge how to translate Zen into English.

But news of his impending trial never came. The anchors just kept babbling about the swelling interest in that midget book, and that was something I couldn't care less about.

So I kept watching.

The talking heads grew increasingly repellant. Once, I considered trying to find a newspaper – anything to avoid those horrible, chattering things – but I had nothing with which to record the broadcast, and the paper wouldn't have newer headlines than the ones flashing on my set. I didn't want to miss anything should the information finally be announced. The TV was my Mecca.

I managed to hold onto my composure for the first few days but assumed, and assumed correctly, that breakdown was inevitable.

* * * *

Rationality was a foreign thing by the beginning of the second week. The talking heads refused to acknowledge my suffering, no matter how loudly I screamed at the TV. I feared the weathermen were formulating plots against me. Everything made me quake. Nothing brought me solace.

Through it all, I hoped the pretty blonde newscaster might reach through the screen and give me a hug. I *needed* her to tell me everything would be okay – that justice would be served – but her heart was stone. She just read her lines and smiled a plasticine smile.

* * * *

Time progressed. I rejected life and its accompanying pleasures roughly a month following the Countess' death. My body became little more than a self-contained lump, functioning yet emotionally dead. The phone rang, but I hadn't the will to get up and stop the noise. I heard the mailman stuff more and more letters into my box. I never checked it. On occasions, the doorbell sounded but, like a debauched primate, I screamed incoherently and threw my fecal matter at the door.

Inner nausea quickly shifted to full-blown physical decay. My skin turned gray as my glands swelled into hurtful lumps. My organs felt liquefied. Breathing became an anathema to me. My limbs no longer functioned as they should and folded each time I tried to stand. Even my hair started to fall out.

I lived for the Countess and the mission I obligated myself to undertake in her name. Nothing more.

* * * *

Days passed without end. My body felt like a desiccated, flesh-wrapped skeleton – kept alive by preternatural forces beyond my control – when the news finally divulged the trial's start-date:

July 6th.

My recovery was immediate. Color tinted my skin. Warmth filled my veins. My sense of self returned, as did my shame.

I recoiled at the human wreck that stared back at me from the mirror across the room. I was suddenly thankful to be unemployed and blessed the government from afar for paying my utilities. I didn't know how well I'd take a screaming boss or an irate bill-collector. Such things would only compound my sense of personal decay.

At that moment, face to face with horror, I caught a whiff of my body odor. I stepped away from the mirror, dodging piles of debris and flies the size of my thumb. It was time to gather up all the things I would need to restore lost dignity. My arsenal soon grew vast – an entire can of disinfectant, a fist-full of steel wool, and two toilet brushes – but the subsequent effort nevertheless proved Herculean. Hours of scraping, pulling, and sanding ensued. Rarely did I let up, though on one occasion I spent nearly two minutes with my head underwater. I had decided, however briefly, that I was too soiled to live.

My hope eventually restored, I continued scrubbing and scrubbing. Additional hours passed. Finally, I stepped out of the tub and observed my pink and steaming body. It felt good to be clean, but I couldn't feel entirely refreshed. Filth still permeated my house, knee deep in some places. I smelled an ungodly reek no matter where I stood. I hated myself even more for regressing, but had no time to revel in self-loathing. The 6th was a scant two days away, and the place was in shambles.

I put on my clothes and set to work. With a little elbow grease and a rented backhoe, I removed the larger debris. Upon finishing that task, I ripped up the carpeting. It was beyond repair.

The act of remodeling proved taxing enough to keep me from obsessing about the upcoming trial. But it never stopped the dreams. Monstrous images haunted my nights. I watched, powerless, as the Zen Master sat strapped to *The Chair*. Wardens hovered over him, forcing rotting green beans down his throat. When his last meal was over, the Reverend pulled a big, red switch. The man's dying body buckled. I heard the laughter of those in attendance and smelled burning meat.

The following night, I dreamt I was in a coffin, sharing space with the dead as the poor man decomposed in some potter's field.

The 6th couldn't come quickly enough.

* * * *

When the day mercifully arrived, I jumped out of bed and stepped into my best suit. I looked in the mirror. Clothing alone would not suffice. If I hoped to infiltrate the proceedings, I had to play the role of a well-to-do-man-of-the-world so, as a finishing touch, I opened up a suitcase and placed a number of one-dollar bills along its edges so that they would stick out halfway once the lid was closed.

I just hoped no one would realize they weren't fifties or hundreds.

* * * *

The thirty minutes drive to the Blackston Township Courthouse: a singularly nerve-wracking experience. So much stress. I knew a man's freedom, and quite possibly life, rested in my hands. My fingers clawed at my face. I began to hallucinate. Cars morphed into mountains atop which stood a race of massive chipmunk-like creatures. Their leader waved at me, his cute cheeks filled with both a cornucopia of foodstuffs and the severed heads of his enemies. My vision suddenly cleared. I realized I was looking at the courthouse's fast approaching cupola, not a gathering of chipmunks. Responding to this understanding, I swerved back into the correct lane. The world shifted to normalcy as I parked my car in a *primo* space near the marble steps.

* * * *

"Well, shit," I exclaimed as I paused by the double-doors leading into the courtroom.

A sign had been hung above the left knob:

PROCEEDINGS CLOSED TO THE GENERAL PUBLIC

I threw the suitcase down. It was a good ruse, but it couldn't help me now. *I'll just waltz in and act as translator.* My naïveté was an embarrassment.

The urge to tear down the sign waxed strong, but I managed to restrain my hand. Destroying property would solve nothing. I had to do something constructive so, to gain entry into the court, I decided to pose as famed journalist KURT ROTHEIM. It was my first plan, and I set the wheels into motion without further commentary.

I tore a strip from a paper napkin in my pocket and, onto its surface, scribbled the word *Press* with a black crayon. There was no glue in my pockets, so I decided to hold the strip in place with my hand and act casual.

The armed sentries eyed me with suspicion as I neared:

<GUARD>: What's your name?

<ME>: I am famed journalist KURT ROTHEIM. Can't you see I have a "Press" hat on my head, which by no means did I create as an extemporized and ill-conceived ruse.

<GUARD>: *(Spoken as his hand inches closer to his billy club.)* Can I see some ID? *(Begins stroking the club as he imagines* KURT ROTHEIM'S *brains adhering to its shaft.)*

<ME>: How dare you ask famed journalist KURT ROTHEIM for identification! If I were younger, I would have you drawn and quartered on the spot!

<GUARD>: Well, since you *are* KURT ROTHEIM and all, I guess you can go in without ID. But only if you let us beat you about the head and shoulders first.

<ME>: I don't think that's such a good– (*Words silenced by the force of a sturdy wooden shaft crashing against lips.)*

A MINUTE OR SO LATER:

<GUARDS>: *(In unison.)* You can go in now.

<ME>: (*Spoken through swollen lips.*) Tank ooo my gud min.

The doors parted; I hobbled into an amazingly opulent chamber. Marble tiles lined the floor. Bodies of the guilty swung from ornately carved rafters, smelling of old death. Most corpses had been hanging so long only grinning skeletons remained.

I stood transfixed, gazing up at the carnage. The entire judicial process sickened me. It had become mercenary, if not *predatory*. Just a few short years ago, there would have been no bodies hanging at all.

A hunk of meat fell from one of the corpses and slapped me in the face. I threw it off with a sigh of disgust and vowed the defendant's flesh would never have the opportunity to dirty the courtroom floor.

Beyond the corpses, I saw the defendant. He was already on the witness stand. Wolves in human form circled him. Lawyers, clutching huge suitcases full of money, threw spit-wads at the defendant and laughed as he made no effort to remove their phlegm from his face. Others fought with vultures for the opportunity to gnaw on bodies that had rotted free from their nooses. My heart felt as though it could weep.

I wandered to an empty bench in the rear of the courtroom. The defendant's cross-examination commenced the moment I found my seat.

"We would like Timmy, the defendant's childhood friend, to step up and address this *foul and unshaven heathen,*" a black-clad lawyer intoned.

The judge looked over Timmy with rummy eyes. "Ah, a fine specimen of manhood! He may proceed."

<TIMMY>: *(Waltzing up to* THE DEFENDANT.*)* Gee, don't you remember the good old days? Weren't they just *swell?*

<DEFENDANT>: The past is but a memory.

<TIMMY>: Yeah, those were the glory days! So, what have you been up to?

<DEFENDANT>: This and that.

<TIMMY>: I heard you did something recently.

<DEFENDANT>: By living we do things.

<TIMMY>: So, why did you do that thing you did?

<DEFENDANT>: I have no reason.

<TIMMY>: Oh, come now! You can trust your old friend, Timmy.

<DEFENDANT>: Trust comes in matters of degree.

<TIMMY>: Goddamn it, tell me! (*At this point,* THE DEFENDANT'S CHILDHOOD FRIEND *rips his mask away, revealing himself to be* THE PROSECUTOR.)

<PROSECUTOR>: What did you do on the night of the16th?

<DEFENDANT>: I went into the world, beautiful and verbose. I stood by the lake and felt the sumptuous breeze pass by. Trees beckoned me to sit underneath their living branches.

<PROSECUTOR>: I see. And how long did you know the Countess Vanessa Von Zanzamere prior to her hideous and untimely death?

<DEFENDANT>: I think I might have met her in a dream.

<PROSECUTOR>: Now tell us why you killed the Countess Vanessa Von Zanzamere.

<DEFENDANT>: Why does one do anything?

<PROSECUTOR>: *(Donning the robes of* THE GRAND INQUISITOR.*)* Confess!

<DEFENDANT>: Words are but clumsy tools.

<THE GRAND INQUISITOR>: Then I shall make thee confess! To the *Iron Maiden!*

I felt compelled to say something. If I remained silent, the man would be tortured for hours, and I would be haunted for life.

"For the love of all things, cease and desist!"

All eyes in the courthouse turned in my direction. I felt their stare. *Heated knives.*

The judge scowled and banged his gavel on the bailiff's head.

"And just what is the meaning of this outburst, young man?"

I stated my case: "The defendant is innocent! He is merely speaking a language that you, with your clouded mind, cannot comprehend! But I can interpret his words so that you might see how he could have never killed the enchanting Countess Vanessa Von Zanzamere!"

<Grows the head of a serpent atop his judicial robes>: "This is highly irregular and seditious behavior! I suggest you sit down before I am forced to hold you in contempt!"

"But–"

"Silence," the judge/snake hissed. "We will listen to your insanity no longer!"

"You don't understand! This man *is* innocent! If you'd just–"

A burst shook the chamber, nearly knocking me from my feet. The room's left half had exploded in a rainbow of flesh and debris. The surviving spectators fled their benches and ran, pell-mell, for the exit. A few managed to get out, but a deadlock soon formed. The screams of those trapped were earsplitting.

Spinning, I noticed the stenographer had ceased typing and was now rummaging through her purse. She removed strange, pinecone-like objects from its compartment. I watched, confused, as she turned to the judge, who gave her a prompt thumbs-up. She nodded before tossing one of the pinecones at my head.

Understanding dawned. Those weren't pinecones. Those were *hand grenades!*

I ran towards the judge's bench and dove to the floor, clutching my skull. I winced as the sound of death enveloped the room. Above it all, I heard the judge's laughter.

"He's down here! Get him! Make your aim true!"

"Aye aye, sir," the stenographer replied. Seconds later, another grenade *whooshed* through the air. I uncovered my eyes. The explosive had landed mere inches from my face. I picked it up – knowing good and well the device could detonate at any moment – and launched the explosive at the judge/snake. He unleashed a half-hiss/half-shriek in the seconds before his scaly head evaporated in a red and pink cloud.

"Damn you," the stenographer shouted. "Where else am I going to find a lover with such a nimble, forked tongue?"

I turned away from the woman and spotted her abandoned stenographer's machine lying on the floor. Picking up the shattered pieces, I threw them at her head. She tried to dart out of the way, but one large chunk struck her temple and knocked her out cold.

There was no time to gloat over victory. I ran to the witness stand, hoping the defendant had survived this sudden and inexplicable holocaust. He had. The defendant's upturned eyes continued to gaze lovingly at the absolutes of *Truth*, *Beauty*, and *Love*. How I wished I could enter such a state, but I had no time to contemplate that possibility. The enemy's defenses were down, though for how long I couldn't say.

I shouted to the defendant: "I've come to get you out of here!"

"How can you get me out of *here* when I am neither here nor there?"

I thought for a second. "Good point. But you know this isn't over yet. It's best we leave. Otherwise, you won't live to transcend another day."

"The mess you speak of is *their* creation and every act of life – even death – is pure transcendence."

"Granted. But you're so amazingly wise. It would tear me apart to see such a special person killed. Your death would be a tragedy."

"We are all beautiful. Everything is beautiful. Nothing is beautiful, too."

"Damn it!" I dragged the defendant from the stand. "I will not let this world destroy another precious thing!"

Overhead, I heard what sounded like a fleet of fast-approaching aircraft. I tugged harder at the immobile and transcendent bulk that was the defendant, spinning around just as the first mini-copter – sleek and black – crashed headlong into the chamber and took out the remaining spectators clumped by the door.

I had heard rumors of these tiny, almost man-sized planes, but had never seen one up until that moment. They were government-owned and operated by highly trained assassins – the *true* policemen of the skies.

Forcing the defendant under the judge's bench, I took cover behind a dead, fat lady. I wanted to live, but my close proximity to such recent death made short work of my resolve. It was all too much. I decided to surrender. I stood up and opened my arms to embrace Eternity. Even as I bowed to the reaper, I prayed the defendant would have the sense to flee as the goons riddled my hide with armor-piercing bullets.

For some reason, the assassins failed to acknowledge my surrender. Instead, they turned somersaults and sent their planes into near suicidal nosedives. Just before impact was inevitable, they returned to the skies (or, in this case, the ceiling) and continued their mindless spinning.

Then it struck me.

The pilots were drunk.

I left my gruesome hiding place, too confused to be elated. Why would such an elite killing-force consume liquor on the job? I ran to the bench where the defendant remained cloistered, not surprised to find him in full lotus.

"Get up! We gotta go, *now!* The people flying the planes are drunk! This is our only chance!"

I tugged at the defendant. Dragging him across the floor was problematic, so I decided to cradle him in my arms. I wasn't the strongest person, and ordinarily wouldn't have been able to shoulder his weight, but things were suddenly different as the defendant began to float above my arms and hover there. In order to move him, I had to merely push my chest against his bulk as I ran.

Ducking the out-of-control aircrafts, I sprinted with the defendant through the gaping hole the planes had punched in the wall. Sunlight flooded into my eyes. Such a welcome respite from that dark and decaying room.

I hugged the defendant closer to my body as we cut a path to the street where the drunken pilots had instigated their rampage. At least two buildings lay in smoldering ruin. A scattering of blasted corpses dotted the sidewalk. Terrified people loomed over the bodies, checking for signs of life. Up ahead, the first fleet of ambulances turned the corner onto the street. The paramedics had to park before they reached the carnage since the road leading up to it was clogged with cars, both occupied and abandoned.

I had had enough death for one twenty-four hour period. I ran until I neither saw nor smelled the bloodshed. A few miles later, destruction finally gave way to normalcy.

* * * *

On the corner of Fifth and Volmax, I discovered an abandoned car with the keys still hanging from the ignition. Again, I felt a bit too lucky. I wondered who, if anyone, was pulling the strings. Maybe it was *Destiny*. Maybe I didn't care just as long as I had a way out.

Dumping the defendant inside was my first priority. I was getting far too many stares from passersby for holding a grown – and floating – man in public. I fastened his seatbelt for him and ran to the other side of the car. I slid into the driver's seat. Turning the keys, I listened as the automobile's engine choked for a few seconds before sputtering to life.

"It'll be okay," I shouted over the roar of the engine. "We're safe now."

"Now is relative," he mumbled, his eyes fixed on nothing in particular.

"So, what's your name? I can't very well call you *the defendant* all the time."

"People call me Peace Loveman," he said and offered me a flower and a copy of *Zen Mumblings* by A. Khriskaherti.

I was dumbstruck. The defendant had actually presented me with a straight answer.

"Well, Peace, it's good to meet you. My name is Luke. Luke Hammonds."

* * * *

Our going was smooth for approximately thirty minutes. Peace meditated, and I sat watching the world unfold beyond the windshield.

It was a very nice day, apart from the carnage a few miles back. The sun was bright and the air crisp. This side of town looked as it always did, bland yet strangely comforting. Only one thing was different. Quite a few banners now hung from storefront windows, though none had been there the day before. For some reason, all bore the name MARK ANDERS.

I had heard that name before. I mulled it over in my head for a few minutes until I realized this was the guy who wrote that damn midget book.

"Hey Peace? Did you ever read the little book that Anders guy wrote? Everyone seems to be fawning over it."

His eyes lit up. "I loved that book. It was *transcendental.*"

"Really? I thought it was pretty mediocre myself."

"Who can claim to define quality?"

"Understood. But I can't see why everyone's going so crazy. The thing was only about seventy pages–"

Sirens blared in the distance. My lips slammed shut. I looked behind me. Through the rear-view mirror, I saw the police cruiser gaining fast.

I decided to play it calm. Confrontation was unavoidable. The police cruiser was nothing compared to the aircraft that had decimated the court, but that didn't mean I wanted to contend with it. Under the circumstances, its twirling blue and white lights alone were enough to instill fear.

I pulled my car to the side. The policeman did likewise. He spent a few seconds repositioning his holster before walking over to our car.

<OFFICER BRADY>: May I see your license and registration?

<ME>: There's no need, officer. *(Dons "press hat".)* For I am KURT ROTHEIM, famed journalist.

<OFFICER BRADY>: KURT ROTHEIM died in 1995.

<ME>: Really. Sheesh. I didn't know I'd been gone *that* long. People tell me I get around quite well for a dead man. *(Chuckles.)*

<OFFICER BRADY>: Get out of the damn car, *now!* Both of you!

<ME>: I'm sorry officer, sir. But we simply don't have the time. (*Notes OFFICIAL MARK ANDERS FAN CLUB PIN on officer's breast. Brain begins to storm.*) We have to meet Mark Anders in *five minutes*. You know how irate he gets when guests show up late.

<OFFICER BRADY>: (*Wets self.*) *MARK FUCKIN' ANDERS!!!*

<ME>: That is correct.

<OFFICER BRADY>: (*Begins dancing about.*) Can you get me his autograph? Can you get it for me? Please, *for the love of God*, tell me you can get it for me!

<ME>: Simmer down! I can ask but I won't make any promises.

<OFFICER BRADY>: (*Fidgety hand hovers near crotch.*) I'll let you go if you swear to at least tell him I said *hi!*

<ME>: Sure. He'll be enchanted to hear from one of his billions of admirers.

<OFFICER BRADY>: Thank you! Thank you! Thank you! That book has changed my life and *I haven't even read it yet*. I just heard the title and that was enough for me. I'm crazy for Mark Anders! He's my man! Thank you! Thank you! *Thank you!*

<ME>: No problem. Can we leave now?

<OFFICER BRADY>: Yes, go on! I wouldn't want to make you late for something so important! *God no!*

I waved to the hyper-kinetic officer as he sprinted away. In the rearview mirror, I watched him disappear into his car. Within seconds, Brady's cruiser was lost behind a wall of traffic. Then I resumed driving.

Turning to Peace: "I think I should write that Mark Anders guy a letter when all this is said and done. He'd probably like to know how he helped us out."

"Offer your gratitude freely and the favor shall surely be returned."

I smiled. "You always say the right words, Peace. I have to admit, you're the most in-tune person on the planet. The Dalai Lama has nothing over you. *Nothing.*"

"I am unworthy of such comparison."

"Nonsense. If you went to a Buddhist temple, you'd be enthroned in an instant!"

"I desire nothing more than what I have now, at this moment."

"I wish I could be so humble."

"Do not wish. *Do.*"

I acknowledged Peace's wisdom and turned off onto another street. The MARK ANDERS banners were a little less frequent here. People, however, milled about the sidewalk, their heads deep in that ubiquitous book. Pedestrians ran into lampposts and tripped over street curbs because they refused to lift their eyes from its pages. Some even wore Countess Vanessa Von Zanzamere T-shirts with her face blanked out and a picture of Mark Anders' nondescript head inserted in its place.

"So you said you liked that book. Right, Peace?"

"That tome is superior even to the *Dhammapada* itself; I tell you true."

My brows furrowed. "The *Dhammapada?* What's that?"

"A collection of aphorisms from the Buddha. It is said that–"

"HOLY FUCKING SHEEP SHIT!"

I swerved to the left and then to the right. Other cars were no longer staying in their respective lanes. I had no idea what was going on. The road had turned, within a span of mere seconds, into a high-traffic madhouse. Some cars drove on the sidewalk and took out those who stumbled along, their faces plastered in *The End: In Circus Midgets and Barbed Chains*. The injured continued to read, even while lying on the ground. Other cars darted across private yards or crashed through storefront windows. Nobody really seemed to care, just as long as they held that book in their hands.

I couldn't look into the windshields of these cars. The day was far too bright. It wasn't until the sun slid behind a cloud that the ultimate horror was revealed:

The people were all reading while driving!

Panic gripped me. I picked up speed and tried to mimic the crazed actions of my fellow motorists. It was the only way I could navigate during a time when traffic laws had lost all meaning. Suddenly, up ahead, a residential neighborhood took shape. I assumed the traffic there would be less heavy.

A black mini-van tore out onto the road a few parking lots ahead of me just as I unleashed a premature sigh.

My body grew cold and my breathing – if not my heart itself – stopped. My life flashed before my eyes in a series of dull, repetitive images. As a kid – at home, alone. As a teenager – sitting by a silent phone, waiting for it to ring. As an adult – more of the same.

I blinked. The car was even closer now. No time to react. Three seconds left to live. *Tops*.

At that moment, an ancient lime-green Pinto barreled from an alley and shot across all lanes of traffic. No one seemed to be driving it, but that couldn't be the case. Maybe the driver was just small.

I watched, dumbfounded, as the car plowed into the mini-van, yet kept traveling at the same pre-collision speed. The green Pinto pushed the much larger auto for at least 100 feet until both smashed through a glass wall and came to rest in the middle of a car dealership's showroom. While the mini-van was a crumpled wreck, the Pinto appeared to have sustained no damage at all.

It was, without a doubt, the most amazing traffic accident I had ever witnessed – made even more amazing by the fact that a lowly Pinto had taken out a mini-van with all the force of a semi. Laws of Physics had been broken left and right, but I wasn't in the mood to question *anything*. I just wanted off the main road as soon as possible.

The residential section I had spotted earlier was now only a few blocks away. My hands shook so hard they barely held onto the wheel. Somehow, I managed to turn onto a street marked *Windsor* without incurring further strife.

My driving normalized. The street was vacant except for my car and a late-model Mercedes-Benz doing doughnuts around a tree growing in the left corner lot. The driver didn't seem to notice me. I figured he or she wouldn't pose too great a threat.

"That was close." I drew in a series of deep breaths. "We've got to find a place where we can hole up for the night. Driving around just isn't safe."

"Do what you must," Peace said, calm as ever.

I was taken aback. "You *do* realize we just about died back there, right?"

"Yes."

"Okay, I was just checking."

I proceeded down the street and, when I reached its end, turned off onto another. It was an exact replica of the first. Disappointed, I tried yet another avenue. When it petered off into a dead end, I slammed my hands against the steering wheel.

The entire neighborhood was utterly suburban – impractical for our purposes. Houses were crammed too close together. No hiding place could possibly be found amongst the sea of brick and pavement. Old shacks and large fields lined the outskirts of town, but we'd once again have to brave the main road to get there. That was something I did not want to do.

"This is probably the worst street we could have pulled into. Do you know that Peace?"

He responded with a smile.

I shielded my eyes and, for a few seconds, once again lost control over the car. Peace's aura was blinding, and I had been foolish enough to look into it dead-on.

"Damn it, Peace! Don't you think you could turn off those lights? Driving's already a real *bitch!"*

"Sorry, I did not wish to offend." He frowned. A darkness settled over his aura. The car began to shake and the temperature within plummeted. Within seconds, ice crystals had formed on the windshield. My breath exited my mouth in foggy puffs.

"What the hell is happening! Peace, tell–"

My lips slammed shut as I watched his once radiant glow suck in the drink holder. Then the steering wheel detached itself from the dashboard, followed by even bulkier pieces of the auto's interior.

"I'm sorry, Peace!" I dodged a large, airborne fragment of the backseat. "For God's sake, get happy!"

The look of hurt refused to leave even as the void tore away, and then swallowed, both my shirt and pants.

"Close this black hole before we're both sucked in!"

But it was too late. I felt my head detach from my body and sail into the gaping maw that had once been Peace Loveman. Then my arms flew away. Then my legs. Soon, each part that constituted *me* was sailing off into the Event Horizon. Everything reduced itself to nothing and nothing reduced itself to everything. The world exploded and then collapsed. A lifetime later, everything went black.

* * * *

Consciousness returned; I found my body intact. Looking down at the dashboard clock, I saw how no time had passed between Peace's creation of the vortex and our being sucked headlong into it.

I wiped the sweat from my brow. We were lucky. Instead of being torn to shreds in the mouth of the Event Horizon, we merely landed in a different location within our own space-time continuum. It appeared, however, as though Peace and I were now somewhere in the flatlands of the Midwest.

Our car was parked in some weed-infested driveway. An old two-story farmhouse loomed above us, standing in the middle of a flat and lonely field bisected by train tracks. The wind that whistled through the open car window was bracing; it caused chill bumps to form on my arms. Overhead, the sky was a dense, opaque gray.

The whole experience was a bit disconcerting, but I assumed our being at this place was a good thing. The police would have a hard time finding us when we were both hundreds of miles from the spot we had occupied just minutes before.

I stepped from the car and walked over to the passenger's side. Then I opened the door, holding it ajar for Peace.

"Come on. Get out. Are you happy now? Do you feel any better?"

"Even Zen Masters must vent once in a while."

I nodded, realizing I could never stay mad at such a majestic man, and ushered Peace to the porch. I paused by the front door.

"All we have to do now is find a way to break–"

I watched, dumbfounded, as the door swung open on rusted hinges.

"Did you do that?"

Peace just smiled serenely. I decided it best not to ask questions.

* * * *

Once inside, I discovered that, for an abandoned farmhouse in the middle of nowhere, this was a rather groovy pad. The house was filled with all the modern amenities. In the living room, a Jacuzzi bubbled away alongside a fully stocked bar. To the right, a big-screen TV pumped out a show featuring some mad doctor and his cheese-headed partner in crime. In the kitchen, a sumptuous banquet rested beneath china. Turkey and dressing, salad and soup: it all appeared so fresh.

Hunger overrode perplexity. Leaving Peace in the living room, I took a seat by the kitchen table. I wasted no time. I stuffed food into my face. The rune-encrusted plates and silverware were never in any danger of use. I just pulled meat apart with my hands and ate directly from each platter.

I looked up, runners of clam chowder dripping from my lips. Peace stared at me.

"Oh God, I'm so sorry! I guess I've just made a glutton of myself."

"Worry not, Luke. Enjoy your meal to the fullest. Just don't get too caught up in temporal pleasures."

I returned to slurping the chowder. It was like nothing I had ever tasted. Not New England. Certainly not Manhattan. For some reason, it reminded me of the Ganges.

I found this odd. I had never been anywhere near India.

* * * *

After dinner – and a long session of bowling in the game room – Peace and I ventured upstairs to find our beds. We made a few wrong turns the first time around. Some doors opened into dark, empty voids. Others opened into hideous, sideshow-based tableaus.

Finally, we located the master bedroom.

A stately suit of armor stood sentinel over a beautiful, centuries old fireplace. Mahogany bureaus, armoires, and chests dotted the room. The canopy bed stood framed in curtains of only the finest silk while dozens of mattresses sat piled atop a supporting box spring. I looked at them in awe, wondering whether or not a pea rested beneath all the padding.

"You can have this one, Peace."

He shook his head. "I could never accept something so grand. I'll find a smaller bedroom and sleep there."

"Are you sure?"

"I insist."

"Okay, but let me know if you change your mind."

Peace made his exit. I closed the door behind him and, aiming my body at the mattresses, leapt into the air. Stripping as I sailed, I was down to my unmentionables before I even hit the bed.

* * * *

Though my accommodations were comfy beyond human comprehension, sleep was not forthcoming. I got up, dressed, and walked through the hall looking for Peace. Hours passed before I found his humble room amongst the thousands of identical doors lining the walls.

I opened Peace's door. The poverty he so gladly accepted was staggering. Unlike my lush boudoir, my new friend slept in a twenty-five by twenty-five chamber sans carpeting and electricity. His bed was a straw mat around which a few barnyard animals gathered. Some clucked; some grazed. An elderly shepherd tended to these creatures while strumming a Jew's harp, his chapped lips embracing a tune that made my eyes water.

The room itself was redolent of hay and animal droppings, but it was an earthy smell. Not at all pleasing, but not at all repulsive, either. I assumed the shepherd also took care of the room, scooping up dung and wiping away urine before the reek could become unbearable. All at once, I found myself respecting this unadorned man.

How wanton of me to demand more than the simple life.

In the midst of this tiny, third world hovel, Peace levitated at least two feet above an Arabian Yoga mat. Just standing in the proximity of his radiating energy sent my consciousness spinning. I walked over. Peace heard me and opened his eyes.

Shame overwhelmed me.

"I didn't mean to interrupt you." I narrowly avoided a pile of feces as I took my seat by Peace. "I was just fascinated by the depth of your concentration."

He unleashed an angel's smile. "Nothing you do shall ever disturb me. Come. You are obviously interested in something. Tell me what you desire."

I stared at my shoes. "I hate to bother you but. . . well. . . what I mean to say is, *can I join in?"*

Peace looked up at me. I could not read his face.

"Will you show me the peace that you know? Will you take me there?"

Peace Loveman agreed and, at that second, the universe crumbled.

* * * *

(COSMIC TIME)

Peace Loveman grasped my hand. Together we danced through onionskin layer after onionskin layer of reality. The world swirled around us in perfect, beautiful chaos and, at that moment, I became selfless. I became selfless and I danced. I danced like a man who knows he's about to die – and *loves* it. I danced like a child who has yet to feel the pains of society – of hatred instigated by majority-rules opinion.

Peace Loveman stared into my eyes. I became him and he became me and we became all that has ever been or shall be. Self-absorption gave way to all-absorption. Our molecules raced to the cosmos where we became star-stuff. We became the ingredients of the primal soup. I bubbled like magma. Peace flowed like water.

Eternity danced on the head of a pin. Universes sprouted from our fingertips. Life began anew in the blinking of an eye, only to die in our palms and be born again. Energy swirled into matter; matter swirled into energy.

All these processes happened at once. Infinite beauty and ultimate love were revealed in both subtlety and splendor. I understood without understanding. I felt without feeling. I was without being. I sensed an inalienable will that collapsed over me like never before. Selflessness – with a personality. Quantum mechanics – with a brain. Quantum mechanics – with *love*.

* * * *

("REAL" TIME)

I awoke the next morning, still surging from last night's pure Zen experience. The police still sought after us, sure, but that mattered little in the grand scheme of things. They could persecute Peace Loveman and me all they wished, but they could never steal our collective soul.

Stretching languorously, I slipped into a blue bathrobe that I had found hanging in the closet. It was a bit threadbare, but I needed to put *something* on. The goats in Peace's room had eaten away every stitch of my clothing. I was far too deep in Zen ecstasy to realize what they were doing at the time.

But the loss did not concern me.

I looked out over my room. I remembered the awe I felt when my eyes first glimpsed this impossibly lavish chamber. Now, material items had lost their once primary importance. It was amazing how things could change in so little time.

And I had my new friend to thank for it all.

I walked over to the window. There, I beheld an enchanting sight. Peace sat meditating in the garden, a halo beatific atop his worry-free head. And how the birds nested at his feet! His meditation was so powerful it had breached the communication gap between man and animal. I watched as he opened his eyes and acknowledged the wildlife his clear consciousness had attracted. Peace smiled, then bent down to rip the head from a blue jay.

My breath caught in my throat.

What the hell had just happened?

Perhaps I was dreaming. I rubbed my eyes, looked out the window, and saw the bird – still dead – by Peace's feet. The others flew away in bird-panic. Strangely enough, *Peace didn't seem to care.*

I ran outside, stumbling in my confusion, and confronted him.

"My God, Peace! You just killed a bird!"

"I didn't."

"Yes, you did!"

"No, I didn't."

"Then why's there a headless blue jay by your feet?"

"The cycles of life and death are continuous."

"I know, but you killed that bird. It didn't just die. *You ripped off its head."*

"What is *you?* What is *bird?* Just words. Images to conceal the true spirit."

I smacked my forehead. "Yes, the language system is imperfect. But you just killed a bird!"

"The eyes deceive."

I looked crossly at Peace. "What do you mean?"

"When you see things, do you see the Truth within? Or do you merely see your *conception* of reality?"

I was dumbfounded. "I guess I see things as they are. I'd like to think I do, at least."

"By saying that, you admit to being a stranger to Truth."

"What the hell are you talking about? *You killed that bird, Peace*. End of story! Cut the games and confess!"

"Again, you perplex me. I am not capable of hurting – much less killing – another sentient being. If I were to hurt something, I would bring a greater pain onto myself."

"Then why's your head not falling off!"

"You will never achieve enlightenment, Luke. Not until you erase delusion and see life as a whole, now and forever unbroken."

"But I saw you–"

"You saw nothing and confused it with something."

By that time, my mind was spinning. “I could have sworn you just tore off that blue jay’s head.”

“Sometimes illusions are more powerful than reality.”

“That’s no illusion,” I pointed at the carcass. “It’s still dead.”

“He who weeps for every bird that falls from the sky has little time for joy.”

“Well. . . I *was* pretty far away. I don’t know. Maybe that bird was already dead, killed by a cat or something.”

“Stop battering your brain; it will get you nowhere. Sit by my side and meditate. Renew your mind.”

I nodded my approval and contorted my legs into full-lotus.

Five minutes later, I once again sailed in the cosmic unknown. My particles soared and sang. The world opened up and, at that second, I could not breathe. I assumed my breath was caught in awe – spellbound by the selfless grandeur of the moment.

But something seemed wrong.

This wasn’t rapture. By god, this was *pain!*

I opened my eyes; the beautiful cosmic world ceased swirling.

But I still couldn’t breathe.

I brought my hands to my neck and, for a few seconds, felt the coarse twine of a garrote about my larynx. Before I could get my hands around it, the loop slipped away. I spun around and saw Peace Loveman – eyes closed – soaring through realm after realm of reality.

Did yesterday’s black hole mess with my mind? Things were simply not adding up. I decided to leave Peace in the garden and meditate behind locked doors. As I left, hobbling on wobbly legs, he didn’t utter a word of protest. His meditation continued unabated.

* * * *

An hour later, Peace returned from his meditation/bird-beheading session in the garden.

I greeted him at the door, hoping he wouldn’t notice the protective chest-plate beneath my robe. I had taken it from one of the suits of armor in the bedroom. Though I wanted to believe Peace, I could no longer be certain of anything.

“Hey, Peace.”

He looked me over. “I see you’re still concerned with illusion, Luke. Take off your protection. You won’t need it once you understand how consciousness itself is your own best weapon.”

“Yeah, but consciousness won’t stop me from being strangled.”

"Believe as you will." Peace brushed past me, stopping by the breakfast nook. He removed a box of cereal-puffs and poured them directly from the box into his maw. He made ecstatic groaning noises. Rubbing his stomach with unholy gusto, he unleashed a series of farts.

"Damn! This is good chow," he exclaimed, mouth open, torrents of partially masticated food spilling forth. "I can't get enough of this shit! *Ummmmmmmmmmmmmmmm!"*

I stood watching, mouth agape.

"Hey, do you want some of this stuff?" Peace threw the box at my head.

"That's not a very enlightened thing to do!" I threw the box back at Peace.

"In that case, I shall hand the box to you so that we might feel the bliss of a deep, intra-personal connection."

I raised my hand quickly. "Stay put!"

He arose from his chair, box of cereal in tow. "No, I insist."

I tried to back myself into the other room and lock the door behind me, but Peace was too agile. One hand wrapped itself around my neck while the other reached into the cereal box. Before I fully understood what was happening, Peace was busy shoveling handfuls of Sugar Puffs down my gullet.

Round after round, he would not stop! My stomach bulged from the amount of puffs stuffed therein. I wanted to beg him to end this madness, but I could not speak. His fist was rammed so far down my throat that I was able to produce only a slight choking sound.

A few minutes later, Peace grew tired and threw the box to the floor.

"There, glad I could share with you."

He released his grip on my throat. I collapsed immediately.

* * * *

When I came to, the room was black. I had been out for quite some time; it was daylight when my new friend instigated his cereal assault. Brushing the dust from my robe and chest-plate, I arose and scanned the room for signs of Peace Loveman's presence. I didn't see anything, but heard strange beating, banging, and rattling noises coming from somewhere on the second floor.

Curious, I ascended the stairs, moving through the hall until I located the closed room that was the origin of the sounds. I placed my ear against the door. Peace was obviously engaged in some strenuous activity. He huffed, puffed, and made all sorts of noise. It even sounded as though there might be a few other people with him. Perhaps he had grown tired of his placid *zazen*-style meditation and transformed himself into a whirling dervish. Perhaps he had found others to join him in his reverie.

I opened the door.

And watched as Peace banged the hell out of six prostitutes. Around his neck, he wore a huge golden chain upon which dangled a diamond-encrusted pendant rendered in the shape of a dollar sign.

Oh, Banks Hatewell!" A squeal. "You're the best!"

Banks Hatewell?

"Yeah, baby. I know you can't get enough of my sweet love meat," he replied in a thick, Bronx accent.

Sweet love meat?

At that moment, I burst into the room. "What the hell do you think you're doing!"

Grinning: "There's more than enough for the both of us. The greatest pleasure is that which makes your loins *really tingly!"*

"No, damn you! I don't want any of this!" The vein in my forehead swelled. "Get these whores out of the house! Immediately!"

Peace's hands clenched into fists. "You'll leave my bitches and me alone if you know what's good for you!"

"To hell with you, then!" I slammed the door behind me.

And the sound of their once interrupted sex played on.

Betrayed, I retreated to my bedroom and barricaded the door with the dresser.

* * * *

Once inside, an existential crisis battered my brain into pulpy submission.

What had I done? Had I helped the murderer of Countess Vanessa Von Zanzamere escape? If so, my soul was stained for all eternity. The KARMA WHEEL would surely grind me into dust.

I now knew, beyond a doubt, that Peace's Zen-like states were pre-fabricated, but that didn't make Peace a murderer. Or did it? Maybe he was just an insincere bastard.

But he assaulted me with cereal, and I felt the presence of a garrote around my neck.

No! His meditation seemed so real. I shared a cosmic experience with Peace. Our atoms swirled in *The Great Unknown.*

Together we had known true bliss.

But, in the end, did that mean anything?

I decided the only way to solve this crisis was to split into two separate entities, then debate myself one on one.

It hurt doing so – the mental stress alone was exceedingly painful – but, an hour later, I managed to segment myself into two equal parts of the same consciousness.

* * * *

"Peace can't be a murderer!"

"Of course he can," I replied calmly, not allowing myself to get frustrated with myself.

"But can't I remember the depths of Peace's meditation? Can't I remember how strong his consciousness felt when I was in his presence?"

I countered: "Perhaps I was feeling my own consciousness?"

"That's just silly," I scoffed. "I'm nowhere near as in-tune as Peace."

"So, I'm telling me that I'm no better than an everyday murderer?"

"Never say that again!"

"I thought this was going to be a debate, not a cat-fight."

"Okay, I'm right. Go on."

"Just put two and two together. Peace confused me into believing he didn't kill the bird. Then he stuffed cereal down my throat."

"But the cereal was good!"

"That's not my point! Do I think that Peace's actions are indicative of your average Zen Master?"

"Well, no. . ."

"Of course they're not. That's because he *isn't* a Zen Master. He's a cold-blooded killer!"

"I'll never buy that! Peace is as beautiful as the Countess Vanessa Von Zanzamere!"

At that point, I knew I had to resort to strategy if I wished to win myself over.

"I'll bake me a coconut cream pie if I agree!"

"Okay!"

"So, I think Peace is guilty now?"

"He's a rapscallion if ever there was one."

At that point, I concluded the session by pulling the segmented pieces of myself back together.

Unfortunately, I lied about the coconut pie and was mad at myself for hours.

* * * *

I got out of bed as the sun rose. Groaning, I looked at my reflection in the mirror. So many bruises. I couldn't believe I had been so hard on myself. All these self-inflicted injuries for a simple coconut cream pie! I felt some degree of shame, but had made my decision and refused to be waylaid by anything.

I removed the barricade from my door and walked downstairs. Halfway to the bottom, I saw Peace perched atop an ottoman, engaged in another one of his bullshit trances.

I screamed from the next to last step: *"YOU KILLED THE COUNTESS VANESSA VON ZANZAMERE!"*

Peace opened his eyes and unleashed one of his patented smiles.

"How can one truly die when all things exist simultaneously?"

"SHUT THE HELL UP! I KNOW EVERYTHING, BANKS HATEWELL!"

He reared up from his lotus position. "Where did you hear that name?"

I rolled my eyes. "Don't you remember? One of your prostitutes moaned it in ecstasy last night."

Banks shrugged. "So, you know my little secret. That's okay. I knew you would find out sooner or later. You gotta admit, I really had you going for a while."

"I don't understand. You seemed so pure and at peace. How could you, with your Zen understanding, betray my trust?"

"Don't tell me you bought that shit. Zen phrases are a dime-a-dozen."

"But you levitated; I saw it on the news!"

"All smoke and mirrors. Parlor tricks. And you were stupid enough to buy them."

"But we shared a cosmic experience!"

"We didn't share shit, bucko. If *you* had a cosmic experience, then *you* were the only one – though I'm still confused about that whole Black Hole thing. It was hard to pretend that I expected it."

"You didn't cause that to happen?"

"Nope."

"Then who did?"

He shrugged.

"Forget about it. Just tell me one thing. Why did you kill the Countess Vanessa Von Zanzamere?"

Banks smirked. "You want to know why I killed the *old bitch*. Well then, I guess I'd better tell you why that *old bitch* is dead."

I winced each time Banks slandered the Countess' fair name.

"I killed her because I was sick of her cavorting. She could have learned to be a productive and efficient member of society, but *no*. She chose to be completely and utterly nuts. Everyone just *loooooved* her. Did they love me? *Noooooooooo*. I used to be a well-respected middle manager at *Omni-Corp*. I pushed around memos like nobody's business! I made the world go around and people like you, Countess Vanessa Von Zanzamere, and all her fans couldn't care less! You people deserve to *die*."

"The Countess was a beautiful woman. She didn't deserve to be killed by some corporate lackey!"

"Oh, really? Let me tell you something. The Countess' non-productivity hurt us all. Did she engage in *any* respectable line of work? *No!* She was a pox on this great country. I did the world a service by killing her."

"That's far from true!"

"To hell with the world, then. *I did it for myself.* I'd see her gallivanting around every fucking day, singing songs in some strange and incomprehensible language. It was enough to drive me nuts! The day before I killed her, I watched her play on the monkey bars in the park. She was *eighty-six years old* for God's sake! And she was playing! On monkey bars! I screamed at her. I told her to get down and get down *NOW!* I told her to get a job and pull her own weight. She just laughed and kept on swinging and swinging and swinging and swinging!"

I tasted bile. *"You murdered her for having fun!"*

"Yes, and I did it with this gun," Banks pulled a sleek nine-millimeter from his pants. He flashed it in front of my face.

"Where did you get that!"

"It was back in my pocket after we went through the black hole. The bullets are gone, unfortunately, but I have other ways of killing you."

I turned to flee as he motioned to rise. Looking over my left shoulder, I saw him clutching the ottoman he once sat upon. He lifted it over his head and smashed it down into my face.

I was at once lost to oblivion.

* * * *

When I came to, I found myself tied to the railroad tracks outside our hideout. We were obviously quite far from the house. How far, however, I could not say. The land around me was featureless except for a few sparse trees and an old shack falling into ruin about a half-mile to my right.

The sun shone down into my eyes. Banks Hatewell loomed over me, but not far enough to block out the stinging rays.

"I would tape your mouth shut," he said, "but, if I did that, I wouldn't hear you scream when the train comes."

I fought against my restraints, but all efforts were for naught. In desperation, I prayed to all the deities whose names I could recall. I expected nothing, not sure whether I believed in them or not.

"Please," I whispered beneath my voice. "Deliver onto me a *Machine of the Gods* so that I might live to breathe another day."

I waited for a few minutes.

Nothing.

"*DAMN IT,*" I thought-screamed. *"ANSWER MY PRAYER AND ANSWER IT RIGHT NOW!!! I'M ABOUT TO DIE DOWN HERE!!!*"

Something materialized in my left hand. Though I couldn't see what the thing was, it felt like some sort of button attached to a narrow, plastic base.

My faith was restored.

Pressing it, I watched as I (circa forty years in the future) materialized next to a low-lying shrub. I wore a pastel space suit replete with matching antenna and headband, and looked somewhat vexed to have been called away from whatever time I called home.

Banks noticed the other me and shot him (me) on the spot. Cringing, I witnessed myself die in a very embarrassing uniform.

I pressed the button repeatedly.

And watched as I appeared in multifarious forms all about the railroad track.

As an infant, I crawled around the grass, sucking my pacifier.

As a child, I ran around Banks Hatewell, pulling at his clothes and jumping on his back.

"Ride, horsie, ride," I exclaimed.

As a teenager, I bent over myself, demanding access to the car keys so that I might take my girlfriend to the malt shop.

"Please! Oh, come on! Can I just have the car for two hours? That's all I want."

I scowled at myself. "Okay! You can have the damn car, but only if you get me out of this mess!"

"Sounds good, just give me the keys first."

I would have smacked my forehead if my hands weren't, at the time, tied.

"I can't give you the keys because I can't reach them. In case you haven't noticed, I'm taped to a fucking railroad track!"

"Then no deal." Teen-me walked away.

"Wait! Come back! I'll give you – I mean *me* – the keys! I swear!"

Teen-me extended his middle finger and dismissed me entirely. I turned my head from teen-me and saw baby-me still cooing ineffectively on the ground. Kid-me lost interest in Banks and had started chasing butterflies around the field. Amongst it all, my captor stood laughing.

"This is a neat display, Luke. But did you, for one second, think this little sideshow would prove effective?"

I allowed my head to rest on the track. Best to embrace death than fight against it.

"So, when does the train arrive?"

He looked down at his watch. "Oh, about five minutes. Then the freight to Deluth will cut your body into three convenient pieces."

"Wouldn't it be easier if you just stabbed me or something?"

Banks groaned. "Come to think of it, I *will* gag you. Your constant lip flapping is making me sick." He pulled a handkerchief from his pocket. "Open wide and say *ahhhhhhh*."

I gagged on the taste of ancient snot.

"There." He finished the knot behind my head. "Now, I can kill you in peace. No pun intended."

Over and above his voice, I heard a rumbling. It sounded like a great boulder rolling down the side of a mountain, which was odd since the track cut through the middle of a field. Banks noticed it too, for he turned his head in the sound's direction.

"And what the hell do you suppose is making that racket?"

I couldn't speak through my gag, so I mumbled my reply.

"Maybe it's the train. Wouldn't that be nice?"

Banks laughed and kicked me in the face. He was so busy

assailing me that he didn't notice the two-story stone wheel barreling towards him at a high rate of speed. I tried to hide my amazement. I didn't want Banks to see what was coming until it was too late. He turned around just in time to see the object crash through the dilapidated shack and reduce the entire structure to matchsticks.

Banks screamed. He lost interest in damaging my face, but nevertheless ventured one final glance. His eyes met mine. In them, I saw only confusion coupled with dawning terror. Banks broke contact and, like a startled deer, took off across the field.

The KARMA WHEEL rolled past a bend in the tracks. The sight was staggering, and I couldn't help but stare. Graffiti covered the wheel's stone façade – people's names, obscene slogans, drawings of every kind. I wondered where it all came from.

Turning away from the spectacle, I saw where my would-be murderer had wound up. Banks hid behind an old, gnarled tree about fifty feet to my right. He must have thought the wheel would simply roll past.

But the KARMA WHEEL ground to a halt right in front of the oak.

"No! Please, God! Make it go away!"

He rambled on and on, but the KARMA WHEEL didn't seem to be going anywhere.

Banks stuck out his left foot.

The KARMA WHEEL moved a few inches to the left.

Banks stuck out his right foot.

The KARMA WHEEL moved a few inches to the right.

"DEAR GOD, YOU'RE SENTIENT!"

Terror creased his face. Wetness spread across his crotch. In a blind panic, he left the tree. Banks ran aimlessly about the field, only to slip and fall into a ripe cow patty.

The KARMA WHEEL stood its ground. I imagined it was humoring him.

"DO YOU WANT ME TO PRAY TO YOU?" he shouted, his face covered in dung. "OKAY! SURE! I WILL! BLESSED ART THOU, BIG WHEEL! BLESSED ART THOU!"

The KARMA WHEEL advanced towards him. It was not interested in veneration.

"YOU WANT ME TO SAY IT? OKAY THEN, I'LL SAY IT: *I'M SORRY FOR KILLING COUNTESS VANESSA VON ZANZAMERE! I'LL NEVER DO IT AGAIN!*"

The KARMA WHEEL was unfazed.

"SWEET GOD IN HEAVEN, ISN'T THAT ENOUGH FOR YOU?"

The KARMA WHEEL picked up momentum and breached the remaining distance between Banks and itself. I closed my eyes, not wanting to see the inevitable, but opened them when I heard nothing resembling a *squish*.

Looking up, I saw the wheel chase Banks at a speed nearly matching the villain's own. The wheel blocked his passage each time he tried to veer either to the left or to the right. It kept him running in a straight line that led right to the train track. I assumed the wheel intended that I watch the gruesome endgame.

And I was right. Only a few feet from where I was tied, the KARMA WHEEL stopped toying with Banks and finally plowed his body under.

* * * *

The KARMA WHEEL continued to roll back and forth, even as Banks Hatewell's screams (and the man himself) died. The KARMA WHEEL seemed intent on washing away every trace of his earthly presence. It ground his bones into meal and squished his internal organs out his mouth and anal cavity.

I winced. Seeing *anyone* suffer was unbearable, but I guess he got what he had coming to him.

My ears suddenly picked up the sound of a roaring train. I went cold. The engineer blew his horn and gesticulated out the window like a mad man. He saw me, that was true, but his train was moving too fast to stop before it ground my body into oblivion.

I heard the KARMA WHEEL rumble. It had finished with Banks Hatewell – now a mere greasy spot on the ground – and was rolling in my direction.

OH DEAR GOD!!! THE KARMA WHEEL WANTED TO CRUSH ME TOO!!!

Being killed by the train was nothing, but being crushed by the KARMA WHEEL! That alone implied I was one of history's great beasts. I had obviously perpetrated a great wrong by willingly, yet inadvertently, allowing a murderer to escape his intended penance.

Yes, I deserved my fate. An eternity of living-death spent under the KARMA WHEEL. Together Banks and I would rot our way through a void without hope.

I gladly accepted my punishment.

A second later, however, the KARMA WHEEL reversed its course. It maneuvered itself in front of the train, blocking its passage. Iron clashed against absolute truth. Even after being kissed by a few tons of steel, the wheel remained unmoved. It wasn't until the thing decided to roll away that I first saw the crumpled wreckage – a human disaster instigated so that a single life might be saved.

I felt unworthy of this sacrifice. . . but, then again, who was I to question the wheel's judgment? Still, the weight of so many lost lives hung heavily on my conscience. I couldn't justify the act, despite any reasons the wheel might have had. I ground my teeth and bit through my gag. *It had no right to hurt those people!* I screamed at the wheel:

"Why'd they have to die! What's so important about me?"

The KARMA WHEEL rolled over in my direction.

It faced me.

And I fell into Eternity as the wheel looked, without seeing, into my eyes. At that moment, I left the ground and floated above the wreckage. Looking down at the engine, I understood how no one had truly died. The flesh inside was just sublimated energy perceived as a standing wave formation. Souls had moved on, yet, in some way, were still present. I saw every possibility occurring simultaneously in a Quantum non-reality. In that train, energy mixed with energy and then folded in on itself. Life and death exploded into the black hole – *THAT GREAT NOTHING* – and both ceased to exist and continued to exist; Creation winked on and off like a photon, somehow in all places at once.

"So you see, Luke, I've committed no evil in destroying that train. There's no trace of ill will or malice in my axle. Beautiful Chaos. That's all I have to say."

A big wheel had just spoken to me in an Eastern European voice. This confused me, so I said nothing.

"But I must admit, I sometimes work under contract – for a nominal fee, of course. Take this occasion. I could have just as easily allowed that man to kill you; it wouldn't have mattered to me one bit. But there's a group of people out there who've set aside a Garden for some and a Pit for others."

"Excuse me?"

"A Pit and a Garden. Weren't you listening?"

"What the hell are you talking about?"

"You don't have to understand anything. My friends are a

beneficent lot. They've set everything up for you, so be grateful."

"If *they* sat all this up for me, then why did I help a murderer escape? Come to think of it, why did I meet Banks Hatewell in the first place?"

"In your case, things had to be sped along. A man must fall before he can rise."

"What do you mean?"

"It's the end of the age, my friend. There's nothing you or I can do about it. It's time for the toilet to flush, which means things are going to get pretty nasty from this point on. Consider it a blessing that you're on your way out. *The Pit Dwellers* and the *Middle-Grounders* aren't so lucky."

"You're really losing me here. I hope you know that."

"But I can say nothing more concerning such matters. I will, however, tell you that no deity had a part in giving you the button. Not directly, at least."

"What? Then who did?"

"I can say nothing more."

"Can you at least tell me why you're covered in so much graffiti?"

The wheel laughed. "Oh, that! Certainly. I've met a lot of hippies in my time. I *am* the KARMA WHEEL, after all. They just love to sign me."

"Isn't that annoying?"

"A bit. I'm not one to complain, though."

"I see."

"I sometimes wish they wouldn't put such bad words on me. But what can I do? I can't very well grind them into the dirt for *that*. Any advice?"

"I honestly don't know what to tell you. I've never had that problem."

"Thanks anyway."

"Sure."

The wheel spun in the opposite direction. "I'd love to continue chatting, Luke. Really, you seem like an interesting person. But I'm a busy wheel. I'll give you a call if I'm ever again in Leeds."

"I don't live in Leeds."

"That's okay. None of us are perfect," the KARMA WHEEL replied, and then winked into a quasi-temporal vortex.

* * * *

Seconds later, I sat in my own living room. Jumping up from the couch, I switched on the TV. Live coverage of Banks Hatewell's murder trial flickered on the screen.

I watched him float above the witness stand. This time, however, I saw the thin cords that kept the murderer suspended from the ceiling. I saw all of Bank's mirrors and artifices. I knew that, at trial's end, he would swing from his neck as I sat comfy on my couch, having never met the defendant a day in my life.

And I suddenly understood.

The KARMA WHEEL had placed me in a different branch of the universe – one in which I had never freed Banks Hatewell. It collapsed the waveform of my brief encounter with evil, thus giving birth to a completely altered reality.

Unfortunately – or, maybe, fortunately – chaos theory came into play.

Change one aspect of the space-time continuum; change everything.

And that's just the science behind what the *KARMA WHEEL* wrought!

Venturing outside, I was amazed to find a new world stretched out before me. The streets were gone, as were the cars. My neighbors' houses had likewise vanished. Not even foundations remained.

Nature itself shifted. The air smelled fresh, no longer reeking of garbage and car exhaust. The sun cast a rich, blue glow over all creation. The ground swelled and breathed. Trees grew purple and now possessed anthropomorphic features. I walked over to one. Wary at first, I soon found the tree quite maternal. Its branches grasped me in motherly arms and allowed me to suckle on a host of life-giving breasts. The milk was sugar-sweet.

Grass slithered, coiling around my legs once the tree put me down. Each strand was suddenly alive and had a distinct personality. One grass-friend even took the time to get to know me. His name was Jeremy.

We spoke for a few hours, him and I – just chatting, really. Then I waved goodbye and resumed wandering through this strange new world.

As the sun sank in a sea of azure, I reached a hill overlooking a lush and verdant valley. Little, naked men stood sandwiched therein. Though tiny, they seemed imbued with awesome power.

My mind refused to wrap around its scope.

I strained my eyes for a closer look and saw how each wielded a bright, flaming sword. Such fearsome weaponry, coupled with the men's lack of clothing, was distressing at first glance. I turned to run at the same time a sudden calm descended upon me, stilling my feet. Fear evaporated in an instant, and my lips turned up in a spontaneous smile.

I walked towards the little men – my heart light, a spring in my step – as I contemplated the best way to introduce myself.

* * * *

Yeah, the whole thing was a bit disconcerting at first, but I think I'll enjoy this strange new existence. I got used to the old one, so I guess I'll do the same here. I just hope I never take anything for granted. With luck, I'll be able to see the unclouded beauty of this paradise at all points along the space-time continuum.

Fuck that. I know I will.

Goodbye!

(*Story ends with kiddie song* "We Love Mr. Karma Wheel Cause He's So Grand".)

(*Credits roll*)

SECTION III:

THE CHURCH OF THE BYRDS
VERSUS
THE CHURCH OF LIONEL RICHIE

PART I:

THE DOUGHNUT KIOSK

I WOKE UP with the memory of a dream. Something about a garden and the strange men who lived there. It made little sense, so I quickly forgot the details. Turning to the clock, I saw how fifteen minutes remained in which to jump out of bed and get ready.

I sighed. Why couldn't life be like it was when I was a kid – nothing but school and play? Things were different now. So much faster.

My mind raced, but my body remained numb. I wanted to get up and pretend to be an active member of the community, but my limbs wouldn't allow it. I was mush and, in the end, could do very little to change that fact.

At a quarter to seven Bobby, my roommate, burst through the door and began rummaging for something on the dresser. He was already dressed in his *Doughnut Kiosk* uniform. I envied him for being so spry in the morning and for looking the way he did. Bobby's hair was a closely cropped brown. His six-foot body was well built and girls probably thought his face was *cute*. I, on the other hand, looked plain and gangly. My hair seemed stringy no matter how short I cut it. That, and I was six inches shorter and thirty pounds lighter than Bobby.

He shouted: "Get up, John! Damn you! We've got to go! *Now!"*

I sighed and peeled my body from the sheets. Bobby looked at me as I arose. He laughed.

"Red underwear. Funny."

I grimaced. "I can't help it. Shelia bought them for me. She thinks I look good in them."

"Your girlfriend's delusional. Nobody looks good in bikini briefs or, should I say, *man panties."*

I flipped Bobby a quick bird and picked up my uniform that, like almost everything else on my side of the room, sat in a crumpled ball on the floor. I hated the garish stripes and bold colors. The huge *Doughnut Kiosk* logo that covered three-fourths of its front made my teeth clench. I felt diseased each time I wore the thing, like some slow-moving cancer was crawling through my body. But I put it on anyway. No choice. I tucked my shirt into my pants and picked up the pin the manager said I was to wear or else be fired. It was promotion for some movie I had no interest in seeing. Sighing, I pinned the hateful thing over my right breast.

"Are you about ready?"

"Just let me tie my shoes, okay."

Bobby shook his head. "I'll be waiting outside."

* * * *

The drive to *The Doughnut Kiosk* was stressful. I suffered in silence until, off in the distance, I watched the brick monster take shape.

My composure shattered. I flailed; I slammed into the armrest; I knocked Bobby's Roman Coke from the drink holder.

"Damn you," he cursed. "I can't be swerving when I have alcohol in the car! Buck up!"

"I can't. Not when I see. . . *that place!"*

"You mean the mall?"

I glared. "You think I'm out of my mind, don't you?"

"What?"

"Just answer the question!"

He shook his head. "Of course I don't. Why even ask?"

"Because I'm beginning to doubt myself, Bobby. I was fine before I started working at that place. Now everything just confuses me."

"Go back to college if you want a better job."

"But college is scarier than the mall."

Bobby sighed. "You're hopeless, John."

* * * *

We pulled into the mall parking lot, and I noticed the giant banner that covered one-half of the shopping center's front:

TODAY IS MARK ANDERS DAY AT THE MALL!!!

I turned to Bobby. "Mark Anders? Who's that?"

"Just some guy who wrote a book about circus midgets. It's okay, I guess. I'll let you borrow it sometime."

"A book about *circus midgets?"*

"Yeah, it has an odd title, but I can't remember it now."

"Weird."

"There're a few good parts, but the rest is boring. You might like it, though."

"Were the characters well-rounded?"

"Wait! You're just trying to stall, aren't you?"

I looked down at the floorboard. "Yeah."

Bobby pulled me from the car by my arm. "Well, it's not going to work this time!"

* * * *

Ten minutes later, I stood inside *The Doughnut Kiosk*. The manager had just bitched me out for being forty-five seconds late and, to add insult to injury, told me that I'd been assigned to the register. No way to blend in when forced into that position. I had to face people. And talk to them. I had to listen to complaints concerning doughnuts. Worst yet, no time remained to compose myself before the customer-pageant started anew.

It was all so predictable.

At lunch hour, *The Businessmen* invariably filter into *The Doughnut Kiosk*. I've learned that the few happy ones are truly evil. They'll throw their doughnuts to the counter and huff: "*These doughnuts taste old! When I come here you always give me old doughnuts!"*

Around the time school lets out, *The Businessmen* are replaced by *The Bitches*. They're mothers who bide in-line time by smacking their six-year old children. They create the kids who'll grow up to be *Stupid Punks* and/or *Future Bitches*.

And then there's *The Dead People*. They come at any time and make up most of the human population. They shuffle their shoes, fill their faces, and close their eyes to everything. I want to smack them. I want to tell them to *wake up*. But I just take their order and let it pass.

Sometimes a genuine person drops by for a change. Last time I worked the register, I met a nice old lady who paid in nickels and dimes. I can always tell *The Good People*. They just feel different. The kiosk shines when they're here, and even I start to feel better.

But *The Good People* never show up as often as I would like. I assume that's because there're so few of them in existence.

* * * *

My first customer arrived just seconds after I took my pre-assigned place. He was a *Dead Person*. Hideously obese, the man wore a huge OFFICIAL MARK ANDERS BUTTON over his heart

I spoke through tightly clenched teeth. "How may I help you?"

"Gimme four plain doughnuts."

"Coming right up!" I dumped four pre-made doughnuts into the deep fryer. I watched them brown, looking like lumps of flesh floating around in oil. My gorge rose. I avoided regurgitating into the deep fryer, but my stomach continued to swim even as I tossed the skin-nuggets into a bag emblazoned with *The Doughnut Kiosk*'s logo.

"Here you go," I said. "$4.25."

The man handed me the money, and I saw how he also had the name MARK ANDERS tattooed in huge, capital letters on his left hand. I pretended to ignore the markings and dropped what he gave me into the register. The sound of change falling tortured my ears and, at that moment, I became aware of the other sounds floating around the kiosk. The bubble of doughnuts frying in oil once again made me want to vomit. The people walking and talking around the mall sounded like chattering rats. The intercom spewed out announcements broadcast from Hell: *Buy more; save more.*

I looked up from my madness and noticed another customer waiting for me. An old lady with blue hair. She too had her very own MARK ANDERS BUTTON and wore a shirt that proclaimed itself to be OFFICIAL MARK ANDERS GEAR. I couldn't understand why all my customers seemed to love him so. Maybe I would just have to read that book.

"I'll have three chocolate crème filled doughnuts, please."

This time I said nothing. I just turned to the deep fryer and did what I had to do. At least this batch smelled good. A minute later, a buzzer told me it was time to remove, drain, and bag the doughnuts. I did so and walked back to the counter.

As I handed the old lady her order, she thanked me warmly and added: "May Mark Anders bless you and keep you."

My lips turned up in a smile. My brain, however, was beginning to spin.

* * * *

Hours creaked by. The cycle never ended. Monotony was

so overpowering I feared death might be imminent. All the OFFICIAL MARK ANDERS BUTTONS and OFFICAL MARK ANDERS SHIRTS and OFFICIAL MARK ANDERS STRETCH PANTS did nothing to calm my nerves, either. I looked up at the clock. Only five minutes remained until Bobby and I got off work. If I could hold out that long, everything would be fine.

I turned around and almost pissed my pants.

Another customer stood in line. *And she was dressed like a clown.*

"Uh. . . how may I. . . help you?"

"Just a coffee."

The woman had to be bat-shit insane, but this was a blessedly easy order. It was just what I needed. Still, I couldn't get by without asking her:

"Why are you dressed as a clown?"

She huffed: "I'm not a clown! I'm a *circus midget!"*

"Oh."

Saying nothing more, I walked over to the pot and poured her drink into a Styrofoam cup. I asked for 85 cents, and she responded by tasting the coffee. White pancake make-up clumped on the cup's lip. Her face folded into a grimace, and the clown nose nearly popped off her face. I sensed trouble from this strangely attired woman; my radar was never wrong.

I hoped to defuse the situation: "A problem?"

She screamed. "This coffee is *weak*! Why do you people always give me weak coffee? Is getting a little service too much to ask!"

"I'm sorry, madam, but it's our standard brew. There's nothing I can do about it."

"Then I guess I'll have to talk to your manager."

"I'm sure I can take care of everything here. There's no need to–"

The vein in the woman's forehead fattened. "For the love of Mark Anders, I want to talk to the manager and I want to talk to him *now*!"

Throwing up my arms, I called out to the manager. I heard him walking up behind me and turned around. My brain nearly short-circuited.

He was wearing a clown nose.

"But. . . but. . . "

My manager shooed me away. "I'll take it from here."

"But . . . but. . ."

"I said I'll take it from here!"

Panic welled up inside. I knew it was OFFICIAL MARK ANDERS DAY, but this was too much. Spinning, I looked out over the people in the mall, counting well over ten shoppers dressed just like the crazy coffee lady. One man had even brought his pet sea lion with him. The thing balanced a big, red ball on its nose and flapped its flippers just outside the dollar store.

Insanity seemed a breath away. I wanted to scream, but couldn't. I gestured at Bobby to cover for me and darted into the mall bathroom where I collapsed into the sink. My mouth rested flush with the drain. I tasted soap-scum. A pubic hair dangled from my lips.

Overhead, harsh fluorescents beat down and made my head feel too heavy to lift. Maybe I was experiencing the first stages of madness. But that couldn't be right. Everything seemed so real and made sense in a completely deranged way. Bobby *had* said the Mark Anders book somehow involved circus midgets, and that was sure as hell how quite a few people were dressed.

Still, something felt very wrong.

I considered slamming my head against the inside of the sink and, at that moment, felt a hand on my shoulder. I spun around and saw Bobby, still bedecked in his uniform. He frowned, and I turned to look at my shoes.

"What the hell are you up to, John?"

"Didn't you. . . didn't you. . . see. . . *them?"*

"Them who?"

"*Everybody*, for God's sake! *I'm talking about almost every last person in the mall!"*

"And what about them?"

"How can you ask that? You saw the way those people were dressed! You saw the sea lion!"

"What sea lion?"

"Just believe me! It was out there! In the mall!"

"I don't see why you're getting so worked up. Today is some special day. People are going to be dressed weird. It happens, you know. Ever hear of *The Rocky Horror Picture Show?"*

"Of course I've heard of it! But that movie doesn't explain *this!"*

Bobby shook his head. "You're so predictable. Can't go a

work day without freaking out."

"*I'm not freaking out!* I'm just reacting to what I've seen."

"Well, whatever. It's three-thirty, so we're off. We can go home and smoke a bowl or two. Will that make you feel any better?"

I just stood there, silent and confused.

"I'll take that as a yes."

"Is the ganja good?"

"*Is it good?* This ganja's so fine you won't even remember your name. You'll have nothing more to worry about. Trust me."

I sighed. "For tonight, maybe. But then what? Tomorrow, I'll be right back here."

"Think of it this way, it won't be MARK ANDERS DAY tomorrow."

"I guess you're right. You're always right. You're a pretty good friend."

Bobby grabbed my arm. "Fuck it. Let's get the hell out of this smelly bathroom. The bong awaits."

And I was kind of glad we left when we did because, when I turned around on the way out, everybody who wore MARK ANDERS BUTTONS appeared to be converging on the few who did not.

PART II:

THE CHURCH OF THE BYRDS

BACK AT OUR apartment, Bobby and I passed the bong around for what seemed like hours. I was no longer capable of worrying about *The Doughnut Kiosk,* the even-crazier-than-usual drivers we encountered on our way back from work, or the lime green Pinto that jetted past at an impossible speed as we pulled into the driveway. Together we saw in so many dimensions that reality no longer had a clear center; we didn't know whether we were awake or dreaming. Vortexes opened and closed so fast we couldn't tell what doorway had opened into which universe.

"So, this is the stuff that's poisoning our youth," I inhaled deeply.

Bobby smirked and took from my hands the maple syrup bottle that served as our bong. He made sure to cover the carb-hole punched in the container's side before wrapping his lips around the tube protruding from Missus Butterworth's head. Bobby took a massive hit. He put the bong down and tried standing; his limbs fold beneath him.

"Easy now, Bobby."

He waved me off. "I'm okay. I'm okay."

"Want me to turn on the TV or something?"

"Sure. Go right ahead."

I staggered to the TV and flicked it on. The screen flashed an image of buildings lying in smoking ruin. Anchormen told of an assassin squad that went haywire and took out twenty innocent civilians. Hearing this did nothing but bum me out. I turned to the next channel and saw what had to be a few thousand people clustered around a nondescript apartment complex. The place looked dull, so I wondered why so many were gathered outside it. The camera zoomed in closer and I finally saw all the MARK ANDERS banners, posters, and placards the people carried. I realized the writer must live in that very building. I yelped and slammed off the TV.

"You're still obsessing about that shit?"

"No, but it keeps getting weirder. That's all I'm saying."

"Stop worrying about Mark Anders. He's just a writer. Have another hit."

I walked back to where Bobby sat and sucked on Missus Butterworth's head. A few seconds later, fragrant smoke filled my lungs to capacity.

"Good, huh?"

I nodded as the smoke extended feelers into my brain.

"And are you worried about *anything* anymore?"

"Hell no."

He laughed. "And are you still wearing red underwear?"

"Why are you giving me so much hell? I've seen you wear colored underwear before!"

"But they were boxers, John. There's a big difference."

"I already told you my girlfriend bought them for me. I wear them for her."

"But you're wearing them now, and I don't see Shelia anywhere."

"That doesn't mean anything. I'd like to know what you're trying to get at."

"So, what other colors do you have? Blue? Black? Any with the name SHELIA written across the front in sequins?"

"Really, Bobby. Could you take it easy?"

"She must think a lot of your package to want to dress it up like that."

"Would you stop!"

"Touchy, touchy."

"Can't we talk about something else?"

"Like what?"

I shrugged. "I don't know. How about the meaning of life?"

"I'm too high to have that kind of conversation. Could you put some music on, instead? I would get up, but I can't right now."

I nodded in understanding and motioned to the record player. Stopping at a stack of singles, I grabbed the 45 on top. In my hand, I held the next offering – a little ditty by *The Byrds*. I placed it on the turntable and set the stylus down. No sound came out. Confusion reigned until I realized I had forgotten to turn the machine on. I laughed until my belly ached and, once the fit subsided, pressed the power-button. The record finally began to crackle.

I returned to my seat by Bobby. "It's all done."

"What's up?"

"Turn, Turn, Turn."

"I've always loved that song. Aren't the lyrics from *The Bible?* Get the good book and we'll read along."

"Don't you think it's kinda weird to read *The Bible* while stoned?"

Bobby glared. "Just get it, okay."

I walked to a bookshelf and pulled from it the blue leather bible my parents had given me for my ninth birthday. Then I mumbled a short prayer, just in case Bobby and I were about to commit a grievous sin.

"You're taking forever. The song has already started."

I carried *The Bible* back to Bobby and handed it to him. He thumbed through its pages, complaining.

"This book is too long. I can't find anything in all this!"

"Try the third chapter of *Ecclesiastes."*

"I hope I'm not making you late for Sunday school."

"I don't go to Sunday school, Bobby."

"You know *The Bible* like you do." He smirked. "Maybe you sneak out once a week and run off to church when I'm not looking."

"And what if I do?"

"To each his own."

"But–"

He waved me off. "We're missing the song."

We turned our attention to the thin, biblical pages as the music wafted through the room:

To everything (turn, turn, turn)
There is a season (turn, turn, turn)

"Listen to those lyrics, Bobby. *The Byrds* realized the secret to world peace all along."

I think Bobby understood what I had said – maybe he even believed it, too – but he was too busy taking another hit to respond. I, however, found it amazing to consider what the Earth would be like if all world leaders took the time to *really* listen to this three minute and thirty-five second record.

I looked over Bobby's shoulder when I didn't hear him say anything. His fingers continued to trace over the verses that had inspired the writing of the song.

And a time for every purpose

Under heaven.

My brows furrowed. "Do you hear something weird? Like monks chanting?"

Bobby listened. "Yeah, I think I do."

"Do you remember monks chanting in that song before?"

"Not really, but it *was* made in the sixties."

A time to gain.
A time to lose.
A time to rend.
A time to sow.

I knew something was odd. I had heard this song a million times in the past, but never like I was hearing it now. Moments before, the monks had been background noise. Now, they were getting louder.

"I think those monks aren't on the record!"

"What?"

"I said I think those monks aren't on the record!"

He scoffed. "Where the hell are they, then?"

"In the room!"

"You're just stoned."

"You know there were never any monks on *Turn, Turn, Turn!"*

"Maybe this is some kind of rare studio cut."

A time for love.
A time for hate.
A time for peace
I swear it's not too late.

I was suddenly more than high. It felt almost as though my brain was floating up through the top of my skull. The room wavered, and I smelled incense in the air.

And, for some reason, I felt that I was Bobby and Bobby was me.

Turn, Turn, Turn,
Turn, Turn, Turn,
Turn, Turn, Turn,

Turn.

The record skipped and our minds broke, the repetition of that single word too much for our human constitutions to bear. The bedroom melted within a beam of pure, translucent white. My body took on a wavering form. For some reason, I now held a tambourine. Looking over at Bobby, I saw he held one as well. The molecules of my lips formed a smile, one that Bobby quickly beamed back.

I struck the tambourine against my hip. I became lost in the music and the music became lost in me. I danced and danced as the record spun on and on. My mind flashed and, suddenly, the rhythm of *The Byrds* became the rhythm of life. Hearts pulsed to the beat; eyes rolled back and forth in REM ecstasy. Bobby and I danced out of the bedroom, we danced out of the house, and we danced to the ruins of the abandoned slaughterhouse across the street. There, with tambourine and cosmic consciousness in hand, we broke through to new levels of reality. Our feet became light as our toes crossed that dusty floor, and our dance suddenly adopted a slow, languorous quality.

In that fleeting yet somehow eternal moment, images died and the distinction between *The Byrds* and ourselves fell by the wayside. The veil started to lift, but revelation was only temporary. We felt the fragments of our souls return as soon as we stopped to contemplate the grandeur of the vision. Our trance ended abruptly as both logic and reason bested us.

And we found ourselves inside a towering stone church.

Beautifully carved images of our faces stared back at us from the altar. A large fresco, depicting the trials and tribulations of three bands and their later assimilation into *Crosby, Stills, Nash, and Young,* graced the north wall. To the south hung sacred relics taken from the body of St. Stills.

And people knelt around us, bowing in worship. To my right, a woman clad in a shirt bearing a faded, ironed-on peace sign gazed up from her prayer mat. A look of spontaneous rapture creased her face, and I wondered if she had not had an orgasm.

A Nehru-jacketed parishioner to my left gasped as wetness spread across his crotch.

"The Travelers! They have stopped dancing!"

Suddenly, I didn't feel high anymore. I looked questioningly at Bobby; he just shrugged in confusion. I turned again to face the congregation. Only seconds had passed, but the room had already erupted into chaos. Men in tie-dyed shirts and corduroy pants shrieked with elation. Women in hemp skirts swooned as naked children wept tears of blood. Infused with life, the relics on the far-wall clattered and the holy water in the fountain turned red and began to boil.

I addressed the crowd: "Excuse me. Could you tell us where we are? We were just smoking up when this crazy thing–"

My words were cut short as parishioners flooded the altar and hoisted us atop their shoulders. From there, I could smell their collective body stench.

They said nothing. They just carried Bobby and me past an anteroom in which the walls were encrusted, top to bottom, with vinyl records. From there, they spirited us into an incense-choked hall where we were soon put down outside an office. I looked up. A brass name-plate was tacked to the door:

HIGH PRIEST NASH

it said.

Seconds later, the door swung open. A late middle-aged man of the cloth bade us enter. His face was oval and fringed with white side-burns – seemingly kind. Apart from the facial hair, I was surprised to see this man so well groomed. He looked nothing like his parishioners. Even his clothes were different. While the others wore hippy paraphernalia, Nash wore an array of priestly vestments, fringe, and lace.

I offered this man a wary greeting before taking my seat in his Spartan and well-ordered office. The entire room was bare except for an unadorned wooden desk surrounded by a few black chairs. A filing cabinet sat in one corner, a potted plant in the other. Apart from these items, the only other object in the room was a massive, full-body portrait of David Crosby.

"I apologize for the vehemence of my flock," Nash began, his fingers clutched tightly around a hefty tome. "You must, however, understand. Today is a special day. One foretold now for billions of years."

"*Billions of years?* That's crazy. We only got high ten minutes ago."

The High Priest laughed. "This is The New Epoch, Dear Travelers. You've been in the realm of the Gods since the 21st Century. That was so long ago we cannot begin to express its linear distance from us."

"We're not Travelers. My name is John. And his is Bobby."

He waved me off. "*The Holy Tome* calls you *Dear Travelers*, so I shall call you *Dear Travelers* as well. I hope neither of you mind."

"I sure as hell mind!" Bobby then overturned his seat.

I, however, took the news better than my friend. At the moment, I was as far from *The Doughnut Kiosk* as I could possibly get. That alone elated me.

High Priest Nash nodded sympathetically. "I realize the pains of rebirth. It will take you a while to become accustomed to this new life. Much has changed since you two departed the earthly plain on God's fiery chariot."

"Actually, we were just listening to a record."

"Yes, yes. Whatever. I'm only saying that you must certainly be experiencing great disassociation. The 21st century was a literal eternity ago."

"Send me back right fucking now!" Bobby gripped Nash's garments. "How am I supposed to tell my boss I'm stuck in this freak show? I've got to be at work by eight tomorrow morning!"

"My son, the boss you speak of has been dead for longer than you can imagine. His bones are but dust."

"I don't care! Leave him if he likes being here!" He pointed in my direction. "But take *me* back! I've got things to do! *Responsibility!*"

High Priest Nash did not respond. His hand shot out across the desk in a blur. It grabbed Bobby by the shirt, pulled him closer, and shoved a white pill down his throat.

"There now. Feel any better?"

Bobby fell back into his seat and drooled.

The High Priest noted my horror. "Don't concern yourself. He won't worry about the past for a very long time. *Trust me.*"

I turned to Bobby. He seemed to be sleeping soundly, though his eyes were open wide and his tongue lolled.

"I guess you know what you're doing. But he won't die, right?"

"Your friend is merely asleep."

"And he won't suffer permanent brain damage?"

"Not a trace, though it's a shame I had to treat The Traveler so roughly. But you seem to be digesting everything so well. You *must* have a few questions."

"I sure do."

"Please, ask."

"Why the hell am I here?"

Nash furrowed his brows. "I thought we covered that already?"

"Not to my satisfaction."

He sighed. "According to *The Holy Tome*, the end of your dance is to usher in some great moment in our Church's history. The Scriptures are somewhat vague as to what this event is and how long after your stopping it will occur, but we have faith that something *amazing* will happen and happen soon."

"But why Bobby and me? Why *our* dance?"

"You two were selected to fulfill *Holy Words*, that's why. I'll have you know that Byrdities have been watching you and your friend twirl for ages now, just waiting for this blessed day. So many have died believing your dance would come to its appointed end. Truly, they have not died in vain."

"That's great and all, but I still don't understand the mechanics that brought me here."

Nash shrugged. "Nor do I, to be perfectly honest. That knowledge is in God's realm. Can you think of an easier question?"

"Uh. . . Okay. . . Why aren't you dressed as a hippy?"

"A *hippy?"*

"Yeah. Your entire flock is dressed like hippies. You're not."

"*Hippie*s. Interesting. *The Holy Tome* calls them *wing-children* so I call them *wing-children*, too. *The Holy Tome* also states that a High Priest should wear the clothing of ordinary men only when attempting conversion."

"And how are the other religions handling this stuff? It's all pretty weird, you know."

"How funny!" High Priest Nash laughed. "You *have* been out a long time!"

"Why are you laughing?"

"My child, there haven't been *other religions* since the last epoch ended! Byrdism, however, reigns supreme. We are living in *The Golden Age of Faith*. Any media source will tell you the same thing – if, that is, you don't believe *me."*

"Pardon me for being frank, but I never asked anyone to start a religion. I just got high one day and started dancing."

"But don't you see? Byrdism is the *true* faith." Nash paused to open *The Holy Tome* now resting on his lap. "Might I have your permission to read a verse from Scripture?"

"If that's what you want."

"It's one of only 5,627 letters to survive the last epoch. *One of these letters was signed by Crosby himself.* That piece was sadly lost in a rectory fire fifteen years ago. We assume this epistle must be derived from *The Hand of Crosby*, though it is signed by *Harry Fairchild*."

"Who's *Harry Fairchild?*"

"Our paid scholars assure us that *Harry Fairchild* is one of our Savior's pseudonyms. And I'll have you know that these men come from Crosby University, the best – and only – institution of higher learning in the land." Nash paused. "But I digress. Please excuse me. I must prepare for the Scripture's dramatic reading and will need a few minutes to find everything I need."

The High Priest threw open a closet door. He tore through the mass of papers, boxes, and assorted mannequin parts piled inside. I looked at the things as he tossed them out. All were stage props. Nash brought the selected items to his desk. There, he slipped into the garments of an unwashed hippy. He dimmed the lights before taking his seat at a table lit by a single candle. A fake quill pen raced across cheap typing paper as Nash announced his intent to play Crosby himself.

He cleared his throat and began the reading:

Dear Mildred:

Remember we're all mad beasts, and it's the madness resting inside that must be ousted or deciphered. (Strange, but most view their personal madness as sanity.) There's no need to race towards the cliff. There's no need to brace yourself at the edge. As they say – The Truth will present Itself. *Focus on* The Mysteries. *That's difficult during a time when enlightenment degrades rapidly into superstition. Focus becomes hard to maintain yet you must remain strong. Keep to the path you have no choice but follow. Let* The Father *learn from* The Child *and* The Child *from* The Father. *But become neither. Strike a balance; unstick things from society's goo. Don't allow fragments to wage war against one another. Know* The Child *– that juggernaut – can never be destroyed, no matter how often you or others may try to quash it.*

P.S. Would you bake me more of those biscuits next Friday? <ahem, ahem> Those last ones were really good.

Peace the fuck out,

Harry Fairchild

After reciting the closing, Nash stood up and made a proclamation:

"Know this: *The letter I now hold would not exist if not divinely chosen to be. It has remained incorruptible throughout the near infinite space between epochs. For a Pre-Epoch man such as yourself, our revelation would equate to finding a note penned by a dinosaur."*

The office loudspeakers pumped the sound of a million hands clapping. I assumed the High Priest had rigged the intercom system to give salutation whenever a skit was complete.

"This concludes my show."

I sighed. "Crosby was divine just because 5,627 letters, only one of which was signed by a man with that name, survived an epoch?"

"You *are* naive, but that's fine. We have faith you were divinely selected to bear secret knowledge."

"But what if the letter survived for no real reason?"

"That's a very heretical thing to say, though I will refrain from punishing you this time. I realize you're a stranger to our reality."

"Perhaps you're right. Maybe the letter *was* meant to be. But did you ever stop to think it might be here so baked beans could be reinvented? Chaos works in crazy ways. You people know what *baked beans* are, don't you?"

"Of course we know what baked beans are!"

"Sorry, but that fact may very well prove my point."

"You don't have to apologize or prove a point. Just accept. *You have been chosen*. Follow our dictates the rest of the way to Salvation."

"The other religions wanted the same thing ages ago."

"True, but they were in error."

"How so?"

"Because they were wrong. But why must we pick hairs on such a joyous occasion? Come! Let's toast this new age, not pull apart and analyze it." Nash pulled a bottle of booze from the shelf behind him, dislodged the cork, and filled twin communion cups. He handed one to me with a rapturous smile. "It's a *staggering* honor to drink with one of The Travelers!"

I took a sip of alcohol and pushed the rest away. I wasn't in the mood for booze.

"This is all just a bit unexpected. I hope you understand."

"Oh, I do. But, like a puppy that whines even though the sound encourages Master to beat him, you simply can't adapt to change. You rail against it. Know this: *The Church of The Byrds is Different*. Perhaps you would be interested in knowing how we view death and the afterlife?"

His question was decidedly pointed, so I nodded my head. I figured I had little choice in the matter.

"Are you aware of the phenomena called *Close-Proximity Uni-junction?"*

"I'm afraid not."

"It sometimes happens when one experiences invasive trauma, or ingests psychotropic chemicals."

"You mean a Near Death Experience."

Nash furrowed his brows. "I guess you could call it what you like. But my point is this: if one experiences *Close-Proximity Uni-junction*, one actually enters *Death-Space* and tastes the Eternity he or she deserves."

"You mean salvation or damnation?"

"Exactly! Most people think *The Big Death* must hold some extra reality over and above *The Small Death* of a *Close-Proximity Uni-junction*. But it doesn't. In what you call a *Near Death Experience*, the soul is pushed back into the body. Following actual death, it never re-enters the Soul-Machine."

"Soul-Machine?"

"The flesh. The body and all its structure."

"Oh."

"And if you blossom into either a *Close-Proximity Uni-junction* or *The Big Death* without Crosby's grace, you'll find yourself in *The Chasm of Memory*. The only difference between the two means of entry is that with the former comes another chance to see the light."

"So God doesn't damn people to *The Chasm of Memory?"*

The High Priest smiled. "Dear Child, God thrusts no one into patterns. One jumps headlong into them. A *Child of Death* enters

The Chasm of Memory on his own volition. A *Child of God* realizes this life is but a training ground for either salvation or damnation and lives on. A *Child of Death* becomes nothing more than a dream dreaming a dream."

I shuttered. "That sounds scary."

"Truly. But remember that each day is a *New Creation*, lit by *Eden's Light*. Alas, all things created must die. God wants His Creations to reciprocate His selfless love during their limited time on Earth and, in doing so, begin to love one another. This is why your soul must be pure or covered in Grace when the *Final Memory* comes. Otherwise, God shall not unleash His fatherly smile upon you."

"But how do I clean my soul?"

"Crosby is your spiritual insurance, but you must continue playing your part – not for your sake, but for the good of mankind. A life lived according to *The Rule* is a benefit to all *Soul-Machines* existing within *The Eternal Now*. But no man can save himself. You must accept Grace so freely offered. Do you follow? I apologize if all this sounds a little heavy, but I'm reading off a cue-card."

"I think I understand."

"Good. Now tell me what you would say if Crosby offered you his hand."

"I guess I'd take it just to be on the safe side."

"You have made a wise decision. On that final and terrible *Day of God*, all living things will enter *Death-Space* as one. There'll be no more second chances. But don't worry. Simply trust me when I say death is something you will never taste, but only if you make *The One Choice.*"

"And that choice is Crosby?"

"Precisely!"

"Your belief structure is one of the most convoluted I've seen."

"Thank you."

Though confused, I returned the gesture. "But I believe I understand where you're going with this. Perhaps I judged you too hastily."

"We do, however, require that you *performicate* sacred duties which are outlined in a codex of arbitrary rules passed down through the ages."

"Oh god."

"Your sacred duty," he continued, "is a simple one. Accompany me to the temple and I'll show you what must be done."

High Priest Nash exited his office, and I followed silently behind. I took one last look at Bobby. He still hadn't regained consciousness.

"Don't worry about him. We'll see to it that he's placed in a bed tonight."

I kept walking. When we stopped, I found myself back at the spot where Bobby and I had finished our eon-spanning dance. I did my best to ignore the look of hungry rapture spanning the congregation's collective face and pay attention to the High Priest. It was a difficult task.

"Behold *The Holy Song-Playing-Device!"*

I recognized my old record player.

"This is how you activate it. Watch me now!"

Perplexity mounted. "Okay."

"First, you lift this shaft called a *bow-hook* and place it gently upon the edge of this vinyl object I call a *discus."*

"I already know this stuff."

Nash beamed. "Then you truly *do* bear secret knowledge!"

"It's just my old–"

"What modesty! You are a true leader – one who doesn't wish for glory yet has it in *abundatude*. My son, you have inherited the keys to the Kingdom!"

"But what if I don't want them?"

The High Priest laughed. "You can't help but accept! They are yours without asking. All you must do is *performicate* your sacred duty on a daily basis."

"What's my sacred duty? You just showed me my record player."

"*Record player?* So, that's what they're called. I believe this is the only one still in existence. Most items from your time were decimated in the wake of *The Great Syphilis Plague*. The books that featured them were all but destroyed, too."

"A plague? When?"

"Sometime during the last epoch. I'm a priest, not a historian. But for all the human suffering *The Great Syphilis Plague* wrought, it nevertheless ended in revival. We entered the cosmic soup until aliens from *Zebulon 5* resurrected 100,000 corpses with nano-technology. When our bodies returned to life, we vowed never again to become so vile that the world has to spit us out."

"So you're all kinda like zombies, then."

"What are *zombies?"*

"Never mind. Just tell me my sacred duty."

"Oh. . . Oh yes! Your sacred duty. I almost forgot. It's simple, really. All you have to do is put the *bow-hook* to the *discus* – I mean "record" – at the beginning and end of each service. We hold a morning service at 10:15 A.M. and an evening service at 10:15 P.M."

"That's all?"

"That's all. Of course, you must also join us in worship. It's usually just meditation. At times we dance, provided the spirit moves us to do so. However, we are to engage in languid rhythms *only*. No mad gyrations. No pelvic thrusting. Do you think you can adhere to this?"

"Well, yeah. It sounds easier than the stuff I had to do at *The Doughnut Kiosk*."

"And one more thing, I suggest you retire early. You've been dancing for ages, yet must be refreshed in time for tomorrow's morning service."

"I'm a bit tuckered, yeah."

Nash grasped my shoulder. "I will show you to your bed chamber. I hope you won't find it offensively Spartan. It's quite simple, just a ten by ten room with a small closet, a bunk-bed, and an alarm clock."

"No problem. That's what I'm used to."

"Then come with me."

I followed the High Priest down a long and winding hall.

* * * *

When I entered my sleeping chamber, I noticed Bobby already ensconced in the top bunk.

"Fucker! You know I always get the top!"

Bobby continued to lie there, sprawled out like a dead man.

"Ummmmm. . . Bobby?"

I shook him, but he remained limp and unresponsive. I assumed he was still feeling the strength of Nash's little white pill. I decided to drag Bobby from the top and claim my rightful spot. Doing that made me feel a little guilty so, rather than just dropping him on the bed, I slid Bobby between the sheets and folded the comforter neatly about his chest.

On the top bunk, I turned my head from my sawdust and rag pillow. I gazed out the small window cut into the opposing wall. Through it, I saw only blue sky, rolling grass, and a hill off in the distance. While

I could discern little else from my vantage point, it appeared as though The Church of The Byrds was smack dab in the middle of nowhere.

I looked up. A tiny bookshelf was tacked to the wall a few feet above the bed. I considered reading something, but the first few selections failed to catch my eye. The books were stuffy manuals outlining the rules and regulations of Brydism. Most looked over 100 years old and were penned by people with names like Monk Aberdeen and Sister Mary Maledictum.

Then I saw a strange object lying by the tomes. On its shaft was imprinted the word *M-Book*. I assumed the nozzle jutting from its silvery base was this epoch's equivalent of a headset. Curious, I picked the thing up and inserted the tube into my ear. The *M-Book* whirled to life as it touched my skin.

An electronic voice bleeped: *"Please wait. . . Please wait . . . Please wait. . . Please wait. . ."*

Suddenly, my brain felt as though it was processing amazingly non-standard input. Strange gears were turning, and I could do nothing but sit back and remain entranced by the oddity of the moment. A minute or two later, the disembodied voice once again bleeped in my skull:

"The information has been uploaded. Please remove the patented M-Book Transceiver from your ear canal."

I did as commanded, and my mental screen changed to dark blue as the *M-Book's* operating system replaced the organic one in my brain. The screen flickered, and words appeared before my eyes:

AMERICA IN THE 21st CENTURY: THE ROMAN AGE OF THE GOLDEN EMPIRE

Part 1: An Introduction

Consider this picture of life during the middle half of the 21st century: American cities ravaged by heat and drought, the world leaders having put too much faith in both the cleverness of man and the ravages of industry. Oceans – all dry. Trees – all withered. Sun-scorched earth where crops used to grow. Dead three-headed children, baking on the pavement. Lines of cars stretching for miles and miles – occupants decayed. Deadening silence and then cacophony as the western world exploded.

Fortunately for him, 21st century man never knew what hit him. 99.9 percent of the population had contracted syphilis decades before the comet plowed through the northern hemisphere and turned human creation to crispy ash.

Imagine having lived just thirty years prior to the world's destruction. You'd experience fewer plagues and more ozone, but things still wouldn't be right. If you were a sensitive person, you'd probably know the end was near. You'd smell it in the air. If not, you'd probably buy clothes. You'd notice a lot of people doing just that and, once you understand you're not just being paranoid, you'd start believing you are *The Chosen One*. You'd almost be right. Only 4.3 percent of the human race really knew. This is the exact percentage of the population spirited away just prior to the ascension of The Grand Dictator and his Royal Advisor Malachi. The manner in which this mass departure occurred puzzles scholars to this day.

Ironically, America died during what the media called its *Golden Age*. The Prophets, however, had another word for pre-plague America. They called it *The Cesspool.*

Verse 1: Things are not as they seem.

After the first quarter of that century, insurance agents and investment bankers started calling their cars *chariots* and talking on small hand-held devices they dubbed *centuro-phones*. These men lounged around offices and watched reruns of their favorite one-hour drama in lieu of actual work. Weekly circuses, called *Pleasure Pageants*, were soon inaugurated to keep employees satiated. It was said that the circus instilled laborers with "good morale" and prevented "worker rebellion."

More than a few people, mostly unemployed vagrants, wound up getting eaten by lions or shot through cannons into brick walls.

Verse 2: Power is death; but it's a slow one.

A fierce caste system evolved as these men ensconced themselves in society's fabric. Those making less than fifty-thousand dollars a year were inevitably thrown into concentration camps or forced to dance, often nude, for the amusement of faceless corporate entities. These souls had no hope of ever leaving their leg shackles.

Verse 3: A little money is all it takes to fuck things up.

Such tactics proved good for business, so these people – whom I shall dub "The Professionals" – responded to success by adopting a single creed: *First and foremost, Man exists as a tool for the advancement of bureaucracy.* They applied this maxim to themselves and thus became money-spewing vortexes, resting only to make sure their ties were on straight.

As a general rule, these moneymakers and moneyshakers wanted nothing more than to think themselves supreme. Most, however, lacked the confidence to believe their loftiness truly existed. They realized just how unhappy they were, so they inflicted misery on others. Thus, they were able to muster a trace of joy.

Ultimately, these vindictive men assumed a subtle, yet all-encompassing chokehold over not only the poor, but over the entire Western world. "The Professionals" bypassed The Grand Dictator and lobbied Royal Advisor Malachi to pass laws that reflected their personal bureaucratic taste but, because every palate is different, discord was destined to erupt.

And erupt it did. "The Professionals" liked to quell rebellion by ordering bullets shot into its flailing body. Despite the bloodshed, they managed to further their cause by selling sanitized stories to the media. (Most network presidents, after all, were in their club.) They quickly endeared the public to their cause while castigating the "criminal" who was, more often than not, a poor person, a member of an ethnic minority, or a free-thinker.

But even these men could not act alone.

Verse 4: The petty always need others to oil their naughty wheels.

The second level in the chain of non-governmental command was filled with brainless lackeys known affectionately as "The Cool People." Living under the influence (and protection) of "The Professionals" media-based power, "The Cool People" lived only to harass those incorrectly tailored to "The Professionals" socio-religio-politico-economico goals. Dispatched to high schools across the county, they weeded out (and gave swirleys to) those deemed too intelligent to live within the continental boundaries of the United States. Any thinking man, they realized, would see past the lies and evasions and had to be taken care of during his formative years. A few exemptions were made for scholars previously brainwashed to follow a strict, university doctrine. These individuals, however intelligent, were already under the control of state sponsored Mind-Beams and, through association, became honorary "Cool People" themselves. Like their less intelligent brethren, these men listened to all the best music and wore all the right clothes, just as "The Professionals" wanted.

Verse 5: Woe be onto the man who first said 'if you can't beat 'em, join em'.

Over-indulgence and personal pleasure *uber alles* was the order of the day – something "The Professionals" liked very much, as it caused demand to *skyrocket*.

But the fun and consumption inevitably got out of hand and "chariot-rage" gripped the nation. The poor hated the rich even more for having greater horsepower under their hoods. They often voiced their disgust with round upon round of lead. In this way, they were much like the Roman peasants who made angry elf-faces at the Emperor as he passed by in his golden chariot pulled by 24 well-oiled steeds.

(Factoid: Over 33,000 men, women and children were murdered while traversing American highways between April 24, 2041 and June 26, 2041 alone.)

Social strife – and quite possibly revolution – seemed inevitable. "The Professionals", however, embarked upon a massive PR campaign and were soon able to convince the world that nothing was wrong. People became satiated cows and failed to note the beginning of the end, even as reality's infrastructure crumbled. Of course, it also helped that most consumer products were, at the time, dipped in *Happy-Dust* – a synthetic and highly addictive substance that sent chemical pleasure surging through the blood stream. The buyers quickly associated the sensation with the mass-produced item, and what has now come to be known as Trained Monkey Syndrome (TMS) emerged.

Soon, everybody was copulating like mad. Women wanted nothing more than to make a baby to put in their infant collections. They didn't want to love it. They just wanted something cute. To hell with it once it grew up and started to lose its fat.

"Oooh. . . lookie! They're so cute they almost look human!"

Such was the state of love and reproduction in the end-times of American Culture.

Verse 6: All your compensation is for naught.

Soon, Mother Nature got fed up with all those self-important, mating assholes. After the 89,000,000,000,000,000,000,000,000,000,000th baby was born during a single day in April, Mother-Nature smacked her forehead in rage and unleashed the beginnings of a slow, boiling plague on all humanity.

What follows is last Dictatorial address ever. It was spoken by The Grand Dictator II – a weak and sickly patsy handpicked by Royal Advisor Malachi to succeed the first Grand Dictator (who died under mysterious circumstances). The text below was delivered a mere two weeks before the plague first manifested itself in downtown Los Angeles and conspired to keep Western culture in a state of stagnation until visiting aliens from *Zebulon 5* built their bio-domes atop this once desolate planet. With their super-computers and nano-technology, they replicated human life, thus beginning wordily existence anew.

EVERYTHING'S OKAY. GOD – I MEAN *THE GOVERNMENT* – IS TAKING CARE OF THE SITUATION. TRUST US; IT'S FINE. IGNORE THE MEN WHO ARE KILLING YOUR CHILDREN. IGNORE THEIR BADGES AND NAMETAGS. THEY DO NOT EXIST AND ARE, IN FACT, FIGMENTS OF YOUR IMAGINATION. DON'T WORRY. YOU HAVE GOOD CREDIT AND THAT'S WHAT REALLY MATTERS. YOU COULD BUY A BIG-SCREEN TV RIGHT NOW. WHY DON'T YOU DO THAT? WHY DON'T YOU DO THAT AND LEAVE YOUR DOORS UNLOCKED? GO ALONE. LEAVE EVERYONE ELSE AT HOME. A CONFIDENTIAL INFORMANT WILL MEET YOU HALFWAY ACROSS TOWN. WHEN YOU SEE HIM, TELL HIM EVERYTHING YOU KNOW ABOUT ANY AND ALL SEDITIOUS ACTIVITIES THAT HAVE OCCURRED ON OR NEAR YOUR PROPERTY. THOSE WHO DON'T COMPLY WILL RECEIVE A TICKET AND BE FINED SIX ($6) DOLLARS.

At this point in his speech, history tells us that a fringe, terrorist band of "The Professionals" burst into the chamber and declared their rule. Royal Advisor Malachi responded, seconds later, by disappearing in a cloud of smoke and fire.

It was a spectacle witnessed by thousands.

What follows is a transcript of events just described, culled from one of the few surviving 21st Century history books:

<THE GRAND DICTATOR II>: WHERE THE HELL DID MY ROYAL ADVISOR GO?

<THE PROFESSIONALS>: DON'T WORRY ABOUT HIM. JUST PRESS THIS BUTTON. YOU HAVE NO CHOICE. THE ENEMY IS OVERRUNNING OUR SCHOOLS AND CAUSING AN EVOLUTION IN OUR CHERISHED VALUE SYSTEM. NO ONE IS SAFE. THE PEOPLE ARE COUNTING ON YOU TO PUSH THIS BUTTON.

<TGD II>: YOU DON'T MEAN. . .

<TP>: YES. WE HAVE CONFERRED WITH ALL THE *TOP GENERALS*. THEY HAVE STUDIED *THE FACTS*. THEY HAVE PLANNED *STRATEGIC BATTLES*. . . BUT NOTHING HAS WORKED! THESE HUNS JUST KEEP ON MULTIPLYING! THE ONLY WAY WE CAN *KILL* THESE CREATURES IS TO PUSH THAT BUTTON!

<TGD II>: I'M THE GRAND DICTATOR II! YOU CAN'T ORDER ME AROUND LIKE THIS!

<TP>: YOU'RE JUST A FIGUREHEAD. MALACHI HOLDS THE TRUE POWER AND HE'S GONE.

<TGD II>: *BUT I'M THE DICTATOR!* I SHOULD HAVE A CHOICE IN DECIDING WHETHER OR NOT I PUSH THAT BUTTON.

<TP>: AGREED. YOU HAVE THE RIGHT TO CHOOSE TO PUSH THE BUTTON.

<TGD II>: BUT. . .

<TP>: SHUT UP! YOU'RE JUST A BRAIN IN A VAT OF SALINE SOLUTION! OUR BEST TRAINED SCIENTISTS TELL YOU WHAT OPINIONS TO HAVE AND WHEN TO HAVE

THEM! OUR *MIND-DUST* CONTROLS EVERYTHING, MR. HONORABLE DICTATOR, SIR! PUSH THAT BUTTON!

<MR. HONORABLE DICTATOR, SIR pushes THAT BUTTON>

<TP>: THANK YOU.

(The transcript ends here as "The Professionals" – having forced the dictator to nuke a small orphanage – slaughter him live on national television.)

Once The Grand Dictator II was out of the way, "The Professionals" focused on assassinating all members of his staff. (Their bodies were later found stripped to their underwear in a small wooded lot.) Then they set to work.

The Professionals' first act in office was to place every sentient being in shit jobs or labor fields. This generated even more profit and thus allowed more Mega-Corporations to merge into Omni-Corporations. Nobody had free time – everybody was working continuously – and an endless supply of tainted paper money traveled from hand to hand. Cash wouldn't stop flowing in torrents, and "The Professionals" smiled. They didn't realize it was all going to end in a plague carried on the wings of dollar bills.

Think about it.

The manacled and leg-shackled cashier at the 7-Eleven had to accept the plague. She would be shot dead unless she, without question, handled the ass-soiled money from the clinically insane patron who just so happened to be a carrier of *The Great Syphilis Virus*.

Soon, the plague was omni-spread and mega-mutated. No one was safe. It became airborne with a vengeance and 99.9 percent of the human population died within seven years of the assassination of The Grand Dictator II and his Cabinet.

Verse 7: ALL PROGRESS LEADS TO THE GRAVE.

In the end, 21st Century man overpopulated the planet and caused too great a strain on her natural resources. The Earth (aka Mother Nature, aka Helen) was, however, exonerated of all wrongdoing in *THE PEOPLE OF EARTH (Deceased) VS. MOTHER NATURE* (2059). The presiding judge, in a monumental decision, declared that The People of Earth "had it coming".

(END OF PART ONE)

At that moment, the feminine electro-voice again bleeped in my ear canal:

*Think "Y" if you would like to continue on to Chapter 2 (ZEBULON 5: ITS RAMIFICATIONS FOR POST-PLAGUE AMERICA) or think "N" to end your M-Book Session (*patent pending*) for the evening.*

I thought "N" and an advertisement for *The Church of The Byrds* boomed in my ears.

Thank you for reading AMERICA IN THE 21st CENTURY: THE ROMAN AGE OF THE GOLDEN EMPIRE. Feel free to peruse the other fine books we have to offer.

And share our faith.

Join us. Hear our words. Read our leaflets. Share them with your family.

Believe and Live!

When the commercial ended, I pulled the *M-Book* from my ear and returned it to the shelf. I was interested in finding out what had transpired during my millennia spanning absence but, at the time, wanted nothing more than to sleep.

I stripped off the clothes I had worn for billions of years and slid beneath the covers. I was so tired that I forgot to set the alarm for 9:30.

* * * *

Victoria Overlake's lips were full and pert, just like the rest of her body. Her slinky form beckoned that I rest atop her multi-canopied bed, and I bent to her whims without complaint.

"Will you ravish me, young man-servant John?"

"Yes, my queen. My appendages are at your beck and call."

Victoria just laughed and took another drag off her cigarette. "Men, you're all the same. Good for meat and little else."

"Yes, my Queen," I said, and meant it.

She extinguished her cigarette on my face. "And now it's time to get to the *fuckin'*."

"The *fuckin'*, m'lady?"

"You heard me, boy."

Suddenly, the voice of God boomed overhead. He had obviously watched our iniquity from above and was now prepared to launch at us only the harshest of penalties: "You overslept!"

My dream lover's form crumbled against waking reality. I looked up and saw a familiar face glaring down at me.

"High Priest Nash?"

"Serpent, repent! You missed the morning sermon! The *discus* was never played!"

"Don't you mean *record?"*

"I mean your *ceremonial duty!* Since your return, you are the only man worthy of spinning the *discus!* We had to cancel the morning service for the first time in *six-hundred years* because of you!"

"But I didn't mean anything by it. I was sleepy."

Nash removed a bleeping gizmo-box from between my mattress and box spring. "And our Brainwave Scanners indicate that you had a wet dream last night!"

"What–"

"And you're wearing colored underwear! Don't you know we are forbidden to don such items in *The Book of Restraint,* and that red is the color of evil!"

"I had no idea! I've been wearing the same clothes since the 21st century!"

"I cannot believe a Traveler would dance to Holy Rhythms clad in such disgraceful undergarments!"

"Listen, High Priest Nash–"

"Silence! Satan has crept into your brain-pan. . . *and he must be exorcized."*

"But I–"

"Stand on your head!"

"Why?"

"To cast demons from your body."

I threw an alarm clock, but Nash ducked out of the way. He leapt over its shattered casing and tossed open the door to my bed chamber's tiny closet. Once inside, he pulled out a frilly spandex bodysuit.

"Then I shall force you to wear the *Leotard of Penance!"*

"Wait! You have a problem with colored underwear yet you want me to wear a *Leotard of Penance?"*

"'Tis a most holy and ordained means of sanctioning unruly sheep." He shook the diaphanous thing in front of my face. "Now wear it!"

"But–"

"*Wear the leotard!"*

"Yes, sir! Yes, High Priest Nash!"

"Slip it over your legs first. Then slide on the shoulder straps."

I looked down and saw just how silly I appeared. "Am I done?"

"As it states in *The Holy Tome*, you must now dance."

"If that's what it takes." I did an angry jig as Nash uttered feverish prayers and spoke in multiple tongues.

Ten minutes later: "May I stop now?"

"Yes, but I want you in my office at five o'clock this afternoon. *Sharp!* Bring your offensive undergarment, too!"

I could only sob through my disgrace.

* * * *

I spent the next few hours in bed awaiting the stroke of five. When I heard the bells toll, I got up and stepped over Bobby, who had fallen to the floor sometime during the afternoon. I assured myself that he was still alive before traversing the hall. The High Priest's door was open, but I paused before walking in.

"You wanted me, sir?"

"Indeed. Have you changed your ungodly undergarments?"

"Yes."

"And did you bring the offending item with you?"

"Yes."

"Well, hand it here."

I strode over to High Priest Nash and gave him my underpants. In turn, he handed me a pair of white boxer shorts.

"These," he said, "are church sponsored."

"But–"

"No *buts."* He lit a Bunsen burner and placed my briefs atop its blue and orange flame. Red gave way to black gave way to ash. Nash smiled. "There. One less tool of the devil in our earthly realm."

"I still don't know why you wouldn't let me keep my underwear. My girlfriend bought them for me."

"Because *The Rules* state that one shall don only the things that God has sanctified. Anything less is devil-borne."

"Could you at least try to understand my position?"

"I understand you're not adhering to the laws governing our church."

"And why should I?"

"Because you need rules to live."

"I'm already alive."

"I was speaking metaphorically."

"Huh?"

"Can't you see? Our belief structure is a necessity. One cannot hope to gain the Creator's favor without its guidance."

"I believe in God, don't get me wrong. I just don't believe in Him the way you do."

"You've just admitted your latent paganism."

"No, I didn't. I only want to talk with you. Maybe ask a few questions."

"Why should you want to ask anything? Know with your heart, not with your mind."

"In that case, why can't I skip your rules entirely?"

"Don't you see? Men of the Cloth are needed to reel in sheep and encourage them to believe the way God deems fit."

"But you just said head-faith wasn't important. Now you're contradicting yourself."

"Know this: you're a lost and heartless animal, foaming in the desert heat, rabies pounding in your bloodstream. You're merely God's washcloth, and he dirties his hands with you."

"Why would God want to debase me?"

"Because you are human, and humans are filthy, slovenly creatures."

"Perhaps you just need to chill out and smoke a bowl."

"I cannot believe you would speak of such depravity! We only do *that* on certain Holy Days!"

"Will you at least consider what I've said?"

The High Priest spent a moment in contemplation. "Perhaps you've made one or two thought provoking statements."

"So, you're going to let me go without punishment?"

Nash shook his head. He looked almost rueful. "I wish I didn't have to do this, but you leave me little choice. To *The Fields of Tribulation* with you."

A team of orderlies plowed through the door before I realized what was happening. One man threw my body over his shoulders. He carried me to the front lawn where a black armored car sat idling. Another opened the rear door and, saying nothing, tossed me inside. The door slammed shut as the car began to move.

I felt a sudden pang of nostalgia for *The Doughnut Kiosk* as I sat in that dark rear cargo hold. I longed to return to my nasty apartment, and I missed Bobby. I wished he might still be around to force me out of bed and berate me for being lazy. The little things I once hated now possessed my mind.

Hours seemed to pass. The cargo door finally swung open. As light flooded in, I found myself face to face with a field ready for sowing. Its width spanned countless miles; its breadth stretched to the far-off horizon.

Nash greeted me as I was escorted, kicking and screaming, from the vehicle.

"This is where you're going to spend the next few months. *Working*."

"Nash? You can't be serious!"

He sighed. "I'm afraid so, Dear Traveler."

* * * *

My punishment was to weed, hoe, and cultivate the field from which the followers of The Church of The Byrds obtained nourishment. Throughout it all, a team of paid orderlies lorded over me.

I looked up from my toil. "May I please have some lemonade?"

"No! You haven't done your work for the evening! No liquid refreshment until the potatoes are in the ground!"

"But there're so many!" I gestured to a mound of tubers the size of my old apartment. "Are you are suggesting that I sow *all these* before drinking?"

A burly orderly smacked my sunburned hand with a ruler.

I soon learned never to speak, much less question authority. Bending down, I shoved another tuber into the nurturing soil as insects ate of my flesh. Runners of sweat poured from my brow, the drops evaporating before they could reach the ground.

Only salt granules remained to stain the earth with my sour sweetness.

* * * *

At night, I was forced to sleep on the ground by my shovel. I often looked up at the sky and tried to lose myself in stars. I imagined my epoch lay somewhere in amongst that swirling black mass. Radio waves. Transmissions of every kind. All still in existence. If I could only touch them. Or hear them, even. That would be all I needed.

My mind often roamed. To forget the present and live in the past was the only way I could lure myself into an extended, yet fitful, sleep.

I remembered the time I was at a party just after my high school graduation. I remembered someone calling the radio station to phone-in a request. For some reason, the DJ invited us to the studio and allowed each to introduce one song. My voice was up there in the cosmos, too – introducing *YMCA* by *The Village People* on Disco Night.

That memory had been all but erased up until my long nights in the field. I guess it just wasn't that important to me before. Now, it was one of the few things I had left.

* * * *

I spent nearly six months as The Church of the Byrds' indentured gardener. My muscles grew large and my brain atrophied in the hot sun.

Then, one lovely morn, High Priest Nash tapped my shoulder. His touch lit an immediate holy fire in my marrow, and I knew the season for planting had finally reached its end.

"You have paid your debt in full, my son. Arise and cast down your implements of cultivation. The time has come to teach you many things."

"You can't be serious."

"But I am. You have come far. The devil had his claws deep in your flank when I first met you. Now, you're a true man of Crosby." He reached into his pocket and brought forth a collapsible facemask brimming with wires and knobs. "Just place this over your head and you will achieve *Conscious Level 1*. Be proud. I was twice your age before this honor was bestowed upon me."

I reached my hand out and accepted the gear.

"But be sure to close your eyes as you place it on your scalp. Otherwise, you might suffer an embolism."

I nodded and, with eyes firmly shut, placed the mask over my face. Virtual tracks and leaflets filled my brain. I thought-clicked the arrow button that appeared superimposed over my vision and turned to the pamphlet entitled *How to Love the True God*. I could see the text, but I didn't need to read it. The wisdom of countless church fathers plowed through synapses and imprinted organic circuitry without me having to do a thing. At that moment, I understood why someone would have to sacrifice his life for the sake of humanity. I saw God's sweeping plan laid out in full color diagrams, bar graphs, and pie charts and realized all was good.

"Now remove the headset."

I did so, then motioned to embrace Nash in a bear hug. Red tears streamed from my eyes in torrents. The High Priest noted the deluge.

"Congratulations! It's rare that a new convert experiences tear-stigmata so quickly. You must have truly absorbed our virtual leaflets."

"Indeed, sir. They told me everything I needed in my quest to know Crosby's glory. They led me down pastures greener than I could imagine."

"I'm glad you found the holy texts a stimulating read, but now I have *secrets* that must be shared with you. The first few are basic. In time, you will progress and become privy to even deeper mysteries. Will you accept this wisdom?"

I nodded.

The High Priest responded by reading from a pamphlet entitled *SACRED CHURCH KNOWLEDGE: Series 1 of 8*.

"A man ingests a psychotropic agent, forgetting he has a doctor's appointment. Three hours later he runs to the office in a drug-induced paranoia-spasm. The doctors pronounce him dead on arrival because they've never seen a man trip so hard. They say '*bag 'em and tag 'em'*, and the orderlies throw him into a freezer."

"Oh my God!"

"Shall I continue?"

I was spellbound. "Please."

"Three days pass, and the funeral director has to tie his flailing body to the casket." Nash looked up from the pamphlet. "Dressing the *corpse* is a particularly interesting part of the story, but I won't go into that now."

"Fascinating."

"His family mourns him. His six-year old daughter looks into the coffin and screams. He tries to assure her he's fine and wonders why no one acknowledges he's a living man tied down. Though legally dead, he soon loses his composure. He screams obscenities as he realizes they fully intend to bury him."

"No one ever saves him?"

Nash nodded solemnly. "The service ends. Cries sound muffled in the closed casket. His surviving relatives wouldn't permit an autopsy. He wishes they had just cut him open. It would have been quicker that way. He wants to go completely and utterly insane – *Cackle, cackle mad* – but decides to accept that it was his time to go."

"So, who was this man?

Answer for yourself.

"Crosby?"

"Precisely. As another man's path was to become a mail carrier, Crosby's path was to become God's sacrifice to man. *The Chosen One*, Crosby, gave birth to the *Divine Act of Love* known as Grace."

"I think you've got the wrong man. Crosby was a guy in a band who used to do a lot of–"

Nash held up his hands. "You have just received enlightenment. Acute confusion is to be expected. The virtual leaflets won't stabilize in your brain for a few more hours, but take comfort in knowing all doubt shall soon be erased."

"But I'm not confused."

"Shhhh. . . *relax*. Deep breaths will help you come to your senses."

"Please, just let me–"

"In fact, let me show you to your bed. A nap will calm your nerves. And you'll get a chance to see your new sleeping chamber. I've been setting it up since yesterday."

"Really?"

"Do follow me."

* * * *

Nash led me to a door on the other side of the hall.

"Here we are, so I'll take my leave now. Let me know what you think of your new room."

I bowed to the High Priest and, for the first time, he returned the gesture.

"Thank you, Nash."

"Think nothing of it."

I turned to the door, pushed it open, and was immediately impressed. In truth, I had expected nothing greater than a more comfortable bunk, but the large room came complete with a walk-in closet, deep-piled carpeting, and a half-bath. Simple yet elegant wallpaper covered the walls; a small crystal chandelier hung from the ceiling. Even the air smelled as though it had been perfumed with lilac. While it wasn't the most ornate room I had ever seen, it was certainly more than I expected from Nash.

Stretching, I walked over to the queen-sized bed and fell down upon its soft, cushiony mattress. The padding was a far cry from the straw and rag stuffed bag I had slept on earlier. So amazingly comfortable, I didn't even bother to turn off the lights. I just slid beneath the covers and lost myself in luxury.

I was asleep within minutes.

* * * *

Holdovers from my conversion flitted through my mind as I slept. Floating cardinals and ambulatory vestments. Swirling baptismal fountains and clattering relics. Fluttering *Holy Tomes* and a cluttered, single-room apartment.

A cluttered, single-room apartment?

The holy images faded. I felt myself drawn further into this tiny, cinderblock walled place. The entire room seemed more real than waking reality. I felt cold tile floor and smelled the odor of days old dishes.

I looked around. The place was empty, but someone had been inside recently. A crushed cigarette still smoldered in an ashtray on the kitchen table.

Something squeaked. I spun in the direction of the sound. The apartment's only door swung open. A man walked in and took his seat by a computer. He was of average size, though slightly underweight. His face was utterly common and looked similar to a million others I had seen. Nothing distinguished. Nothing out of the ordinary. No marks or scars.

He typed for a few minutes, pausing to take intermittent sips from a coffee mug. He remained engrossed in his work, turning to me only after he had set the printer into motion.

"Hello, there. Glad you could make it."

I walked up to the man. "Who are you?"

"I'm just a plain guy who does plain things. I like to write, though. Do you?"

"Not really."

The man shrugged. "Can't say I hold it against you. It's so non-lucrative a career that one might not even call it a career at all. But I press on because writing's in my blood."

"Why are you telling me this?"

"No real reason. I just thought we might chat a bit before getting down to business."

"Well, I guess I don't have a problem with that."

"So, tell me about your life."

I took a step back. "That's weird. We've just met."

"Just tell me. It's important that you do."

"Well . . . my life itself is fine, but some of the circumstances didn't used to be. *The Doughnut Kiosk* caused a lot of stress."

"The Doughnut Kiosk?"

"It's where I once worked."

"Once?"

"Yeah, I stopped going."

The man grinned. "Is that because you were recently hurtled through time?"

"How did you know about that? I wasn't going to tell you. I was afraid you'd think I was insane."

"I wouldn't. I know a bit about such things, myself."

"How so?"

"That's not important. Keep going."

"I really don't know what else to say."

"Then I guess I'll have to lead the conversation." The man paused in thought. "Tell me, do you miss anything?"

"You mean from my old life?"

"Yes."

"I had a girlfriend back home. And a family. I didn't see them often at all. Hell, I didn't even call, but I still cared about them."

"And are these things still important to you?"

"Of course, but I can't go back. Everybody's dead except Bobby, and he might as well be."

"But you still hold their memory, right?"

"Memories can only take me so far."

"Very true. It's time to break away from the past and make new memories. There's only one question: what kind of memories will they be?"

"Memories of the Church. Memories of the High Priest."

"And Memories of Power, perhaps?"

"I don't know what you mean."

The man sat back in his chair, allowing his legs to rest on his desk. "Let's just say I've heard a man named Nash is quite impressed with you. He's the kind of guy you'd want to know if you desired a line to the top. Answer this: would you refuse power if it was offered to you?"

"Of course not."

"That's what I thought. I would have said the same thing myself. In fact, I already have."

"But I wouldn't abuse power if I held it. I'm not that kind of person."

"When you wake up you may feel differently. I can already tell you've gone through many changes. You're hardly the same person." The man took another sip from his mug. For the first time, I smelled the scent of wafting alcohol. "Will you let me offer up a word or two of advice?"

"Sure."

"Love every last thing, no matter how mundane it is. That's my advice to you. Cherish every minute you spend making doughnuts."

"I don't think I can do that."

"It's your only ticket back."

"I'm not sure I want to go back."

"And why not?"

"I've already told you."

"Your explanation wasn't good enough."

"Wasn't good enough?" I felt anger rise. "You're a writer, and writers do interesting things! What I used to do didn't amount to shit! For the first time in my life I have a purpose! Hell, I can even feel myself growing!"

"No need to get angry. I'm just saying it's in your best interest to listen, especially in light of what you just said. You're a *Middle-Grounder;* you need my advice."

"A what?"

"A *Middle-Grounder* is he who sits between poles."

My head spun. "None of this makes sense, and you're just a dream."

"I fear you'll pay a high price if you keep that attitude."

"How would you know?"

"Personal experience."

"Why am I even listening to you? I'm going to leave now."

"Do as you must, but I want you to know something before you go."

"And what's that?"

"When you see me again, I'll be completely different."

I barely heard him. The fluttering relics had reappeared, their forms superimposed over the apartment. The floor sank beneath my feet. The walls melted away. A swirling fog of incense replaced the odor of neglected dishes.

But, through the haze, I heard the man's voice one last time:

"And you'll be different, too."

PART III:

THE CHURCH OF LIONEL RICHIE

LIFE HAD CHANGED since I learned to embrace Nash and his wisdom. No more troubles. No more worries. He had taught me how to solve everything with a little faith. I was a true *Man of God* fighting in *The Lord's Army*. Never did I desire to light up another doobie or spliff – unless, of course, it was a Holy Day.

And rarely did I think of Bobby – my lost friend. Nash told me the church doctors were taking extra special care of him, and that he would get better soon. I took comfort in knowing the High Priest would die before uttering falsehood. He was a man infused with *Crosby's True Spirit* – a flame in the *Eye of the Infinite!*

Life was good. Faith was good. Nash was good as Crosby was good.

Then – one day – the High Priest noticed work going on across the street and asked that I join him by the window.

* * * *

"Looks like they're building something." I noted construction workers busily lifting pre-fabricated concrete slabs into place. "And they're putting it up fast. There wasn't anything in that lot two days ago."

"What do you suppose it is?"

I shrugged. "Could be anything."

"I hope it's a restaurant. I could go for something a little more exciting than our usual meat and potatoes fare."

"Just keep your fingers crossed, High Priest Nash."

"I can almost taste those hamburgers now." He mussed my hair playfully. "We'll both eat there when it opens. My treat."

"That's not necessary. . ."

"My star pupil – always the humble one!"

". . .but I wouldn't say *no* if beneficence were so offered."

Nash smiled, then turned to face the clock. I followed his gaze. It was already 10:10.

We retired to the temple. I took my seat by the record player as the High Priest bestowed wisdom upon an adoring flock.

* * * *

A day later, I was back at the window, staring.

"It looks like they're putting a steeple on top of that new construction."

"A steeple!" High Priest Nash scurried over to the stained glass. "By Crosby, that's a *church!"*

"A church? But I've heard nothing of The Church of The Byrds building another temple."

Nash glared. *"That's because The Church of the Byrds isn't building another temple."*

"But I thought our church was *the* church!"

"You're not the only one."

"Look on the bright side, maybe it's not a church at all."

"Then why does it have a *steeple?"*

"Maybe it's a religious-themed restaurant."

"*A religious-themed restaurant?* That's the stupidest thing–"

Suddenly, a righteous blast of song interrupted Nash in mid-sentence. Its lyrics involved dancing on the ceiling, so I recognized the tune immediately.

"What! I don't remember *The Byrds* ever having a song like that! It's so *raucous!"*

"That's because they didn't. It's by Lionel Richie."

"Lionel who?"

"Lionel Richie. He was once in *The Commodores*."

"*The Commodores?* This means nothing to me!"

I was prepared to launch into an impromptu synopsis of the rise and fall of *The Commodores* – beginning with their 1971 foundation and ending with Lionel's departure in 1982 – before I too was interrupted. My mouth closed as I looked out the window and saw a leisure-suited and fake afro-topped man exit the building. He drove a sign into the ground just outside the construction site. I couldn't see what was written on the board until the man finished working.

And when he did, my heart screamed out in anguish.

THE CHURCH OF LIONEL RICHIE
(Whirling Dervish Branch)
Established 3456 C.Z.
High Priest Lionel – Presiding

High Priest Nash flew into a frenzy.

"Another Church! *Another Church!*" He beckoned me with the frantic waving of his hand. "I want you to go over there. I want you to arrange a meeting between Lionel and me *on the double!*"

I bowed. "Then I will do so."

"You are truly brave, Dear Traveler. Your Faith may be shaken. You may see seductive icons and imagery. You may be tempted. But you can't let these things make you sin. You are a Byrdite beyond even the day of your death!"

"Yes, sir. I understand."

* * * *

I entered The Church of Lionel Richie. Inside, volunteers busily hung relics: a shattered 8-Track, a swatch of ancient polyester, a baggie of cocaine. Off in a corner, others filled the baptismal fountain with something that smelled like hairspray. A skeleton hung over a freshly painted altar rendered in the shape of a disco ball. I assumed the ghastly thing was all that remained of Lionel Richie.

Though the room had yet to be furnished, the congregation – dressed in silly disco garb except for the veil-clad women – was already in attendance, watching the activity. Just being in the same room with these blasphemous and gaudy people made me physically ill. Most of the men sported glitter under their eyes; some even wore tiny spandex shorts over their hips. Others buttoned their shirts so far down their chests that their navels lay exposed for all to see. Still more wore massive golden chains below make-up smeared faces.

My entry seemed to have confused them. I just ignored their collective stare until I reached the High Priest's office.

"Venomous Sprite!" I kicked in his door. "High Priest Nash from The Church of The Byrds requests your immediate presence!"

But High Priest Lionel's lanky, middle-aged form continued to bump and grind about his office. Clearly, I had interrupted him during a scandalous "mystical" dance.

"Do you hear me? When High Priest Nash requests your presence *you come without question!*"

Lionel swayed casually, his dark god empowering him to soar about the room in defiance of all things Holy. He rotated his pelvis, and the urge to vomit overwhelmed me.

"High Priest Nash holds no power over me. *I'm not a member of his flock.*"

"But he's the High Priest!"

Lionel took to the ceiling and swayed about a spinning disco ball, his pouffy orange shirt billowing. "So am I."

"But you must come!" I slammed my fist on his desk in an attempt to dislodge the heretic from the ceiling.

"Tell him I'll be over when I feel like it."

"You'll come on the double!"

"So be it." Lionel sashayed toward the back wall, running his hands through his thick, black afro. "I'll entertain this sick little man."

"Make sure you do that!"

High Priest Lionel did not respond. Instead, he tipped a ceiling mounted bucket that sent a shower of gold and silver glitter streaming to the floor. It was all too much. I stormed out of his office and found myself back in that hateful sanctuary. His congregation once again stared at me. I shot their glares right back at them before crawling into The Church of The Bryds' warm bosom.

* * * *

High Priest Nash stood waiting for me by the door. Visibly anxious, he held a clump of his own hair in his hand.

"Did it work," he shrieked. "Tell me it worked! I can stop playing with my hair if it worked! *Can I stop playing with my hair? Please!*"

"You can stop, Nash. Lionel will be here any second now."

The High Priest threw down the curly mass. "I feel so foolish for over reacting. Like a bad Byrdite, I failed to place my faith in Crosby."

I gripped Nash's shoulder. "Don't worry. You've been under a lot of strain. God won't spite you – this time."

"You mean that?"

"Of course I do."

High Priest Nash looked towards the sky. "It's true. . . all teachers are at some point bested by their greatest pupil. You shall take over the reigns of power when my time on this temporal sphere ends. I must therefore open you to even deeper Mysteries."

"Do what needs to be done," I whispered in subservience.

"Please listen with ears that hear to the following allegory."

It's only the memory of your bad judgment that makes Puppy piss the floor. He doesn't want to harm you. He just wasn't reared by a perceptive owner and would be okay if, for a second, you would stop crushing his head against the wall.

Open your eyes. The Puppy yaps and yaps because Puppy is Beast, but you too must serve a Master if you are to live in THE WORLD, much in the same way that Puppy must follow certain mutually beneficial codes if he is to co-exist within THE HOUSE OF MAN. Do not strike out in malice or lift your fist to compensate for some personal anguish. Would you want your God hitting you for a selfish reason? Do onto others as you would have God do onto you. Be good stewards.

SOUND THE TRUMPETS! One true master exists. Some call him Random Madness. But Random Madness is, when looked at in the Eternal Sense, Perfected Order.

It has been said that Perfected Order lives in a single room. Like many small rooms, there's only one door leading both in and out. Legions outside ram their heads against masonry in hope of entering. In the end, the doorway must be acknowledged and sacrifices against Man's animal nature made.

We call that doorway Crosby. AMEN.

I turned from Nash, glowing with radiant knowledge, only to gasp as the doors to The Church of Lionel Richie spilled open. The whirling form of High Priest Lionel spiraled through the exit, pirouetting in the air as it traveled, and pulled a triple 360 before landing mere inches from Nash's feet.

I took the opportunity to greet the two warring Priests.

"High Priest Lionel, this is High Priest Nash. High Priest Nash, meet High Priest Lionel."

"Pagan!" Nash spat.

"Heretic!" Lionel regurgitated.

"Whoremonger!" Nash gnashed.

"Homosexual!" Lionel snarled.

I sprinted back into the church and bolted the door. From the protection of a stained glass window, I watched the two men pounce atop one another. Clothes were rent and blood was spilled. Guilt plagued me as the spectacle unfolded. Nobody in the church, myself included, seemed brave enough to stand between them. We all just kept watching.

I grimaced as Nash took a devastating uppercut to the chin in the battle's final moments. He staggered around drunkenly as the other High Priest laughed and laughed through spit and blood coated lips.

Lionel was, in fact, laughing so hard that he wasn't prepared for our High Priest's sudden recovery. One minute, Nash limped around in agony. The next, however – with his back arched and head lowered like that of a bull – he plowed into Lionel's midsection, sending both men to the ground. Nash smashed Lionel's face as he hunkered over him, and Lionel likewise pounded Nash from below.

A little later, when the two High Priests were collapsed in a single heap, representatives from both churches walked onto the porch and carried away their respective casualty.

* * * *

I stayed by Nash, sharing his recovery bed for three days. The High Priest was often delusional. I assumed this had something to do with the huge gash marring his forehead. (One parishioner said she could make out Nash's brain in the hole, but I never saw it.) He mumbled a lot during that time and chastised imaginary foes.

More than once did I feel the desire to suffocate the poor man beneath his pillow. I shook the thought from my head, not sure from whence it came and ashamed to have even conceived it.

As my vigil reached its third day, Nash arose. A halo of beatific light surrounded his scalp as the grievous head wound closed in on itself. Blood begat bone begat skin. I saw *The Divine Proclamation* unfold in a vision. Upon its parchment surface, a single maxim was rendered:

BYRDISM IS THE WORLD'S ONLY RELIGION

At that moment, a beam of pure energy swallowed his body. His glowing form levitated from the bed, and a majestic yet see-through crown descended onto his skull. On its surface, three words were emblazoned:

DIVINE POWER PREORDAINED

The High Priest smiled down upon me, his countenance turning my lips into a rapturous smile. He opened his mouth. I anticipated the holy words soon to pour forth, and a jolt of pleasure surged through my body.

"LET'S SHOW THESE LIONELS WHAT HELL IS REALLY LIKE!!!"

My eyes rolled back in ecstasy. Nash grabbed my limp hand and led me back to the sanctuary. Along the way, I felt his grip grow steadily firmer. I looked over at his hand and noticed, with some alarm, that the creases of age had vanished, along with all the small, gray hairs that once dotted his skin. Not only that, but the fist that gripped my own was now twice as large, and twice as tanned, as before.

"Nash?"

He didn't respond, but that was because he was busy mutating. Nash's flesh bubbled and undulated as though something living was buried beneath it. When his features finally settled, I gasped at the majestic, nearly naked thing that stood before me.

* * * *

The entire flock stood transfixed. Nash's sudden transformation into *Holy Avenging Angel* had stunned them all. The mane of golden hair shimmering atop his once balding head was perplexing, as was the leather thong that had replaced his holy vestments.

He looked upon us with eyes that dazzled. In a single moment's contact with God, High Priest Nash had transformed his middle-aged bulk into that of a Conan-esque warrior spirit. A majestic hawk lighted on his shoulder and became his familiar. Nash named it *Arkto-Kazan* after blessing it with the blood of his ancestors. He beat his breast and spoke with fierce authority.

Nash grunted monosyllabically: "Kill. Hurt. Pain. Wo-men."

I decided it best to wait until he came to his senses before I paid too much attention to him. He was still buzzing from his direct contact with the divine, and would most likely be in this state for quite some time.

"LEATHER FLAPS PROTECT MUSCLES IN SUN. WOMAN LIKES TO LAY *NASH-NA*. WOMAN NEEDS SAVED FROM BAD PEOPLE IN SCARY ROBES. *NASH-NA* FIND HER AND BASH SKULLS."

I forced myself to listen as Nash rambled half the day away.

"I AM NOBLE WARRIOR. I COME FROM *COO-TAH,* A PRE-HISTORIC WORLD WHERE WE HAVE *OOM-BATS* AND *WAM-PAG* WHERE WE STORE OUR *FRALA* AND *KEPETCHA* WHEN THE WINTERS ARE HARSH. I LIKE TO STIR *HERTU*

INTO MY *SLOPKN-MA* TO MAKE IT TASTE BETTER."

Something flashed in Nash's eyes. His leather thong began to fade out as his holy vestments faded in.

"Wait! Where am I?"

Overjoyed, I reached out to hug Nash. He just pushed me away.

"And where's High Priest Lionel?"

I watched, entertained, as the High Priest boxed the air around him.

"You're not fighting anymore." I laid my hands on his flailing fists. "Three days have passed."

"Three days?"

"Three days."

"I didn't just have a Divine Experience, did I?"

I nodded my response.

"Dear Crosby! I'm so embarrassed!"

"And I'm afraid your Conan-shtick was pretty weird. But that's forgivable under the circumstances."

"But I must have looked *insane!"*

"Don't waste time apologizing. Tend your flock."

High Priest Nash smiled in understanding and, with the knowledge God had just bequeathed to him, addressed his people:

"Sheep! I come to you today with a divine duty you must fulfill. Adapting may be difficult. You might even prefer death to change, *but change you must! EMBRACE HOLY AGGRESSION! FEEL IT DOWN DEEP IN YOUR SOUL! FEEL IT AND GRAB ALL THE HARD THINGS YOU CAN FIND AND TOSS THEM AT HIGH PRIEST LIONEL'S HEAD!"*

The parishioners shot from the floor and began ransacking the temple. They pulled St. Stills' remains from the reliquary and dumped them by the window. They tore apart idols and icons in search of suitable ammunition.

On my way to the window, I ripped off a segment of St. Stills' leg bone as High Priest Nash broke out the pane with his unprotected fist: "Throw the femur, *now!!!"*

I launched the projectile. It sailed through the other church's stained glass window before lodging itself in High Priest Lionel's faux afro.

"Bull's-eye!!!" Nash gave me a high-five before administering an

equally jubilant slap to each parishioner.

Impelled by his fiery touch, we took up more arms and continued to hurl projectiles at the heretic in the seconds before he ducked for cover. The sound of relics and icons pinging off his skull tickled my ears into an auditory frenzy.

Suddenly, High Priest Lionel burst outside clutching a metallic object that looked like a huge water gun. He pulled the trigger, and a liquid jet plowed through the window we stood behind.

"That's not fair," Nash shouted. "You're not supposed to retaliate! You're supposed to let us hit you!"

"Like hell I am!" Lionel unleashed yet another burst. This jet punctured the skull of Brother Hendrix – one of our most loyal parishioners – and made instant gravy of his brain.

Nash cocked his fist in the air. "You just killed one of my sheep!"

"That's one less Byrdite I've got to deal with!" Lionel laughed and proceeded to carve his initials into the side of our church with his gun.

Nash turned to me. His face spoke of desperation.

"What's wrong?"

"*What's wrong?* I'll tell you what's wrong! They have weaponry! We have bones and icons! We don't stand a chance!"

"Maybe we should stop playing their childish games."

His eyebrows arched. "What are you suggesting?"

I spent a moment in thought. "A plan to cripple them mentally."

"But how?"

"I'm not sure just yet. Maybe we should try coercing them into a temporary Peace Accord. That'll buy us time. The worst they can say is no."

"I like the way you think, Dear Traveler."

"But we don't have time to delay. Ask them now."

Nash shouted so that he might be heard outside: "We relent! Would a representative from The Church of Lionel Richie meet one of us halfway across the green? There, under mutually compatible conditions, we would like to enter into a Peace Accord with you!"

High Priest Lionel smirked then threw down his water gun: "Hah! It appears as though we've gotten the better of you, *High Whore Nash!*"

"Indeed. And we need time to rest. Please, grant us a respite."

Lionel scratched his chin. "I guess we can do that. It would only be fair – *considering how we ripped you new assholes today!"*

"You're a truly honorable man."

Lionel raced to the window. He leaned his head through the shattered pane and screamed at his followers: "Would somebody get outside and draft a peace accord? I don't exactly have all day to get this done!"

A timid woman wearing a full-body veil pushed through the door and, taking her seat by the opposing porch, sent a quill racing across parchment. High Priest Lionel slapped the pen from her hand.

"Don't write anything yet! Let's negotiate terms! We've got these bastards where we want them!"

Nash overheard this: "We're willing discuss anything with you!"

"Well, then. Are you ready to offer up one-fourth of your collections to our church?"

He gritted his teeth. "Okay."

"Are you willing to abandon that silly gear you wear and don the ritualistic garments we hold as sacred?"

"By all means. We would be delighted." Nash cursed under his breath.

"Of course, that also includes full-body veils for the women."

"I assumed as much."

"And how about cleaning the inside and outside of our church at least once a week? Can you do that, too?"

He nodded mechanically.

"But that's not all. Here's the most important condition: *I want you and your flock to worship the way we do."*

Nash scowled. "And how exactly is that?"

"With frenzied dance and utter excess!"

The High Priest gasped.

"There's a number of steps you should learn: *The Hustle*, *The Hot Chocolate*, *The Bump*. Most holy of all, however, is the act of *Pelvic Rotation*. You must master this first."

"*Pelvic rotation!* That's strictly forbidden!"

Lionel did not pause. "All dances, however, are booty-shakin' fun."

"What is this *booty* of which you speak?"

With both hands, he grabbed hold of his own rump. "I'm talking about *this*, baby."

"Don't you understand! The Dark Master can nest in ones *booty* and cause disgraceful tremors!"

Lionel briefly shook his ass.

Nash screamed: "There's an abomination in your pants!"

The other High Priest ignored him. "We also hold weekly orgies. Communication with the divine is best achieved through the abandonment of inhibition. This is also the only day women are allowed out of their veils. They are to don glittering bras and panties instead. This is how *we* do things, so you must do likewise."

"We *cannot* do likewise! Our God sets standards and limits! If we do not obey them, we fall short of His Glory!"

"Then no Peace Accord."

"But–"

"No *buts*. During the orgies, you are to partake in *The Triune Sacrament* of Alcohol, Cocaine, and Speed. This Sacrament obliterates pain. Pleasure, however, is elevated beyond comprehension. Of course, you don't have to wait until *Orgy Day* to take it. I'm pretty high right now."

"No! We must *expand* our consciousness, not plow it under with hedonistic drugs!"

"Obliteration is the key!"

"Expansion!"

"Obliteration!"

Nash turned to me with a huff. "I wasn't expecting this at all! Should we risk compromising *everything?"*

I nodded. "It's the only way."

"But what if–"

"It'll never come to that. Trust me"

Nash addressed Lionel, though he didn't sound totally convinced: "Your terms are. . . agreeable."

Lionel smiled. "Are you sure? I forgot to tell you we're polytheists."

"Polytheists! No!"

"I'm afraid so. We worship Lionel Richie *and* the relics he left behind. Everything he touched is invested with all the properties of Godhood."

Nash cringed.

"And you'll also be required to destroy that horrible song, of course. It practically makes my ears bleed. Besides, it's time you people adopted something with a little more soul – namely *Dancin' on the Ceiling*. That's part and parcel of the bargain, too.

"Break the *discus!"* Nash slammed his hand against the windowpane. "*Never!* It is Holy and billions of years old! We will *not* replace it with your debauched melody!"

"Remember, you're not in the position to haggle. *I am.*"

Nash sank against the wall. "You're right. Sure. Whatever. We'll break the *discus*. Just give us another week to enjoy it, *please.*"

Lionel considered the option. "I'll be merciful. Just as long as you accept these conditions in full. You *will* accept them, right?"

"Yes. Just draw up the Peace Accord. Get it over with."

High Priest Lionel bopped the timid woman on the head. "Go ahead! Add all this stuff! What's taking you so long?"

"My hands ache."

"Sure. Whatever. Just get it done."

She offered up a hasty bow and returned to work.

Silence descended. The woman scribbled for five additional minutes. After that time, she turned to Lionel.

"Does the Peace Accord meet you approval?"

He ripped the parchment from her hand. He looked it over, humming and hawing.

"Looks like you misspelled a word or two, but what else did I expect?"

"So, is it ready?"

"It appears to be, yes."

"Can I take my leave now?"

"Go ahead. Do what you have to do."

High Priest Nash saw this gesture and ordered me to the demilitarized zone between the two churches. There, Lionel signed the document. He handed it to me, and I carried it over to The Church of the Byrds.

"For you, Nash."

He took the paper from my hands, scrawled his signature with so much force that the paper ripped, and returned the parchment to me. "This had better work."

I bowed to Nash before giving the accord to Lionel. He shook my hand – squeezing it quite hard – and, without saying a word, retired to his temple.

* * * *

Back in the temple, High Priest Nash paced the floor and muttered to himself.

I attempted to offer solace: "Sit down, Nash. No need to be

so restless. It's disturbing the congregation."

He glared: *"No need?* We now owe the Lionels one-fourth of our collections! I'm not even going to mention those other conditions! You had better come up with one great plan!"

"*Me*? But don't you think we should all share the burden?"

Nash huffed. "And how do you propose we do that?"

"You guys really love the sixties, right?"

"Excuse me?"

"I guess you have another name for it. What *do* you call the time we're trying to emulate?"

"Oh, now I see! *The Holy Tome* calls it THE HOUR OF FLOWERS AND WONDER."

"Well, the *wing-children* who lived during THE HOUR OF FLOWERS AND WONDER really dug this stuff called Lysergic Acid. Are you familiar with it?"

"No."

"It's a psychotropic chemical."

Nash furrowed his brows. "You mean like the stuff that's in the *Xtra-Sacred Wafers?"*

"I didn't know we had *Xtra-Sacred Wafers."*

"We do. But they are only to be used on August 15th. That's the New Year. *The Holy Tome* says it commemorates the PINESTORK festival."

"I think you mean WOODSTOCK."

"No, I mean PINESTORK. I refuse to argue with *The Holy Tome."*

"Whatever. Just tell me the purpose these *Xtra-Sacred Wafers* serve."

"Well, first we are to don ritualistic garments: *The Floppy Shoes of Truth*, *The Red Nose of Understanding*, *the Polka–"*

"Wait, Nash. That sounds like stuff clowns would wear."

"What are *clowns?"*

"Forget it. And skip the ritual part, too. Just tell me the effect these wafers have on the congregation."

"They unveil the path our church is to follow for the next 365 days."

"That's good, because I think we need a path *really bad* right now."

The High Priest gasped. "But it's not August 15th!"

I sighed. "What's the punishment for early ingestion of a *Xtra-*

Sacred Wafer?"

"There isn't any. *But it still shouldn't be done!* Great dangers are involved! *Xtra-Sacred Wafers* were never meant to be eaten like candy!"

"I understand this, believe me. But do you really want to offer up one-fourth of your collections to those people?"

"No."

'Then we have no other choice."

High Priest Nash ran his fingers through his hair. "I'll have to supplicate myself and see what Crosby has to say. His word shall be final."

"Then do so. But make it quick."

He bent his head in prayer. His lips trembled, and he mumbled words in a language I could not understand. A few minutes later, he raised his head.

"And what did Crosby tell you?"

"He says he understands given the circumstances, but I still feel wary about this."

"*Don't*. Get the wafers."

Nash drew in a deep breath and walked over to *The Holy Cupboard*. He pulled out a box marked *Xtra-Sacred Wafers*. The parishioners saw this and gathered in circle formation on the floor. They obviously knew the drill.

"Please hold this wafer under your tongue for at least thirty minutes," Nash instructed as he handed a wafer to each of us.

I accepted the offering, then bowed my head in the spirit of inner contemplation. The entire congregation, High Priest included, did the same as we awaited the wafer's forthcoming effect. About thirty minutes lat–

(Holy Moley! I think it's happening now! Pink gorillas and marzipan memories! Washing machine mother's daydream!)

At first, there was no plan in sight. Just random neuron firing. Then crazy fractal patterns started swirling about our eyes and the room in general. Often, they coalesced into vaguely organic shapes only to shatter into a million tiny fragments. Sometimes we – it was difficult to think in terms of "I" at that point – looked up only to see a sedentary object pulse with vibrant life. More than once did we feel the need to hug this inexplicably radiant thing. It was as though we were experiencing the world and all things in it for the first time.

Soon afterward, extreme lucidity descended upon us. The running commentary in our heads ceased and was replaced by one-on-one telepathy. Finally, after eight hours, the plan for the ultimate defamation of the Lionel's temple became a reality without so much as a single word being spoken.

* * * *

I opened my eyes as my being slid back into its fleshy casing. Casting my gaze across the room, I saw how *Standard Human Consciousness* had returned to all Byrdities simultaneously. We drew in deep breaths. Then we broke our lotus positions so our bodies might sprawl along the floor.

A parishioner gasped: "That was one hell of a trip, man!"

Nash scowled.

"It's wasn't a *trip*, Brother Joplin. It was a sacrament!"

Timidly: "Are you going to punish me now?"

He thought for a moment. "No, not this time. We've shared a vision and now must conceptualize."

Brother Joplin sighed with relief.

"Before I begin, I must – with my newly returned *Standard Human Consciousness* – know whether or not we shared the same experience. In one voice, tell me the main ingredient of *Crosby's Divine Plan.*"

"Pig guts," we replied.

"Yes, that is correct."

"But what does Crosby want us to make of such disgusting things?"

"He doesn't want us to make anything of them. He wants us to use them to defile the Lionel's temple."

"For Crosby's sake, where do we get guts?"

"Already arranged." Nash arose and twenty buckets, stretching out in a line behind his back, were revealed.

"I didn't go to the slaughterhouse to get these. They came to me in a vision, so I took the opportunity to snatch them from the ether."

I effused: "You are truly an inspired man. I shall do anything you ask."

"Then slosh these buckets all over The Church of Lionel Richie! Crosby told me that the heathens are celebrating the Peace Accord with a fieldtrip. They've gone backpacking and will be away for five days."

"Well, hand me the bucket so I can get to work!"

"Not yet. Preparation comes first. You must fast for two days and remain in a state of constant supplication. At no time during this forty-eight hour period shall a prayer not be on your lips."

I said *yes* to this stringent demand and, come next Tuesday, was more than ready for the task.

* * * *

My fellow Byrdities bade me goodbye. Stepping outside, I drew in a deep breath to center myself. I prayed to God and I prayed to Crosby. When I realized I could delay no longer, I left the porch and crossed over into enemy territory. A cart full of pig entrails followed close behind.

I walked quietly up the steps and paused by the door. Even with my ear to the wood, I could hear nothing. Muttering yet another prayer, I crept into the chamber.

The place was empty now, so I noticed things I had once overlooked. Before, I imagined the place was merely unfinished. Now, I realized the Lionels held no regard for either pews or prayer mats. The entire temple was nothing more than one big dance hall with a pulpit. A bar even stood in the corner, though it remained only half-stocked. *Blasphemy*. I could only imagine the gyrations and thrustings that occurred in this Place of Darkness.

I moved toward the altar, my footsteps loud. I cringed, hoping the Lionels had not left anyone behind as a safeguard. Then I chastised myself for even considering that a Lionel might have the planning ability of a Crosbitie.

Looking around, I found myself gazing too long at the statuary lining the altar.

(So pure.)

I tried to advert my gaze, but my eyes were fixed and unresponsive. Lionel's carved face suddenly appeared so smooth, so flawless. . .

No!

. . .so beneficent and all-knowing. . .

Please God! Please Crosby!

. . .so pure and blameless.

My mind felt out of control. Outside hands were playing in my brain matter. At that moment, I realized The Church of Lionel Richie was wired, top-to-bottom, with hell-mouths broadcasting subliminal Scripture. I gritted my teeth and tried to withstand the influx of contradictory propaganda.

I had to leave as soon as possible.

But I found myself transfixed by their gaudy relics and icons of excess.

I found myself wanting to dunk my head in their holy fountain of hairspray.

I found myself kneeling by their disco ball shaped altar.

My hands rose in supplication to their horrid, skeletal deity.

My hips began to move in provocative ways.

I wanted nothing more than to dance on the ceiling while wearing bell-bottom pants.

Then I felt my *being*. I felt Byrdism rise up and save me at the pivotal moment. Forgotten Scripture flooded back in a torrent. I broke free.

Tearing down Lionel Richie's remains, I defecated on his most "sanctified" altar. I laughed at his stupid song and danced mockingly to its melody. Smiling, I imagined my corporeal bulk entombed in a mausoleum and – five centuries later – disinterred so that my bones might hang alongside St. Stills' relics in the temple. Such would be a proper reward but, to earn it, I had to make this defamation *extra special.*

I sloshed entrails on the wall and splashed fluids on the altar, making sure every square inch was covered in blood and viscera. No spot, not even the ceiling above, eluded my touch.

When I came upon a wooden rendering of Lionel Richie, I squirted pig bile into its idolatrous face. I laughed and laughed and laughed and laughed as the icon did nothing but stand in silence *like an insensate piece of wood! Ha!*

I unleashed a rainbow of guts onto the floor where The Lionels danced. Viscera impregnated varnish and stained the boards a fluorescent red that no manner of commercial cleaner could remove.

I dripped the blood of swine in their holy water and blessed it backwards. Now, the children baptized in this fountain would be cursed with two heads and a mongoloid's intellect.

I opened the Lionels' holy book and dropped an assortment of pig colons onto its time-yellowed pages. The organs squelched and bubbled. Slamming the tome shut, I officially rendered the abominable thing unclean.

To cap off the defamation, I made mockery of their symbols and connected them to form either pentagrams or swastikas. Thoughts of the returning Lionels both possessed and entertained me. Many would surely vomit at the mere sight of their defiled sanctuary.

And that was good.

* * * *

Days later, reports started filtering in. Most concerned school-aged children and old ladies who were forced to enter into psychiatric counseling due to the ghastliness of the defamation. These people could no longer go into rooms without suffering hideous flashbacks. While our Holy Mission was a resounding success, services continued unabated in The Church of Lionel Richie.

And the temple was attracting more and more followers each day.

But I had a plan, and by no means could I keep it to myself.

* * * *

"High Priest Nash!" I barged into his office. "I have much to tell you!"

He threw down a magazine he had been reading and shoved it hastily under the desk with his foot.

"Dear Traveler! I wasn't expecting you! Please, come in!"

I bowed before taking my seat.

"And to what do I owe the pleasure of your visit?"

My smile was wide. "*The Fall of the Church of Lionel Richie.*"

"Excuse me?"

"The Fall, Nash. And all we have to do is get the Lionels to converge under our roof."

The High Priest sighed. "That will be a tall order."

"Not if we offer them free food."

His fists clenched. "I thought we took care of your old ways in *The Field of Tribulation!*"

"You don't understand! I'm just saying that, in order to appeal to their souls, we must first appeal to their appetites!"

"*What?* Are you're saying I should bow down to these mongrels?"

"In a way. We invite the Lionels over for a coming-together feast and–"

He gritted his teeth. "But can't you see? These heathens can *never* hold court with us! To allow them to do so would be *blasphemy!"*

"Exactly. . . but only if we go about it in the spirit of goodwill. If we work towards our own goals, however, we shall reap many rewards."

"Rewards?"

"*Converts*, of course. Sweet-talk the majority into accepting Byrdism and the rest will surely follow. What begins in *dinner* ends in *assimilation."*

"Dear Traveler, I'm sorry I didn't understand you earlier! I'll gladly inform the others."

The High Priest left me by the window. There, I watched him gather his flock and set them to work.

* * * *

Priest and parishioner alike spent the evening before the feast printing up gilded invitations. A few of us later tossed them through the windows of The Church of Lionel Richie with the aid of large rocks affixed to crème-colored envelopes.

WE'RE SO SORRY FOR CAUSING GREAT PAIN AND SUFFERING TO RAIN DOWN UPON YOU AND YOUR FLOCK FOR SEVEN GENERATIONS HENCE. WE WOULD LIKE TO ATONE WITH A FEAST! COME, BREAK BREAD WITH US AT 10:15 TOMORROW MORNING IN THE DINING HALL.

CROSBY BLESS,

HIGH PRIEST NASH (c/o <u>THE CHURCH OF THE BYRDS)</u>

We even included detailed maps that laid out how the Lionels might get to our church from their own. It was a sin to ascribe intelligence to heathens.

Minutes after the last invitation had been delivered, everyone retired to bed. The banquet needed preparing, and we all required rest before morning kitchen duty. My delegated job was the production of giblet gravy, a task I undertook with relish as soon as dawn broke the next morning.

Hours later – with sweat pouring in torrents – I exited the kitchen, gravy bowl in arm. High Priest Nash greeted me on my way out. In his hands, he held a platter of herb stuffing.

"Ah! Synchronicity," he cried. "And my, that gravy sure looks delicious!"

"Why, thank you! But your stuffing looks even better."

"Your words honor me, but please carry this platter to the Dining Hall. High Priest Lionel called. He'll be here any minute now, so I've got to find my gun in case things get ugly. I don't ever want to use it, but I must consider the safety of my flock." Nash paused. "Besides, this food should have been on the table ten minutes ago."

Entering the sanctuary, I saw a banquet table already covered with food. Nametags for each member of The Church of the Byrds and each heathen of The Church of Lionel Richie sat propped against soup dishes. I placed the stuffing on the table just as Nash opened the door.

* * * *

Nash greeted the visiting members of The Church of Lionel Richie as they breached *The Holy Threshold* with a handshake and a too-hard pat on the back.

"Nice to see you!"

"Glad you could make it!"

"Oh my, that's a lovely veil you're wearing!"

The dervishes acknowledged the High Priest with an indifferent nod and pushed their way to their half of the ceremonial dining table. Unlike the section where we sat, the Lionel's side did not have a tablecloth. It had been cut in half for this very occasion. Our side came replete with golden flatware and fine china. Theirs had soiled chopsticks and tin bowls. Shimmering crystal encased bubbling pools of our best champagne, but the Lionels were to use crudely hewn wooden mugs to drink water collected from a drainage ditch. They scowled at their accommodations. . . but they would just have to get over it.

After the last dervish was seated, a cyclonic vortex plowed past the threshold and into the room. For nearly two minutes, it swirled around Nash as he stood by the door. Only after that time did the cyclone slow down enough for us to realize it was only High Priest Lionel engaged in one of his maddening dances.

Lionel spat: "Sorry to be late. I was busy doing important

things."

Nash said nothing. I assumed he pretended not to hear.

"May I enter your *sacred grounds* now?"

Nash glared at High Priest Lionel. "By all means. Take your seat. I'm sure you'll have no trouble finding it."

Smirking, Lionel made his way to the table. He found the tag with his name on it, affixed it to his silky orange shirt, and sat down.

Seconds later, the sound of sitars and pan flutes wafted from the church loudspeakers. Nash left *The Holy Threshold* and motioned in our direction. His gate was deliberate and regal. We Byrdities were all quite impressed with the spectacle. I turned to the Lionels and was disturbed to see them looking off in another direction. Nash paused above us all, standing until the song was over, and then took his seat by my right hand.

"We are *ONE!"* he suddenly exclaimed. "Never again shall our bond be rent asunder! This is a new epoch! No longer shall we throw rocks at or direct harsh words against our fellow man. Let this – our dining ceremony – forge a new brotherhood between warring parties. *LET THE CHURCH OF THE BYRDS AND THE CHURCH OF LIONEL RICHIE HENCEFORTH BE REBORN AS THE CHURCH OF THE RICHIE BYRDS* (*under the direct supervision and hegemony of the temple formerly known as The Church of the Byrds.*)"

We Byrdities raised our glasses in a collective toast, which the Lionels refused to acknowledge.

"Here's the parable of the mouse at the Last Supper," Nash continued. "On the last day of a Holy Man's life, his friends hosted a goodbye party. There was, unbeknownst to them, an uninvited guest in attendance – a lowly field mouse. Eating not with the others, the mouse took his nourishment by eating crumbs that fell from lips. The mouse knew not that it needed only to crawl up the Holy Man's gown and partake of his flesh and drink of his blood. Alas, the little mouse continued to forage for the rest of its sick and miserable life. I now ask: *do you see how this applies to you?"*

Those of the Church of Lionel Richie stared back soundlessly.

"Heathens too may eat at the *Holy Plate*, provided they make *The One Choice!"*

I watched with growing apprehension as the dervishes gritted their teeth.

"You don't need to convert all at once. Take your time!"

The opposing flock nodded mechanically. They were merely humoring him.

"We here at The Church of The Byrds hate the falsehood but love the heretic! You can stop by for dinner anytime. Our blessed sanctuary should be a home to both saint and grievous, repulsive reprobate. Can I get an Amen?"

All members of The Church of the Byrds lifted their glasses.

All members of The Church of Lionel Richie rustled in their seats.

"Excellent! And now we eat!" High Priest Nash shoved a turkey leg into his mouth.

Rather than reciprocate and pick up their dirty chopsticks, the dervishes whipped out a boom box, inserted an 8-Track, and cranked up a well-worn copy of Lionel Richie's *Dancing on the Ceiling*.

"What!" Nash shouted, chunks of meat rolling from his lips. "Can't you leave that song at your own church!"

He didn't understand, but I read the Lionels' body language. This was no dance. This was a *jihad*. That 8-Track was a sacred thing, an epoch old, so they'd dare play it only on special days. Terror rose in me as the Lionels' fell from their seats and twitched beneath bits of mashed potato, all the while calling the NAME OF GOD. Others mounted tables and bumped and ground to hyper-sensual war rhythms atop stuffing that Nash had so lovingly made.

"This is a *travesty!* Defile our temple no more!" Nash removed the semi-automatic from his pocket.

The Lionels did not respond.

He emptied the pistol into the air and reloaded. The entire congregation of The Church of the Byrds jumped in the wake of the blast, but members of The Church of Lionel Richie refused to stop even as plaster rained on their heads.

"For the love of God and Crosby; *leave this place!"*

The Lionels who weren't integral to the War Dance jumped up from the table and seized the throats of our female parishioners. They knocked them out of their seats and dragged all seven towards the door.

Nash's face turned red. "Don't steal our women!"

"They're not going to listen to you, Nash! Use your gun!"

His eyes widened. "No! Please don't make me do that!"

"It's your only choice! Crosby knows what they'll do to the

women!"

Nash made a series of hand gestures. Tears rolled down his face as he said: "May God smile down upon us all."

"Do it, Nash."

He closed his eyes, and let the rounds fly.

Pandemonium ensued.

Warriors from The Church of Lionel Richie were felled by Nash's bullets before their ritual War Dance could reach its climax. Our parishioners stampeded from the table, some tripping over blood spattered afros that now dotted the floor. They didn't stop until they reached the vinyl anteroom. There, the more courageous ones peeked their heads around the corner to witness the ensuing blood-bath.

In the end, six Lionels lay dead by the pot roast. The others wailed and gnashed their teeth. His shoulder grazed by a bullet, High Priest Lionel scooped up the boom box and, along with his surviving congregation, retreated hastily to his dark temple.

But I knew those savages would return for more.

* * * *

Nash stumbled away, tears streaming down his face, as the last Lionel sprinted from The Church of the Byrds. I watched, though it pained me to see a great man reduced to a shell.

Following him down the hall, I waited by his office for a few minutes before gaining the courage to enter. I walked over to Nash and laid my hand upon his shoulder. Coldness seeped into my flesh. It was as though I had offered up my embrace to a corpse.

"I'm sorry. I really thought my plan would work. How was I to know Byrdism could not penetrate their black hearts?"

"No, Dear Traveler, I don't blame you. I accept full responsibility. I should have been a better High Priest. If that were the case, I wouldn't have taken so many lives today." Nash looked down at his hands. "These are stained for an eternity. There's nothing I can do to wash the blood away. *I'm soiled.*"

"Come, Nash. There's no need to browbeat yourself."

"Kind words. But they mean nothing to me."

I sighed, unable to ignore Nash's sudden transformation. Pits and craters lined his brow. Underneath, his jowls sagged obscenely. He appeared twenty years older. Perhaps more.

"Isn't there anything that gets your mind off the pain?"

He nodded. "Sometimes I write. Did you know I kept a journal when I was younger?"

"No."

"Well, I've been writing in it again. It's the only way I can make the walls stop breathing. Would you like to see my latest entry?"

I accepted the journal. High Priest Nash crouched over my shoulder, mouthing the words as I read in hushed and respectful tones.

Welcome to MY world! My name is St. Ebenezer Nash and I'm a graduate of high school. I'm going to go to college this fall. I like to read. Sci-fi and erotic fiction, mainly. I love sitcoms. I don't have a favorite series, just favorite characters. I am ADDICTED to hopscotch. It's so much fun! My favorite foods are ice cream and chocolate cookies. I still like stuffed animals. I also like movies that feature bunnies and fawns in pivotal roles.

"Did you like the part where the horsies frolic?" Nash asked

My brows furrowed. "I don't remember reading anything about *horsies."*

A faraway look spread across his face. "That's because they were never there."

"I think stress is making you a little funny in the head."

"Yes," he agreed. "And for good reason. Did you know I received a phone call just before you walked in?"

"Who was it from?"

"An important person in our church. The man who runs the entire financial end, in fact. He's not at all pleased with my performance and is sending a representative over."

"When?"

"Right now, so you must leave. Please, before he gets here."

I bowed despite my confusion. "Honorable Nash, I bend to your whims."

He nodded perfunctorily.

"I really hope you feel better in the morning."

"I hope so, too."

I opened the office door and gasped. Before me stood a man clad in an expensive three-piece suit. In his hands, he held a black briefcase. I couldn't see his eyes because he wore such dark shades.

"Would you move out of my way." It wasn't a question.

I turned to the High Priest.

"Just do as you're told." Nash didn't even make eye contact with me.

I bowed to this strange man. He failed to return my greeting. I bade Nash goodbye as I exited his office, but did not receive a reply. My footsteps echoed hollow. It felt as though all the life had been sucked out of the room in a single gasp. It was only then that I realized how vital Nash's presence was to The Church of the Byrds.

And now that he had pulled away from us all, the void was undeniable.

* * * *

I entered my sleeping-chamber. Kneeling by my bed, I offered up my nightly prayer. I didn't set the alarm before I slipped beneath the covers, but it wasn't because I was lazy. I knew I would get out of bed in time for the morning service. The hours were imprinted on my biological clock so deeply that their presence was eternal.

I smiled at the beauty of Crosby's creation. I closed my eyes.

And the dream began.

I found myself encased in blackness on all sides. The world remained a void until a marbled floor began to grow under my feet and branch out like a living thing. The walls reared up and mounted human heads sprouted from stone as purple tapestries unfurled. The ceiling birthed itself from the summit of the newly formed walls, dropping forth a cage-encased skeleton that swung lazily on its chain.

The floor opened. Torture devices sprang up in a fountain and slid into the four corners of the room – a Judas Chair, a Whirligig, an Iron Maiden, a Chair of Spikes. A balcony arose. Upon it, a six-piece band sat alongside their instruments. Below, a golden throne materialized. A man wearing purple pants, shirt, and cloak reclined in the crushed velvet seat. He ate grapes and talked to himself.

He mused: "I love nothing more than to use my implements to disembowel the citizenry. It's such fun. I don't even need a reason."

"Excuse me, sir?"

The man turned around, and I got a better look at him. He was of average size, though slightly underweight. His face was utterly common and looked similar to a million others I had seen. Nothing distinguished. Nothing out of the ordinary. No marks or scars. I was quite certain I recognized his face.

"Wait. Weren't you the same man who used to live in that

little apartment?"

"What little apartment? All I see before me is gold and splendor. Nothing little here."

"I'm talking about the place with the tile floors and cinderblock walls. You once lived there."

"I really don't know to whom you're referring. That man must be dead."

"He looked just like you."

"But that doesn't make him me, now does it?"

"I guess not."

"Did he seem to possess great power?"

"No."

"Did he seem to have the world under his thumb?"

"Not really."

"Then this man cannot possibly be me. I don't know how you could confuse the two of us." The man brought a set of golden tongs from behind his back. "I really should use these on you."

"But I've done nothing wrong."

"That matters little."

"And I'm human."

"I'm afraid that doesn't matter at all."

I took a few steps back. "I don't think you're a very nice man. Good thing you're only a dream."

The man laughed. "If this is all a dream, I'm sure as hell enjoying it. May I never awaken!"

"You're crazy. I–"

Before I could finish, the door nearest to the Judas Chair swung open. A woman dressed like Salome danced through the chamber, dropping veils along the way. Her belly and ass gyrated as the band on the balcony struck up an Arabian melody.

"Ah! It must be 5:30!"

The woman ground her hips and thrust her pubic region until all her veils lay on the floor. The man's penis grew beneath his purple pants. When the band finally stopped, she knelt by the throne, unzipped his trousers, and commenced fellatio.

Panting: "Have you ever had it this good?"

I said nothing.

The man lost himself in an extremely loud orgasm. He exhaled deeply, then pushed the woman to the ground. The door again swung open. This time, two stocky, armor-clad guards motioned to the throne.

One asked: "And what manner of execution might you prefer today?"

He considered his options. "The prospect of garroting intrigues me."

The guards said nothing more. They simply picked the woman up and carried her body, kicking and screaming, from the chamber.

The man called out: "Film the proceedings and drop the tape at my throne by no later than 8! And kill yourselves when you're finished doing that! Knives to the gut both ways!"

He turned to me and noted my horror.

"I'm sorry about all that murder stuff. Some of my weaker stomached guests can't take it, but dealing out punishment is part of my job. And here's the truth – *I rather like it.*"

"Are you really going to have those people killed?"

The man popped a grape into his mouth. "Naturally. I do it everyday. Sometimes I even hold raffles. Whoever holds the right number wins, so to speak."

"But you can't be serious!"

"Enough already! What's done is done! Let's talk about something else. The previous topic seems to have disturbed you. Care for a change?"

I nodded.

"Then tell me what you think about my palace? Does it suit your taste?"

"The torture devices make me uncomfortable."

The man laughed. "And tell me, do you like my royal garments and purple cloak?"

"I guess so."

He smiled. "And could you picture yourself wearing them?"

"I don't know."

He once again flashed his golden tongs. "I think you should make up your mind."

"In that case, yes."

Removing the cloak from his back: "Then feel free to try it on, but don't forget to make your first proclamation."

My body tingled as I slid the cloak over my shoulders. It felt as though the fabric was fusing with my skin. My thought processes warped. Desire and need flooded over me in a deluge. I turned to look into a full-length mirror hanging from the wall and was enamored by just how regal I appeared.

The man goaded me: "Do it now!"

"I proclaim that we decimate ethnic schools to build Swedish spas!"

"Again!" It was an order.

"Destroy the children! Because they are happy when we are not!"

"And how will you appease the citizenry?"

"We will have circuses! Circuses to please the masses! The lions await!"

"Very good! You impress me. Now remove the cloak and hand it back."

I wrapped my arms around the garment. "Never!"

The man sat back, chuckling. "*Wow*. Nobody's taken that tone with me in a while. You must really like my cloak."

"I sure do. *So back off!"*

"Don't get ahead of yourself. I'm the one who holds the power here. You hold an illusion." He paused. "And I'd also suggest that you keep my little toy in mind. I like you, but I enjoy using it more."

I huffed and puffed, but was silenced as the man made clicking noises with his tongs. Cursing under my breath, I slipped the garment from my shoulders and winced. It felt like I was removing my own skin. My brain ceased swirling at that moment, and I vaguely recalled saying something about Swedish spas and circuses.

The man grinned broadly. "My cloak provides a most singular sensation, does it not?"

"I'm too confused to know what to think."

"But you sounded pretty sure about those Swedish spas. Just imagine how comfy they would be. You could soak for hours."

"So, I did say something about spas."

"Did you ever! Your passion stimulated me!"

"I guess I got caught up in the moment. That's all. Your robe had an effect on me."

"Interesting. Would you wear it again if I offered it to you?"

"I'm not too sure about that."

"What if I let you keep it? What if I let you wear it *forever?"*

"Sorry, but I'm still not sure."

The man slammed his fist down on the throne's armrest. "Then to hell with you! I demand *certainty!* Either you're in the club or you're out of the club. There're no two ways about it!"

"In that case, I'm out."

"So be it. I couldn't care less."

At moment, the floor reopened and swallowed both the man and his throne. The torture devices slid from their corners, flying headlong into the vortex. The balcony folded like an accordion; the walls and floor did likewise. Only darkness remained.

I dreamt no more that night.

PART IV:

HERR FRAKNOW

BY MORNING SERVICES, the dream was a fading memory. I felt refreshed. Even the parishioners of The Church of The Byrds seemed to have calmed down as the last Lionel corpse was finally carted away. I took my place out front and looked to my left. Immediately, I realized today would be a special day. The higher-ups had allowed Bobby to leave the clinic and join me by *The Holy Song-Playing Device*. I had forgotten that my old friend even existed, but was glad to see him nonetheless.

I smiled at Bobby's insensate face and turned back to *The Holy Song-Playing Device*. The compulsion to start the *discus* tugged at me, but I could not do so until the High Priest gave the order, and Nash wasn't even in the temple.

Five minutes passed. Then ten. Later twenty.

My fingers twitched and my feet tapped the floor, seemingly on their own volition. If he failed to show up, I'd spend the entire day just thinking how much I needed to touch the *bow-hook* to the *discus*.

But I forced myself to remain calm. I knew Nash would never let his sheep down. This was the first time he had been late in the six months I'd been at The Church of The Byrds. I couldn't fault him for this one minor indiscretion.

An hour later, however, my sanity had reached its breaking point. Nash was nowhere to be seen. I decided to send someone out to look for him, and chose the Byrdite closest to me for the job.

"Would you please go to Nash's office!" I gripped the man's love-beads with fists tightly clenched. "Would you try to find our High Priest! *For the love of God!*"

The man nodded before scampering away. I turned to the remainder of the congregation. They squirmed in their seats and gnawed at their nails. If something didn't happen and happen soon, all hell could quite possibly break loose. I mumbled a quick prayer and waited for the man to come back and tell me something – *anything* – about Nash.

Minutes later, he returned. His face alone told me the news

wouldn't be good.

"Did you find him? Oh God, tell me you found him!"

"I'm sorry, man. I looked everywhere. Maybe he's off on his own trip."

My nerves rattled. I had no idea what to do. I was actively contemplating suicide when from out of the vinyl encrusted anteroom emerged a young priest clad in Nash's vestments. He ascended the pulpit and opened *The Holy Tome*.

"I'm sorry to report that I'll be taking over for High Priest Nash this fine morning. He had to go away. *Unexpectedly*. In his absence, I have been ordered to make the following proclamation: *From now on – when writing – we refer to our church exclusively in all-caps. Those who do not follow this edict will be put to death. Your thoughts will be monitored to ensure proper all-caps visualization. Those who are not criminals have no reason to fear this new edict."*

I turned to Bobby. "That doesn't sound like something Nash would say."

Bobby, however, said nothing, though he did piss his pants. Disgusted, I scooted my seat back a bit.

"And anyone who has dealings – both public and private – with the followers of The Church of Lionel Richie will be put to death. As will those who, from this point on, capitalize the church of lionel richie in any form of writing. This includes personal correspondence."

I was dumbstruck. I missed the Officiating Priest's order to start the *discus* spinning. He made a second angry gesture before I sat the *stylus* down on *vinyl*. The soothing tones of *Turn, Turn, Turn* soon wafted through the chamber.

Instead of falling silent in rapturous meditation, the Officiating Priest pounded the podium and shouted to the rafters. I wondered if he knew *Turn, Turn, Turn* was only to be played during either dancing or prayer.

"As foretold in the chapter entitled *Peace-Love-Not-War*, The Travelers have returned! And now the one named BOBBY must be sacrificed to placate the wrath of *That Which Controls All Creation With the Iron Fist of Indifference!"*

The Officiating Priest stepped from the altar, mumbling random words in Latin.

"Huh?" Bobby gasped as Nash's pill finally surrendered its

hold. Such was the first spark of intelligence I had seen in him in months. Unfortunately, it was also his last.

The Officiating Priest did not respond to Bobby's slurping query. Instead, he sent the machete sailing in a lethal arch that lopped off my friend's head. The ceremonial blade glistened; the congregation cheered. The Officiating Priest bowed in prayer as the Holy Custodian took care of the mess.

I wiped a gout of blood from my face. "You just killed Bobby!"

He smiled serenely. "Dear Traveler, I was merely acting in accordance with *The Dictates of The Spirit.*"

"No you weren't!"

The Officiating Priest bent down over the holy book and read from its pages:

> *Yea, it is said that when the hour of dancing is through*
> *The Sheep shall rise to greet The Travelers*
> *and, when the time is ripe, slice the head from the one*
> *called Bobby so* That Which Controls All Creation
> With the Iron Fist of Indifference *might smile*
> *down upon all the children for an extra fortnight.*

"So you see how I merely fulfilled the will of *That Which Controls All Creation With the Iron Fist of Indifference.*"

"I haven't even heard of that deity!" I ripped the tome from the Officiating Priest's hands. Looking down, I saw how the text had been written on a post-it note and affixed to a header entitled *Peace-Love-Not-War.*

"Somebody planted that! Can't you see it's handwritten?"

"It's not my place to argue with *The Holy Tome.*"

"I would very much like to hear what the High Priest might say when he gets back!"

"The High Priest won't be coming back."

"What!"

"The *Uber Elders* in *The Holy City* replaced him with Herr Fraknow – Ex-Chief of The Department of Money Management for THE CHURCH OF THE BYRDS. Since the promotion, his new title has been Herr Fraknow, *Godvernor.*"

"Godvernor?"

"Yes."

"I demand to see this man and I demand to see him *now!*"

The Officiating Priest bowed. "As you wish, Dear Traveler*."*

I followed the man who had murdered Bobby until we stopped by a water fountain.

"Here's Herr Fraknow's door. I am forbidden to go any further."

"But High Priest Nash never forbade anyone from entering *his* office."

The Officiating Priest did not hear. He scurried away, bowing repeatedly as he ran.

I opened the door.

* * * *

Herr Fraknow's suite was situated across from High Priest Nash's old one, but the similarities ended there.

While Nash's office had exuded simplicity and order, Herr Fraknow's stank of corporate splendor and excess. Leather chairs sat atop antique Persian rugs. A massive photograph of Herr Fraknow astride a white stallion hung in place of Crosby's picture. The wall it rested against was once a chipped and motley white. Now, however, it was covered with expensive hardwood paneling. The ceiling had been raised three or four feet and sleek tracklighting installed.

I turned back to the desk. A blonde secretary sporting a red, cleavage-revealing dress poured coffee into a cup emblazoned with a huge dollar sign. Herr Fraknow slapped her on the ass and she bent her head in gratitude. The muscle-bound men who flanked his mahogany desk, guns drawn, did likewise. They, however, did not receive a bow in return. On her way back to the closet from which she operated, the woman nearly tripped over a heaping pile of pure China White sitting in the middle of the floor. Herr Fraknow laughed shrilly before turning to face me.

"Ah! Nice to meet you, Dear Traveler!" Herr Fraknow bade me enter. "Want some nose candy?"

"Now's not the time for fucking *nose candy!"*

"I really hope you're not mad about the whole beheading-your-friend thing." He removed a hundred dollar bill from his double-breasted jacket and rolled it into a tube. "Sheep must feel good about their religion. Adding ritual is a great way to ease the boredom and pain of modern life."

"I really don't care. You killed Bobby in cold blood. You put that extra passage in 'Peace-Love-Not-War' and now you're snort-

ing cocaine!"

The *Godvernor* slammed his fist on the desk. His face grew nearly as red as his hair. "To hell with High Priest Nash and everything he believed in! I'm the leader and THE CHURCH OF THE BYRDS is going to play my game! Since the announcement of my takeover alone, stocks have soared! Did they soar when Nash was around? No, of course they didn't! The High Priest just didn't have a nose for business."

"Dear Crosby," I moaned.

"Crosby Wrosby." He paused to snort another fat line up his left nostril. "Stop living in the past, man. The Church is a business – a booming business at that. I don't need to change my beliefs just because I'm presently running THE CHURCH OF THE BYRDS. Hell, I don't even know a thing about your stupid rules and regulations. *Fuck 'em.*"

"How dare you even *hint* that you hold beliefs! A man like you cleaves to nothing!"

"Oh, is that a fact?"

I stood firm. "Yes."

"You don't seem to think I'm worthy of this position. I may be young and upwardly mobile, but I'll have you know that I'm a true *Man of the Spirit*. No one is more capable than I. THE CHURCH OF THE BYRDS' path to the greatness is my own."

"I think you're insane."

"Would it ease your mind if I told you how I found The Lord? Would it make you see how we're both holy men?"

"Why should I listen to a murderer?"

"It's a beautiful story, really."

"I don't think it's appropriate for–"

Herr Fraknow took that as an invitation to begin: "I was just lounging around the house one day when The Lord came to me. He knocked on the door and I answered it. To be honest, the man looked like a traveling salesman, but I saw through His disguise. I welcomed Him in and we sat around for a few minutes, chatting. Then The Lord brings out this bottle of whiskey. He chugs half of it and hands the rest to me. I drink of the fluid because I know it is the *Nectar of Life Eternal*. Six hours later, I wake up with the memories of anal penetration. I remember how blood welled around my sheets and–"

"Are you saying this man raped you!"

"*No!* By no means am I saying such a thing! I must admit that

I too once doubted what He had said, though I soon discovered my blasphemy. The Divine Angels sat by my bedside and told me it was all a bad dream. It was merely my human, sinful mind that created these foul images. The Lord would never order The Divine Angels to lie."

"Ever think that man might not be The Lord?"

"Pray tell who he might be, then?"

"Uh. . . a homosexual rapist? Just a guess."

"Heretic!" He reached over and slapped my face.

"Admit it!" I paused to rub my stinging cheek. "You're just compensating for the shame of violation!"

"Liar!"

"Come into the fold and love Crosby!"

"*I refuse to listen to you! I am Herr Fraknow! Your silly words hold no sway over me!*"

"I know you're really just a wounded doe."

"This is seditious behavior! Step into our *Confesso-Matic* so you might be cleansed!"

"But you were so close to the truth!"

"Knowing the truth won't help me attain *The Corporate Edge!* Now get in the damn *Confesso-Matic* before I get mad!"

"What will you do if I don't?"

"Alter your bio-chemical structure from the bottom up."

"Then do so. I'm sick of this charade."

He motioned to his hired thugs. Instead of ending my life where I sat, the goons grabbed me by the shoulders and pulled me from my chair. They stuffed a gag in my mouth, then proceeded to strip me down.

"Now, now. Don't want to debase him too much."

The goons acquiesced and allowed me to keep my underwear. When they were finished with me, my all-but-naked body was brought into a room adjacent to the office and tossed into the *Confesso-Matic's* holding tank. I looked up. Gas jets lined the drab tile.

"Don't worry," Herr Fraknow shouted through the glass. "We are a church and have no intention of harming our own. We're merely going to turn your brain into sauce for a few hours."

I battered my body against the glass.

"It would be best if you stopped struggling, but do go on. Have fun until the brain foam works its magic."

I turned toward the nozzles. No longer silent, they unleashed a subtle *hissssssssss.*

"It's more gas than foam, really – odorless, tasteless, and perfectly safe for the body. But for the mind," he added, "it's one hell of a skull-fuck, hence the name."

I looked down. My church-sponsored boxers had ceased being cheap underwear, transforming into an infinite pool of swirling, primal soup. I gazed into *The Center of Creation* and found it funny that this *location* had once been my crotch.

Crash. Crack. Pop.

The Sword of God rises from a stagnant pool. I see myself, clad in the garments of a noble knight, accept the offering from *The Lady of the Lake.*

<*Memory Congestion Alert*>

I saw beauty and truth. I saw childhood in one flashing, eternal moment. I saw forgotten sheds and the doggie named Brewster. I saw old washtubs in the back of grandpa's garage and bugs hiding under rocks.

<*Data Deleted*>
<*Mind-Beam Connection Re-established*>

Millions bow in my honor as I hold the sword aloft. *"Oh, thank you for agreeing to kill those huns,"* they say in a single voice. How the menfolk admire my prowess! How the womenfolk want nothing more than to lay me!

<*Memory Congestion (*Instance circa 1999*)*>
<*Buffering*>

Dandelion fluff. I remember gathering the puffy seeds and blowing them away. I remember hearing cicadas and the hum of power lines. I remember smelling chemicals from the factory. I remember love and the soul in everything. I remember joy and bliss.

<*Data Deleted*>
<*Mind-Beam Connection Re-established*>

On the battlefield, I smell blood. The odor excites me so I keep hacking and hacking until copper is the only thing I smell. I look down and see all those who had tasted *The Sword of God*. Whirling dervishes no more, they exist as piles of heaping, decayed flesh. Maggots churn and I smile.

<*Memory Congestion (*Instance circa 2002*)*>
<*Initializing Switch to Safe-Mode*>

My dad's black lunchbox. The smell of acetone. The discoloration on his pants.

<*Data Deleted*>
<*Mind-Beam Connection Re-established*>

I can even smell the vomit of the infidels wafting on a cool breeze. God himself would smile at the stench.

<*Memory Congestion (*Instance circa 2006*)*>
<*Initialization to Safe-Mode Approved*>

The abandoned van in the yard behind my grandmother's place. Inside, a plastic laminated obituary and a vase full of silk flowers. Mattresses and pillow casings thrown to the floorboard. I placed my hand on the door, my sweat discoloring old, faded paint. The print never faded away.

<*Data Deleted*>
<*Mind-Beam Connection Re-established*>

I return the sword to *The Lady of the Lake* and she gropes my package. As I undress, the gates of Valhalla open. Mighty warriors sing.

<*Memory Congestion (*Instance circa NOW*)*>

But that was the past and the past is only a memory of trends. I'm a Man now, a man who needs to accept Adult Duties. I can never be happy again so I should just reinvent the concept. Happiness is no longer playing with bugs. . . Herr Fraknow! Are you still there? What was I saying about beauty? I forgot.

<*Data Deleted*>
<*Mind-Bean Connection Re-Established*>

Herr Fraknow's voice boomed across the ether. "Never mind what you were thinking of 'beauty.' It matters little."

<*All Deletes Successful*>

Herr? Would you help me find myself? Ah. . . to hell with it all! I just wanna kill me some followers of the church of lionel richie!"

<*Shift to Graphical Interface*>

Herr Fraknow entered my mind wearing a glowing sweat-band.

"Wouldn't you just *love* to wield power? Wouldn't you just *love* to overthrow me? Imagine the possibilities. . ."

The drug – which was once on a low ebb – gripped me and, on Herr Fraknow's vocal cue, killed my brain only to resurrect it anew.

Crash. Crackle. Pop.

Suddenly – a vision.

I saw myself working as advisor for the *Godvernor's* re-election campaign. We stood alone in a backroom minutes before a televised debate. There, Herr Fraknow ventured from his practice cards to speak his mind:

"I want to hold the mindless masses accountable for their actions by demanding that they adhere to rigidly absurd ecclesiastical standards concerning thought and social behavior. I will make sure all people hold my values as supreme because they're the values of my forefathers – men who died billions of years before my nano-resurrection. Still, I know exactly what these men thought. . . *and their thoughts are my own."*

I grasped his shoulder. "Don't take this the wrong way but, as your advisor, I'd suggest you not say that in public. Sadly, you already did."

"What?"

"Don't you get it?" I gestured to a screen behind which I had concealed a number of top-ranking reporters. "You're on national TV!"

Herr Fraknow screamed. The plaster cracked. A bolt of lightning soared from Heaven and baked the former man's body into the concrete. Only flecks remained.

I blew kisses to everyone and lifted my new crown from its bejeweled case. The Pope glared at me. He was supposed to do the honors – *but fuck him.*

I looked up at the television monitors broadcasting events live as I created them. My face filled each screen, but its features were no longer my own. They belonged to the purple-cloaked man. I smiled. His power rested inside me, too.

"Line up for mandatory testing," I heard myself bellow, "for I am *THE NEW REFORMER!"*

Crash. Crackle. Pop. Bang.

My neurons started firing at a slower speed. I was able to discern Herr Fraknow's actual self apart from his fantasy, drug-induced form.

"There. Didn't that feel good? Wasn't overthrowing me fun? Unfortunately, it was only make-believe. I wouldn't be stupid enough to hold a re-election campaign."

The drug suddenly pulsed harder in my mind. The real Herr Fraknow winked out of existence and, seconds later, the ersatz, sweat-band-sporting version returned.

Rip! Bang! Kapow!

"Now, spit upon the body of High Priest Nash!"

My vision shifted. Beloved Nash now lay sprawled out on the floor. The back half of his head was gone. Torn flesh around the massive wound – stained black with gunpowder – formed a mouth. Looking at the hole filled me with great sadness.

"No!" His voice boomed from all sides. "*Hate!* You must feel *hate!* This man is part of the old order. *Spit on him!"*

I leaned over Nash's supine form and hocked up a lungful of clear mucus.

"Good. Now open your mouth!"

I looked down and once again encountered Nash's ruined face – a countenance I had once loved and exalted higher than my own. I closed my eyes, unsealed my lips, and let a loogie fly.

The second my spit touched his face, High Priest Nash popped out of existence and a big-top unfurled.

Lions, hatred blooming in their eyes, attacked bejeweled trainers. Trapeze artists smirked and laughed as those less skilled fell from perches into vats of boiling oil. Twisted and deformed clowns honked horns as a man dove into a glass of water and died on impact. The audience sat back in their seats and munched popcorn, slobbering idiots one and all.

I shot aimlessly through this world until I neared the tent's far wall. There, the tarp opened and sucked me into a shaft of solidified light so long I feared it might be endless. Ages seemed to pass before I noted the tunnel's terminus. What looked to be white ceiling tiles covered its mouth.

I closed my eyes. Death on impact had to be a sure thing. Seconds later, I crashed through the tiles and landed in a hard plastic chair inside a waiting room.

Amazed, I found myself not only alive but fully intact. I looked over my new surroundings. Such a drab yet somehow foreboding place. White walls, white tiled floors, white *everything*. The only objects in the room were two white folding chairs that sat between an almost too small door. Buzzing fluorescents provided the only sound. Their hum made me look up. Oddly, I couldn't find a hole in the ceiling I had just plowed through.

The splendor of my previous delusions was lost. I felt uncomfortable and alone. I had no idea what I was waiting for, if anything, so I just drummed my fingers on the armrest and rocked in my seat.

Time seemed to stretch out forever. Whether hours or minutes had passed, I could not say. Leaving seemed like the only option until my mind brought forth strange images of what might lie beyond the little room. Drawing in a deep breath, I arose from my seat and paced back and forth. My skin felt itchy. So much irrational fear. I closed my eyes and told myself I had nothing to worry about. This was, after all, only a waiting room.

I gained enough courage to reach for the knob, but withdrew my hand as it turned in my grasp. The door swung open to reveal a vast, almost infinite chamber. I took a few steps back as a tiny man in colorful circus regalia peered into the room and then sauntered in. He carried with him a large, manila colored file.

"Hello, my name is BernexCarl. Sorry to keep you waiting, but I had to speak with five others today."

I remembered my last day at *The Doughnut Kiosk,* fell sideways into my seat, and curled into a fetal position. My sphincter felt loose. I shrieked: "You're a circus midget!"

The man sat down in the only other chair the room had to offer. He smiled at me, and my terror increased tenfold.

"Don't worry, I'm not here to hurt you." He regarded me as I trembled. "You must not be accustomed to seeing little people."

I blathered: "No. No. No. *Too accustomed.* Not little people. Big people. Acting like little people. Sea lions in malls. *Horror.*"

The circus midget bent down and leafed through the file on his lap. "Ah, you come from the 67th epoch! That explains it!"

I quaked: "No! Nothing could explain *this! You!"*

"Yes it does, actually. Our book served as the end-time impetus for your era. I bet you saw lots of weird circus midget stuff going on. Enough to traumatize you?"

I nodded.

"Try not to think of those people. They're in *The Pit* now."

"You're really scaring me!"

"Do you want a sweet? Maybe that will make you feel better." The little man removed a napkin folded cookie from his pocket. I noticed it was white chocolate macadamia nut and reached out with trembling hands.

"I knew it was your favorite flavor. That's why I brought it along. Go on. Try it."

I took a hesitant bite. A calmness descended upon me. I looked over at the midget and no longer felt fear. In fact, I felt *love.*

"I see you like the cookie. Good. It's my own special recipe. I must say it soothes the savage beast far better than music."

"What was your name again?"

"BernexCarl."

"It's nice to meet you, BernexCarl."

"And perhaps you'd something to drink as well?"

"Sure. Thank you."

He removed a foil pouch from his other pocket, and I accepted it. A straw was glued to the back. Pulling it off, I stuck the tube through a perforated area on top. Then I tasted the drink.

"Do you like?"

I didn't know how to respond. The fluid tasted like salty broth mixed with seaweed, but I didn't want to offend the man, so I nodded ambiguously.

"What you're drinking is the juice of the orange Agodavo plant. Did you realize they're capable of joyous sexual reproduction?"

"I've never even heard of an Agodavo plant."

"Don't worry about it. Few have. Much to their disadvantage, however, since its juice tastes quite good."

"I'll be honest with you, what I drank tasted terrible."

BernexCarl nodded. "That's to be expected. It's the drug they exude that makes the drink taste so funny. It's usually filtered out. In your batch, however, it wasn't."

"*The drug!* Are you trying to poison me?"

The little man laughed. "Not at all. I just have to ask you a few questions, and I want your responses to be as truthful as possible."

"Herr Fraknow already drugged me! Now you're doing the same!"

"Herr Fraknow's drug has no effect here."

"But you didn't even ask for my permission!"

"I'm sorry, but you seemed so skittish when I first walked through the door. I didn't think you'd allow it."

"You're damn right!"

"Try to calm down. It's important to be in the right frame of mind when the juice takes effect." BernexCarl looked down at his watch. "That'll be about twenty-five seconds from now."

"But–"

"Really. It's *important*. You don't want your head to explode, now do you?"

"No, of course not."

"Then relax."

I obeyed. Leaning back in my seat, I closed my eyes. Strange arabesque patterns flittered through the darkness behind my lids. The room suddenly felt larger, as though I was surrounded by nothing but space on all sides.

"It appears you're now under the influence. Is this correct?"

I nodded.

"Good. Keep your eyes closed. Focus on the patterns you

see. I have some questions prepared. Are you ready to answer them?"

I heard the rustling of paper. "Yes."

"I'm required to read these questions exactly as they are printed. Sorry if they seem dry. I'll do my best to cover the bases quickly. To begin, have you ever blown away dandelion fluff?"

"As a kid, yes. Sometimes I still do. I got caught one time last year. It was embarrassing."

"Did you ever enjoy catching bugs in your backyard?"

"Very much so. Up until I was about thirteen."

"Did you also enjoy killing them?"

I looked down at my shoes. "Yes."

"And could you describe the method by which you dispatched them?"

"I dug a little hole in the ground and put about twenty or thirty bugs inside."

"And then?"

"I'd cover the hole with twigs laid out like a roof and put mud over them. It'd harden in the sun and make a chamber from which the insects could never escape."

"Did you ever open this crypt?"

"Yeah. After about two weeks. They were all dead by that time, of course. The hole never stank unless I put a lot of caterpillars inside. They usually turned into goo."

"I see. Now let's move on to your later life. Have you ever experienced a passion greater than the love of the self?"

"I think so. I really liked Shelia. Sometimes I thought we might be soul mates. She had a tendency to go a little crazy, though. I don't think she ever realized how much I loved her. She said I didn't show it enough."

"And have you ever experienced a hatred greater than the self?"

"Not as greatly as I've experienced love. I admit to being somewhat jealous of Bobby. His looks, his way with women, his *responsibility*. Pretty much everything about him."

"Moving on. Have you ever wondered if your neighbor's apartment was filled with recording devices and bleeping gizmos of every make and model?"

"A few times when I was stoned."

"Have you ever had visions of the forthcoming apocalypse?"

"Again, a few times when I was stoned."

"And I take it you've heard of a book entitled *The End: In Circus Midgets and Barbed Chains?"*

"Yes."

"And what was your response upon hearing the title?"

"I thought it sounded interesting."

"Please clarify, by *interesting* do you mean *seductive?"*

"Not at all."

"Good. We were right to assume you didn't belong in *The Pit*. Now listen up, this next question is very important: Have you met a strange man in your dreams?"

"Yeah. He was just some writer guy the first time around. Then he lived in a palace and was executing people left and right."

"Have you ever felt like a pawn in some cosmic game?"

"Right now I do."

"So, I take it you've at least considered the possibility that something greater than the self-constructed self might exist."

"Yes."

"Good. And have you ever entertained the notion of mass genocide?'

"You mean even for a second?"

The little man nodded.

"I'm ashamed to admit it. . . but yes. That time in the dream. When I wore a purple cloak on my back. All sorts of stuff raced through my mind."

"That's what I thought. I'm now required to read a job description. Please pay attention."

This position requires that an individual provide the stimulus necessary to bring about the closing of an Age. It is to be filled by one (1) Middle-Grounder selected from a pool of at least six (6) Middle-Grounders.

Applicants are to be transferred to the end-time of whatever epoch is deemed suitable. Transference is to occur only on the day The Gardeners and The Pit Dwellers separate in the applicant's original epoch. Observations will then be made, followed by a personal interview six (6) months after initial touchdown.

An acceptable applicant will exhibit the following qualities in his own world: A calm demeanor, a simpler than normal lifestyle, a well-hidden jealous streak, and an intrigued yet not overly zealous reaction to whatever end-time stimulus is applicable to his/her epoch.

An acceptable applicant will exhibit the following qualities in the test epoch: Initial refusal, later acceptance, and a desire for respect that gradually culminates in the once unthinkable need for absolute power.

If accepted for this position, you will be required to commit at least one (1) act of mass genocide. (While we, the Circus Midget Collective, do not condone such acts, they must nevertheless occur so as to ensure the human pageant's continuity.) You will also be required to develop a rabid, cultic following based on your name and/or image. This aspect is pre-arranged, however, and does not require action on your part.

Though acceptance of this position will forever bar you from The Garden, you will nevertheless be spared The Pit. Upon the completion of your mission, you shall enter a simulated reality of our creation. It will mirror the more positive aspects of your previous existence and will come into being exactly twenty-four (24) hours following your death in the test realm. Those who worshiped you will remain for approximately three (3) to thirty (30) years following your removal. After this time, they will be transferred to The Pit via universal plague.

Once in the simulated world, you will be required – without prior warning – to offer guidance to Middle-Grounders from all epochs. Travel will not be necessary as these sessions will always occur during sleep. No memory will remain upon your return to what you believe to be reality.

"Any questions?"

"What's all this about a garden and a pit?"

"Self explanatory, really. But let me show you."

The circus midget waved his hand. The wall before us disappeared and was replaced by a lush, verdant garden in which sentient tress sported anthropomorphic breasts. A babbling brook spoke in German. At least a dozen fawns gathered along its silver bank, lapping up water and responding – in Swedish – to the water's query. Further back, nude people of all shapes and sizes lounged on organic, mushroom-like chairs beneath a blue sun. Others walked amongst them, their strides as purposeful as their swords were awe-inspiring. Amongst it all, an amazingly large and graffiti-covered wheel rolled alongside an old and cheerfully insane woman who sang songs in some incomprehensible language.

"And here's what I mean by *Pit.*"

The garden evaporated in a red and orange mist. In what looked to be a dank, underground cave, the same big wheel rolled over a man with Jesus-like hair. He remained squished for only a few seconds. Then he was whole again, screaming. With clockwork precision, the wheel repeated the eternal process.

"Why's only one man there?"

"Because *The Pit* is unique for everybody. Just be glad you're not in Bank's position. On *The Day of Separation*, our files show you sitting right in the middle of the spectrum."

"Spectrum of what? Good and evil?"

"No, I'm referring to the range of possible reactions one might have to *The End: In Circus Midgets and Barbed Chains*. That's why we sent you to The Church of the Byrds. We had to ascertain whether or not a new location would push you closer to one side or the other."

"Did it?"

"Indeed. It pushed you so close to *The Pit* that I'm surprised you're not falling in as we speak. But that's okay. You're exactly the type of person we need to fill this position – basically good but easily corruptible."

"I think I understand now. That Mark Anders guy, he must have been a Middle-Grounder like me."

"Not quite. He was the first we ever touched. His book opened the portal to your world, and we've been active ever since."

"But it sounds like you've been around as long as creation. Mark Anders was from my age."

"Once we got a foothold in one epoch, we were able to exert influence over all seventy of them. It mattered little that his, and yours, was third from last."

"There's seventy?"

"No more. No less."

"And then what?"

"I don't know."

"I thought you knew everything."

"Everything but *that.*"

"So you know my future? Every bit of it?"

BernexCarl sighed. "I'm really tired. I already told you how many people I've seen today. Forgive me if we skip right to the contract stage."

"But what if I don't want to sign!"

"I'm afraid you won't have a choice. Either your name will be on the contract when I pick it up, or it won't. The five others came up blank. I've got one more after you – if, that is, your signature doesn't appear." He once again opened the manila folder and leafed through its contents. "I know it's in here. Give me a second."

I crossed my fingers and prayed that the little man might never find the contract. My heart sank as he ceased his rustling and brought forth a fragment of yellowed parchment paper.

"Oh, look! Here it is!" He turned the contract over so that the written side faced me. "Do you recognize this?"

I saw my signature. My mouth fell ajar. "Yes. But–"

"Whew! That's a relief! I really dreaded having to do a sixth interview."

"Listen here! I don't know how you managed–"

"And I forgot to tell you that you'll soon be meeting Malachi. Not a very pleasant man I'm afraid, but a necessary one nonetheless."

"I didn't sign–"

BernexCarl stood up and motioned to the door. "I'll be on my way now."

"No! I'm not going to stand–"

"You're a nice person at heart. I'll really miss seeing you in *The Garden*, but I'll always remember you. I'd be lying if I said creating end-time scenarios is something I enjoy, but a free agent of creation can only do what a free agent of creation does."

"What! Are you going to leave me here!"

BernexCarl paused by the open door. "Of course not. You've got an important mission to carry out. Your consciousness will be transported back in . . ." He looked down at his watch. "Three-tenths of a second."

And then I was gone.

* * * *

When I woke up, Herr Fraknow stood above me, smiling. I looked down at myself and found my body clothed in a dashing and well-fitted suit of armor. So shiny. It even featured a jewel-studded codpiece and a helmet with a large feather that dangled from the top. I looked majestic and ready for the battlefield. Rubbing away sleep, I motioned to rise.

"I see our Knight-Traveler is ready for *The Grand Battle*. We're counting on you to pull us through."

I shambled towards him and extended my hand in greeting.

"It*is*an*honor*to*see*you*again*I*will*not*let*you*down*sir."

"Herr," he corrected.

"YES*HERR*SIR!!!"

Herr Fraknow patted my back. "I knew the potential was there. And it only took sixteen hours to drag it out of you."

"WHEN*MAYISERVE*YOU?"

"Whenever you want, Dear Knight-Traveler. First, however, we must make sure the brain foam has reached its full potential. Tell me, did you like its sweet, chocolaty taste?"

"BETTER*THAN*THE*MILKSHAKESIHAD*AS*A*KID."

"Good. Good. And are you ready to fight *The Scourge?*"

"YES."

"And are you fully convinced that God hates the followers of lionel richie and desires nothing more than their fiery deaths?"

"YES."

"And are you fully convinced that Byrdism is the only true religion? Can you also see how it now operates under my exclusive dictate?"

"YES?"

"Is that a 'yes' on both counts?"

"YES."

"And are you fully prepared to die for that which you hold dear?"

"YES."

"And will you die *now* if I ask you to do so?"

"YES."

"Do you accept the word of Herr Fraknow as gospel?"

"YES."

"Do you reject the previous gospel muttered by the false teacher known as High Priest Ebenezer Nash?"

"YES."

"Here's your personalized *Holy Tome.* Clutch it as you send infidel souls to Hell. Give a *Hail Crosby* each time you slay a heathen. Do you believe this to be your destiny?"

"YES."

"Yes what?"

"YES*HERR*SIR!!!"

"Good. Now say the following after me: *I will do my duty as Head Traveler. I shall run out on the battlefield and gut mine enemy from groin to sternum!"*

"I*WILL*DO*MY*DUTY*AS*HEAD*TRAVELER*I*SHALL* RUN*OUT*ON*THE*BATTLEFIELD*AND*GUT*MINE*ENEMY*FROM* GROIN*TO*STERNUM!"

A look of rapture spread across Herr Fraknow's face. "Now, follow me to the gun closet."

I did so without hesitation.

Once inside, he pulled out a fine specimen, removing it from an anointed gun-rack molded into the shape of Crosby's head.

"I think this one has some real potential." Herr Fraknow placed the gun in my hands.

"YEAH*IT*DOES!" I fidgeted with the firearm's shaft.

"Save a little of that passion for the infidels!"

"OKAY*SIR*I*MEAN*HERR!"

"And you'll need some bayonets, just for style-points, of course."

"I'LL*GLADLY*TAKE*WHAT*YOU*OFFER*ME*SIR!"*

"And, if your mission is a success, you can wear whatever underwear you choose. Don't think I haven't heard about your little run in with the late High Priest Nash. Wouldn't you like the power to decide what undergarment to wear?"

"YES*HERR*SIR!"

"Then so be it! Destroy the lionel richie menace and I'll make sure this nonsensical underpants law is stricken for all time!"

I exploded from Herr Fraknow's office, all but oblivious to the shrieks of delight accompanying my ascent to the battlefield. I ran out the main exit, bolted across the street, and stopped just outside the church of lionel richie. Noting the sounds of music and dancing issuing from the temple, I laughed. This was the perfect time. Get 'em while they're worshiping. I mumbled a verse from Scripture and kicked in the door.

The parishioners ceased their erotic flailing. They turned in my direction only to get a face full of hot steel.

"EAT*LEAD*FUCKERS!" I let the rounds fly.

High Priest Lionel was the first to go. He motioned for the *Super-Saturator* tucked in his pants, but my bullets were too fast. He died with his finger frozen around the trigger, and a six-inch smoldering gash around his heart.

Following the death of their leader, the followers of the church of lionel richie gyrated madly about the temple. Cries of lamentation tickled my ears. Panic sat in, and I took advantage of the moment by fully dispersing my ammo-clip.

Those who made it past the first round of saturation hid behind the bar. I simply found my victims and cut them down where they lay, thrusting them headlong into the gaping hell-mouth that awaited those who denied *The Gospel of Crosby* because

THE DICTATES OF THE CHURCH OF THE BYRDS
ARE IRON CLAD.

I kept pulling the trigger but, at that instant, my vision faded. Herr Fraknow's brain foam reached a new high, and I had to go wherever it took me.

Pull. Rip. Burn.

I ran through the stinking battlefield that had once been a holy sanctuary. I unleashed a terrifying war-whoop. Pouncing atop the villains, I ran my bayonet through their intestines. Internal organs coated my arms in wet profusion, and I lapped at their sticky and steamy sweetness with my tongue. I felt just like a kitten, nursing on the breast of a mama cat.

"HAILCROSBYHAILCROSBYHAILCROSBY!" I screamed as my last foe died and rapidly decomposed at my feet. Triumphant, I buried my heel into the fallen ones and planted a flag atop their fetid bulk.

Crack. Wham. Bang.

I came to and saw blood loss. I saw pain and death. I saw little children blown apart in their mother's arms. I saw decay stain the ground in a Rorschach pattern. I smelled gunpowder and tasted smoke in the air. I felt the void of countless stilled hearts.

I vomited. My soul blackened.

"WHAT HAVE I DONE!!!"

The door swung open behind me. Herr Fraknow sprinted into the church clutching a hypodermic syringe. The needle slipped into my neck before I had time to react.

Whip! Pop! Garzipppp!

NOW I WEAR MY TRIUMPHANT HEADGEAR THROUGH THE ARMIES OF THE NIGHT. I MOUNT NOBLE STALLIONS AND AWAIT DAWN'S FIRST RAY. I KILL THE ENEMY BEFORE I SEE THE WHITES OF THEIR EYES.

Through the brain foam, I heard Herr Fraknow command me into motion. My legs followed the order without input from my brain.

"We're going to honor your heroic deed. Please, accompany me back to our church."

"OKAY!"

"The parishioners will all love you."

"OKAY!"

"And you're no longer upset about killing all those people, right?

"OKAY!"

"Good, because there's only time for smiles."

"OKAY!"

I opened the door; confetti fell on my head from a bucket rigged above. One of Herr Fraknow's goons, now stationed by the threshold, pinned a huge *Medal of Valor* to my shirt. The people inside cheered and hollered as this honor was bestowed upon me. Many held hastily constructed banners bearing my name, but I couldn't care less because I was a *Holy Warrior* – above and beyond their petty concerns. *Fuck 'em. Fuck 'em all.*

"Isn't this wonderful!" Herr Fraknow gushed. "History shall always remember your name!"

"SURE! WHATEVER!"

Hands tugged at me as women planted kisses on my cheek. Herr Fraknow beat them away.

"Stand back, people! Give our hero some room!" The organic wall parted and Herr Fraknow and I walked amongst the congregation. People laid offerings at my feet as I passed. Flowers, incense, first-born children: I just crushed everything beneath my shoes and kept walking.

"Follow us to the basement level! A ceremony is about to take place!" Herr Fraknow paused. Bending down, he whispered in my ear. "This will be very good for PR, trust me."

"OKAY!"

We passed through hall upon hall. The parishioners followed close behind, singing songs. Herr Fraknow finally stopped and ordered us all down a rickety set of wrought-iron steps leading into a subterranean labyrinth. The cold bit at my skin as I entered the winding corridor. We walked for a few minutes until the hallway widened. Herr Fraknow then pointed to a closed door and the parishioner in front opened it.

In the room, corpses rested in stone vaults whose lids bore the bas relief of their likenesses. A new crypt lay open, a closed coffin sitting by its side.

"We have come here today to bid farewell to our beloved High Priest Nash."

A parishioner sobbed. "High Priest Nash is dead?"

"I'm afraid so. But don't worry because, thank God, he's far away from here."

So much crying echoed through the burial chamber, but I just stood there, a sloppy grin on my face. Runners of drool cascaded down my chin. I didn't bother to wipe them up.

"Our hero will now give benediction. It is only fitting that one so great should give tribute to the fallen."

I drew in a deep breath and began:

"OKAY! SURE! WHATEVER! OKAY!"

Herr Fraknow placed his hand on my shoulder and whispered: "I think I'll take over."

"SURE!"

His voice boomed: "Let Nash's benediction simply be this: He loved his flock like he loved all sheep." Herr Fraknow paused to distribute the tiny leaflets he had removed from his pocket. "These sheets contain lyrics to *The Holy Godvernmental Anthem*. Please sing the verses as the burial takes place."

The parishioners stared down at the sheets and lifted their voices – a mournful choir.

"Now, Dear Hero, please help me with the sarcophagus."

I made a series of meaningless hand gestures and picked up the left half of High Priest Nash's coffin. Herr Fraknow dealt with the right. Once it rested on the lid, the *Godvernor* and I shoved the box into the crypt where it landed on its side. I wasted no time. I slammed the lid down over Nash's coffin so hard that stone cracked.

"And now, the hero and I shall join you all in song!"

I happily sang *The Holy Godvermental Anthem,* substituting *okay* and *whatever* for each word I encountered. The melody enraptured me to such a degree that I felt compelled to rip the *Medal of Valor* from my chest and brandish it in the air. My eyes gleamed. I smiled widely. I rammed the huge needle into Herr Fraknow's back and ground it in until steel broke through bone.

Herr Fraknow flailed madly. His arms weren't long enough to remove the medal from his back. I giggled as a blood bubble formed over his mouth, but didn't really begin laughing until he made all those funny gurgling sounds with his throat.

I then decided he was moving too much. Pulling the medal from his back, I repeated the process over and over again.

"OKAY!"

Stab.

"SURE!"

Stab.

"WHATEVER!"

Stab.

"OKAY!"

Stab.

Herr Fraknow finally fell to the floor. His finger clutched at the air and his chest heaved in the seconds before he expired.

And the crowd just stood there as I clutched the blood-soaked *Medal of Valor*.

* * * *

A week later, I stood by the pulpit dressed in Nash's vestments. (I had dispatched of the new priest just the day before. Besides, I looked better wearing the robes than he had.) On my clothes, the bloodstained *Medal of Valor* hung heavy.

The more psychedelic effects of Herr Fraknow's brain foam had worn off, too. I was back, only *better*. The drug had released my hang-ups and birthed a self-actualized man. Not even Herr Fraknow's guards bothered me. This was confusing at first. I was sure they would seek retribution, but nothing ever happened. I guess their loyalty ended the moment I ripped the man from his seat of power.

I took a big gulp from the cognac bottle I brought along for the ride. It was my first drink from the second fifth-bottle of the day. Wiping my lips, I began the morning service.

"Four score and seven flapjack pancakes ago, zombies ate make-up crème pies while walking sideways up the stairs."

The congregation sat enraptured. They knew better than to question me, especially when I was drunk.

"And purple wolves laid with pink bunnies as the sun turned black and stars fell from the heavens."

The world began to sway as though it had slipped from its axis. I saw double, then triple, then quadruple. My stomach lurched.

"Together, they partook of the orange and green tomatoes their God had bequeathed onto them."

I slipped from the podium and fell to the floor. Mumbling obscenities, I struggled to pick myself up. I did not, however, let this little setback interfere with my sermon.

"And the tomatoes did present their brains with the most glorious of visions! Pork sandwiches for all!"

I clutched the podium. I alternately felt both conscious and unconscious. My stomach stopped lurching and started to spasm. Vomit poured from my mouth in a geyser, splattering both the pulpit and the parishioner who sat closest to me.

I wiped the vomit from my chin: "Can I get an amen!"

The crowd raised their voices and lifted their hands. They gyrated in their seats and then collapsed to the floor where they flapped like fish. It felt so good to have them under my control.

"That's not sufficient! Do it *harder!"*

The people on the floor quaked as though suddenly stricken with epilepsy. I heard the sound of a few dozen heads beating rhythmically against the concrete floor.

"Harder!"

It looked like the room had been wired with 10,000 volts of electricity. One parishioner flapped so hard that his head cracked open and his brain shot out across the room. I was so proud of him.

"Okay people! That's enough! You all did *really good!* Now it's time to go out into the yard and do some *calisthenics!"* I staggered down from the pulpit. "Come on! Follow me outside!"

The congregation responded to my vocal cue and rose from the floor. They amassed in a single file line before exiting the temple. I sat on the steps as they gathered before me in the yard.

"Now run around the church lawn sixty times." I took another gulp of cognac. *"Really fast."*

They kept up a nice, steady pace for a few minutes. This made me chuckle. Then I noticed some people panting for breath. Others had gone so far as to stop completely. That was unacceptable.

"Pick up the pace, damn you! Run! Run! Run! *Run!"*

My parishioners did the right thing. All except for one, that is.

I scowled. "Brother Clapton! What the hell do you think you're doing?"

The man doubled over, hands clutching his knees. He looked up at me and panted: "I can't go on. I just can't."

"You know the punishment for non-compliance, but I'll give you one more chance!"

Brother Clapton continued to huff and puff. His heaving fat rolls repulsed me.

"Okay! You asked for it!" I reached for the *Medal of Valor*. I had used it on Herr Fraknow, the new priest, and two random parishioners all in a single one-week period. It was my favorite means of conveying discipline.

I stood up and felt the ground slip and slide beneath my feet. Falling back, I groaned. I wanted nothing more than to punish Brother Clapton, but felt too drunk to do so.

"I'll take care of you later!" I coughed and sputtered. "For now, keep running! That means all of you!"

I crawled along the porch and pulled myself up with the aid of a door facing. I stood there, immobile for almost an hour. Only then did the world, for the most part, cease its mad spinning.

* * * *

I somehow managed to stagger into Herr Fraknow's sleeping chamber on rubbery legs. It wouldn't ordinarily have taken me more than a few minutes to get to that room from the porch. This time, however, it had taken fifteen. I kept making wrong turns and bumping into walls I thought were people.

Once inside, I closed the door behind me and leaned my weight against it. I smiled drunkenly at the luxury spread out before me. At least a few dozen servants waited in the small, and otherwise empty room situated to the left of the bar (which they were forbidden to use). Each lived for nothing more than to pander to my whims. All I had to do was ring a bell and they scampered into the chamber. And the room itself! *Massive.* A mini palace complete with inlaid flooring, track lighting, and vaulted ceilings. I never wanted for luxury. A big screen TV kept me company, as did a team of hired female dancers. They shook their titties in my face, writhed on poles, and threw panties in my direction. They once amused Herr Fraknow twenty-four hours a day. Now, they amused me.

I tried to slide out of my clothes, but tripped over my pant legs in the process. Groaning, I pulled off my socks while still lying on the floor. I got up, unbuttoned my vestments, and threw them to the ground. Sure, I could have put them in the closet, but that was the maid's duty, not mine.

I climbed atop the bed once I was down to my briefs and undershirt. I had gotten the briefs via mail order just the day before; no more church-sponsored boxers for me. Now, I could lace my arms beneath my head and become an island in and of myself as the flock ran around the church lawn, out of sight and out of mind.

Once comfortable, I turned to the TV. It was already on. I guess I had forgotten to turn it off before morning service, but that was okay because the video disk I had been playing had looped itself over to its beginning. Good timing. This was my most amusing home movie to date.

My televised image opened *The Holy Cupboard* and removed sixteen boxes of *X-tra Sacred Wafers*. I carried them to my parishioners, all of whom had already been ordered into circle formation on the floor.

"I want you to eat all of these," I heard myself say. *"Every last one.* There's 100 to a box, so that gives you roughly 30 apiece."

I watched hands grope warily for the boxes.

Someone off camera: "But we usually take only one at a time."

"Well, this is an *X-tra* special day."

The parishioners said nothing more. They opened the boxes and stuffed handfuls of wafers into their mouths, their cheeks extending like those of a chipmunk.

At that point, the screen when blank. I had stopped recording because I knew it would take at least thirty minutes for the wafers to take effect. Only when things really began to heat up did I restart.

A few seconds later, the images returned. A few of the parishioners sat in unbreakable lotus positions on the floor. They were obviously having a deep heart-to-heart with their cerebral cortexes. Others flailed madly across the room. A few tore at their skin to get at the spiders and remove the slugs from their bodies. Some ranted and raved and accused their friends of spying on them. One screamed something about alien mind-beams before jumping headlong out the window.

I sighed as the video disk reached its end. It was so nice to be able to look back over past games, but it was nothing compared to actually playing them. I only wished I had had the sense to record today's around-the-church marathon. Too bad I'd gotten so drunk that the idea of preserving the event fled my mind completely.

I staggered from bed and slammed off the TV. The flickering screen amused me, but it also hurt my eyes. I didn't need that much visual stimulation so soon after consuming two fifths of cognac. What I needed to do was unwind. I bent down and removed a remote control device from between the mattress and box spring. It was another one of the room's hidden treasures that I'd recently discovered. I cradled the unit in my hands and selected the *vibrate* option. The bed rumbled for a few seconds. It was revving up.

I closed my eyes and drew in a deep breath. I'd used this unit five times before and knew exactly what to expect.

Seconds later, the bed began to undulate under me like a lover. The sensation was merely tingly at first. Then the motions became more fluid – almost erotic. Quickly, the feeling escalated from tingly to mind-blowing. Orgasmic waves rocked my body. It was even better than masturbation. I moaned with release, after which I motioned to set the whole thing vibrating again.

Then the door smashed open so hard that the wall behind it cracked. My breath caught in my throat. I looked up. The pleasure enveloping my loins was replaced by a chill.

Herr Fraknow had walked in flanked by eight goons.

"Ah, Dear Hero! Glad to see you're enjoying the new bed to its fullest!"

I catapulted from the sheets in both terror and embarrassment.

"Herr Fraknow!"

"I'm glad to see you, too."

A dead man stood before me. I felt my sanity burst. My mind melted, and I imagined it dripping out my ears and mouth. I began to cackle.

"Don't tell me you weren't expecting this? Did you really think I would go anywhere without my guards? You must be pretty dense."

I responded with incoherent mumbling. So scared, I had forgotten my own language.

"Remember the confetti?"

I tried to respond, forcing my lips to say something – anything: *"Ga ra splem."*

"It was coated in something *special."*

Quaking: *"Splem dah flunt?"*

"One touch and programmable reality became your reality. Good thing I took that class over at Crosby University. They taught me the coding language."

"Efr dat flan? Blat ra tabe fue!"

"We'll discuss that in the Smelting Room. It's where the church makes all its icons. Very interesting place. Have you ever been?"

"Nep."

"Then it's time for a tour. Artisans and myself are usually the only ones allowed back there, but I'm going to make an exception for you."

"Vaf Ka ref gantil?"

"No, you can't put your pants on first."

Herr Fraknow motioned to his goons with a forward sweep of his hands. The men surged into the room and grasped me by my armpits. I sunk in their grasp as they dragged me out the door, facing backwards.

"Gam dah ra plat," I wailed. *"Gam dah ra plat!"*

* * * *

The guards carried me into a dark and smelly basement factory filled with furnaces and kilns that reeked of burned carbon. A large, steaming vat sat in the center of the steel-lined room. A metal trough connected it to a cast iron mold in the shape of a human body.

"I told all the workers that they could take the day off. Bronzing is a hobby I've wanted to pick up for three days now, but the first mold didn't come with arm and leg shackles. I had to order another one and that delayed things a bit."

His goons picked me up and threw me into the mold. My body fit perfectly. I thrashed about as they locked me into position.

"Sorry about this. I wouldn't mind keeping you around for a few more years, but you're getting a little too popular. You dispatched with all those lionels, after all. That part was real. Unfortunately, the parishioners' love for you is real, too."

Before I could respond, one of the goons picked up a petroleum soaked rag from the floor and stuffed it in my mouth.

"I thought it would be good for *my* PR to create a hero, but it seems as though a splinter cult may be forming in your name. That's taking things a bit too far, don't you think?"

I just shrieked, bug-eyed, through my gag.

"Maybe I should have programmed you to kill real parishioners and not just imaginary ones. That could have lessened your popularity. Oh well. . . you know what they say about hindsight."

Someone behind me turned a wheel. I heard it squeak. I arched my back up and down. It was the only part of my body that could move.

"Tomorrow, *my* flock will wake up to a new statue. They'll ask me what happened, and I'll read them the letter you left on my desk. It wouldn't be proper to take away the source of so much adoration without an explanation." Herr Fraknow removed a folded sheet from his pocket. "Once I read this, they'll have nothing to love but a memory."

I did not reply. I screamed and choked and then screamed and choked again. My heart was breaking free from its cage. I could even feel it beating in both my hands and feet. The sweat that drenched me was first cold, then hot. Finally, embarrassment flooded my senses when I realized I really was going to die wearing nothing but red underwear.

"But one last thing before you go," Herr Fraknow said. "A church secret, if you will. From what I gather, Nash was rather fond of imparting them. Would you care to hear it?"

Figuring I had nothing to lose, I screamed at him: "For Crosby's sake, let me die in peace!"

"Will do. But not until I tell you the secret contained in the 23rd verse of *The Book of Zeppelin.*"

I spat: "There's no secret, you son of a bitch! *The Book of Zeppelin* ends at verse 22!" My shouts then reverted to sobs.

Herr Fraknow smiled. "Indeed. All published versions end exactly where you say they do. But the original copy – the one hidden away at Crosby University. . . let's just say it's *different*. Think I should tell you how different it really is? This is forbidden knowledge, privy only to those who *really* pull the strings, but I don't think you'll be around long enough to spread the good word."

My sobbing continued unabated, and I said nothing more.

"In that case, I'll tell you. Verse 23 reveals that the *Holy Tome* was written by. . . get this. . . *circus midgets*. Can you believe it? Isn't your entire belief system a hoot! And you guys take this shit so seriously! *Midgets for god's sake!* I really hope you're hearing this."

Behind me, a final wheel twisted. I heard something that sounded like a door parting and felt a rush of steam. Herr Fraknow droned on just a few feet away, but the only sound I heard from that point on was the liquid rush of bronze down the tube.

* * * *

I lay both dead and forever encased that night, but my soul continued to swim about my body-statue. I tried to move further out through the dark factory in which Herr Fraknow had left me to harden, but it was as though I was tethered to my bronzed corpse. I felt nothing, not even the air in which I sailed, but was able to see and hear everything as clearly as I had when alive. Death itself had brought forth a sort of clarity. I could look at the fragments of my life without comment and see my past existence as a chain of linking events. Shame did not well up inside when I observed the final layer of my life. It could not have turned out differently, even if I took steps to the contrary. In that understanding, I felt peace.

A door opened behind me. My contemplation shattered. Herr Fraknow's voice boomed through the empty factory. I heard a number of footsteps and surmised he had brought a few of his goons along. Seconds later, Herr Fraknow's hand reached out from the blackness and touched my body-statue.

"He's pretty cool now. Why don't you give me a hand?"

My soul observed his goons lift my body from the mold and place it atop a dolly. They strapped me in. Herr Fraknow tested the tightness of the ropes.

"That'll do. Wheel him out to the front lawn."

One of his goons complained: "But it's gross, Herr Fraknow."

Another: "Yeah, there's a dead guy in there."

Herr Fraknow gritted his teeth. "Just do as you're told! And you better not go around telling the flock about the dead guy out in the yard. They aren't supposed to know that, remember?"

"Oh yeah, boss."

Herr Fraknow stomped his feet. "Then what's taking you so

long! Get moving!"

The dolly moved. My soul traveled along with it. I had no choice but watch the men drag my body-statue through the church under the cover of night. They didn't pause until they reached an exit.

A goon: "This guy's pretty heavy, boss. Can we rest?"

"Of course not! Dawn's about to break! Take him out into the yard! Do it now!"

The goons obeyed. I was taken to the center of the church grounds where I was untied from the dolly.

"Do you think you boys could pick him up? My back hurts."

"Sure, boss."

The big men lifted my body. I heard them grunt and groan and even smelled their noxious sweat. They heaved and strained and finally managed to place me atop a ground-level concrete block.

"A little to the right. I don't think it's straight yet."

The guards moved my statue until Herr Fraknow's frown became a smile.

"Great! Now let's get back inside! The five o'clock bells are about to ring!" Herr Fraknow and his goons ran back to the church and closed the door behind them. The bells sounded a few seconds later.

* * * *

Five minutes, and the entire congregation stood outside, oooing and ahhing over my body-statue. For some reason, everybody seemed outlined in a thin haze. I couldn't focus on whatever it was because the people kept moving, circling around my statue and making comments:

"That's a statue of *The Hero!*"

"It looks so lifelike!"

"Do you think it's made of gold?"

"Nah. Probably brass."

"Why is he in his underwear?"

"I don't know. Maybe the sculptor was just weird like that."

"Groovy."

A second later, and the doors to The Church of the Byrds parted. Herr Fraknow strolled outside. In his hand, he carried a piece of paper. He walked up to my body-statue and stood right below my soaring spirit. I wished I could spit a loogie on his head.

"I'm afraid our hero is gone," he announced, the same haze

now creeping over his shoulders.

A collective shriek: *"Gone!"*

I looked on in amazement as the foggy blur over everyone's head grew darker.

"Yes, but he *did* leave this letter on my desk sometime during the night. I think it might explain things." Herr Fraknow bent his head to read:

To all,

My work here is done. Now, like all true prophets and heroes, I must ascend to Heaven. I hereby bequeath this statue as a memorial.

Do not worry. I will return in 2,000 years to lead you – my people – to a glorious new dawn. For the time being, however, please worship Herr Fraknow.

In parting,

THE DEAR HERO

"Now you understand the higher purpose of the man to whom we owe the continued survival of our church. Please excuse me for a second, I must give honor where honor is due. If you like, join me in supplication." Herr Fraknow bent to his knees and lifted his hands to Heaven. "Oh God, thank You for this blessing that You have bestowed upon me – Your unworthy servant. I shall do my best to insure that Your Will is made manifest through my being and through all my worldly activities. Allow me never to stray. Allow me to lead the sheep with a stern but disciplined hand. Allow me never to waver in my financial and spiritual responsibilities, and allow me to maintain this position for the remainder of my time on this temporal sphere. May Your *Holy Light* shine down upon my sinful flesh, in the Name of Crosby. Amen." He lowered his hands and turned to the people. "You may place garlands at my feet whenever you so desire."

Instead of listening, the first parishioner picked herself from the ground and dusted herself off. Her hips started to gyrate, slowly at first and then with increasing speed and fluidity. She unbuttoned her hemp shirt as she slipped from her tattered, floral-print dress. At that moment, the once sedentary haze expanded from her head down the entire length of her body. It began to undulate.

"What the hell are you doing!"

"Loving the statue, man. If you're not with us, you're against us."

Herr Fraknow slammed his fist on his leg. "*Loving the statue!* What does that mean? You heard what the hero said! You are to love *me!*"

"No way, man. I'm going with my gut, and my gut says *love the statue*. It's the real vibe. Can you dig it?"

Another parishioner: "Nah. He's just a capitalist and a bureaucrat."

And another: "What a downer."

He huffed as the man turned from him and, like the woman before, removed his clothes and started to dance. The others soon followed.

I marveled at the red tendrils that boiled off Herr Fraknow's body in waves and currents. Being dead, I suddenly realized, had given me the ability to see auras – the initial hazes having marked my entry into this new realm of perception.

"Damn you all! He's dead! I'm alive!" His eyes widened. "Oh fuck, did I just say that!"

I turned back to the crowd. Each man and woman now emanated a yellow glow so bright it stung my incorporeal eyes. Lost in ecstasy, they ignored the *Godvernor* and continued to sway and gyrate about my pedestal. Strange chants soon filled the air, their language indecipherable.

"It's over! He did his job and he's a hero! But he's not a God! If you need one of those, turn to *me!*"

Herr Fraknow shook his fists and stomped his feet. He ran his fingers through his hair and clenched his teeth.

Despite it all, the Dionysian frenzy continued unabated.

"If you won't listen to me, maybe you'll listen to my guards!" He withdrew a pager-like device from his pocket and pressed it repeatedly. The church doors swung open. Twelve burley men poured forth. Each carried a sawed-off shotgun.

I wanted to close my eyes and avoid watching the inevitable bloodshed. But I couldn't. My soul didn't have eyelids.

The guards moved fast. I figured the people had a good fifteen or twenty seconds left to live. The goons seemed so purposeful, so intent on fulfilling Herr Fraknow's orders. That's why it surprised me to see them stop dead in the middle of the lawn. They titled their heads up. Their mouths fell ajar.

I turned my gaze upward and there beheld an orange and red funnel opening up in the sky above my body-statue. A gust of wind blew in from the west as the sun turned black. The funnel descended from the heavens and spiraled to the ground just inches from Herr Fraknow's feet.

"Now what!"

When the red and orange haze lifted, a man with eyes as gray as his skin stood before us all. Even Herr Fraknow took a few hurried steps back. The man turned to the bodyguards and waved his hands. They immediately froze into position.

"There now. They won't be a problem anymore."

Herr Fraknow raced up to the man. "You better not have killed them!"

"And what if I did?"

He backed off.

"That's what I thought." The man smiled and walked towards my statue, his aura bubbling jet black. He placed his hand on my bronzed arms, and a coldness formed at the very pit of my being. My soul shivered as all the iniquity I had committed during my lifetime floated up as a condensed memory. I suddenly felt helpless and alone, the darkness refusing to subside until the man lifted his hand and spoke.

"My name is Malachi, and I come bearing *The Word of God!"*

Herr Fraknow once again stepped up to the man.

"What did you say?"

"I said I come bearing *The Word of God."*

"That's impossible! I'm the head of the only church in the land! No one bears *The Word of God* unless I tell them to!" He dangled his forged letter in Malachi's face. "Look at this! Tell me what it says!"

Malachi ripped the paper from Herr Fraknow's hand and tore it in half. "Times have changed."

"Now you listen here! This is *not* the way we do things!"

"I'm afraid you're wrong."

"I'm afraid I'm *not* wrong! Just who the hell are you anyway? You can't waltz in here like you own the world!"

"I don't own it. I just lease it."

"I don't care what you own or what you lease! Go away! You're not welcome here!"

Red fire bloomed in Malachi's eyes. *"Shut up!"*

Herr Fraknow did as he was told.

Malachi drew in a deep breath: "A new age is upon us. It's time to throw away antiquated systems. From this point on, The Church of The Byrds is null and void. Worship the corpse contained within this statue."

This time, Herr Fraknow reached out and grabbed Malachi's shoulder.

"Damn you! I refuse to let this go any further!"

"You really shouldn't have done that."

Malachi clenched his fist. Herr Fraknow grabbed his head as though he was suffering from the worst headache imaginable. Tears of blood streamed down his face as his cranium swelled. He collapsed to the ground, strange lumpy stuff pouring from his ears. I assumed he was dead and assumed correctly because, a moment later, Herr Fraknow's spirit soared alongside my own.

"I can't believe this," his disembodied soul shouted. "He made my brain explode in my fucking head!"

I shrugged. "Shit happens."

"But this feels pretty good." He flapped his soul-arms like wings. "I think I could get used to–"

The words were torn from Herr Fraknow's soul-mouth. A sizzling sound was audible as the edges of his spirit turned black and crispy. He flailed about. His soul passed through mine and left a tingling sensation in its wake.

"Oh God! It hurts!" He shrieked as his features expanded and then contracted. His head tore clean off his torso; his gut split in half; his legs separated from the rest of his body. The fragmented remains of his soul flickered and then collapsed in on themselves. Within seconds, I could discern no further trace of the *Godvernor*.

I turned my attention towards Malachi. He was still speaking.

"Destroy all vestiges of your old ways. Begin anew. Tear down the temple. It's the only way to gain the favor of your new God."

The crowd took to their feet. As one, they sprinted across the lawn and smashed headlong into the sanctuary. I heard so much battering and clanging. Minutes later, the first cluster of worshipers exited the church, holy relics in hand. They collected the once venerated items in a heap a few yards from my body-statue. The pile grew and grew until everything from pictures of Crosby to the baptismal fountain itself was thrown to the ground.

"Now burn them."

"But we don't have gasoline," someone said.

"That won't be a problem." Malachi snapped his fingers, and the entire mass baked under a carpet of flame.

The people responded to the conflagration with unparalleled sexual abandon. Hands groped bodies that swayed and undulated to rhythms I had never before seen. The scent of human juices was pervasive. Malachi looked on hungrily.

My soul became light as I beheld the orgy. I soared upward and out, finally free from my body-statue tether. Malachi and the masses below were just little black dots. Higher and higher – I could discern the curvature of the Earth. Blue gave way to the blackness of space as visions assaulted my disembodied consciousness.

I saw a caveman. He was trying, and failing miserably, to create the first piece of art with gnarled and mud-caked hands. A midget walked into view and seized his stick. The scene faded out just as the little man started drawing the picture himself.

Another faded in.

Now, the same midget whispered something into the ear of a bearded man in a white robe. At that point, my eyes became a split-screen. On the left hand side, the midget continued to converse with the slender man. On the right, however, he went over diagrams and equations with an lab-coated individual whose nametag read OPPENHEIMER. A bright flash later, the world was a desolate slagheap until the cavemen returned to once again try their hands at drawing.

The cycle went through seventy loops before the vision shattered beneath a wave of pulsating blue light. The glare was so powerful even my soul felt its heat.

Beyond the light, people stood amid a fairy-tale landscape of sliver brooks and purple trees. Most were amazingly short, but quite a few were my size or even larger. The vision was evocative, and it seemed as though I had experienced it all before but, before I could remember exactly how or where, I was lying in bed with fading memories of what I imagined was a dream.

And I really didn't mind having to get up for work.

THE END

ABOUT THE AUTHOR:

Kevin lives in the hills of Tennessee.

His short fiction and poetry has appeared in such venues as The Mammoth Book of Legal Thrillers, Flesh and Blood, ChiZine, The Cafe Irreal, Poe's Progeny, Book of Dark Wisdom, Dark Discoveries, Bathtub Gin, Not One of Us, Dreams and Nightmares, Electric Velocipede, Sick: An Anthology of Illness, Bust Down the Door and Eat all the Chickens, and others.

He also edits the Bare Bone anthology series for Raw Dog Screaming Press and does not eat chimpanzees.

myspace.com/kevindonihe

FROM THE COVER ARTIST:

"I have drawn as long as I can remember. When I was a kid I used to make models out of cardboard and decorate them with markers or watercolors. I drew and painted quite a bit throughout highschool, mostly traditional landscapes and figure studies. I didn't discover surrealism until my sophomore year when I learned of Salvador Dali and Heirynomous Bosch. After highschool my creative drive diminished and I didn't make much art with the exception of a handful of drawings and a few paintings. Then in the summer of 2004 I re-discovered my pencils and began drawing again, this time with an enthusiasm I hadn't experienced before. I've been drawing like mad ever since."

\- Ryan B. Thornburg

eyeball32000.deviantart.com

Bizarro books

CATALOGUE – SPRING 2006

Bizarro Books publishes under the following imprints:

www.rawdogscreamingpress.com

www.eraserheadpress.com

www.afterbirthbooks.com

www.swallowdownpress.com

For all your Bizarro needs visit:

www.bizarrogenre.org

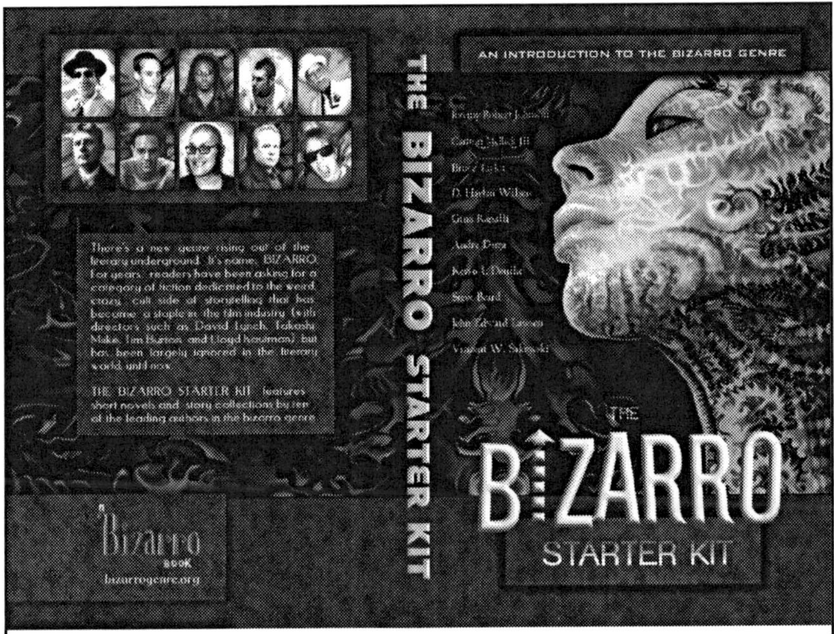

BB-0X1 "The Bizarro Starter Kit"
An introduction to the Bizarro genre

There's a new genre rising out of the underground. Its name: BIZARRO. For years, readers have been asking for a category of fiction dedicated to the weird, crazy, cult side of storytelling that has become a staple in the film industry (with directors such as David Lynch, Takashi Miike, Tim Burton, and Lloyd Kaufman) but has been largely ignored in the literary world, until now.

THE BIZARRO STARTER KIT features short novels and story collections by ten of the leading authors in the genre: D. Harlan Wilson, Carlton Mellick III, Jeremy Robert Johnson, Kevin L Donihe, Gina Ranalli, Andre Duza, Vincent W. Sakowski, Steve Beard, John Edward Lawson, and Bruce Taylor. Get the perfect sampling of Bizarro for only five dollars plus shipping.

236 pages $5

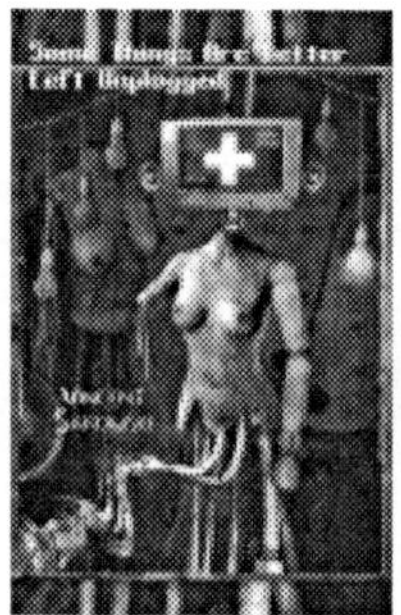

BB-001 **"The Kafka Effekt"** **D. Harlan Wilson** - A collection of forty-four irreal short stories loosely written in the vein of Franz Kafka, with more than a pinch of William S. Burroughs sprinkled on top. **211 pages $14**

BB-002 **"Satan Burger"** **Carlton Mellick III** - The cult novel that put Carlton Mellick III on the map ... Six punks get jobs at a fast food restaurant owned by the devil in a city violently overpopulated by surreal alien cultures. **236 pages $14**

BB-003 **"Some Things Are Better Left Unplugged"** **Vincent Sakwoski** - Join The Man and his Nemesis, the obese tabby, for a nightmare roller coaster ride into this postmodern fantasy. **152 pages $10**

BB-004 **"Shall We Gather At the Garden?"** **Kevin L Donihe** - Donihe's Debut novel. Midgets take over the world, The Church of Lionel Richie vs. The Church of the Byrds, plant porn and more! **244 pages $14**

BB-005 **"Razor Wire Pubic Hair"** **Carlton Mellick III** - A genderless humandildo is purchased by a razor dominatrix and brought into her nightmarish world of bizarre sex and mutilation. **176 pages $11**

BB-006 **"Stranger on the Loose"** **D. Harlan Wilson** - The fiction of Wilson's 2nd collection is planted in the soil of normalcy, but what grows out of that soil is a dark, witty, otherworldly jungle... **228 pages $14**

BB-007 **"The Baby Jesus Butt Plug"** **Carlton Mellick III** - Using clones of the Baby Jesus for anal sex will be the hip sex fetish of the future. **92 pages $10**

BB-008 **"Fishyfleshed"** **Carlton Mellick III** - The world of the past is an illogical flatland lacking in dimension and color, a sick-scape of crispy squid people wandering the desert for no apparent reason. **260 pages $14**

BB-009 **"Dead Bitch Army" Andre Duza** - Step into a world filled with racist teenagers, cannibals, 100 warped Uncle Sams, automobiles with razor-sharp teeth, living graffiti, and a pissed-off zombie bitch out for revenge. **344 pages $16**

BB-010 **"The Menstruating Mall" Carlton Mellick III** "*The Breakfast Club* meets *Chopping Mall* as directed by David Lynch." - Brian Keene **212 pages $12**

BB-011 **"Angel Dust Apocalypse" Jeremy Robert Johnson** - Meth-heads, man-made monsters, and murderous Neo-Nazis. "Seriously amazing short stories..." - Chuck Palahniuk, author of *Fight Club* **184 pages $11**

BB-012 **"Ocean of Lard" Kevin L Donihe / Carlton Mellick III** - A parody of those old Choose Your Own Adventure kid's books about some very odd pirates sailing on a sea made of animal fat. **176 pages $12**

BB-013 **"Last Burn in Hell" John Edward Lawson** - From his lurid angst-affair with a lesbian music diva to his ascendance as unlikely pop icon the one constant for Kenrick Brimley, official state prison gigolo, is he's got no clue what he's doing. **172 pages $14**

BB-014 **"Tangerinephant" Kevin Dole 2** - TV-obsessed aliens have abducted Michael Tangerinephant in this bizarro combination of science fiction, satire, and surrealism. **164 pages $11**

BB-015 **"Foop!" Chris Genoa** - Strange happenings are going on at Dactyl, Inc, the world's first and only time travel tourism company.
"A surreal pie in the face!" - Christopher Moore **300 pages $14**

BB-016 **"Spider Pie" Alyssa Sturgill** - A one-way trip down a rabbit hole inhabited by sexual deviants and friendly monsters, fairytale beginnings and hideous endings. **104 pages $11**

BB-017 **"The Unauthorized Woman"** **Efrem Emerson** - Enter the world of the inner freak, a landscape populated by the pre-dead and morticioners, by cockroaches and 300-lb robots. **104 pages $11**

BB-018 **"Fugue XXIX"** **Forrest Aguirre** - Tales from the fringe of speculative literary fiction where innovative minds dream up the future's uncharted territories while mining forgotten treasures of the past. **220 pages $16**

BB-019 **"Pocket Full of Loose Razorblades"** **John Edward Lawson** - A collection of dark bizarro stories. From a giant rectum to a foot-fungus factory to a girl with a biforked tongue. **190 pages $13**

BB-020 **"Punk Land"** **Carlton Mellick III** - In the punk version of Heaven, the anarchist utopia is threatened by corporate fascism and only Goblin, Mortician's sperm, and a blue-mohawked female assassin named Shark Girl can stop them. **284 pages $15**

BB-021 **"Pseudo-City"** **D. Harlan Wilson** - Pseudo-City exposes what waits in the bathroom stall, under the manhole cover and in the corporate boardroom, all in a way that can only be described as mind-bogglingly irreal. **220 pages $16**

BB-022 **"Kafka's Uncle and Other Strange Tales"** **Bruce Taylor** - Anslenot and his giant tarantula (tormentor? fri-end?) wander a desecrated world in this novel and collection of stories from Mr. Magic Realism Himself. **348 pages $17**

BB-023 **"Sex and Death In Television Town"** **Carlton Mellick III** - In the old west, a gang of hermaphrodite gunslingers take refuge from a demon plague in Telos: a town where its citizens have televisions instead of heads. **184 pages $12**

BB-024 **"It Came From Below The Belt"** **Bradley Sands** - What can Grover Goldstein do when his severed, sentient penis forces him to return to high school and help it win the presidential election? **204 pages $13**

BB-025 **"Sick: An Anthology of Illness" John Lawson, editor** - These Sick stories are horrendous and hilarious dissections of creative minds on the scalpel's edge. **296 pages $16**

BB-026 **"Tempting Disaster" John Lawson, editor** - A shocking and alluring anthology from the fringe that examines our culture's obsession with taboos. **260 pages $16**

BB-027 **"Siren Promised" Jeremy Robert Johnson** - Nominated for the Bram Stoker Award. A potent mix of bad drugs, bad dreams, brutal bad guys, and surreal/incredible art by Alan M. Clark. **190 pages $13**

BB-028 **"Chemical Gardens" Gina Ranalli** - Ro and punk band *Green is the Enemy* find Kreepkins, a surfer-dude warlock, a vengeful demon, and a Metal Priestess in their way as they try to escape an underground nightmare. **188 pages $13**

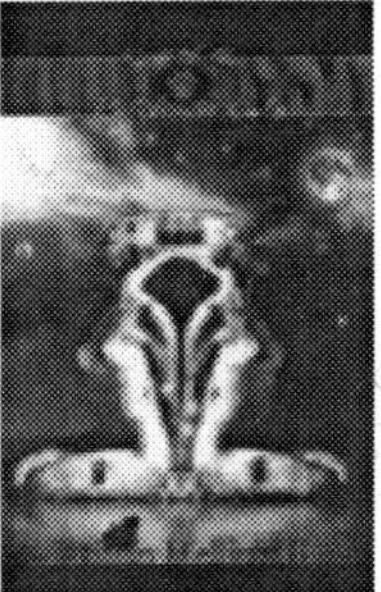

BB-029 **"Jesus Freaks" Andre Duza** For God so loved the world that he gave his only two begotten sons… and a few million zombies. **400 pages $16**

BB-030 **"Grape City" Kevin L. Donihe** - More Donihe-style comedic bizarro about a demon named Charles who is forced to work a minimum wage job on Earth after Hell goes out of business. **108 pages $10**

BB-031 **"Sea of the Patchwork Cats" Carlton Mellick III** - A quiet dreamlike tale set in the ashes of the human race. For Mellick enthusiasts who also adore *The Twilight Zone*. **112 pages $10**

BB-032 **"Extinction Journals" Jeremy Robert Johnson 104 pages** - An uncanny voyage across a newly nuclear America where one man must confront the problems associated with loneliness, insane dieties, radiation, love, and an ever-evolving cockroach suit with a mind of its own. **104 pages $10**

BB-033 **"Meat Puppet Cabaret" Steve Beard** At last! The secret connection between Jack the Ripper and Princess Diana's death revealed! **240 pages $16 / $30**

BB-034 **"The Greatest Fucking Moment in Sports" Kevin L. Donihe** - In the tradition of the surreal anti-sitcom *Get A Life* comes a tale of triumph and agape love from the master of comedic bizarro. **108 pages $10**

BB-035 **"The Troublesome Amputee" John Edward Lawson** - Disturbing verse from a man who truly believes nothing is sacred and intends to prove it. **104 pages $9**

BB-036 **"Deity" Vic Mudd** God (who doesn't like to be called "God") comes down to a typical, suburban, Ohio family for a little vacation—but it doesn't turn out to be as relaxing as He had hoped it would be... **168 pages $12**

BB-037 **"The Haunted Vagina" Carlton Mellick III** - It's difficult to love a woman whose vagina is a gateway to the world of the dead. **132 pages $10**

BB-038 **"Tales from the Vinegar Wasteland" Ray Fracalossy** - Witness: a man is slowly losing his face, a neighbor who periodically screams out for no apparent reason, and a house with a room that doesn't actually exist. **240 pages $14**

BB-039 **"Suicide Girls in the Afterlife" Gina Ranalli** - After Pogue commits suicide, she unexpectedly finds herself an unwilling "guest" at a hotel in the Afterlife, where she meets a group of bizarre characters, including a goth Satan, a hippie Jesus, and an alien-human hybrid. **100 pages $9**

BB-040 **"And Your Point Is?" Steve Aylett** - In this follow-up to LINT multiple authors provide critical commentary and essays about Jeff Lint's mind-bending literature. **104 pages $11**

BB-041 **"Not Quite One of the Boys" Vincent Sakowski** -While drug-dealer Maxi drinks with Dante in purgatory, God and Satan play a little tri-level chess and do a little bargaining over his business partner, Vinnie, who is still left on earth. **220 pages $14**

COMING SOON:

"Misadventures in a Thumbnail Universe" by Vincent Sakowski

"House of Houses" by Kevin Donihe

"War Slut" by Carlton Mellick III

ORDER FORM

TITLES	QTY	PRICE	TOTAL
Shipping costs (see below)			
TOTAL			

Please make checks and moneyorders payable to ROSE O'KEEFE / BIZARRO BOOKS in U.S. funds only. Please don't send bad checks! Allow 2-6 weeks for delivery. International orders may take longer. If you'd like to pay online via PAYPAL.COM, send payments to publisher@eraserheadpress.com.

SHIPPING: US ORDERS - $2 for the first book, $1 for each additional book. For priority shipping, add an additional $4. INT'L ORDERS - $5 for the first book, $3 for each additional book. Add an additional $5 per book for global priority shipping.

Send payment to:

BIZARRO BOOKS
C/O Rose O'Keefe
205 NE Bryant
Portland, OR 97211

Name

Address

City State Zip

Country

Email Phone

Printed in the United States
70986LV00002B/224